Christmas Magic

Cathy Kelly

HarperCollins*Publishers*

HarperCollins*Publishers* Ltd
1 London Bridge Street
London SE1 9GF

www.harpercollins.co.uk

First published by HarperCollins*Publishers* 2011
This edition published by HarperCollins*Publishers* 2018
1

A catalogue record for this book
is available from the British Library

ISBN: 978-0-00-832219-9

This novel is entirely a work of fiction.
The names, characters and incidents portrayed in it are
the work of the author's imagination. Any resemblance to
actual persons, living or dead, events or localities is
entirely coincidental.

Set in Sabon by Palimpsest Book Production Limited, Falkirk, Stirlingshire

Printed and bound in Great Britain by CPI Group (UK) Ltd, Croydon CR0 4YY

MIX
Paper from
responsible sources
FSC **FSC™ C007454**
www.fsc.org

This book is produced from independently certified FSC™ paper
to ensure responsible forest management.

For more information visit: www.harpercollins.co.uk/green

For Dylan, Murray, Laura,
Naomi, Emer and Robert, with all my love

Contents

Christmas Magic

Primrose Cottage sat at the very end of Johnson's Lane, an enchantingly pretty little house with wisteria snaking into the low roof and rose bushes clustering up to peer in the windows.

It was owned by the Malone sisters, Dolores and Genevieve, and although they didn't get a lot of post, the sisters were on first-name terms with the postman, Bernard, who often stopped at Primrose Cottage for a quick cup of tea of a morning.

When he had anything for them, Bernard's routine was to arrive at about nine thirty, by which time Genevieve would have completed the crossword and Dolores taken the dogs for their first little stroll of the day, up past that nice young couple's cottage and back. The kettle would be boiling away happily on the range and Dolores' scones would be warming in the small oven, ready for dollops of Genevieve's crab-apple jelly.

Genevieve was the chattier, more outgoing of the two:

older than her sister, Bernard thought, but more worldly and keen on wearing silver combs in her white hair. She was a smiling sort of person, always neatly dressed in flower colours and with tortoiseshell glasses perched on her nose. Dolores, who still had a hint of softest auburn in her hair, was shyer and more inclined to let Genevieve do the talking, but she never stopped chatting to her beloved dogs, feeding them little bits of scone all the time.

Time permitted Bernard to stop only a couple of times during his morning round and, despite a number of very talented housekeepers in the town, there was no place he liked stopping better than at the Malone sisters'. Their home reminded him of how life used to be when he was a boy.

'You're wonderful, the pair of you,' Bernard would say, when he had a cup of tea in one hand and a bit of hot buttered scone in the other.

'Oh, it's nothing,' Dolores would reply. 'It's just what Mother used to do.'

'Yes,' agreed Genevieve. 'Mother always made her own bread, scones and jam, but she had the hens too.'

Both sisters looked a little mournful at this recollection. Mother had always made them feel inadequate. She had been amazing, a domestic goddess long before such a term had been invented. Everyone over a certain age in Ardagh agreed: there had been nobody like Mrs Malone.

She was a powerful woman, people said, using the rural sense of the word, which conveyed strength and purpose rather than an ability to lift tall buildings. She had been on every committee going, a stalwart churchgoer, organiser of the church flowers and a woman with firm views no matter the subject.

There were a few people who felt that perhaps Mrs Malone had been a bit too powerful when it came to setting the ground rules for her daughters. And a really critical person might say that Dolores and Genevieve Malone were still under her thumb even though Vera Malone was long since dead and buried.

Her 'girls' might be cruising towards seventy, but they still adhered to her strict rules and, somehow, along the way, they'd never courted, never got married and never moved out of Primrose Cottage with its long back garden, half an acre of ground that still boasted a vegetable garden and several crab-apple trees. Though no chickens.

Bernard Kavanagh could see that the sisters were bothered about the lack of chickens bustling about.

'Chickens are an almighty nuisance, you know,' he insisted. 'My sister-in-law has them and the eggs are lovely, there's no doubt about that. But they're mad creatures, always fluttering all over the place, escaping out on the road or getting killed by the fox.'

'Mother never lost a single hen to the fox,' Dolores informed him gravely. It had been a source of great pride to Mrs Malone – no fox had ever got the better of her.

On that fateful morning in mid-December, Bernard had a couple of fliers in his hand, at least one bill, and a large insulated package addressed in a wild scrawl to *The Malones, Primrose Cottage, East Ardagh*. 'I wonder what this is?' said Bernard, who normally could tell with a single look. Packages from mail-order clothes companies, court summonses: he knew the feel of them all.

'Interesting,' said Genevieve, taking it from him.

She examined the package for a moment. It was heavy, a

3

big solid thing, like a heavy book, perhaps, but they hadn't ordered any books. When they wanted something that Devine's bookshop didn't stock, they asked Mrs Devine to look it up on her computer and she'd order it for them. She'd then phone them when the book in question arrived. She'd never sent anything to the house before and, even if she did, she'd hardly be so rude as to write *The Malones* on it. Genevieve decided she'd open it and get to the bottom of the mystery when Bernard was gone.

'Tea, Bernard?' she asked, putting the package down on the table. 'We have mince pies.'

Bernard wanted tea because he wanted to know what was in the package. It was very heavy for a book. But he'd long since discovered that Dolores and Genevieve weren't as consumed with curiosity as he was, and would quite happily leave the package on the table for ages before opening it. He was running late as it was, so he politely declined the offer of tea.

After he was gone, Genevieve returned to the crossword. She was having a bad run of it. Yesterday, she'd had to leave three spaces blank and, when she checked the answers today, had been horrified to find they were so simple. I must be losing my marbles, she thought mournfully. It was a horrible prospect. Mother's mind been like a rapier until the day she died.

'Genevieve, don't slouch,' was the sort of thing Mother said. 'Just because I'm dying doesn't mean you have to lose your posture, for heaven's sake!' Or: 'Cook the ham yourself. That butcher charges the earth for boiling it up and slicing it. Daylight robbery, that's what it is.'

Mother had never forgotten a thing in her life. She'd have

been horrified to see her daughter losing the run of herself. Genevieve wished the mysterious package had never come.

She said nothing to Dolores about these worries.

She'd always protected Dolores and she wasn't about to stop now. Instead, she eyed the big package on the kitchen table. It definitely looked like a book and Genevieve had absolutely no memory of ordering such a thing. Dolores would never have done so without telling her. Dolores never so much as bought a litre of milk without mentioning it first to her sister.

The package sat reproachfully at the other end of the table, as if daring her to open it.

Dolores was happily talking to the dogs. Pixie – half Chow, half something else, with an adorably scrunched-up face and big eyes like a bushbaby – was dancing happily around Dolores' feet. Snowy – white, wispy-haired, with delicate paws grey with mud – was quietly waiting for the post-walk dog biscuits.

Around eleven, Sidney, a fat grey tomcat who looked as if he'd been fluffed up in the tumble drier, ambled in for a snack. He and the dogs muddled along quite well together with a comfortable sharing of territory and only the odd unsheathed claw.

Mother had not been a dog or a cat person. In fact, Genevieve knew that Mother would have disapproved of both the pets and their unusual names. Genevieve's own name had been given to her by her father, a kind man who had also been rather under his wife's iron thumb. By the time Dolores arrived, two years later, Vera Malone had put a stop to her husband's brief flirtation with fancy names. Vera wanted to call her second daughter Dolores after the blessed saint. Stuart

Malone had mentioned Lola, but this was deemed racy. Dolores it was and had remained so for seventy years.

That morning, Genevieve went about her normal chores, and waited until Dolores had taken the dogs out into the garden for a quick pre-lunch meander. Then she seized the big packet from the kitchen table. She opened the flap carefully and her fingers touched the hardcovers of a book.

Where had it come from? Banishing the prospect of senility from her mind, Genevieve pulled the book from its wrapping.

She stared at it for a full moment in absolute stupefaction. It was no ordinary book.

Magic for Beginners was the title, written in dark green script on a background of what looked like Tudor embroidery in saffron yellows and rich olive greens. A book about *magic*. Where had this book come from? It definitely had their name on it and their address. Surely neither of them would have been mad enough to go into Devine's bookshop and order something like this? There was no note from Devine's, and no return address on the back of the big padded envelope. But how else would such a book have arrived at Primrose Cottage? There was no other explanation for it: Genevieve Malone must be losing her mind.

For a whole week, Genevieve kept the book hidden in the pantry cupboard at the very top, wrapped in an old scarf. Dolores had a bockety knee and relied on her older sister to climb on a stool to reach anything up that high. But despite its being stashed away, the magic book haunted her thoughts. *I am still here and you are losing your marbles*, it seemed to be saying.

She said nothing to Dolores about the contents of the package. Dolores could worry on a grand scale and, when she *did* worry, she was prone to faintness. Genevieve invested a lot of time in avoiding such circumstances.

Instead, Genevieve phoned Devine's bookshop on Saturday morning, talked to Mrs Devine herself and had a most unsatisfactory conversation.

'No, there was no order here for you, Miss Malone,' insisted Mrs Devine. 'I have all your last orders and the most recent one was *Tours of the Holy Land*, which you picked up. Are you sure you couldn't have ordered it on the computer?'

'No,' said Genevieve sadly. 'I didn't.'

There was no computer in the Malone sisters' home. It wasn't, the sisters had always felt, the sort of thing Mother would have approved of. Mother had been sceptical of electricity, never mind computers. When the whole town had been connected up to the national grid in 1947, Genevieve could recall her parents fighting over it.

'You can't stand in the way of progress, Vera,' her father had said, exasperated.

Her mother's answer had been typically dogmatic: 'I will do what I want.'

In the end, the Malone household had been the only house on their road to refuse connection. After a year, her mother finally yielded because Mrs Kemp had bought one of those newfangled vacuum machines to clean the rugs. For a brief while, the balance of power on Johnson's Lane had shifted. Mrs Kemp held sway with talk of how the dust just vanished with one whoosh of the wonderful machine.

'You wouldn't believe how dusty even the cleanest rugs are,' she'd said, throwing a gauntlet down to Mrs Malone.

A month later, the Malones had both electricity and a vacuum machine.

The kerosene lamps were kept for particularly dark mornings or for nights when the power was weak. But a computer . . . Truly, Mother would not have approved of any machine with the capability to think for itself.

Genevieve put down the phone to Mrs Devine, her mind troubled.

Upstairs, *Tours of the Holy Land* lay on the small cabinet beside Genevieve's bed, along with her rosary beads. She dipped into the book most nights, running her fingers over pages of pictures of the Wailing Wall and the dark, mystical cavern that was the Church of the Holy Sepulchre. She'd always wanted to travel but had never gone further than Dublin for the odd special-occasion lunch in the Hibernian Hotel. She'd been to Galway once, nearly fifty years ago, to the wedding of her best friend, Mariah.

'It'll be you next,' Mariah had said joyfully the evening of her wedding when she was ready to leave the hotel, her trousseau packed and the bouquet ready to be thrown. Genevieve had caught the bouquet, but there had been no wedding for her.

No trips abroad either. When she was young enough to travel, her mother hadn't wanted her to. No local man had ever measured up to her mother's standards, either.

Genevieve Malone wasn't the sort of person who got angry, but a flicker of naked fury rippled through her now. She and

Dolores would have liked a computer, but Mother wouldn't have approved, so they didn't have one.

They'd have liked to travel, but Mother didn't approve of that either. So they had gone nowhere, married no one.

Now that she and Dolores were their own mistresses, their mother's likes and dislikes still guided them.

Genevieve grabbed the stool and hauled the magic book out of its hiding place.

'I don't care what you think, Mother,' she shouted, surprising both herself and Sidney, the cat. 'I want to look at it.' She placed the book on the table and opened it at the first page.

The book was not the heathen volume she'd expected. There were no exhortations to say black masses or other ceremonies designed to undermine Christianity. Instead, the introduction was a gentle ramble through history and the place that magic had in the world. Genevieve read of professional Egyptian magicians: of the burning of the library at Alexandria; and of Celtic, Italian, Romany and Jewish spells.

Although the shadow of her mother's disapproval hovered, Genevieve kept reading.

She knew, as she read of the power of dancing skyclad, that she would never, ever, attempt any of the spells in the book. Yet there was something deliciously freeing in poring over them. She, Genevieve Malone, would not take to wearing snake bracelets to ward off harm or ask a birch tree to yield up a piece of bark upon which to write a plea for a man to love her. Yet she felt a sneaking envy towards the sort of woman who would.

How would her life have been different if she'd rubbed beetroot all over her body to attract romance?

She thought wistfully about the one man she'd loved from afar, a gentle kind boy named Dermot, who'd left Ardagh without ever knowing that Genevieve Malone watched him walk up the church aisle on a Sunday, her grey eyes following his every move. What if she'd had the courage to disobey her mother then and speak to him?

She wrapped the book up in its scarf, put it up high again, and told Dolores she was off to the shops because they were low on milk. She passed their next-door neighbours' house where dear Janet Byrne had lived until her heart had finally given out. She'd left the house to her niece, a lovely tall, dark-haired girl named Lori who'd introduced herself one day, and had rarely been seen since. Genevieve supposed she had one of those marvellous new careers where she was always racing off to meetings and such like. Her husband, Ben, was to be seen coming and going, and he was there now, hauling groceries out of the car. He always offered her and Dolores a lift to the shops down the hill when he spotted them. There was something a bit sad about him, Genevieve thought. It must be hard for him to be on his own so often. It was only ten days to Christmas: she might suggest to Dolores that they invite Ben and Lori in for tea as a kindness to dear departed Janet. No, Genevieve thought excitedly, drinks! They'd invite them in for drinks. Mother had been an abstinence pioneer and had never touched a drop. Today, apart from a little Guinness for the Christmas pudding, there was nothing alcoholic in the Malone household, but people had drinks these days, didn't they? She and Dolores would have a little party!

'Hello, Ben,' she said. 'Lovely bright day, isn't it?'

Ben Cohen looked up at the sky as if it was the first time he'd seen the day.

'Lovely,' he said distantly.

Genevieve instantly understood that he wasn't in the mood for talk. Understanding other people's moods was one of her skills: a necessary one with Mother, who used to turn furious in an instant and had to be watched. She'd ask him and his wife in for Christmas drinks another time.

She loved the walk down the lane to the town and admired other people's Christmas decorations as she went.

Padraig from The Gables had Christmas roses clustering over his front door. Padraig was confined to bed now and Genevieve dropped in most days, but today she could see his niece's car in the driveway and knew there was no need.

The Cardens, a big family recently moved back to Ireland from Toronto, had the Maple Leaf and the Irish flag amidst all their fairy lights, along with a big sign exhorting the reindeer to stop and nibble the reindeer food.

Dolores and Genevieve had an Advent wreath in their kitchen and a small, discreet Christmas tree that sat in the parlour window. There were no electric lights on it, although Dolores longed for such fripperies. But after a lifetime without sparkling Christmas lights, Genevieve was scared to buy them now. What if they caught fire?

Finally, she was in the town itself and she spotted Sybil Reynolds climbing slowly out of her car, fluffy white hair semi-captured by a knitted red hat. Sybil was eighty if she was a day and she was a keen traveller. Mother had never really liked Sybil or her mother.

'Far too flighty, those women are never off the road,'

Mrs Malone had pronounced and that had been that.

Secretly, Genevieve and Dolores had envied Sybil her easy-going ways. She'd married the handsomest man in the parish, had five children, and although Harry's mind was long since gone and he sat quietly in the nursing home, staring out into the world with blank blue eyes, Sybil had not lost her *joie de vivre*.

Suddenly, Genevieve had a fierce longing to talk to Sybil, a woman who'd never let anybody put a stop to her dreams. She'd bet Sybil's Christmas tree was a positive fire hazard with twinkling lights.

'Sybil!' roared Genevieve across the street, shocked at her own daring.

Ladies never yell, was another of Mother's dictums.

'Will you come to the café for a pot of tea with me?'

'I'd kill for a latte with a double blast of coffee in it,' said Sybil, beaming as she slammed the door of her Mini.

'Have you been to the Holy Land?' asked Genevieve when they were installed in a window seat of the café, Sybil's coffee and a spirulina shot in front of her.

Genevieve wished she'd ordered something more thrilling than tea.

'Harry and I went twice,' Sybil said, a hint of a tear in her eye. 'I wish I could bring him to Italy with me in March, but he can't leave the nursing home.'

'You're going away?'

Sybil shot Genevieve a shrewd glance that said she was used to people expecting her to put her life on hold because her husband was in a nursing home.

'Harry and I talked about everything, Genevieve,' she said. 'Including what would happen when one of us died or if one of us got dementia. Harry said there was no point in us both being dead. The other one was not to sit shiva forever.'

'I'm sorry,' Genevieve said. 'Where are you going in Italy?'

Sybil shrugged expressively. 'Haven't set an absolute date yet.'

'And, er, is it with a group or something?'

'Just me.'

'You're so brave,' sighed Genevieve. 'I'd love to travel, but I'd never have the nerve to go on my own.'

'Well, you've got Dolores to go with,' Sybil pointed out. 'And you're welcome to come with me, anytime you'd like.'

'Really?'

Sybil drank down her spirulina, grimacing as she did so. 'Supposed to keep you young, but it tastes awful.' She put the glass down. 'Are you saying you and Dolores would like to come to Italy with me?'

'Goodness no,' said Genevieve hastily. 'We wouldn't want to impose—'

'You wouldn't be imposing. I wouldn't ask if I didn't mean it,' Sybil replied.

She made it sound so simple. There were no hidden pitfalls in conversation with someone like Sybil, no chance of saying the wrong thing. Not like with Mother.

Genevieve decided to try normal conversation. 'You see, we've never travelled, never been anywhere,' she said. 'Mother didn't approve.'

Sybil's look of pity nearly made her stop but she kept going.

'I got this book by mistake during the week and it's making me think about things.'

'What sort of book?' Sybil leaned forward with interest.

'*Magic for Beginners*. It was a mistake, we'd never ordered it from Devine's or anything,' Genevieve said hastily. 'I go to Mass and—'

'Genevieve, I am not your mother. I am not the judge and jury, either,' Sybil said. 'I'd love to get a look at that book. It sounds fabulous –' Her face broadened into a huge smile. 'There's Claudia, look.'

Genevieve turned to see the youngest of Sybil's brood, a woman with wild red hair and a smiling face.

'Sorry, Genevieve, we're off shopping today. Claudia's driving. Must fly. I'd love a look at that book of yours sometime.'

And she was gone.

Genevieve bought some milk and walked slowly up the hill to Primrose Cottage, wondering what her life would have been like if she'd been more like Sybil, more like the sort of person who'd buy *Magic for Beginners* and use it.

The lights were on in the cottage next door but Ben and Lori didn't have a Christmas tree put up yet. Janet had always adored Christmas, Genevieve thought sadly as she went inside. It had been such a shock when Janet had died. It had been so sudden. One moment she was there, the next, she was gone.

Life was moving so fast, slipping away from Genevieve, and she felt as if she had done nothing with hers. But she could always change that, couldn't she?

* * *

14

Ben had fallen in love with Lori the first time he'd seen her. There had been thunder, great howls of energy rumbling across the sky and into his chest, followed by the retina-blasting lightning. And then the rain.

Stalling for time before he had to run out into the rain to get a cab, Ben had been standing under the awning of the restaurant. It was nearly three, most of the lunchtime business diners were gone. Ben would have been long gone too, only his guest – another ad man – was off on his holidays that afternoon and was preparing to start holidaying early.

'I think I'll have another glass,' Jeff had said conspiratorially. 'You sure you won't join me?'

Ben shook his head and thought about the work piling up on his desk.

He finally left Jeff with another last glass and the rapt expression of a man who might not get home early to pack – 'The wife will have it all sorted, she knows what to bring better than me!' – and ran out of the restaurant, wondering why advertising business lunches weren't listed in Dante's Circles of Hell.

It was high summer and the wet, earthen scent of the box hedge outside the restaurant rose up to greet him, reminding him of the summers in his grandmother's house in West Cork. Earth, sand, the whisper of the ocean across the dunes, the picnics in the garden overlooking the sea, sheltering with old blankets when the wind whipped in across tanned skin.

A woman came out of the restaurant and stood beside him, her eyes scanning the wet street. She was tall, nearly as tall as he was, although she was wearing heels. Without them, he surmised, she might be up to his nose. Dark hair fell to her shoulders on a light-coloured jacket that matched her trousers. He had the chance to watch her because she was so intent on whatever she was looking for: a cab, a person.

Still the rain fell. Ben waited calmly and watched. She was pale, with a dusting of freckles on an aquiline nose, dark lashes touching cheeks tinged with rose as she looked down at her watch.

And then she turned to look at him, eyes a surprisingly light blue, like the sea in West Cork, and smiled. It was the smile that did it.

Released from lunch, not yet imprisoned back in the office, Ben's true self smiled back at her. As an account manager for an advertising agency, he knew how to smile with his face when a client wanted something impossible. At lunches, he smiled at tales of sailing, golfing, stag parties in Portugal where the groom had literally lost twenty-four hours of his life.

But with this woman, outside the restaurant and the heavens shaking all around him, he smiled from his heart.

The woman crinkled up her eyes at him. 'You look familiar,' she said, in a soft accent he instantly identified as Irish, possibly Galwegian.

'Racial memory,' he replied, in his own Dublin accent.

She laughed then. 'How is that that the Paddies always find each other?'

'Paddy sat-nav?' he volunteered. 'And how is it that if anyone else called us Paddies, we'd want to kill them?'

'The Murphia, that's what they call us in my work.'

'Better than Micks,' Ben said. 'Although they don't do it

16

so much with me once they hear my second name. I'm Ben Cohen. They don't quite know what to make of a Jewish Mick.'

'Breaking the Oirish Catholic mould!' she said delightedly, and reached out to shake his hand. 'Lori Fitzgibbon. Actually Lori Concepta. I even went to a convent.'

'Convent girls,' he sighed. 'We were all warned about you.'

'That we were wild?'

'Wild as hell. All that pent-up sexual frustration.'

He fell in love then, with her cool hand in his, and the sight of those blue eyes and the pale Irish skin, fine against the burnished dark of her hair. He'd had to come to London to find a girl from home to fall in love with.

Two years later, they were married. Neither of them had planned to stay in London. Marriage and the purchase of a townhouse in Naas seemed like a wonderful reason to come home.

Lori had a plan: a year of having fun, going away on holidays together and getting the house ready. And then trying for a baby.

'I like the sound of trying for a baby,' said Ben. 'Can we try a lot? Can we try now, in fact? Just to get the practice in.'

How those words stuck in his mind. The trying had been fun, no doubt about it. It was when the trying was getting them nowhere that things started to go wrong.

Ben wasn't worried. Twelve months wasn't a long time trying to get pregnant, he told Lori. She rounded upon him.

'It's forever!' she shrieked. 'You have no idea, Ben, no idea.'

Their GP took it all very seriously. He recommended them

17

to a fertility clinic. Ben's test was easy, if embarrassing. His sperm proved to be fine.

'Great swimmers!' he joked, trying to lighten Lori's mood.

The laparoscopy showed scarring from endometriosis. Getting pregnant was not impossible, but when the scarring was this severe, it made things harder.

IVF was the most sensible answer.

'This will work, darling, I know it will,' said Lori to Ben, her eyes shining that first day she began taking the drugs to push her body into premature menopause.

By the end of the cycle, Lori had produced a worryingly high number of eggs, so high that she was at risk of something the doctors called 'hyperstimulation', a possibly fatal condition. They could not attempt to implant any embryos into Lori this time. She'd have to wait three months for another cycle.

Ben had never seen wild grief like Lori's. He buried his own pain inside him as he tried to soothe her.

'You don't understand what it's like for me,' she sobbed night after night, as she opened a bottle of wine to try to numb the pain.

That was when Ben felt totally useless. He wanted children too; he wanted Lori's children, but the pain of failed baby-making was seen as an exclusively female pain. What about a man's pain? What about being denied the chance to be a father?

The next two cycles, when frozen embryos were implanted into Lori, failed – and cost them all their savings. Then came the miracle: Lori's great-aunt Janet died and left her a house in Ardagh, a small commuter town outside Dublin. The house was a picturesque two-storey house on Johnson's Lane, a country road where they had neighbours on only one side, a pair of sweet, elderly ladies.

They thought about selling the Ardagh house, but it was old, and needed renovation. They'd get more money if they sold their own house and moved to Ardagh, thereby freeing up cash for more infertility treatment.

It would mean a longer commute to their jobs in the city, but it would be worth it.

'It will happen,' Lori said confidently when their house finally sold. 'This was all meant to be: Aunt Janet dying, our getting the house – it's meant to be. It's like a journey and we had to travel this far to reach the point where our dreams come true.'

She'd looked so beautiful, smiling at him, as young and happy as the girl he'd fallen in love with in London.

'Let's go out to lunch to celebrate,' she went on. 'A day like today needs a glass of champagne to celebrate the future.'

Ben had felt a frisson of fear then at her utter confidence: there were no guarantees in life or in fertility treatment. Nobody knew for sure. They might spend every penny they had and end up with nothing. But he couldn't explain this to Lori. It was as if she was living for this dream and without it, she'd crumble. He was worried enough about her as it was.

She was drinking more and more to help her cope with it all and a longer commute meant, Ben hoped, that Lori would no longer be able to party with her colleagues from work. Partying meant drinking, and while Ben could understand his wife's need to numb her pain with a couple of glasses of wine, she was going out more and more since the failure of the last cycle. And drinking more and more too.

The city was the problem, Ben had decided. Away from the bars, the nightlife and all her old friends from work, it would be like it had been when they were first married. There would be no more slurred phone calls at nine o'clock with Lori saying, 'Just dropped into the pub with a few pals, I've only had two drinks, honestly.'

She never had two drinks. Two drinks per bar, perhaps. But Lori never stopped at two. Ben had read a detective novel once where a virus called a chimera infiltrated a person and changed them utterly.

Lori was like a chimera, the many-sided beast. He never knew which version he was going to get. Sometimes, she'd come home and she'd be the smiling Lori, the one he remembered from London all those years ago before infertility had taken over their life. She'd laugh and hug him joyously, saying, 'We had such fun! They all wanted to go dancing, but I said no, I had to come home to you, love.'

The muscle in the side of his jaw would stop tensing quite so much. He could handle this Lori, just about. She'd giggle and want to eat crisps or something else they didn't have in the house. Eventually, she'd grow sleepy and he'd put her to bed, undressing her slowly. The sleepy times were the best. He could almost imagine it was his old wife, the one he married.

Then were nights when she came home in a rage. He'd

never discovered precisely what she'd drunk. It probably didn't matter. Wine versus tequila wasn't the issue. Something would have set her off; some small thing in her work day: a pregnant woman, an angry customer. And then the rage would emerge, a rage that Lori could apparently only assuage with alcohol.

He got into the habit of talking to her mother every day. It was strange how Yvonne became the person he phoned. He was almost too frightened to phone Lori at work on her mobile. Except on those days when she was guilty and sorry, promising never to do it again.

'I'm so sorry, Ben,' she'd cry. 'I don't know how you still love me, I don't know why you stay with me. I'm so horrible. I'll never, ever do it again.'

There would follow a week of not drinking, a week of Lori coming home on time and making lovely dinners, being the perfect homemaker. Until the next time.

Yvonne, Lori's mother, seemed to understand.

Yvonne said she'd seen her daughter drunk at too many family get-togethers recently: not falling-down drunk, but the subtle glassiness of the secret drinker who'd been filling her own glass with vodka steadily throughout the evening.

One night at such an event, Ben and Yvonne had helped Lori up the stairs to her old bedroom and the subject had been broached. Ben said he knew that a problem drinker did not need to have lost their job and be living in a cardboard box to be an alcoholic.

'What should we do?' asked Yvonne that night, her face drawn and her eyes wet with tears.

Ben shrugged helplessly. 'I don't know,' he said.

21

That had been nearly six months ago, not long after the move to Ardagh, the move he'd hoped would change it all.

Today, Ben made his daily phone call to his mother-in-law.

'How is she today?' Yvonne asked.

Ben could hear trepidation in her voice. He'd grown to hate theirs.

'Fine today,' Ben said.

He kept his voice low. Nobody in the marketing department knew what was going on in his life. They thought, laughably, that he had it all: stunning wife, lovely new home in a beautiful town, promotions on the way, no doubt. Life's biggest irony, Ben thought: there could be such a vast difference between the outer picture and the inner one. If only they knew.

'We're going into the clinic on Friday for a consultation about the next cycle,' he told Yvonne. 'She never drinks before that. They do so many blood tests. I think she's afraid of what they'll find in hers and take us off the programme.'

'Maybe that's the answer,' Yvonne said, startling him. 'Tell them she drinks every time she's not on an IVF cycle. Alcohol is definitely a factor in fertility.'

'She wasn't drinking that heavily until the last few months,' Ben protested.

There was an ominous silence on the other end of the phone.

'She was,' Yvonne said, so softly Ben wondered if he'd imagined it. 'She always drank too much, even as a teenager. Her father used to too, but he's stopped.'

'Why didn't you tell me?' he said, stunned.

'I was afraid you'd leave her,' Yvonne whispered. 'She needs you. I thought if we shocked her with being thrown off the IVF programme, she might stop.'

Ben left work early that day and drove home towards the rolling Wicklow hills and Ardagh. As he drove, he thought of the years he'd known Lori and how he'd never noticed her drinking more than anyone else. He liked the odd glass of wine, but that was it. True, Lori liked to have an open bottle of white in the fridge, but he didn't see how she could have been drinking without his knowing. Surely he'd have noticed.

At home, he searched the house. There were several empty vodka bottles in her underwear and sweater drawers, a half-full one in the airing cupboard, and several bottles of wine stashed away in the kitchen. The wine was the same type as the half-full one in the fridge. Very easy to finish a bottle and replace it with another one, Ben realised, making it seem like the same innocently half-full bottle. He discovered many, many empty wine and vodka bottles shoved into the back of the cobwebby old shed. Lori had known he wouldn't look there. They didn't use it for anything, just promised themselves that one day, they'd clean it out. She'd known the evidence was safe enough. They'd only been in the Ardagh house for two months and she'd managed to create such a stash in such a short time.

The anger hit him then. Nobody went from being an ordinary drinker to hiding bottles of vodka that quickly. This was, as Yvonne had said, clearly a much longer-running problem than he'd thought. And the thought made him so very angry.

He'd believed he knew everything about Lori and he hadn't, he hadn't at all. He thought of all the tests and the sheer agony of waiting. And all the time, his wife was skewing the results by secretly drinking. How did he know whether she'd stopped or not during the actual cycles? He'd given up alcohol, he'd even given up cycling when Lori had read a report about how sports saddles heated the testes, which was bad for fertility.

'No more cycling!' she'd said firmly, and he'd agreed.

She might well have been drinking vodka on the tough days, while he stopped even cycling, for God's sake.

He phoned her mobile and it went straight to voicemail.

'Hi, Lori, we need to talk.' He paused before delivering the next line. 'I found the vodka bottles at home. Call me back now.'

He didn't sign off with love. At that moment he felt absolutely no love.

There was no phone call in return. He drove down to the supermarket, bought some groceries and was unpacking the car when he saw one of the old ladies from the cottage next door looking at him from their front window. He waved. It was Genevieve, he thought. He wasn't entirely sure which was which. He went indoors and made some pasta with butter and tried to watch a film on the television, but he couldn't concentrate. Ten o'clock came, eleven, then midnight and still no sign of Lori. His phone sat silently on the low coffee table in front of him, the screen still blank.

And then he heard the noise.

* * *

It was ten to midnight, and Genevieve could hear her sister sleeping. Dolores didn't snore exactly, but she made a low, trumpeting nasal noise, for sure. Genevieve called the dogs from Dolores' bed and they came with a clattering of paws, delighted at this late-night game.

'Hush,' whispered Genevieve as Pixie began to bark. 'Biscuits.'

She knew that the dogs would protest loudly if she went outside and they were stuck inside, so she'd collected a few of their doggie biscuits and had them hidden in the pocket of her dressing gown. She handed biscuits to Pixie and Snowy, who devoured them like dogs who hadn't eaten in months instead of having had half of Dolores' nighttime toast and jam just an hour before.

Then, she shut her sister's door and shuffled down the stairs, one hand holding a small bag. The dogs jostled at her heels, keen to be involved. In the kitchen, Genevieve found the candle and the kitchen matches. It was a wild December night and any candle would blow out in an instant outside, so she got out an old hurricane lamp and carefully placed the candle inside. The book stipulated that it should be a special candle. This one was left over from Mariah's fortieth wedding anniversary, which Genevieve felt was special enough. To add to the light, she put a few tiny tea lights around it. In the small bag, she had the paper upon which she'd written her hopes and dreams, as the book had told her, and she'd said a couple of prayers over it, which wasn't entirely magic either, but by now Genevieve had read enough to decide that magic was rather more open to personal interpretation than Catholicism.

YOU have the power, said the book.

Genevieve Malone, who'd never felt as if she had any power in her whole life, was determined to reclaim some of it now. She was going to start by dancing skyclad under the moon over a wishlist of her dreams. Perhaps then, she'd have the courage to go to the Holy Land instead of just looking at books about it. Sybil did it. Wasn't it time that she and Dolores did it too?

The dogs were hysterical with delight to be let out into the garden on this windy night hours after they'd been put to bed. Pixie kept chasing her tail wildly, and bumped into Genevieve.

'Be careful, sweetie,' whispered Genevieve, steadying the lamp.

The wind roared around the garden, rattling the holly bushes and the bare trees.

Genevieve picked her way through the dark over to the copse in the middle of the garden. It was obviously entirely accidental that her mother's garden had hazel, rowan and elder trees in it; all magical trees. There, she put down her lamp and laid the precious paper under it.

'God, I'm not turning my back on you,' she said, looking up at the night sky. 'I'm only opening my mind up to other belief systems. Asking for help wherever it is, if you like. I mean, I'll still be at Mass on Sunday, and you know we've got the Advent wreath in the kitchen. And these are your trees and this is your moon, after all.'

She stripped off her dressing gown and was caught in a riptide of mid-winter air.

'This is your body, too, God!' she cried, shivering. 'I don't

26

know why we're supposed to be ashamed of it. Mother wouldn't let us wear skirts shorter than our ankles, you know. Why? I mean, *why*?'

There was no point whispering now. Shouting was the only way to go.

She began to twirl with her arms outstretched, feet bare on the damp, cold grass. 'I want to travel and have adventures. I'm asking the universe to help me do it! You and the universe, God. I'm asking everyone!'

It was at this moment that Pixie started at something, leapt to her feet and bounded off, knocking over the hurricane lamp on to Genevieve's pink candlewick dressing gown, which burst into flames.

Snowy began to bark, Genevieve began to shriek. She rushed back towards the house to find something to put the flames out, and fell over Dolores' ornamental wheelbarrow, planted with January's snowdrops and crocuses. She lay on the grass, her lower back, always prone to stiffness, locked into a spasm of pain, and screamed.

'I've got a gun, I'll shoot you!' roared Dolores from her window, brandishing a broom.

'It's me,' yelled Genevieve in agony.

A light was turned on.

'What are you doing in the wheelbarrow, for the love of God?' Dolores said. There was a pause. 'And why are you naked?'

Ben rushed out into his back garden but it was clear that the noise was coming from next door. Dogs were barking and someone was screaming. Without pausing to dial the police, he grabbed a golf club and hopped over the wall connecting the two gardens.

There, he discovered a naked Genevieve sobbing with pain and shivering with cold by a wheelbarrow.

'She's never done anything like this before,' gasped the other elderly lady, emerging from the back door with a blanket and a broomstick.

'Of course not,' said Ben. He worked in advertising. He'd seen it all.

He stomped out the fire and rescued a piece of paper that was blowing in the wind. It had some writing on it. Something about hopes and dreams. He put it in his pocket.

He averted his eyes till the naked lady was suitably covered and then tried to calm her. She was consumed with pain and embarrassment, that was clear. The other lady kept saying, 'What were you *doing*, Genevieve?' in bewilderment.

It took a few minutes to extract Genevieve from the plants and she was surprisingly light and sweet-smelling.

'That's lovely perfume, Genevieve,' he said, as if it was daytime and they were meeting out the front of their respective houses.

'Grapefruit oil,' she said, and he sensed her relax.

'But, Genevieve, *why*? With no clothes on?' Dolores was saying.

'I wanted to be out at night,' began Genevieve shakily.

'Of course,' agreed Ben, with no hint that midnight excursions into gardens in the middle of winter might be considered strange by most people. 'Wonderful for putting you in touch with nature and, er . . .' He looked at Genevieve for a hint on which way to go in order to soothe her worried sister.

'God,' she said swiftly. 'God loves us to appreciate our world.'

'And His great universe,' added Ben, who only stepped into churches for weddings and funerals. 'You had a light to see by and your dressing gown caught fire, perhaps?'

'I had to take it off then,' said Genevieve, grabbing this explanation.

'Very wise.'

Ben helped her on to the couch in the kitchen, and Dolores went off to get painkilling tablets and more blankets.

He took the piece of paper from his pocket and gave it to Genevieve.

'Thank you,' she said, looking at it sadly. 'Nobody's ever come to my rescue before. Dolores would be upset if she knew what I had been doing. Going skyclad into the night. I got this magic book by mistake and it made me want to try something different, you see. I wanted to change my life before it's too late.'

At that moment, Ben felt a kinship with this old woman.

'I can understand that,' he said. He thought of Lori and all the bottles, of how she'd lied, and of how he wanted it all to be different.

If only it could be different.

'Are you all right?' It was Genevieve's turn to ask him. There was something about those wise eyes that made him think she'd understand.

Dolores bustled around making tea. Genevieve told her to go to bed. She'd manage.

Ben said if they wanted, he'd stay to carry Genevieve up to bed when she felt ready.

'She'll be safe with me,' he told Dolores gravely. 'Plus, the dogs are here too.'

Genevieve's painkillers took a while to work, but when they did, the spasms were less painful and she was able to get off the couch.

'Should you do that?' asked Ben.

'The doctor says you have to move around, not stay in one place.'

She made more tea, served with home-made mince pies this time, and then directed Ben to the high-up cupboard where *Magic for Beginners* rested.

They sat at the kitchen table and flicked through the book and talked about their lives.

Ben Cohen, who treated his grandmother with respect but never told her what was in his heart exactly, told Genevieve about falling in love with Lori, about their infertility treatments and about finding all the bottles.

Genevieve, who had never confided to a single person in her life apart from Dolores, whom she tried to protect, told him about the look of pity in Sybil's face when Genevieve had talked about Mrs Malone.

'Sybil knows and she pities us,' Genevieve said. 'She knows the two of us are prisoners here, even if Mother is dead. She doesn't think we'll ever go to Italy with her.

'The book and Sybil, it's made me see it all differently now: the past, that is. I never married or went off around the world. I should have.'

Ben looked at her face, pale now with pain, but still

warm and lively for all the signs of age. He could tell she had probably been a beauty when she was younger, with those high cheekbones and the fine arched brows. He saw suddenly that she was still beautiful. He'd never seen it before when they'd made small talk in the lane. But then, he'd never seen the truth about his beloved Lori either.

'It's not too late,' he said suddenly. And he wasn't just talking about a trip to Italy.

'Do you think?' said Genevieve.

'It's not too late for either of us,' Ben said. 'You should tell Sybil you'll go, both of you. I could mind the dogs for you.'

Genevieve's eyes filled with tears, but they weren't sad tears. They were tears with hope in them, hope for a new life because it was never too late.

'Thank you, Ben,' she said.

He helped her up the stairs to bed and placed a kiss on her warm papery cheek.

'Maybe you'd come in over Christmas for a – ' Genevieve paused. 'Some tea and more mince pies?'

'I'd like that,' said Ben. He meant it.

He went home and got into his cold bed. He tried Lori's phone again, and this time she answered.

'Darling!' she said, her voice clearly telling him all he needed to know.

'How many have you had?' he asked sadly.

'Three. Honestly. I didn't want to, I wanted to come home and explain about the bottles. You see, Scarlett at work had a party when Marcus was away, and she needed somewhere to put them because he hates her partying, so we stuck them in my car, and I forgot to get rid—'

'Stop.'

'No honestly—'

'Stop. No excuses, Lori. I get it. Finally.' He was more forcible this time.

This was no time to make plans or tell her of discussions they needed to have. That would have to wait until tomorrow when she was sober. He had met plenty of alcoholics over the years. He had never thought Lori would fit into that category.

'Can you get a taxi and come home?'

'Well,' she sounded so unsure then, almost childlike now that the anticipated scolding hadn't materialised. 'I suppose I could,' she said.

'Do it now. If you've no money, tell the driver I have and I'll pay him. I'll put you to bed and we'll start again in the morning.'

She began to cry then, noisy sobs. 'I thought you'd be so angry with me. I don't mean to. I tell myself I'll just have one and then – '

'It's OK,' he said softly. 'Just come home, love. We'll start again. We'll get you into rehab, whatever it takes. It's never too late.'

There was more noise and muffled voices, then a car door slamming.

'I'm in the taxi,' Lori said. 'I'm coming home.'

'See you in a little while, Lori,' said Ben.

He hung up and walked upstairs to where he could

overlook Genevieve and Dolores' garden with the little grouping of ancient trees sending spindly, bare branches up into the night sky.

What he and Genevieve had talked about that night was true, he knew. It was never too late.

Dolores didn't like going away when the daffodils were still out.

'And what about the slugs?' she wanted to know. The garden would be ravaged by them.

Genevieve had heard variations on this theme every week since they'd booked the holiday with Sybil to Italy.

'There's no right time to go away,' she told her sister now, looking up from her final checklist regarding passports, photocopies of passports, tickets and money. The taxi was coming in an hour to take them and Sybil to the airport. 'We have to trust that this is the right time for us, Dolores. It's going to be marvellous.'

'What if something goes wrong?' said Dolores, looking up at her sister with beseeching eyes like the dogs'.

'Sybil has travelled the world,' Genevieve said firmly. 'She'll know what to do if something goes wrong.'

'The problem with Sybil is that I think she'd quite like something to go wrong,' fretted Dolores. 'She's far too fond of adventure.'

Genevieve laughed. 'I'd quite like an adventure myself.'

Seeing the alarm in her sister's eyes, she immediately pointed out that if anything went wrong, they could phone Ben and he'd sort it out.

'Yes, Ben's so good to us,' Dolores muttered, mantra-like,

'taking care of the dogs for us. Pixie and Snowy love both Ben and Lori.'

Genevieve knew that Lori found long walks therapeutic since she'd come out of rehab. She and Ben were looking forward to caring for the dogs and taking them for walks, although Genevieve explained that neither dog had ever had an actual long walk in their life.

'We'll take care of them,' Ben had assured her the day before.

There was a light in his eyes these days. It made Genevieve happy just to see it.

When Genevieve and Dolores came back from their travels, he and Lori were going to Kerry for a few days' holiday.

'Lori wants to keep it simple,' he explained to Genevieve. 'We've never been to Kerry, so it's not tinged by bad memories of the past. It's hard for her, but she's being so strong. And I'm happy no matter where we go, as long as she's OK.'

'She'll be fine with you beside her,' Genevieve said.

'What about Dolores?' he asked. 'Is she still nervous about going away?'

'Terribly,' admitted Genevieve. 'But wait till we get there. She'll love it, I know she will. We both will.'

Handbag packed, she took one last trip around the house to make sure all the windows were locked before they left. It was odd to be going away for two whole weeks. She'd never been away from Primrose Cottage for that long ever before.

On her bedside table and carefully left under a knitting book, lest Dolores spot it, lay *Magic for Beginners*, now well thumbed. Genevieve thought she'd finally got to the bottom of the mystery of how it had ended up in her hands. There

34

had been another Malone on the other side of Ardagh, it seemed. A Mrs Malone of West Ardagh. The man in the big post office had eventually uncovered this information, but only after Genevieve explained that it was just a book that had come to her house by mistake. Not a bill or some vital, private document.

'Only a book,' said the man, clearly relieved. 'You see, if this was a private document, then we couldn't give you out any details.'

'Of course,' said Genevieve. 'No, it was only a book.'

She'd taken the car on one of its rare trips over to West Ardagh to find the mysterious Miss Malone and had come upon another Primrose Cottage, a tiny sliver of a house wedged between two fine new-builds. The old Genevieve might not have had the courage to ring the doorbell so firmly, or even to peer in the windows when nobody answered the door, but the newly courageous Genevieve had no such qualms.

However, the house was clearly empty. It felt empty. There was dust on the windows and dirt on the mat at the door. Whoever had lived here had moved on. But they'd left behind a gloriously beautiful garden, enclosed by rowan, elder and hazel trees. Magical trees.

Genevieve wrote a note on a piece of paper from her handbag and posted it through the letter box.

Thank you for Magic for Beginners. *I still have it, if ever you need it. Fondest wishes*

Genevieve Malone

Anniversary Waltz

In the tiny staffroom of Deloitte's Pharmacy, Felicity Barnes put her mobile phone away and returned to her coffee and her chicken wrap thoughtfully.

Lunchtimes at Deloitte's were fluid things and she might as well eat while she had the chance. It was Monday, the day when doctors' surgeries were jammed with people who'd held on to their sore throats and aching backs over the weekend and had decided they needed medical attention urgently once Monday morning dawned.

Consequently, pharmacies were like Grand Central Station all day Monday with little chance of a break, and in the two months Felicity had been working in Deloitte's, she'd learned to take lunch when she got the opportunity.

As she ate, she thought about her daughter's phone call.

Mel was twenty-two and sometimes Felicity thought she was a *very young* twenty-two. Casting her mind back, Felicity realised that she'd been married to Leo with a baby on the way at the same age. But then that was years ago, when things had been different. People had grown up quickly then. She and Leo had been living in London in a tiny third-floor flat with no lift and very little money. They'd had no support system when Ryan, now twenty-seven, had cried through the night and an exhausted Felicity had wondered what she was doing wrong. She could recall the relief of hearing another mother say it was '. . . just colic, love. All babies get it. Blooming nightmare, isn't it?' The relief at hearing those words and the realisation that Ryan's terrible crying was normal.

Conversely, twenty-two-year-old Melanie had no responsibility for anyone but herself and still brought bagfuls of laundry home from teacher training college at weekends for her mother to wash, dry and iron.

Or at least, she always used to.

Melanie had been working in Spain over the summer holidays when Felicity and Leo sold the house.

The sale had been part of the separation arrangements. Felicity had loved the house on the quiet, tree-lined housing estate where the children had grown up. It had been the family home for over two decades, but it had to be sold and the money split between herself and Leo. There was no other option.

Melanie had recently returned to Ireland to learn that her stuff from the house was now stored in a warehouse on a vast industrial estate, along with some of the bigger pieces of furniture that Felicity and Leo hadn't wanted to sell. There was the piano Leo's mother had given them and a huge wooden dining-room table from a great-aunt which was supposed to be a fabulous antique but which Felicity suspected was just an ordinary old table with carved legs. One day, Felicity said, the children might like these things but there was no room for them in her new apartment overlooking the sea. It wasn't a box like so many apartments and it had three bedrooms – albeit two incredibly tiny ones along with the master bedroom – so her children would always have somewhere to stay, but it didn't have room for big furniture.

It was also, as Mel had sobbed on the phone just now, '*not home*!'

'You knew we had to sell the house, Mel,' Felicity had replied with a calmness she didn't really feel. She had known how painful it would be for her children. She'd asked Mel to fly home from Spain to visit the house one last time, just to forestall this sadness. She'd made it plain that her new home would be Mel and Ryan's home too. But Mel had been too busy to fly home.

Now that she was home, Mel didn't even want to hear about her mother's new apartment. Having managed not to think about the family upheaval while she was working in Madrid, she'd just returned to her college digs, in time for the autumn term, and *now* she was thinking about it. And she was wildly upset.

Mel was, Felicity reflected, the more emotional of her two children. Ryan had great emotional depth but was less prone to outbursts than his sister. He worked in window design for a chain of interiors stores and he was endlessly busy, but he'd still managed to be there the day Felicity had locked the door on their beloved family home for the last time. He'd taken his mother to lunch and they'd talked about the fun times they'd spent there, and about how they hoped the bones of Teddie, the family collie, would not be disinterred by the new owners digging near the roses. Somehow, Ryan managed to blame nobody for his parents' marital discord. It wasn't his place to judge, he said. He liked that it was all civilised and that there weren't insults flying between Felicity and Leo.

'I never got to say goodbye to the garden,' Mel had said bitterly on the phone.

There was no value to be had in pointing out that Felicity had asked her to come home to do just that. Fresh off the plane and with no cosy home to return to, Mel didn't want to hear about financial problems, the reality of her parents needing two separate places to live, how her mother had never wanted it all to turn out like this.

'Wherever your father and I are, there will always be a welcome for you. Our homes are always your homes,' Felicity said in anguish, hating to hear her darling daughter so distressed.

'Home will never be where that cow is!'

That cow was Sonya, the woman Leo had recently moved in with. Sonya, incidentally, was *not* the woman he'd been having an affair with for many years. With an equanimity that surprised her, Felicity felt pity for Darina, her husband's assistant, who had been considered surplus to requirements once Leo had got his freedom. Apparently, this happened a lot.

'The agony aunts tell women he'll never leave his wife and, if he does, ten to one he won't move in with you – he'll have another woman you never knew about lined up,' said Felicity's sister, who was keen to disembowel Leo and was fed up with her sister's calm handling of all this. 'Serve Darina right. She's getting a taste of her own medicine.'

Felicity pitied Darina as yet another woman who'd been fleeced by Leo Morgan. But she refused to be bitter about him. Bitterness hurt only oneself.

Leo had left in January when Felicity could no longer live with the knowledge that her husband was cheating. Now that they were apart, it was immaterial to her if he was living with Darina, Sonya or a cast of thousands. It was marvellously liberating to realise that Leo's whereabouts was no longer her business. She was only sorry she hadn't forced his hand years ago. She'd always tried to be grown-up about his infidelities and to ignore the pain because they had children. But finally, something had cracked inside her. It wasn't the giant crack of an earthquake: it was the gentle shearing away of one piece of polar ice from another, an inevitable event which had turned out to be far less painful than being married to the other ice cap.

Ryan reported that Sonya was nice enough but his father's new relationship probably wouldn't last.

'She's sort of naïve. Too naïve for Dad, really. I don't see it going the distance.'

Felicity wondered how her elder child had become so wise, not to mention forgiving.

And why Melanie wasn't the same.

'Where is this damn flat, anyway?' Melanie had snapped down the phone. Mel always hid her fear by lashing out.

Felicity, relieved that her daughter was giving in and

agreeing to come and stay, had given her directions and explained that she was in apartment 14, with the name F. Barnes on the bell.

'Barnes? But that's your maiden name!'

Felicity was sure her daughter's shrieks had been heard by all in the pharmacy back room.

'Yes,' she had said, again using the calm voice she'd employed many times during Mel's teenage years. She longed for Mel to understand why she'd gone back to her maiden name, that she was reclaiming part of herself that she'd lost years ago. 'See you at half six.'

She sighed as she mulled over all this while eating her lunch.

'Family trouble?' Chantelle, one of the other sales assistants, had come over. She was an attractive Belgian woman, who would wear a silk scarf knotted just so, and was able to handle the most difficult customers.

'My daughter's home and she's angry that we've sold our house,' Felicity explained. 'I wanted her to come home before we sold it, but she wouldn't. She hates the idea that I've moved into somewhere new. I knew she'd be upset but it's still heartbreaking.'

Felicity wouldn't have dreamed of filling anyone in on her private details normally, but Chantelle invited confidences partly because she didn't have the gossip gene and partly because she had such fabulous advice on all things.

'Does your daughter not see that you were unhappy and that her father treated you badly?' Chantelle asked.

Felicity shook her head sadly. 'She wants it to be like it always was, no matter how hard that was for me. My mother's the same,' she admitted. 'She thinks I told Leo to leave in a fit of sheer lunacy.'

In the two months she'd worked in the pharmacy, Felicity had gone to see several films with Chantelle and had been to a salsa-dancing night with the other staff members, Monica and Zoë, a fact which she had no intention of sharing with her daughter. Mel would see it as more proof of change. Previously, Felicity's friends were all women she'd known for years or mothers she'd come to know when Ryan and Mel were at school.

Her work in Deloitte's was part of Felicity's new life. For most of her marriage, she'd worked one day a week as a pharmacy assistant, but now there was no reason for her not to work almost full time. Instead of feeling overwhelmed by the hours, she loved it. This new chapter in her life was exciting.

Chantelle laid a gentle hand on Felicity's arm. 'She will come round, you'll see,' she said kindly.

That evening, Felicity cooked Mel's favourite meal: broccoli and feta cheese pasta bake, although she didn't have time to make her trademark caramel meringues and had to make do with some ordinary shop-bought meringues instead. She had fresh orange juice for Mel's breakfast because her daughter said she loved the glorious Spanish orange juice she'd become used to in Madrid.

Felicity changed from her smart work blouse and tailored trousers into jeans and a sweater. She walked round the apartment, tidying, repositioning things and hoping that Mel would like it. The bedroom she'd assigned for Mel was tiny and had only space for a single bed, but Felicity had bought pretty, delicately sprigged bed linen and the small table beside the bed had fresh flowers on it. Nobody could find fault with the place.

'The flat's very small, isn't it?' Mel said when she arrived, stalking around.

'Yes,' said Felicity evenly. 'But a four-bedroom semi doesn't make much sense for a woman on her own.'

No need to discuss the financial implications of modern separation and divorce. Small steps, Felicity reminded herself.

Mel liked the bed linen but was shocked at the size of her bedroom.

'We're all downsizing now,' said Felicity gaily.

They'd started dinner – Mel much happier now that she'd seen her mother was still cooking the same sort of comfort food – when the intercom buzzed.

'Only me,' shouted Felicity's mother, Rosalie.

What fresh hell is this? thought Felicity. Her mother and Mel sang from the same hymn sheet: life was better when Leo and Felicity were together, irrespective of flings and marital disharmony. Ignoring reality was clearly a trait that had skipped a generation and had gone straight from Rosalie to Mel.

Mel and her granny hugged, sobbed a bit at the changes in the family, and were soon whispering about how upset they were as Mel finished her food and Rosalie drank some strong tea.

Felicity's apartment was intentionally closer to her mother's seafront bungalow, but the intent was more along the lines of being near in case of trouble, instead of being near so that Rosalie could drop in morning, noon and night.

Rosalie and Mel looked alike, both being small, birdlike and fair-haired, although Rosalie's fairness now had help from the odd highlight. Felicity was tall and dark, like her dear departed father. He had been a calm man too, and she thought ruefully that he'd never been entirely at ease with her choice of husband. Leo had always been too edgy, too full of great plans for the future.

Rosalie wanted to hear all about Spain and the gorgeous local men. Chat about what college would be like for the next term took them through dessert and on to coffee.

Mel told them she had shared a cab from the airport with a completely fabulous guy who'd been on her flight from Madrid and they were now seeing each other. He was in college too, doing something in computers. Mel had only liked computers for the social networking sites and for doing college essays, but suddenly, she was very interested in them.

'Shane's really clever, he was writing code when he was eleven,' she said dreamily. 'He's in a band, too. He plays the bass guitar.'

For the first time that evening, Felicity and her mother's smiles were in harmony.

Rosalie invited her daughter to a charity cake sale the following Tuesday.

'I can't, Mum,' Felicity said. 'I'm working.'

Rosalie and Mel's faces formed themselves into similar disapproving looks.

'I don't see why you have to kill yourself working in that chemist shop, Felicity,' Rosalie said crossly. 'You're only doing it to spite Leo. What's wrong with you, why can't you stop all this talk of separation and *divorce*?' She almost hissed the word. 'In my time, we knew how to keep our families together.'

Mel's bottom lip wobbled.

'I'm not working to spite Mel's father,' Felicity said, keeping herself calm with great difficulty. 'I'm working because I need to earn my living. Leo and I would each be living in shoeboxes on the side of the road if I didn't. I've always worked, Mum. I've just upped my hours and it happens to suit me.'

Rosalie left soon after, muttering to her grand-daughter about hoping *that some people would come to their senses soon.*

Mel said she was tired and stomped off to her tiny room. 'I need to be on my own,' she said loftily, the same way she used to end arguments when she'd been a teenager.

Felicity tidied up the dinner things and wondered how all this had become her fault.

The next morning, Mel was so happy that Felicity knew something was up.

'Dad just phoned me,' she said, when they'd had breakfast. The orange juice had been pronounced 'nearly as nice as the Spanish stuff'. 'It's Nanna and Gramps' fiftieth anniversary in December. They're having a big party and they want us all to go. You too. No, actually, you especially! Dad says he really wants you to go, and so do Nanna and Gramps.'

Mel's pretty face was so child-like in its enthusiasm that Felicity simply couldn't say no to her. There was no point in admitting that she'd never got on with her husband's mother and that not having to endure any time ever again with Nanna, aka Concepta Morgan, was one of the great pluses of the separation.

She could see that her husband's family were thinking along the same lines as her own mother and daughter: get the recalcitrant pair together and they'd make up. Simple! Everything could go back to the way it was before, a way that suited everyone except Felicity herself.

Perhaps actually seeing Felicity, Leo *and* his new love, Sonya, together might make them realise the truth.

'We can go together,' she said to her daughter, thinking it was a small sacrifice to make Mel feel happier.

'I was thinking of asking Shane to go,' Mel said. 'What do you think?'

Leo even left a message on her mobile phone answering service:

'I know Mel's going to tell you, but we do all want you to be there: it wouldn't be the same without you, Felicity.'

At work, they talked about ex-husbands and families and how hard it was to reconcile them all.

Zoë had an ex-husband who'd never been any sort of provider and still turned up on her doorstep from time to time, asking for money.

'He's had scores of women over the years but he still comes back to me,' she sighed. 'Lord knows why. He never had kids with the rest of them. I think that makes a difference. They associate you with the concept of family. Like you're their mother or something.'

'I love men, but I could never marry one,' said Chantelle, who was known to have a complicated romantic life. 'They are better to dip in and out of when you feel the need.'

'Right now, I don't feel the need for a man,' said Felicity.

46

'I certainly don't feel the need to go to my ex-mother-in-law's wedding anniversary party, but it's being presented to me as this great family affair and they'll all be devastated if I don't go.'

'Your ex, he is bringing his new woman?' asked Chantelle, getting right to the heart of the matter.

Felicity didn't know. 'Nobody can hope for us to get back together if he turns up with another woman, but he might not bring her in case he offends me.'

'He never worried about that before,' Zoë remarked.

'True. Do you think I should ask him to bring her?' Felicity said thoughtfully.

The pharmacy erupted into laughter.

'You're an original, Felicity,' said Zoë, 'I'll say that for you.'

Rosalie was thrilled with news of the anniversary party and clearly saw it the way the Morgan family saw it: as an excuse to get Leo and Felicity to see the error of their ways.

'Marriage is for life, Felicity, you see,' she said, adopting the wise-woman voice that made Felicity want to kick a hole in the wall. 'Nobody said it was easy, but some people manage to stay together through all the pain and heartache.'

'What heartache did Dad put you through?' Felicity demanded. If anything, the shoe was on the other foot. Her father should have been canonised for putting up with her mother.

'I'm not saying *we* had heartache, but I understand it,' Rosalie went on piously. 'You have your children to think of.'

'They're grown up and my husband cheated on me for

years,' Felicity snapped. 'I thought you'd be glad I'd finally stood up for myself.'

'I suppose I am, but I like Leo,' wailed her mother.

'We *all* like him,' roared Felicity. '*I* like him. I just didn't like being married to him!'

By November, Mel and Shane were deeply in love, Ryan was toying with the idea of moving to London for a year to work, and Felicity had acquired an apricot-coloured Burmese kitten called Miss Lillie.

She'd been on a double date with Chantelle and two divorced Belgian male friends, information she had not shared with any of her family. It had been enjoyable but it had made Felicity realise something very important: she wasn't interested in the flirtatious behaviour she remembered from her early years with Leo.

Her date, a charming furniture importer named Michel, was lovely company but when he asked her out on her own, she had to say no.

'You are not ready yet, perhaps?' said Michel kindly, over a coffee in Chantelle's pretty townhouse after the meal.

Felicity treated him to some of her new-found total honesty. 'It's not that, Michel,' she said. 'I'm not still in love with my ex or hurting over the separation. I've spent so many years pleasing other people, I haven't the energy to please anyone else. I want to please myself right now.'

'You might change your mind,' Chantelle said the following day.

'I might,' Felicity agreed, 'but at this exact moment in time, I simply have no desire to dress up to excite a man or to worry over whether I have cellulite or not. Why are we all supposed to worry about cellulite, anyway? Is that what suffragettes died for?'

'Sex is an important part of being a woman,' Chantelle argued.

'Michel is right, then,' Felicity agreed. 'I'm not ready yet. I'd prefer to wear socks in bed and watch BBC4. But when rampant desire hits me, I'll know who to call.'

Sonya was not going to the great Morgan family anniversary party.

'She wants to go, but Dad is insisting she can't,' Ryan revealed.

Felicity found herself feeling sorry for Sonya. It wasn't easy being involved with Leo Morgan.

'He should take her,' Felicity said. 'If he's living with her, he's living with her and everyone should just get with the programme. All this carry-on reminds me of parents not wanting unmarried grown-up children to sleep with their partners in the family home. You either respect that when your children grow up they have different values, or you don't.'

'Does that mean I can bring girlfriends to sleep in your flat?' asked Ryan.

His mother laughed. 'Of course you can, love. But remember, it's a small single bed. One move and you'll both be on the floor, which is bare wood, by the way.'

The pressure surrounding the anniversary grew.

Rosalie inveigled her daughter on a shopping trip that somehow took in an expensive lingerie shop.

'Isn't this the cutest thing you ever saw?' said Rosalie, inno-cently holding up a red silk bra and pants set with off-white lace trim. 'The label on the knickers says they're *Brazilian cut*.'

Felicity eyed her mother, aware that Rosalie's own lingerie tastes ran to severely cut white bras with the vaguely conical cups she'd worn as a young woman.

'Brazilian cut means the knickers are high cut over the bum and you'd probably spend the whole day adjusting them. Should I go the whole hog and buy a G-string?'

'There's no need to go that far,' said Rosalie crossly. 'I'm only trying to help.'

Felicity put the red outfit back on the rail. 'I know you are, Mum. Let's have a cup of tea and a bun, shall we? I'm not really a red silk person.'

When Mel phoned with details of accommodation in the hotel where the anniversary party was to be held, Felicity finally lost her temper.

The vast Morgan clan had taken over the entire hotel and one of Leo's sisters was organising the room allocation.

'Aunt Leslie has put all of us on the same floor. Shane and I have a double room, but she could only get a single room for you. The place is jammers! It's going to be fabulous.'

'A single room for me,' repeated Felicity, incensed by the presumption that she'd be on her own.

'You hardly need a double, do you?' said Mel cheerfully.

'What if I did?' The question was out of her mouth before she had time to think.

'Mum! You're married to Dad, for heaven's sake,' said Mel.

'Not any more,' her mother replied.

'Nanna Morgan's right, you know,' Mel said crossly. 'You're just thinking of yourself. I met Shane's parents the other day and they have a lovely home and do you know what I felt? Lonely, that's it. Lonely, because our family is all gone and I hate it, Mum. Did you think of me when you and Dad split up? No. It's as if it's not supposed to matter because me and Ryan are grown-ups, but it does. I hate all this, really hate it.'

And Mel hung up.

Felicity wondered where she had gone wrong. Mel had no thought for her mother's pain during all the years Leo had cheated on her. Ryan had. But not Mel.

Mel had Shane, her own busy life, and she wanted her parents back together because it suited her. She could see nothing else.

Felicity didn't sleep much that night. She looked back over her marriage and wished she and Leo had split up earlier, so that perhaps Mel might have grown to see that other people's feelings were important. It was not enough to be blissfully happy yourself and wounding all around you in the way Leo had done, the way Felicity had facilitated, she realised sadly.

When morning came and Miss Lillie crept up the bed to purr for attention, Felicity had come to a decision. She would go to the anniversary party on her own terms and she would show everyone that she mattered. She didn't want to hurt Mel, but Mel needed to come face-to-face with some truth.

She told Ryan when she'd finished making the arrangements.

'I feel guilty,' she said in the bar where they met for lunch.

Now that she'd put it all in place, she was suddenly filled with anxiety. 'I must be a bad mother, a bad daughter. I shouldn't be doing this, or telling you either. I'm turning into one of those dreadful people who drag their children into their confidence when their children don't want to be involved.'

'Mum, it's all right,' Ryan said. 'Mel, Dad and everyone else should realise that you have your own life now. I love Dad, but he didn't do the right thing by you for a long time. What's wrong with asking people to recognise that?'

Michel's car was a lovely old sporting thing with a long bonnet, low-slung leather seats and an air of romance about it.

'It's fabulous,' said Felicity in delight when she saw it.

'It's very old,' Michel said as he helped her in, 'so it doesn't have the suspension of modern cars.'

Felicity grinned. 'Us old things have quite good suspension, as it turns out.'

They both laughed.

On their fourth date, they'd ended up in bed in Felicity's apartment and she found that the red silk underwear made her feel better than she'd imagined. After the party, she would say a big thank you to her mother for showing it to her.

She was becoming very fond of Michel, whom she'd taken into her confidence about her plan early on, and his eyes had twinkled with mischief at the idea.

There were so many things to talk about that Felicity didn't notice the time passing on the journey to the town where the anniversary party was to be held. She'd cancelled her single room and she and Michel were staying in another hotel, a more elegant establishment where there was a double room complete with four-poster bed and claw-footed bath available. They arrived early so as to enjoy both the bedroom and then the spa and beauty salon, where they had massages before Felicity had her hair blow-dried into a becoming wavy style.

'What are you wearing to this party?' asked the hairstylist.

'A red silk dress, it's got a low back, and a high halter neck at the front,' Felicity revealed. The strange thing about red, she'd realised, was that it suited her and somehow made her feel like a braver version of herself. Plus, the Brazilian knickers actually didn't need to be adjusted every five minutes.

'That sounds lovely,' said the stylist. 'You're so tall and slim; you can carry that sort of thing off.'

Felicity and Michel arrived at the Morgans' ruby wedding anniversary celebration exactly on time. The anniversary couple were to make a grand entrance at five past eight, so the party-goers had been asked to assemble just before the hour.

Ryan came up to them straightaway. He hugged his mother, told her how wonderful she looked and shook Michel's hand.

'I think I should make a run for it while I still have time,' whispered Felicity to her son.

He held her in a steely grip.

'You're not running anywhere.'

Next to spot them was Leo's sister, Leslie, she of the room-organising fame.

'Felicity!' she said, open-mouthed, staring.

With Ryan's hand still gripping her arm tightly, Felicity smiled and introduced Michel.

'Mum's partner,' added Ryan, just in case Leslie hadn't

got the gist of it. 'Boyfriend sounds too young, doesn't it?' Ryan went on cheerfully. 'Lover sounds a bit too risqué.'

Felicity could feel herself turning a bit pink, but it was nothing compared to the colour of Leslie. She'd kill Ryan. He was definitely enjoying this too much.

'Does Leo know?' gasped Leslie finally.

Finally, Felicity felt the steel enter her own soul. 'I doubt it,' she said. 'We didn't discuss our arrangements. I presume he's here with Sonya? It would be terrible if he couldn't bring her. They're partners too, after all. I think it's vital that we all move on and behave like grown-ups.'

Leo was next to spy the three of them. Michel had procured some champagne and Felicity had downed her own glass quickly.

'Sorry,' she said, 'just needed a little pick-me-up.'

True to form, Leo didn't notice Michel at all, just smiled at Ryan and pulled Felicity into his arms for a hug.

'You look pretty gorgeous, my dear,' he said, charming as ever. 'I had no idea red suited you so much.'

Felicity recovered more quickly this time. Leo had seen a man beside her and had instantly ruled out the thought that said man could be with her. She pulled out of his embrace and introduced Michel.

'Michel, my ex-husband,' she said, putting a hand on Michel's arm. 'Leo, meet Michel. Michel was kind enough to drive us up – you know how I hate long drives. We're staying in the hotel across the road. I couldn't get a double here.'

Leo didn't gasp. His eyes narrowed as he took in the other man, a man who was taller, wore a very elegant Italian suit and was plainly sleeping with his ex-wife.

'You didn't tell me you were bringing someone,' he said.

Felicity ran through the answers at high speed in her mind.

She settled on: 'No, I didn't. Is Sonya here? I'd like to meet her. As I've said a million times to everyone, we should all be grown up about this.'

'Sonya's not here,' snapped Leo.

'Mum did say you should bring her,' Ryan pointed out.

At this moment, Michel chose to murmur to Felicity that perhaps she needed some privacy with Leo.

'No, darling,' she said, smiling. 'It's all fine. Let's find Mel and her boyfriend. I'll see you later, Leo.'

As she swept off, she could see Ryan put his arms around his father and say it was lovely to see him. There was no doubt about who was the more mature, she thought.

She and Michel came upon Mel at the bar, holding out for a pint of beer for Shane, who was, Mel had explained, not a champagne man.

'You look beautiful, darling,' Felicity said with a tremor in her voice. She wasn't sure if she was able for any more. If Mel got upset, Felicity vowed that she'd leave.

And at that instant, Michel said the best thing he could ever have uttered: 'So this is the beautiful, clever daughter I have heard so much about?'

He was a quick study, Felicity realised.

Mel beamed.

'I drove your mother up here,' Michel went on.

There was no mention of four-poster beds and what they'd already done in one. He understood totally.

'Hi, Michel,' said Mel. 'This is Shane.'

'You are good at computers, I believe?' said Michel.

Nobody was happier than Mel to be discussing how marvellous Shane was.

After the happy couple had been welcomed and the buffet was over, Mel sought her mother out again and pulled her to one side. Mel's face was worried.

'Dad says Michel is your date.'

'I suppose he is,' said Felicity, feeling a touch of Judas Iscariot as she cast off Michel so easily. 'I would have loved to have met Sonya,' she added. 'Ryan says she's lovely. The eight of us should go out one night to dinner: all the Morgans, Shane, Sonya, whoever Ryan wants to bring and Michel. It would be lovely.'

She held her breath then and waited. It felt like such a long wait. Mel could see her father sitting at a table of much younger guests – flirting with the women, if the wild laughter was anything to go by.

'I suppose that would be nice,' Mel said slowly. 'But you're a Barnes now, you've gone back to your maiden name.'

'Oh, pet, I'll always be a Morgan when it comes to you,' Felicity said. 'I'm your mum, nothing will ever change that.'

After the buffet, tables were pulled back for dancing. Michel and Felicity stood to one side and watched it all, apart and yet part of it.

'Thank you,' whispered Felicity, breathing in the scent of his aftershave. Eau Sauvage. She loved it.

'I have children myself and am divorced,' he murmured. 'Of course I understand. Shall we dance just once?'

Felicity could see her former mother-in-law in the distance. She'd gone to offer her congratulations but hadn't brought Michel in case Nanna Morgan said something rude.

'Yes,' Felicity said.

The band struck up the 'Anniversary Waltz' and the happy couple danced for a moment, then the band summoned all the guests up. Felicity held Michel's hand and they joined the throng on the dance floor. Michel danced very well, much better than Leo. For the first time since she'd entered the party, Felicity allowed herself to relax.

She could see Leo staring at her glumly from the bar, could see Ryan happily chatting to a girl near the door, and on the dance floor, Shane and Mel were locked together. Nanna Morgan was now being twirled by Leslie, who was waving at Leo to join them. Rather like a sulky child being asked to join a party, Leo ambled over and soon he, his mother and sister were linking arms and dancing, while his father sat down to catch his breath.

Mel was going to be fine and the Morgans could look after themselves. Felicity allowed the music to flow over her and laid her head on Michel's shoulder. They'd go back to their lovely hotel in a little while, but for now, it was marvellous to simply be herself.

Madame Lucia

Stanley Maguire hadn't planned on renting out the upstairs office. A large, L-shaped room on the floor above Maguire's Travel, the office had just been vacated and Stanley had finally decided that the time had come to extend his travel agency empire on to the second floor. The architect had already drawn up the plans and Stanley could see himself in a spacious room overlooking Main Street, with cool green walls and a couple of cream leather couches perhaps, for valued customers to sit on. It was time to make a statement about the success of Maguire's Travel.

And then the woman had come into the travel agency and asked him, in a quiet but somehow steely way, if she could rent the office out for a couple of weeks. Stanley had meant to say no. He'd done his best, in fact, but the words wouldn't come. There was something about her smiling round face and those warm brown eyes that made him lose the run of himself. No had become yes.

'No bother at all, Sister,' he'd said, because she had a look of a nun about her with her tidy grey hair and the sober navy suit. Sure, what harm would it be to have a nun in the place while he was away on holiday? He even heard himself offering to send the office cleaner up to dust and vacuum.

'Thank you, Stanley,' the brown-eyed woman said, clasping his hand. 'You're a kind man: I can tell.'

Stanley beamed like a schoolboy even though it was at least thirty years since he'd graced a schoolyard. It was only when she was gone that he realised that she hadn't told him her name or what she wanted the office for.

The girls in Maguire's Travel were fascinated when the small card went up above the doorbell for the upstairs office.

Madame Lucia: fortune teller

'I thought Himself was going to turn it into a posh office,' said Carmel, who'd worked in Maguire's longer than anyone else and who'd had it up to the tonsils with men and their empires. 'Wait till he comes back from his holidays and sees this! I suppose she'll be some flamboyant type who'll stick exotic lights in the window and have a stream of lunatics dropping in and out.'

But there was no stream of lunatics. There was only the neatly dressed figure of Madame Lucia herself going in and out quietly during normal business hours. Flamboyant was certainly not a word that could have been applied to her. Her hair was a soft grey, her dress was unremarkable and the only detail that stood out was that she appeared fond of sensible, lace-up shoes.

Between customers, Carmel, Gwen and Selena discussed how they didn't trust fortune telling.

Carmel didn't even read her horoscope any more. All the magazines had told her that Geminis and Libras could be a good match, but she and Michael had fought like cats and dogs and now Michael was back living with his brother while Carmel had their apartment to herself.

She was thirty-four and her mother kept making snide remarks about how living with a man before marriage hadn't been the gateway to anything but ruin when *she* was a girl.

'When you come to your senses, your old room is there for you,' her mother, Phil, said at least once a week.

Carmel knew she couldn't afford to pay the rent all by herself for much longer but neither could she face living with her mother again.

Phil wore her bitterness like an Olympic medal. It was the only thing she'd been left with when Carmel's father had walked out on her thirty-two years ago. She had seemed almost triumphant when Michael had moved out of the apartment he shared with her daughter.

History repeats itself, Phil had remarked grimly. Under the circumstances, Carmel had no interest in hearing that red was her lucky colour or that Saturday was her best day of the week. Such frivolity didn't cut any ice with her any more.

On the third day, Gwen decided to risk it.

She was ready for Madame Lucia, she told her colleagues confidently. Fortune tellers were canny and could read clothes, handbags and jewellery with as much skill as they could supposedly read the cards. Gwen's good leather handbag and her engagement ring would have given the game away.

She'd left her handbag and the ring with Carmel and she'd taken off her navy uniform jacket with 'Maguire's Travel' embroidered on one pocket, so there'd be none of that 'I see you going on a foreign holiday' malarkey. Madame Lucia would get no clues from her.

Upstairs, lemon aromatherapy oil was heating in a small burner and the air was redolent with scents of somewhere far away. Madame Lucia sat at a table with a crystal ball in front of her. She smiled silently at Gwen, who sat down politely and looked into the crystal ball too. They both gazed at it for ages.

Gwen did her best to see whatever it was that people saw in them. Fog or swirling mist. Wasn't that what you were supposed to see? Gwen tried hard but all she saw was a fat globe that smelled strongly of the window cleaner her granny was always using. Madame Lucia was not a million miles away from Gwen's granny, now that she thought about it.

Sensible beige cardigan, cream blouse buttoned up to the neck, a kind smiling face and not a jangling gypsy earring in sight. She even had the same sort of gold-rimmed glasses Granny wore but without the gold chain. Behind the glasses, Madame Lucia's eyes flickered, but she said nothing. Could Madame Lucia see something? Maybe it was all a con.

'You'll be married within the year,' said Madame Lucia. 'I am seeing San Francisco, I think. Yes, that's it.'

Gwen rolled her eyes. So much for fortune telling. She and Brian were going to Sardinia on their honeymoon.

'No, San Francisco,' Madame Lucia said firmly, as if she could read Gwen's mind.

Gwen blinked.

'I know you've booked somewhere else, but it'll be San Francisco in the end. There's a bit of a shock coming and you have to make a decision, but I think you'll take the right road. It's all for the best, really. You're a strong girl.'

'What about other things – money, family?' Gwen wanted more than this limited vision of the future.

'You came to ask me about love,' said Madame Lucia simply. 'That's what I saw for you.'

'I didn't say what I came to you for – ' began Gwen, but she stopped.

Because she *had* come to find out about her and Brian. Not that she'd have admitted it to anyone, even her closest friends, but there was something not quite right. Brian was so distant these days.

He looked uncomfortable when she began going through her wedding notebook, listing all the things they'd done and all the things they still had to do. Gwen was worried about the wedding cake. Was it unlucky to have a pyramid of profiteroles instead of the traditional fruitcake?

Madame Lucia smiled a kind, granny-ish smile. 'You'll do what's right,' she said.

'Well?' Carmel and Selena were curious when Gwen arrived back at work.

'Oh, you know, the usual rubbish,' said Gwen, searching

62

in her handbag for her mobile phone. She might just send Brian a text message about this evening.

Gwen and Brian met in Mario's Coffee Shop after work. Brian had pulled a sweatshirt on over his plain bank cashier's shirt and tie.

'What's up now with the wedding of the century?' he said gloomily, stirring two fat sugars into his latte. 'Don't tell me: the florist can't get the exact shade you want for the roses and everything's going to be ruined. Can we talk about something else?'

Gwen looked at him, hurt.

'How can you say that?' she began, and then stopped. He was right. All they ever talked about these days was the wedding. Gwen had dreamed of her wedding day since, aged five, she'd seen Barbie resplendent in her meringue of crispy lace.

'You're fed up with all this wedding stuff, aren't you?' she said.

The question took both of them by surprise.

'A bit,' he admitted. 'I feel as if I'm stuck on a roller coaster and I can't get off.'

Brian looked at Gwen to see how she was taking this. She wasn't gasping with shock or anything, so he took the plunge.

'I always thought it would be nice to get married on a beach or somewhere simple. Without all the fuss.'

Gwen thought of the elaborate plans for a wedding feast that was going to cost a fortune and which made her break into a cold sweat when she thought about the inevitable drama of the table plans. Imagine her wild uncles sitting beside Brian's beautiful but shy girl cousins? Or Brian's brother telling risqué jokes as best man, jokes that would shock Granny and make her reach for her heart tablets?

'If we had a quick, tiny wedding, just for immediate family, we could use the money we've saved for a huge holiday. Like . . .' she searched for a place '. . . San Francisco. We could tour the area, drive up Highway One, go to LA, everywhere . . .'

Brian didn't say anything. He didn't have to. The huge smile lighting up his face said it all.

Selena passionately believed in fortune tellers. She always had, but she couldn't say that because the girls would tell her to give it a go, and if Madame Lucia took one look at her, *she'd know*.

And Selena was terrified that someone would find out.

She still had the money, hidden in an envelope in her desk under a spare pair of tights so that anybody seeing the tights would know this was her personal drawer, and wouldn't look any further. Because two thousand euros was a lot of money and anyone with half a brain would realise that Selena, the office spendthrift, could never have saved that much in her life.

She hadn't meant to take it, she really hadn't. She had never stolen as much as a notebook from the office supply box, but that day a month ago that Stanley Maguire forgot to put the money in the safe was coincidentally the same day Selena received the awful letter from the credit card people.

How could she owe them that much money? Yes, she'd

bought the shoes and that long suede skirt that everyone admired so much, but surely she didn't owe nearly two thousand?

She'd added it up with shaking fingers on her calculator. Incredibly, all those small amounts of money (€19.99 for sunglasses that were almost exactly the same as the ones all the Hollywood stars had; a yoga video; a new wallet) managed to add up to the same heart-stopping total on the bottom of the statement.

Which made it seem like fate when Stanley, who turned absent-mindedness into an art form, had opened the safe to put the morning's cash in and had left one wad of notes on his desk.

He'd gone out to lunch then and Selena had picked up the money to give it to him later but somehow, once her fingers touched the cool, sleek notes, she'd known that this could solve all her problems.

Only it hadn't. Guilt burned her soul like the fires of hell and she hadn't had a decent night's sleep since.

'I know you don't believe in fortune telling,' said Gwen, who looked utterly delighted with herself since she'd called off the wedding, 'but Madame Lucia is different. She knows things. And she doesn't tell you bad things; only good news.'

What if you didn't have good news to tell? Selena thought miserably.

There was a lull in the office at eleven and Gwen urged Selena again.

'Go on, I bet you won't believe what she'll tell you. Look at me and Brian and how it's all worked out for the best.'

* * *

Selena kept her glasses on. She only needed them for the computer, but she thought that if she had a protective layer of glass between her eyes and the piercing gaze of Madame Lucia, the fortune teller mightn't see the guilt and the misery behind them.

'There's no need to be nervous,' said Madame Lucia pleasantly when Selena sat down, clasping and unclasping her hands anxiously.

Easier said than done, Selena thought. She tried to breathe deeply, but all that came out was a shaky, shuddering breath.

'It's not the end of the world, you know,' Madame Lucia remarked, staring into her crystal ball. 'Life tests us all every day: little temptations to see what kind of people we are. And you know what sort of person you are, after all. A good one.'

Selena's eyes brimmed. She wasn't a good person, she *wasn't*. If she had been, she'd never have been tempted by the money.

'You should talk to someone about a possible debt plan,' Madame Lucia continued. 'Pay off a little a week, that sort of thing. The banks are happy once you're paying something.'

Selena realised the fortune teller was talking about the credit card bill. She didn't know about the other money.

'Spring cleaning,' added Madame Lucia.

Mystified, Selena looked at her.

'The office hasn't had a good clean for ages. You'd be amazed at how things can fall down into drawers and filing cabinets and get lost. A good spring clean will soon restore everything to its rightful place.'

Her words sent a little jolt of excitement through Selena. Of course. It had been months since the office had been given a good sorting out. The back office was always cluttered with boxes and Stanley's desk had a paper mountain as big as Everest on the floor behind it.

A wad of money could easily have got lost in the mess. A wad of money that nobody would ever suspect had been hidden in Selena's drawer for a month.

'You'll talk to the bank, won't you?'

Madame Lucia stared at her and Selena saw in that instant that the woman knew about the other money. But there was absolutely no judgement in Madame Lucia's eyes. She was offering a way out, a solution.

Selena beamed at Madame Lucia. 'Yes, I'll talk to the bank. And thank you, for everything.'

She bounced down the stairs, her mind racing. A proper spring clean was definitely a good idea. Just because they'd all been busy lately didn't mean that standards should slip.

Carmel's asthma flared up halfway through Selena's office spring clean.

'There might've been money behind Stanley's desk, but there's nothing but dust in that corner,' she wheezed as Selena cleaned like a woman possessed.

Selena had already filled two bin bags and had come up with a new office code of conduct for dealing with duplicates of documents already on the computer system.

'If we back up the files on the hard drive, we needn't keep any paper copies,' Selena announced.

'I'm going out for some fresh air,' Carmel said.

Outside, she looked at the door that led to the upstairs office. Why not? she decided. She had a few minutes to spare.

She didn't waste time staring at the crystal ball. She eyeballed Madame Lucia, who gazed back with a quiet intensity. Then, Madame Lucia took Carmel's hand and gently turned it palm up.

Her unmanicured hand was cool and firm and Carmel felt some of the tension leave her.

'The ball tells the future, the palm tells the past,' the fortune teller said.

Carmel waited, not believing.

'You're carrying someone else's pain,' Madame Lucia said matter-of-factly. 'It's not your burden. You have to let it go before you can live your own life.'

Carmel held her breath. This was unexpected.

'There are two good men in your life. One is far away but he's never forgotten you. He prays for you.'

'He can't,' said Carmel, shocked, but knowing exactly who Madame Lucia was talking about. 'My father's gone, he left years ago. He's never written; he doesn't care.'

'He does and he has,' insisted Madame Lucia calmly. 'The other man cares deeply for you too, but there is this – ' she paused, considering, 'this *guard* around your heart that keeps him away. It's the pain you're carrying, the other person's burden. You have to let it go.'

Carmel was still trying to take in the first bit of information. 'What do you mean, "he has"?' she asked slowly.

'He has written to you,' Madame Lucia replied.

She squeezed Carmel's hand, this time in comfort.

'This is good news for you,' she said. 'This is a new beginning and you are in charge of it. You, not anybody else – not someone who is angry with the whole world.'

It was such a good description of her mother that Carmel smiled wryly.

'What should I do?'

Madame Lucia's mouth relaxed into a smile. 'That's up to you. The future is always up to you.'

Carmel's mother was polishing the brass on the door when Carmel walked up the path. Everything in No. 9 The Crescent was polished to within an inch of its life. Phil used to say it was because that waster hadn't left her much and she had to look after it. Carmel tried to imagine what it must have been like for her mother all those years ago. Alone with a small child and little money. Had that hard shell been her only defence?

'What brings you here?' demanded Phil, as if Carmel never visited rather than coming home at least twice a week.

'I wanted to talk about my father,' Carmel said evenly. She never called him Dad. Dad was for a person who had been there.

'What about him?' Her mother kept grimly polishing.

'About the letters.'

The old yellow duster stopped moving.

'How did you know?'

'That doesn't matter. I want to see them.'

Carmel waited outside until her mother emerged with a large manila folder crammed full of envelopes, some open, most untouched.

'I didn't want him in our lives any more,' her mother said in a small voice, handing the folder over.

Carmel said nothing: she'd become good at that over the

years. When Phil raged against Carmel's father, Carmel had learned to hold her tongue until the anger had burned out.

'Where are you going?' asked Phil anxiously as Carmel walked down the path, holding her precious cargo of letters.

'Home,' said Carmel pleasantly. 'I'll talk to you later.' There was no point in recriminations or bitter words. As she knew, that type of thing got you nowhere in life.

The most recent letter was dated the previous Christmas. Her father wrote every Christmas, despite never having had a reply in thirty-two years of writing. He'd worked it out, though. He knew his wife would never forgive him for walking out.

I hope that one day she'll give you these letters so that you'll know I've never forgotten you, he wrote. *I would love to see you but you would have to want to see me and you might not, because I left. Your mother was a hard woman to live with but I should not have left you. I was young and stupid, and I regret that every day of my life. She didn't want my money, didn't want anything of me.*

He lived in London, a city Carmel had visited many times, never knowing that her father lived just off the Hammersmith flyover and kept a picture of her as a baby in a frame by his bed. When she'd read the last letter, she'd phoned Michael, who'd come over immediately and hugged her tightly as she sobbed for all those lost years. Michael said she should write to her father. But Carmel wanted to visit him. Now, immediately.

'I'd love you to come with me,' she said hesitantly, not knowing if Michael would want to be involved any further because, after all, she'd pushed him away and they'd split up.

'Why don't we go tomorrow?' said Michael, holding her tightly.

Stanley's holiday in Florida had been fantastic.

'The holiday of a lifetime,' he said ruefully, patting his belly and remembering the pancake breakfasts he'd grown to love. 'Two weeks isn't enough, though. Two months would be better.'

He was delighted with the cleaned-up office, and even more delighted with the recovery of the missing two thousand euros.

'Fair play to you, Selena,' he said. 'You've worked hard on the place and I like the new hard-drive filing system. I suppose you'll be looking for some of that two grand as a raise?'

'No,' said Selena quickly.

He was less pleased to hear that Gwen wanted three months sabbatical to go to America.

'Ah, Gwen, what'll we do without you?' he complained. 'Anyhow, I thought you'd booked the Central Hotel for a big wedding?'

Gwen grinned. 'We've got it all worked out. Carmel has had five applications from people looking for holiday work now that the college term is over, and she and Selena say they can cope if we take one person on.'

'Where is Carmel?' Stanley suddenly realised that his office manager was missing.

'She had to go to London with Michael,' said Gwen. 'Something came up.'

'I thought she'd split up with Michael?' Stanley was getting very confused.

'It's all back on,' said Selena.

Well, Stanley didn't know what to make of it all, but if the women were happy, he supposed he was happy too. He looked at his watch. Half past nine. He had a meeting later with the architect about the office upstairs. It was time to get the *Stanley Maguire – The Empire* plans back on track. Then, he remembered that kindly woman who'd wanted the office for a couple of weeks.

'Is the nun still upstairs?'

All the phones went at once.

'She's not a nun,' said Gwen, leaping to answer a phone.

'She's a fortune teller,' Selena added, before saying, 'Hello, Maguire's Travel, how can I help you?' in her professional voice.

Stanley went out on to the street, then in at the door of the upstairs office. He marched up the stairs, feeling the weight of those extra pounds. There was nobody there, just a table in the centre of the floor with a chair on either side of it. A small card on the table caught Stanley's eye and he picked it up.

On one side was inscribed a child's prayer to a guardian angel and on the other was a picture of an angel, all flowing robes and wings, hovering on a cloud. Stanley smiled to himself and put the card in his pocket. Fortune teller, indeed. He knew she was a nun. Anyhow, she was gone, God love her, and it was back to work in the real world.

Off Your Trolley

Purple was not my colour. Not even a subtle, iris-hued gossamer cardigan that was supposed to drape delicately over the shoulders, revealing elegant collarbones before ending in fragile scallops around a Scarlett O'Hara-sized waist.

That's what it would have looked like on Chloë, my older sister: a girlie confection of silk that made the wearer look part water fairy/part supermodel.

On me, it just looked like something I'd knit myself, *without* the pattern. The tiny, elbow-length sleeves made my own solid forearms look as if they belonged to a sheet-metal welder, while the tiny mother-of-pearl buttons were stretched in a too-small rictus with the buttonholes as they strained against extra-enormous PMS-variety boobs.

In the cardigan and a slithery lilac skirt, I resembled nothing so much as a bruise in full colour. A big bruise.

Not the elegant, lissom girl I wanted to transform myself

into before the ten-year school reunion. Which was only six days away!

'Come out of the cubicle, Sarah,' ordered Chloë. 'We want to see you.'

I came out gloomily.

Chloë and the assistant looked at me for a moment, matching bird-like blonde heads at an angle, mascaraed eyes narrowed as they took in the purple ensemble.

They looked more like sisters than Chloë and I did: both petite, fine-boned and capable of giving admiring men in passing cars whiplash.

Being six foot tall with an athletic build, the only way I'd ever give a man whiplash was if I banged into him at full tilt.

With my height, men just weren't interested in me. I mean, I was the only female researcher in Reel People TV who'd never been chatted up by the Head of Marketing, although my colleague Lottie reckoned this was because even Slimy Eric didn't have the nerve to flirt with a woman who could look down on his bald patch. It wasn't that I secretly longed to feel his sweaty paw on my backside in the secrecy of the executive lift. I just wanted to be one of the girls for a change, instead of Amazon Woman.

'Perhaps the green one?' suggested the sales assistant.

Green! If purple made me look like a female boxer after a title match, green was even worse. Green made me look seasick, bilious, like second-stage bruising.

'I mean,' the assistant continued helpfully, seeing as I wasn't saying anything to the contrary, 'with your auburn hair, green would be lovely.'

'Green doesn't suit her,' Chloë announced in a bored voice, studying perfect gel nails for flaws.

Sometimes I hate Chloë.

'Don't worry about me. I'll have a wander around the shop and see if there's something else I'd like,' I lied, obviously convincingly enough, as the assistant drifted off to flog more Tiny Tears-sized clothes.

'I don't think there's anything else here that would suit you, and we don't have much time,' Chloë said crushingly. 'I have to be back in the office in half an hour.'

God forbid that she didn't get back to PR Solutions in time, I thought crossly, wrenching the curtain across the cubicle.

I mean, who else would be able to organise all those crucial details for the latest society launch she was involved in – like making sure the Page Three stunna who was guest of honour didn't end up sitting beside the footballer she'd kissed and told about the week before, or checking they'd got the right sort of mineral water so that the ladies who lunched wouldn't be belching through the speeches.

I carefully inched my way out of a hundred and fifty quid's worth of purple spider's web and simmered. Why did my only sibling have to drive me insane every time she opened her mouth?

Catching a glimpse of myself in the mirror as I reached for my T-shirt, I remembered why. Because Chloë was gorgeous and I wasn't. Because she had attractive men falling over themselves to take her out to dinner while my last date had been with a systems analyst named Humphrey who'd taken me to a sports club in Clapham and run out of cash after buying me two vodkas. And because at the age of twenty-seven I was sick and tired of being 'the clever one'.

Just a year apart in age, we were a million years apart in everything else. All through school, Chloë'd had endless boyfriends and everyone loved her. She'd actually been voted the most popular girl in the school in her last term. My claim to fame was winning the fifth-year physics prize, not an achievement guaranteed to make you a member of the cool gang. Chloë wasn't just a member of the gang; she *ran* it. Despite that, I still wasn't allowed in.

Ten years after leaving school, it still rankled. The invitation to the reunion had seemed like the ideal chance to redress the balance, to prove to the old girls of St Agatha's that I was different from the Sarah Powell of old: glamorous, successful, and chased by scores of men. Except that I wasn't any of those things. Well, I was successful enough. I'd just been given a promotion – *without* the help of the Head of Marketing – and I'd saved up enough for the deposit on a flat of my own. But the 'glamorous and chased by men' bit was a non-starter. You couldn't be glamorous with unruly long red curls, freckles and the build of an Olympic swimmer.

I'd drafted Chloë in to help purchase the perfect outfit. If anyone knew how to wow the St Agatha's Old Girls, it was Chloë. But that hadn't exactly panned out either. I suppose you couldn't expect a size-eight nymph to know what would suit a six-foot-tall Olympian with no discernible waist.

We hurried along Old Brompton Road together. Me stomping along in my TV researcher's uniform of black jeans, black leather jacket and white agnès b T-shirt. Chloë immaculate in a white Michael Kors trouser suit, killer stilettos and more MAC than Lady Gaga needed for a photo-shoot.

I was too disheartened to talk but she chattered away like a canary on acid.

There was a guy she liked from another PR company, she said, but she didn't think he liked her.

'Why not?' I said, surprised. Men loved Chloë.

'He just doesn't, right?' she snapped.

'Fine,' I said, although I didn't think Chloë had ever met a man before who didn't fall at her feet. She was obviously imagining it. He was probably shy. I was about to tell her to just chat to him, but I thought better of it. How could I give Chloë advice?

We kept walking.

'We're organising the opening of the Jacob Kelian exhibition at Jo Jo's on Friday night and everything's been going wrong,' she fretted, half-running to keep up with my long strides.

'Who's Jacob Kelian?' I asked, wondering if he was that bloke I'd seen on TV who made sculptures out of old wine bottles. If it was the same guy, he'd go berserk with delight when he saw all the raw materials he could dredge up from the drinks cupboard at my place. We never got around to cleaning out the old bottles, and when we were manless – most of the time – myself and my flatmate, Susie, went through quite a lot of bottles of wine for our spritzers.

'Honestly,' huffed Chloë. 'Don't you ever read the arts pages? He's only the hottest young artist around. He paints the most amazing nudes in oils.'

'Oh,' I muttered, keeping an eye out for taxis as I was now very late for work. 'Sorry, never heard of him.'

'He's gorgeous, you know – Jacob. I met him yesterday. Real he-man stuff, American-football shoulders,' Chloë said dreamily. 'You can come along on Friday, if you want,' she added off-handedly. 'It'll be fun.'

Since my usual Friday-night plans involved watching TV or going out with Susie and our pals to the Duke's Head, I accepted. Beggars couldn't be choosers. And there were bound to be cocktail nibbly things to eat, so I wouldn't have to cook that night. Although it did cross my mind that Chloë probably wanted me there so I could hand out the cocktail nibbly things.

On Tuesday I left work early and hit the shops desperately hoping that the perfect reunion dress would leap out at me screaming *Buy Me! Buy Me!*

Nothing leapt out, apart from a blue fleece jacket that would look great with jeans but would hardly cut the mustard in Brighton's poshest restaurant among sixty Prada-clad high-fliers.

Dejected and ravenous, I hiked over to Marks & Spencer's food hall and proceeded to trawl the aisles for dinner. Forget the latest turn-into-a-nymph-in-a-week diet, I thought savagely, as I threw a brace of full-fat chocolate dessert things in my basket along with a tub of ice cream.

The reunion's on Saturday, my conscience reminded me, so I put it all back and took two low-cal mousses instead.

'I can never make up my mind either,' said a deep voice with a faint American twang. 'I love the fatty stuff, but you've got to really work it off.'

I wheeled around and found myself staring up – yes,

up – at a dark-haired man in denim who was holding a shopping basket crammed with fruit. He was undeniably good-looking, with short, wavy hair brushed casually back, glittering black eyes and enough designer stubble to make him a dead ringer for the Diet Coke bloke. Broad-shouldered and lean in a grey marl sweatshirt worn with faded jeans, he was one of the few men I'd ever met who dwarfed me. He certainly looked like he worked out. All he needed was the Harley Davidson, I thought with a gulp, noticing the biker boots and the chunky diver's watch on one massive tanned wrist.

'I don't usually do this, but I couldn't help noticing you,' he said, dark eyes appraising me coolly. 'Would you like to go for a drink when you've picked up your groceries?'

I stared at him the way you would stare at a strange, admittedly gorgeous man who'd just chatted you up in the supermarket. My mind raced. This had to be a joke. There was no way he was for real. Men like this went for beautiful girls like Chloë. They didn't eye up women like me over the low-fat yogurts, even when I was wearing my favourite pinstripe stretchy trouser suit and had recently washed my hair.

I peered around him, convinced I'd see someone from Reel People TV hiding behind the cheese, giggling hysterically at the idea of having set me up so marvellously. I couldn't see anyone, but I knew they were there. It had to be Lottie's idea; she loved practical jokes and had just started dating some American bloke. They'd probably spotted me coming into M&S and had decided to play a wicked trick. It wasn't going to work.

'Are you on a day release, by any chance?' I asked, trying to sound supercilious. 'Is this Care in the Community Week?'

'No.' He looked a bit surprised at this. One dark eyebrow went up in a look that was almost genuine. Probably an out-of-work actor, I thought. Lottie loved actors.

I marched off towards the vegetables. Nobody was going to make a fool out of me. He followed.

I picked up some celery and stuck it virtuously in my basket. Whoever he was, he wouldn't be able to tell Lottie that I was a glutton who ate the wrong things. I dumped another packet of celery in for good measure. The fact that I didn't like celery was immaterial. You could use it for Pimm's, couldn't you?

'I didn't mean to give you a shock, but I really would like to buy you a drink,' he said, standing very close to me so that I could smell his aftershave, a musky scent I didn't recognise.

New York? I wondered. I'd never been very good at American accents. *I'd rilly likta buy y'a drink*. Great accent, great voice. Dark, rich and treacly. Great-looking guy. I sighed. Why couldn't this be happening for real?

To take my mind off him I stared at the avocados. I loved them with vinaigrette, onions and black pepper. But they were anti-diet items and I only bought them in moments of complete piggery.

Mr America expertly squeezed a couple of avocados with one tanned hand and stuck them in my basket. I stuck them back on the rack with their friends.

'Avocados are full of protein and their nutritious qualities outweigh their calorific content,' he pointed out calmly, putting them back in my basket.

'What are you telling me that for?' I demanded, eyes glinting dangerously. 'Are you telling me I'm big or something?' The joke was going too far.

'No, you're just right.'

I stuffed his bloody avocados at him crossly. 'Yeah, and every actress in Hollywood would look better with another stone or two on.'

'Probably,' he said evenly.

'Anyway, what are you doing in the vegetable section?' I pointed accusingly at his basket where a head of lettuce and two giant cucumbers nestled in the middle of a large bunch of bananas, a honeydew melon, several lemons and a net of oranges. 'You've got enough fruit and vegetables for a vegan orgy. Are you following me?'

'Yes.'

'Are you a friend of Lottie's?' I snapped.

'Lottie? Who the hell is Lottie?' he asked, his accent becoming even more pronounced.

He couldn't have faked that much surprise. Not unless he was a very good actor, and a very good actor would have been rehearsing for some play or other and wouldn't have time to play games with Lottie.

'You mean you're not doing this for a joke?' I asked in a less strident voice.

His eyes, which were intelligent for such a handsome beefcakey type, sparkled. 'You think I'm doing this for a joke? I'm not. I wanted to buy you a drink. If you're not interested, say so. But I am.'

I loved the way he said 'interested'. *Innerested.*

'I didn't say that,' I mumbled.

81

'Great.' His face was creased in a huge grin, a gloriously sexy grin with gleaming white American teeth in a movie mouth which I had a sudden vision of being glued to.

Control yourself, Sarah! I ordered. Being manless for a few months shouldn't turn you into a complete sex-mad nympho.

'OK. Let's have a drink.'

We sat in Callaghan's Irish Bar in Piccadilly, bags of shopping clustered around our feet. Jake – that was his name – had obviously been there before because he led me to a cosy little snug in the back bar, pushed the revolving stained-glass windows shut and ordered drinks from a chatty barman he knew by name.

Unlike Humphrey, he didn't run out of money in 2.5 seconds. We talked about the oddest things, things I'd never discussed on a first date – well, not that it was a date, exactly. When he asked me why I'd thought he was joking when he chatted me up, I explained. I told him about being the 'tall, clever one', about Chloë the PR queen, and about the reunion that was hanging over me like the Sword of Damocles. It was strange for someone so physically blessed, but he understood.

He explained that his elder brother was a doctor and his younger sister was a teacher: steady professionals. He'd been the wayward one who'd run off to Europe to follow his dream and it hadn't worked out quite the way he'd planned. After years of waiting on tables by night, he still hadn't got anywhere. It had hurt like hell admitting to his family that he'd failed.

'What was your dream?' I asked softly.

He grinned boyishly. 'To be an artist.'

'I'm afraid I don't know anything about art,' I said ruefully. 'I'm a philistine. But what do you do now?' I asked quickly, not wanting to labour the point that he obviously wasn't an artist if his dream had failed.

He looked down at his hands, large hands that had a smattering of yellow paint on one thumb. 'I'm a decorator,' he said abruptly.

It was a wonderful evening. He was funny, charming, clever, and seemed so interested in me. We both loved *Two and a Half Men*, hated hip hop and adored Billie Holiday. His favourite movie was *Some Like It Hot*, which was certainly in my top ten, and our birthdays were exactly six months apart, although he was three years older.

After our drink, we meandered over to Compton Street and ate enormous chicken sandwiches in a jazz-filled bistro. Our knees touched under the table. It felt electric – to me, anyway.

At half ten, he said he had to go.

We stood outside the bistro door, shopping bags knocking off each other. He stared down at me, dark eyes in shadow.

'I've really enjoyed this evening, Sarah,' he said. 'You're so different from the women I've met recently – they're all so uptight and they think I'm something I'm not,' he added, a bit confusingly. 'You're not like that. You're an original.'

I blushed and was so busy wondering if I looked horrible and red that I didn't notice his lips coming down to meet mine. As kisses went, it was gentle, his lips firm but not probing. But the effect it had on me was incredible. My stomach muscles clenched involuntarily and I felt as if a million fireworks had been set off deep inside me. I didn't know how good he was with a Laura Ashley floral border, but he could certainly kiss for America.

'I'd like to see you again,' he said when he stopped kissing me.

Like a shot, I dumped my shopping, rooted a pen out of my pocket and wrote my number on a matchbook. (It's obvious that I only got as far as page three of *The Rules*, isn't it?)

He stuck it in his jeans pocket. 'See ya,' he said, waving.

I waved back happily.

He wouldn't call. I knew it. It was one of those rules of dating: the sort of bloke you wished wouldn't call always did, and the one you dreamed about every night for a week never remembered your number. Or at least that's what he'd say the next time you bumped into him by accident and he had to come up with a rapid excuse. Jake had no excuse for not remembering my number. But he wouldn't ring because, no matter what he said about liking big girls, I probably wasn't his type. I was Humphrey's type; Humphrey, the two-vodkas-and-I'm-broke type.

At least wondering if Jake would call took my mind off the reunion for the rest of the week. I'd stopped caring about what devastatingly sexy little outfit I'd turn up in to stun the old girls into awed silence. Nightmares of looking like hell in my old school uniform had been replaced by hot, sweaty dreams of being kissed by a giant American with meltingly beautiful eyes, a cheeky grin and arms that could crush you to death.

Chloë called round on Thursday night in time to see me open a bottle of rosé in Jake-didn't-phone depression. Unusually, she seemed depressed too. From the train of the conversation, you didn't need to be Einstein to figure out that some bloke was the root of the problem.

'Men like you,' Chloë said sadly. 'They don't like me.'

I was stunned. 'But that's not true,' I protested. 'Guys love you, they fancy you rotten.'

Chloë looked at me pityingly. 'Sarah, if you don't know the difference between lust and like at your age, there's no hope for you.' She adjusted herself on the sofa and took a deep slug of her rosé. 'Men fancy the knickers off me,' she announced, 'and generally that's what they want to do – get my knickers off. They want to *talk* to you. I couldn't tell you the last time any man wanted to talk to me.'

I looked at her fine-boned face, the silky blonde hair rippling artfully around her shoulders and the slim legs curled up under her, legs I'd have killed for. Chloë had never eaten a Ryvita in her life, only had to open her cigarettes outside the pub for ten guys to proffer lighters, and hadn't spent a single New Year's Eve without a date since she was fifteen.

'I don't have the knack, that's all,' she said. 'It's so easy for you – you just talk to them, you speak their language,' she added, almost accusingly.

I thought longingly of Jake, gorgeous Jake who spoke my language and still wasn't interested. She hadn't a clue.

'We've this new client,' Chloë was saying. 'He's into opera and we're organising an event for him. I had to take him out yesterday and he just looked bored rigid all during lunch.

He wasn't interested, I could tell. I tried *everything*. I was even wearing my Marc Jacobs suit,' she wailed.

I poured her more wine.

'Welcome to the club, Chloë,' I said, feeling suddenly sorry for her.

Perhaps I'd been wrong about Chloë's fabulous effect on men. Maybe she wasn't such a man magnet, after all. Maybe we were more like each other than I'd thought.

I wore my stretchy trouser suit again. It seemed the right thing for an art gallery do and anyway, everything else was still at the dry cleaners or the bottom of the laundry basket. I'd just wolfed down three baby quiches and half a glass of red wine when I saw him. He was talking to Chloë, still wearing his biker boots and faded black jeans but this time with a white cotton shirt that was open at the neck, revealing the tanned throat and the cluster of dark hairs I'd admired just a few days before.

Even across the room, I could hear Chloë's voice as she introduced a couple of grey-suited men to him.

'Meet Jacob Kelian, tonight's star,' she said brightly.

I felt a lump in my throat. Jake. Jacob. Decorator, huh? I had been conned, but not by Lottie. By a man. A handsome, bored artist who thought it was fun to pick up women in supermarkets and chat them up. Maybe it was for a bet, a variation on the 'see who can screw the least attractive woman' game played by holidaying lager louts in Torremolinos. The lump threatened to become an all-out howl of misery.

Glancing around for somewhere to put my wine glass, I heard my name being called.

The base of a sculpture would have to do. It was better than all over his shirt, which was where I really wanted to dump it. I'd made it to the gallery door before he caught up with me and grabbed my arm with one large hand.

'Get off,' I hissed, wrenching my arm away. 'You lied to me.'

'I'm sorry.' He looked it. 'Please give me a chance to explain, Sarah.'

'What is there to explain?' I said angrily.

People turned to look at us. Jake pulled me into the relative privacy of the foyer. 'Please listen, Sarah,' he begged.

I couldn't resist those dark eyes. 'Why didn't you tell me who you were?' I asked quietly. 'Was that a joke?'

'Why do you think everything's a joke?' Jake asked in exasperation. 'Do I have a funny face or something?'

I couldn't help smiling, even though it hurt. 'No, I do.'

He took my face in his hands. 'You don't. You have a wonderful face, a face I'd like to paint. I'd quite like to paint the rest of you too.'

I went puce, knowing that the walls were covered with Jacob Kelian nudes. Nudes of Olympian women. Suddenly it all made sense.

I faced him, eyes blazing. 'Why? Because you need another heap-of-the-week model? How many do you go through per exhibition?'

'In fact,' he said calmly, 'these are all pictures of my last girlfriend. We split up a year ago and I haven't painted a new subject since. I need to feel connected to someone to paint them, and I haven't. Until Tuesday.' He paused. 'I lied because I was sick of meeting people impressed by what I did and what I was becoming. I wanted to meet a normal person who'd like me for being ordinary Jake Kelian from Queens instead of media darling, award-winning Jacob. That's all.'

He looked at me earnestly, one hand still caressing my arm through my jacket. 'My cleaning lady washed the jeans and I couldn't read the matchbook any more.'

Yeah, right, I thought sourly.

'I've rung every TV production company in London looking for you,' he added. 'I finally tracked you down today and a woman named Lottie told me you'd gone early to a hush-hush meeting, you were then going to a journalistic seminar and wouldn't be back.'

I gazed at him open-mouthed. That was exactly what I'd told Lottie to say in case our boss, who was on holiday but constantly rang to check up on us, phoned after I'd skived off early.

He *had* rung after all.

'I was crazy to see you again. I couldn't believe it when I saw you here – and I knew what you'd think. I want you to trust me, Sarah. Please say you'll stay here for the evening. I'd love to have you with me.'

'And will you ring me tomorrow for a date?' I asked tartly. 'Or will you lose my phone number again?'

'I thought you were going to a reunion tomorrow,' he said.

My heart fell. 'Oh yeah, I'd forgotten.'

'Tell you what,' he said, pulling me closer and kissing my forehead, 'how about if I drive you down and stay over? Brighton's not that far. We can make a day of it, have lunch in a pub along the way. If the party's boring, you can always meet up with me.'

'Drive down in what?' I asked.

'On my bike.'

'Don't tell me,' I said. 'It's a Harley.'

'How did you guess?' he asked.

I didn't answer. A vision of myself in leathers, clinging to Jake for dear life as we pulled up to the restaurant, all my old school pals gazing out admiringly at my hunky, clever, and successful escort, fluttered into my head. And then that vision was replaced by a fabulous one of me and Jake together, dating and being happy. Suddenly, the reunion didn't matter at all.

'Perfect,' I breathed. 'That would be perfect.'

May You Live in Interesting Times

The night of the Ryans' twentieth wedding anniversary was the first time Ruby Anderson ever felt really old. It hit her when she discovered that she couldn't even fit into her fat black trousers, the emergency ones with the forgiving waist that could cope with a stomach rounded by months of comfort-eating chocolate.

'It's official: I am thirty-nine and three-quarters and a slob,' she told her reflection gloomily, ignoring the screams of delight from downstairs as the babysitter produced the evening's dual bribes of a deep-pan pizza and the DVD of *Shrek 2*. Shrek was the cultural icon for Ellie, nine, and Lewis, seven. Ruby knew it was her own fault for not having played endless Mozart to them when they were in the womb.

'Whadidyasay?' roared Tim from the bathroom, where he was clearly doing things with that horrible nose-trimming machine his mother had given him for his birthday. Even its buzz sounded nasal.

'I can't fit into my clothes,' Ruby roared back. She delved into the wardrobe at high speed because they were late already. 'My black trousers are too tight.'

Saying the words was a mini defeat in itself. She was finally on the road to having no waist. And she didn't have fabulous legs to compensate, unlike her mother, who had such shapely calves.

'Wear jeans,' Tim said over the drone of his nose machine. 'It's a barbecue. That's pretty casual, isn't it?'

The death glare flared briefly in Ruby's eyes. If she couldn't fit into her ordinary clothes, then she was not going to be metamorphosed into a supermodel in her jeans now, was she?

The brown hip-skimming jersey tunic and matching elastic-waisted trousers – bought in panic when Lewis was three months old and she'd still looked heavily pregnant – were the only decent, non-sweatshirt items of clothing that actually went over her hips. It was a sexless outfit, Ruby admitted miserably to herself. She resembled nothing more than a large dark chocolate: solid and definitely a little bitter on the inside.

The second shock of the evening came courtesy of the Ryans themselves at the end of the speeches. There had been wine, food (wonderful Chinese dishes from a proper catering company, a step up from the normal fare at barbecues on their road), plus a jazz band and real waiters with a seemingly endless supply of booze. And just when everybody thought it couldn't get any better, Deirdre and Lorcan Ryan delivered their news.

'We're emigrating to Australia,' Lorcan said, beaming.

Deirdre was grinning so much that her fillings were visible. 'The house is sold. We're off next month. To Melbourne.'

After the previous fifteen minutes of anodyne *thank you all for coming and we would like to thank our families* speeches, Ruby thought this must be Lorcan's idea of a joke.

'Australia? Deirdre and Lorcan?'

'Fair play to them,' said Tim beside her. He'd freely availed himself of the waiter service and his world was now a happier place. Even better, the Ryans lived only four houses away from him and Ruby. They could stroll home whenever it suited them without the palaver of looking for a taxi. Happy days.

'But I'd have never thought – ' stammered Ruby. The Ryans – of all people to do something so exciting.

Deirdre Ryan could spend a month deliberating over whether or not to have her hair layered. What fit of wildness had prompted her and her husband to up sticks and emigrate?

'It's such a big step,' Ruby went on, thinking enviously of what she'd read about beautiful Australian homes with year-round sunshine and a pool in the backyard.

'Wait till I show you photographs of the house in Melbourne.' Lorcan Ryan was proudly telling everyone about their fabulous new life-to-be. He talked animatedly about a half-acre site with a verandah around the house, a championship-quality public golf course just up the road, the wonderful school the kids would go to.

'Sasha wasn't sure at first, she's nearly seventeen, so it's harder for her to leave her friends, but when we told her about what life will be like out there, she was hooked like the rest of us.'

Lorcan looked different now, Ruby thought in surprise, as if the news had given him a new glow. He and Deirdre were doing something with their lives, not just stagnating. Like her and Tim, Ruby realised sadly, conscious of the promise of youth drifting away.

It was this second surprise that completely floored Ruby. Perhaps tomorrow was the day to start the diet to end all diets.

She was dickering over choosing the strawberry pavlova or the lemon cheesecake when she found herself beside Hannah, a woman eight doors down with a daughter in Ellie's class.

Normally the sort of mum who turned up in old jeans and a T-shirt to pick up the kids on rainy days, today Hannah was wildly glamorous in a striking pink chiffon kaftan and cream linen trousers that Ruby knew wouldn't have gone up over one of her own legs.

Hannah had a man in tow and she introduced him gleefully.

'Hi, Ruby, lovely to see you. Meet my date, Simon.'

As Hannah already had a husband named Davey, theoretically rendering the whole date thing obsolete, Ruby was momentarily speechless. 'Duh – er,' was all she could manage. Hannah and Davey must have split up and nobody had told her, and should she say something about how awful that was, or just forget it and act delighted to meet this new guy?

'Hello, how are you?' said Simon cheerfully, holding out a hand. He was much better looking than Davey, Ruby thought. Davey was quiet and sturdy. This guy had an open-necked shirt, leather rockstar necklaces round his throat, and a pair of Ray-Bans stuck in his shirt pocket. He was cool, or whatever young, hip people said nowadays.

'Nice to meet you too,' mumbled Ruby.

'Great party,' said Hannah chattily. 'The food's lovely, and isn't it gas about them going to Australia? Might as well grab life while you can, right?'

'Er, yes,' said Ruby.

Hannah might think Ruby was very cold if she didn't mention Davey and commiserate over the break-up of the marriage. Surely Hannah should have whispered that in her intro: like, 'This is Simon. Davey and I are separated. It was awful, but I got over it, and wayhay, I've got a new man!'

Ruby felt the pressure build to say The Right Thing.

'Sorry about you and Davey,' she whispered, so that Simon wouldn't hear.

'Oh, we haven't split up,' said Hannah loudly. 'Simon's just a bit of fun.'

'He'll hear you!' Ruby went puce with mortification.

'He's deaf, unless we're talking about sex, aren't you, honey?'

She put an arm around Simon's waist and he smiled vaguely.

'Better go,' Hannah added. 'Places to go, people to see.' And she winked at Ruby.

Ruby had pavlova *and* lemon cheesecake, to restore herself after the shock. What was happening to the world? Was she the only sane one in it?

'Did you meet Hannah's date?' asked Brenda, another neighbour. The party was winding up and the waiters were distributing tea, coffee and fortune cookies.

'God, yes,' said Ruby, dying to discuss it. 'She introduced him to me and I honestly didn't know what to say.'

'He's fabulous looking,' Brenda said, as if that was explanation enough. 'She's introducing him to *everyone*! Well, wouldn't you?' Brenda was an elegant fifty-something who had two grown-up kids and a recent divorce.

But what about Davey? 'What about him?' Brenda shrugged. 'If Hannah wants a bit of passion, who are we to stop her? That's where I went wrong with Ronnie, you know. We stuck it out like two squares for years, clinging to marriage because that's what people did. If I'd had an affair, I might have realised what I was missing and got out when I was still young, instead of sticking to Ronnie until it was too late for us both.'

Ruby was used to straight talking from Brenda, but this was intense stuff.

'Fortune cookie, madam?' asked a waiter, interrupting them.

'Thank you.' Ruby took one and cracked it open absently.

'*The dawn brings wealth tomorrow*,' Brenda read from hers. 'Remind me to buy a lottery ticket. What's yours say?'

Ruby unfurled it. '*May you live in interesting times*. Some hope of that,' Ruby muttered. 'My life's totally uninteresting.' Compared to everyone else's, it was. She must be dull as dishwater and a conservative to boot at being shocked by Hannah's affair, when even Brenda, who was at least fifteen years older than Ruby, thought married women having lovers was a good thing.

'I don't think that's a good fortune,' Brenda said thoughtfully. 'I think it's a curse, actually. I'm surprised they put that in a cookie.'

Ruby put the fortune in her handbag. How could interesting times be a curse? Boring, dull times: now that was a curse, all right.

That night, Ruby lay in bed and thought about it all. When she and Tim first got married, they'd had such hopes and dreams. They were going to change the world, be different from their parents, never own a gravy boat or tell their children that modern music had awful lyrics and no tunes. Now, she read about other people's hopes and dreams in *Hello!*, shuffled along with her life and watched her neighbours do interesting things. Like emigrate to stunning countries, or have wild affairs with men other than their husbands, and fit into their clothes without leaving the waistband buttons open. Nobody wanted to have wild sex with her, and she would never have considered the possibility of such a thing, although it seemed she was the only one in the area who didn't. She couldn't fit into most of her wardrobe and she could suddenly see herself in ten years' time, looking in the mirror at a woman wearing sensible mumsy clothes, and wondering where the slim-hipped girl she'd been had gone.

Even the most boring neighbours on their road had a more exciting life than she and Tim did.

Ruby was a part-time typist in a secretarial firm and the most thrilling part of her day was wondering whether to have chocolate or crisps at elevenses. While the Ryans were emigrating to the other side of the world.

The flirtations with punk music, trips in a beat-up camper van to wallow in the mud at Glastonbury, and her Pilates classes had all been in vain: she and Tim had become their parents. They were old. *She* was old.

Ruby sat bolt upright in the bed. Life was passing her by. Hadn't her fortune cookie told her she could have interesting times? She'd better jumpstart the process herself.

Beside her, sleeping off the barbecue wine, Tim snored contentedly.

'Do lots of people have affairs, do you think?' Ruby asked her sister, Cat, the following Monday. Cat worked in television, knew everything, and if by some miracle she didn't know what you asked her, she had the mobile number of someone who would.

'They're all at it in work,' Cat said dismissively. 'Long boozy media lunches are supposed to be a thing of the past, but they're not. There are hotels around here where you can definitely rent rooms by the hour. Most people meet lovers in the office, you know. It's the new sexual hunting ground.'

Not in Carrickmines Secretarial Services, Ruby thought. The staff were all female, so unless she became a lesbian or went bi, it was not a suitable sexual hunting ground for her.

At the school gates that afternoon, Hannah arrived late and rushed off without saying hello to Ruby.

She looked amazing, Ruby thought gloomily, feeling lard-like in her pink striped sweatshirt by comparison. It wouldn't be hard to get a lover if you looked like that. Not that Ruby wanted a lover, she told herself. But it would be quite nice to have someone flirt with her, as if they desperately wanted to drag her off to a hotel for some room-by-the-hour sex. She could always say no. But being asked would be nice. It would make you feel better about your marriage, if you knew someone else wanted you, wouldn't it?

'I think Hannah Timmons is having an affair,' she told Tim that night when she was taking the lasagne out of the oven.

'Really,' murmured Tim, stuck on nine across.

'Well, I know she is,' Ruby amended.

'Yeah.'

She banged the pasta pan down on the counter. Tim didn't even look up from his crossword.

'Lorcan and Deirdre are going to be off to Australia soon. It sounds amazing out there. Have you ever thought about us emigrating?' she asked.

'What?' Tim dropped his pen. 'When my team's doing so well in the Champions League?' he asked, stunned.

Ruby borrowed some diet books from Cilla at work. Cilla had been in Carrickmines Secretarial Services nearly as long as Ruby, and she'd tried every diet going: Atkins, South Beach, GI.

As the GI didn't involve eating eggs morning, noon and night, Ruby plumped for that. It was easy enough, and after a couple of weeks, she was able to sit down in her jeans without feeling as if someone had tied a tourniquet around her waist.

The shedding of six pounds made Ruby feel a whole lot better. Still not young, but better. Able to flirt, anyhow. That's all she wanted. Not to be like Hannah, but not to be invisible, either.

On the Saturday morning, three weeks after the Ryans'

bash, she drove Lewis to swimming and then dropped Ellie at ballet. She had a whole hour and a half off and most weekends she wheeled a trolley up and down the supermarket aisles. Today, a different sort of woman was going to buy the family's food, a woman who refused to give in to old age and who'd spent ages with the eyeliner trying to perfect that little Audrey Hepburn-esque flick up at the corners. Her dark hair was shiny, she was drenched in Eternity, and she was ready for some interesting times.

The man behind the counter in the deli on Market Street was pretty gorgeous. Greek, she thought, with olive skin, lips made for kissing and a flirtatious way of looking at his female customers.

'Hi.' Ruby leaned against the counter, twirled a bit of hair with one finger and tried to look sexy.

'Hello, can I help?' Adonis asked.

'Well, I'd like some Parma ham, six slices, and a piece of that brie. Four euros' worth.'

'No problemo.'

He hefted the wheel of brie up and began to cut it, without looking at Ruby. She tried to stand provocatively, balancing a hand on one hip, making sure her glossed lips were still moist. His eyes stayed on the brie. She twirled some more hair. Honestly, would he ever look at her?

Finally, he handed her the package of brie. It was now or never.

'How are you?' Ruby tried a bit of glinting-eye technique and followed it up with some eyelash flickering. 'I haven't seen you for ages.' Flicker, flicker.

Adonis angled his handsome head in concern.

'Have you got something in your eye?' he asked helpfully. 'A speck of dust? Customers aren't supposed to use the loo, but seeing as how it's an emergency. There's nothing worse than something getting stuck in your eye.'

'No, it's fine,' Ruby murmured, and looked down at her feet. 'I'm fine. Do you know, I'm in a rush. Forget about the ham. I'll just pay you for the cheese.'

A huge moving truck was parked in the Ryans' driveway when she got back home with the kids. The house must have sold as soon as the estate agent put out the details, because no 'for sale' sign had ever appeared in the garden. Ruby thought of her own house and what sort of frantic hard work would be required to make anyone want to buy it before a sign had been put up. There were scuff marks all over the magnolia-coloured walls. Her parents' house was magnolia-coloured too. What had she been thinking?

'We need to redecorate,' she announced to Tim when she got home. 'This place is a pit and it's so old-fashioned. We need to liven it up!'

'Painting?' asked Lewis happily. He loved painting, especially when the teacher let them put paint on their hands and do handprints. 'I can help.'

'And me. Can I have a purple bedroom instead of pale pink?' asked Ellie. 'I don't like pink any more.'

'You can have whatever colour you want,' Ruby said, kissing her daughter. 'The whole house is going to be brightly coloured from now on. It'll be fun! We're going off to buy paint after lunch.'

100

'This afternoon?' asked Tim, who'd had a hard week at work.

'No time like the present.' Ruby wondered why she hadn't thought of this before. Once the house was a vibrant family home instead of a shrine to magnolia, she could get a book on feng shui and put everything in the proper place. Then, lots of interesting things would happen and life would be exciting.

'We could paint the hall plain white, like a gallery, and put pictures everywhere. And have the kitchen crimson or dark blue, and paint a mural in the bathroom, with a jungle theme. Wouldn't that be gorgeous?'

The hall was bigger than it looked and it was only half-painted by nine that night. Ruby was quite weary at the thought of having to start again in the morning, but they couldn't leave it now. One half was a shabby cream and the other half was blindingly white. Plus, she was tired and had belatedly realised that decorating was only bearable when you could stop for lots of cups of sugary tea and chocolate biscuits.

'Are you in the mood for love?' asked Tim hopefully when they slumped into bed, still with spatterings of white paint on their skin. He nuzzled her neck gently.

'I'm on the GI diet,' Ruby shrieked with the full force of a woman deprived of biscuits and KitKats. 'If I'm not allowed anything nice, neither are you!'

On Sunday, they ran out of paint. To get everyone out of the house, where both tension and the scent of paint were high, they all went to buy some more. In the DIY store car park, they spotted Davey Timmons, Hannah's husband, parking his car.

'Hide!' shrieked Ruby, crouching low in her seat.

'Why?' asked Tim.

'I told you,' she hissed.

Lewis and Ellie both had their faces pressed against the car window.

'You didn't.'

'I did.'

They drove to another DIY store where Ruby told Tim about Hannah for the second time.

Further proof that he hadn't been listening the first time was the look of pity on Tim's face as he heard the story.

'That's just so sad,' Tim said, taking Ruby's hand in his and squeezing it tightly. 'Six months down the line, they'll be splitting up. And look at what they're going to lose.'

Ahead of them, the children were picking wild colours for their bedrooms, Lewis giggling as he produced dung-coloured paints for Ellie, who retaliated with Barbie-pinks for him.

'I always thought Hannah was a stupid cow. She must be mad to risk her family for a meaningless fling.'

Ruby squeezed her husband's hand back. 'So you don't think variety is the spice of life?' she asked.

'No,' he said firmly. 'Do you?'

'No,' she answered, too slowly.

Tim looked at her curiously.

'It's just that Brenda and I were talking that night, and she said she wished she'd had an affair when she was married so she'd have known straight off that she and Bill weren't suited. And I was shocked, and then I thought – ' Ruby paused. It sounded stupid now. 'I thought I'd turned into my mother and that I was getting old, because my mother would have been shocked too.'

Tim laughed so loud that Lewis and Ellie stopped messing with paint for a moment to cast quizzical glances at their parents.

'What's so funny?' Ruby demanded.

'I like your mother.'

'But you don't want to be married to her, do you?'

'Ruby, you're unique, do you know that?'

He gave her a hug.

'Unique in a good way?' she asked, standing in his arms in the emulsion section.

Lewis and Ellie made being sick noises at the sight of their parents kissing.

'Unique in a fabulous way.'

'Not old?'

'Not old,' Tim agreed. 'Now can we buy paint and go home, so we can start on the second phase of changing the house?'

On Tuesday, Ruby spotted Deirdre Ryan on Main Street. Surely she should be in Melbourne by now, lying by her pool or admiring the garden from her verandah?

'Hi, Deirdre.' Ruby hesitated as she got closer. Deirdre looked utterly miserable. 'Everything all right?'

'Oh, Ruby, no, it's not,' wailed Deirdre. And in the middle of Main Street, she began to cry great heaving sobs.

With Ruby comforting her, it emerged that Sasha, their sixteen-year-old daughter, had not been pleased about upping sticks and moving to Melbourne after all.

'She has a boyfriend,' sobbed Deirdre, in between snuffles. 'She doesn't want to leave him. She says we can shove off if we want, but she's not coming with us. She says she'll be an orphan if that's what we want: she doesn't care.'

Ruby winced. What a horrible scenario. 'I'm so sorry, Deirdre,' she said. 'What are you going to do?'

'I don't know. It's all a mess,' Deirdre muttered. 'I knew it was a mistake to try something different. I told Lorcan you can't up sticks at the drop of a hat, but he convinced me. He said we've only got one shot at life – he says that all the time since his heart attack – and we should go for it. And now look!'

'Sasha might change her mind,' volunteered Ruby.

'But when?'

After a coffee and a bun, Deirdre felt well enough to say goodbye to Ruby. But her face was still tear-stained. Interesting times, Ruby thought sadly. Poor Deirdre.

'What did you buy?' asked Tim that evening, as he looked at the tissue-wrapped package on the kitchen table. 'Some feng shui thing, I bet.'

Ruby smiled and added a big dollop of cream to the soup. She'd had enough of dieting. 'No,' she said. 'It's a gravy boat. I felt we needed one.'

'I thought you hated that sort of rubbish.'

'So did I,' Ruby said. 'It must be genetic.'

A Villa by the Sea

Marcella was the golden one of the Rhattigan family. Lovely looking when the rest of them were sadly quite plain, and effortlessly clever when the other girls had to study long hours to achieve any sort of results. Eugene and Una Rhattigan were quite astonished at their eldest daughter because they themselves were very ordinary. Where had this tall, brilliant creature come from?

'Marcella's very advanced for her age in reading. Well, she's advanced in every part of the curriculum,' her teacher, Miss Sweet, told them when Marcella was just seven. 'She really is quite gifted, and such a lovely child too. Of course, you must know all this.'

Eugene and Una Rhattigan stared at the young teacher in astonishment. They didn't know this. Nobody in either of their families had ever been advanced at anything. Neither had they ever been praised.

Praise was a bad thing in Eugene and Una's minds. Instead

of telling Marcella she was clever and that they were proud of her, they said nothing. Silly to be putting ideas into the child's head.

But Marcella knew she was clever. She knew because she finished her work faster than anyone else. She knew because she could easily read all the books that most of the class struggled over. Yet she never gloried in her success. Even at the age of seven, Marcella Rhattigan wanted all her little friends to be just as clever, and just as praised by their beloved Miss Sweet.

'We must be kind to other people,' Miss Sweet said every single day.

Marcella hung on Miss Sweet's every word, wishing she was petite and fair-haired with big blue eyes like her heroine, instead of tall with a curtain of straight, jet black hair.

Sometimes in Marcella's school a teacher took a class for a second year in a row, and so it was that lovely Miss Sweet had Marcella's class again when they moved up. Under her gentle tutelage, Marcella bloomed even more.

'I want to be a teacher when I grow up,' Marcella announced at home, as baby Cliona wailed in her high chair for tea, and toddler Pat ran after the dog to pull its tail.

'Why would you want to do that?' demanded her heavily pregnant mother, after she yelled at both Pat and the dog, and shovelled another spoon of carrot mush into Cliona's baby-bird mouth.

Marcella had no answer and sat quietly for the rest of the evening.

'Miss Sweet, why did you want to be a teacher?' she asked the next day.

Miss Sweet did her best not to have a favourite, but she adored Marcella's gentle wisdom and inquisitive little face.

'Because I wanted to help other people achieve their potential,' she said. 'To help them become whatever wonderful thing was inside them. Not everyone knows what's inside them, you know,' she went on. 'But the right person can help.'

From that moment on, Marcella had her mission in life: to be just like Miss Sweet.

As soon as they were old enough to understand, Marcella coached her three little sisters in Life.

She held Pat's hand when she went into Junior Infants, even though many other big sisters totally ignored the little ones for fear of appearing babyish themselves.

She taught Cliona that it was nicer to share toys with the other little girls than to snatch them back. When little Loretta stopped being a baby, it was Marcella who pushed her gently in her pram along the road. Nobody had to ask Marcella to babysit her younger sisters. She walked them to the shops when she was big enough to go alone and they were eager to be just as grown up and go with her.

Una and Eugene were content to watch, happy to let Marcella do it all.

An outsider to Glendalough Gardens might have looked at the Rhattigan family and thought that here was the perfect example of both great parenting and warm sisterhood in action.

From the age of ten, Marcella coached her little sisters in maths, the Irish language and her favourite subject, art. She was a patient teacher, definitely wise beyond her years, the neighbours agreed.

Tall and pretty, while her siblings were small, stocky and prone to freckles and mousy hair, Marcella tried not to eclipse her sisters. She never came home waving a test paper with top marks or the certificates that proved her ability with watercolours or dancing.

Instead, she was the glue that held the Rhattigan family together. She triumphed in Pat's first A in history, baked a cake when Cliona got second prize for her creative writing essay and insisted that a special place be found to hang Loretta's rosette from the Irish dancing competition so they could all admire it daily.

Her sisters were gifted and wonderful, Marcella said. She was so proud.

And Eugene and Una, who knew vaguely that Marcella herself had drawers of certificates and rosettes, felt that they must agree. Marcella was right: the girls were marvellous.

Slowly, the little triumphs of everyday life began to be celebrated. Under Marcella's warm, proud gaze, it became the norm for the Rhattigans to tell people about how gifted their four daughters were. In this way, a little of Marcella's own glittering brilliance dusted them all.

More importantly, it helped the girls grow up with a sense of a solid, loving family behind them.

Pat's longing to hang around with the bad girls in her class diminished. Cliona became far more sociable when her classmates saw her as a talented writer rather than a quiet, rather timid creature; and Loretta's dedication to dance meant she lost the puppy fat that had threatened her confidence.

Una began to enjoy people telling her how marvellous her daughters were.

'They're all so hard-working,' other mothers would say, convinced that Una was a wildly pushy mother who hid it well.

'We try to lead by example,' Una would say loftily, having heard Marcella use that exact phrase. Eventually, she came to believe the words herself.

Eugene began to think that perhaps there was something to education after all. As families around them dealt with children going off the rails, he was proud that his daughters were such paragons of virtue. There had never been an irate phone call from the school principal to the Rhattigan household.

'You and Una are very lucky, I'll tell you that. How have you managed it that not one of them has ever been in trouble?' demanded his old pal, PJ, who had one young lad suspended from school over drugs. 'I can't talk to my kids at all. They never listen to me.'

'Una and I are united on the drug issue,' said Eugene. 'We talk about it at home, you know: the effects of drugs, how easy it is to get hooked on them.'

He'd conveniently forgotten that the person who instigated all the conversations about addiction was Marcella. *She* was the one who'd found age-appropriate literature for her sisters about how being one of the cool kids could go horribly wrong.

If Marcella had heard, she wouldn't have minded. Marcella was that rare creature: a person who didn't need praise for the work, only the knowledge that the work was being done.

As the years went by and the Rhattigan girls grew up, Marcella went off to study art history on a scholarship, and from there

109

on to a job in an art gallery in the city, and during her trips home, she continued to coach and encourage her sisters.

It wasn't always easy.

After the first few months in her new job, Marcella came home to find that seventeen-year-old Pat had fallen back in with a bad crowd, girls who wore skirts like belts and went drinking and smoking with the neighbourhood bad boys.

'They're the fun crowd,' said Pat sullenly. She'd dyed her hair platinum and had a line of earrings up one ear.

Fifteen-year-old Cliona had decided that she was such a wonderful writer, what was the point in trying to pass school exams? It was all a waste of time, surely. She'd be a famous author soon, and nobody would wonder about her exam results then.

'Who asks celebrities about their exams? Tell me that?' she demanded.

Thirteen-year-old Loretta was bored with all the work that went into dancing. 'What's the point?' she asked, with her mouth full of doughnut.

'Mam, Dad, what's going on?' Marcella asked her parents anxiously that first evening when her sisters were out of the way. 'Pat's going to get herself into dreadful trouble. She's hanging around with Jimmy Devine's gang and they're bad. Not teenagers messing, but plain old dangerous. Jimmy deals drugs. If Pat gets into trouble with the police, she'll never get a decent job. A conviction for drugs will follow her forever.'

Una and Eugene were aggrieved at Marcella's rant. They were doing their best.

'I can't watch her every moment,' said Una. 'She won't talk to me – or listen to me, for that matter.'

110

'And Cliona's not doing a tap of work. Did you hear that they want to move her out of the higher-level English group into the lower one? We must explain that you need some education to make a living before the Pulitzer Prize judges come knocking on the door.'

'Cliona's a smart girl,' said Eugene, stung. He was the perfect father: everyone told him so. 'Book learning's not everything, you know. Plenty of people earn good livings without college degrees. She'll always manage.'

Marcella looked at her parents sadly. She loved them so much but she didn't want her sisters to simply 'manage'. She wanted to help them shine. It seemed as if she was the only one who could make this happen.

She didn't even like to mention how sad Loretta looked as the weight piled on. She knew what her parents' response would be: 'Ah sure, she's a fine handful of a girl. No point trying to make her give up the sweets.'

Marcella knew that her youngest sister's battle with weight ran far deeper than the physical. Marcella had been the one a few years ago who held Loretta as she sobbed her heart out about feeling huge and ugly. Dancing had been the lifeline that had saved her, both mentally and physically. And now nobody was there telling her how important it was to keep it up.

Marcella took another week off work and slowly began to set the family to rights.

Pat was too wise to waste her life hanging out with Jimmy Devine. He probably wanted her to go the whole way, Marcella said thoughtfully, and Pat might make a huge mistake by giving in.

'You're right,' blurted out Pat. 'He does. He says I'm a little tease.'

She'd cried great sobs at this and Marcella held her closely. 'What about drugs?' Marcella asked casually. 'Does he still deal? Stupid guy. He won't be the big man around town when he's in jail for six years for shifting heroin.'

Pat looked at her suspiciously. 'You know he deals?'

Marcella shrugged. 'He always did. I'd hate to get caught up in that, Pat. Plus, if you're linked with him and get a record, you'll never be able to work abroad. They ask if you have convictions on the visa applications. Still. It's up to you.'

Marcella told Cliona about a wonderful creative writing degree course at her university.

'It's definitely the coolest faculty,' Marcella said. 'I mean, the art people in my group were cool, but the writers were – I don't know, just great fun. You'd love them. 'Course, I know you're not interested in that type of thing, are you?'

Cliona suddenly found she was very interested. 'What would you have to do to get a place?' she asked.

Marcella looked surprised. 'Well, you'd need higher-level English, obviously, so if you get bumped down to the pass-level class, you wouldn't be eligible.'

A fire gleamed in Cliona's eyes. 'Who said I'm going to be bumped down? I just said boring old Mr Lennon thinks I'm not working enough. I could if I wanted to.'

'Oh, right,' said Marcella casually.

Loretta was on her bed, reading a book and working her way through a family-sized bar of chocolate.

'Fancy a walk?' said Marcella. 'Anne Lyons from my class in school is doing a charity five-k walk tonight for the community centre. They're trying to raise funds for PE equipment. Anne's mother is very involved in it.'

Loretta hesitated. She felt tired; she felt tired all the time, actually. She knew it was from eating too much sugar, but she needed the energy. She'd be fourteen soon and instead of being grown-up and skinny, she felt fat and out of place.

'I hate going on my own,' Marcella confided.

The sisters talked as they walked and rattled the collection buckets for the charity. 'Anne's mum says they need teenagers to teach Irish dancing to the younger kids during the summer holidays,' Marcella said. 'I know I shouldn't have, but I said you were an absolutely brilliant dancer and I know you're not doing much right now. If you helped out even for a couple of weeks, they'd be so grateful.'

Loretta wasn't sure, she said, but if it was to help someone out, she'd do it during the holidays.

'They'd be thrilled to get someone as good as you,' Marcella said.

In time, Pat went into teacher training and fell in love with a fellow student, an eager, handsome boy from Kerry. They dated for three years, and then got married, with Pat in full Wedding Barbie regalia.

Cliona, who'd gone on to study English with Creative Writing at college and ended up working for a publisher, was a bridesmaid in palest yellow. Loretta, who was training as a pilates teacher, wore a matching dress in pale pink. Their respective boyfriends had suits and smiles, clearly happy to be part of the Rhattigan clan.

Marcella, who had no boyfriend with her, wore the last

bridesmaid's dress, in cloudy blue, and had her hair looped into an elegant knot. She'd moved on from her first job and now worked in a fine art auctioneers, a job she loved because it brought her into contact with beautiful paintings every day.

Una and Eugene stood in the receiving line and graciously accepted compliments about how Pat was a credit to them.

'We've been so lucky with our girls,' Una said, resplendent in lilac taffeta.

Una had filled out over the years, but despite that, nobody would miss the resemblance to the bride and two of the bridesmaids. Only Marcella stood out as different from them all, taller and darker than her sisters.

'All of them are so gifted,' said a guest. 'They've done so well.'

'Oh yes,' Eugene agreed.

He wished his mother was alive to see this: himself in a fancy suit and one of his girls trained as a teacher and marrying another teacher. It proved, Eugene told himself proudly, that hard work paid off.

'Loretta's as good as engaged,' Una told the guest, 'and Cliona's fellow's mad about her. I'd say he'd marry her in a flash except she's very keen to progress her career. It's Marcella I worry about. She never seems to have time for a man in her life. I don't know why.'

When the official family photos had been taken, Marcella slipped away from the wedding party to stand on the balcony of the seaside hotel and gaze out at the ocean. She loved the sea, the wildness of the waves. It was like a siren call telling her she needed to find a home for herself by a stretch of rocky beach, and paint.

Marcella knew that her sisters expected her to do great things.

'You'll be setting up your own fashion label, I suppose,' Cliona used to say, a little enviously because Marcella was so good at drawing, after all.

'Or one of those fabulous art agencies,' Loretta added.

'You're all wrong,' Pat would laugh. 'Marcella's going to be President!'

Marcella smiled out at the sea and thought of lovely Miss Sweet, whom she still kept in contact with. Miss Sweet had retired and moved to Portugal, where she lived with her sister in a small, quiet community. Marcella had been there on holidays and as always, she found herself drawn to the calmness of her former teacher. Life was simple to Miss Sweet: simple and full of kindness.

Marcella had spent all her young life taking care of her sisters in the same way Miss Sweet had taken care of her.

She had helped them achieve what was in them. But she could now see the difference in what she and Miss Sweet did for other people.

'I helped my students and then they moved on to another class,' Miss Sweet had told her that last holiday in Portugal, when they were sitting on the tiny terrace with the evening sun glinting on azure waters in front of them. 'With your family, you will be helping them forever if you don't pull back a little. You need to concentrate on yourself, Marcella. Stop trying to make them all happy and fulfilled. Enjoy your own life and leave them to theirs.'

Miss Sweet's words had stayed with her and Marcella had begun to see that her dear teacher was right.

She had done her best for her family and now it was time to let go.

Once the decision was made, it was surprising how quickly her life changed. No longer on call to worry about the Rhattigan family, Marcella had more time for socialising at work.

A colleague had taken her to an exhibition where she met a sculptor who lived on the west coast and made giant granite pieces.

Marcella let her mother and sisters head off to Dublin to search for Pat's wedding gown, and she went with Rian, the sculptor, to his house by the Atlantic, where they'd sat on a rocky beach and watched seals bask in the sun. By the time of the wedding, Marcella and Rian were spending all their time together.

But Marcella hadn't wanted him to come to the wedding.

'Let's not steal Pat's thunder,' she said. 'They can meet you afterwards.'

'Would it be so shocking to them that you have a man in your life?' Rian asked.

'I've never had time for a man,' Marcella said, eyes dancing. 'I was too busy looking after my family.'

From inside the ballroom where the wedding was going on, Marcella could hear music. She adjusted the straps on her bridesmaid's dress and readied herself for the party.

Tomorrow, she was driving to Rian's house in the West for the rest of the weekend. It wasn't the same as Miss Sweet's lovely little villa by the sea in Portugal, but it had the same effect on Marcella.

The sense of coming home.

The Gap Year

Her mother still lived in the tiny house on Dublin's Holly Road that Frankie had grown up in, although it was older and smaller than the picture of it in Frankie's mind. In particular the kitchen, with its elderly cooker and the cream-painted wooden dresser, seemed so tiny now that Frankie had difficulty wondering how three children and two adults crowded into it for so long: herself laboriously doing home-work at the table, her two older brothers arguing over the last bit of cake.

In the weird timescale of the past, it managed to seem both a long time ago and only yesterday since Frankie had lived there. Those twenty years magically disappeared or seemed forever, depending on both her mood and her location.

When she was with Michael, her eighteen-year-old son, Frankie felt every inch the wife and mother, a slim woman of forty-two who looked great in her faded denim jacket, had a part-time job in a travel agent's, a lovely home, and a husband who still liked her to put her arms around him when they were lying in bed thinking about getting up as they listened to the drone of the shipping forecast on the radio. Then, she was a grown-up and childhood was behind her.

When she was within ten yards of Holly Road, Frankie felt like a grubby ten-year-old whose right place was in the wrong.

Practically every one of the original tenants on the road owned their home now, having bought them from the council years ago before the prices went crazy. But there weren't many of the original tenants left: most of the redbrick two-up, two-downs now contained young couples with small children, and the cries of children's games echoed up and down on the summer evenings.

Frankie's mother, Noreen, was probably one of the oldest people on the road now.

'Sixty-one plus VAT,' Frankie's husband, Sam, teased her.

'Ah, go away out of that,' Noreen would say delightedly, flapping her hand at him.

Not Looking Her Age was one of the highest compliments anyone could pay to Noreen.

She was actually seventy-seven and, while she was no longer the sprightly figure she'd been for so many years, her mind was as sharp as a tack.

Or a stiletto, as her older son, Luke, said.

No, a laser, argued Matthew, who was next in the family dynasty.

Frankie, or Frances, over a decade younger than her

brothers, was the unexpected last child. Her mother had been keen on apostolic names but circumstances meant she'd stopped at three, with a Frances instead of a Francis.

'God didn't bless me with any more children,' Noreen would say wistfully at times like Christmas and weddings when she had her regulation thimbleful of sherry and told her life story to anyone who'd stop long enough. 'I was thirty-five when I had Frances, and that was almost a miracle in those days. But I'd have loved more.'

Frankie wasn't entirely sure that her mother would have liked that many children, but there were times when she wished she did have eleven siblings. At least they could share out the duties of taking care of their mother.

Being the youngest, a daughter, and the only one of the family who still lived within a mile of their old home meant that Frankie had more than her fair share of the duties.

Every Tuesday after work, Frankie visited Noreen and took her out somewhere. If Sam didn't need the car, Frankie would drive and they'd go for a spin doing Noreen's errands. Otherwise it was the bus and a certain amount of Noreen's eyebrow raising at both the state of the buses and the quality of the people who got on them.

Today, Frankie didn't have the car and as she walked briskly towards her old home, she could see that the garden had been done. The sliver of grass was cut neatly, the beds were weeded and the hedge was clipped with a military number one crew-cut.

As Noreen could no longer handle the garden, Frankie and her two brothers had clubbed together to get someone to come in once a month and tidy it up.

Maurice was the name of the man, and Frankie felt sorry for him. At least she could occasionally escape when her mother was telling her where she was going wrong with everything she touched, but poor Maurice was paid to put up with Mrs Brennan loudly pointing out that any idiot knew that geraniums wouldn't grow in that old scrubby soil under the window.

'He's old and ugly enough to know better,' Noreen would say whenever Maurice did something she disapproved of.

What did that *mean*? Frankie never knew, except that it was a horrible old saying.

One of Frankie's best friends, Heather, who thought Frankie's mother was a scream, mainly because she wasn't *her* mother, laughed. 'It's just one of those phrases,' Heather said. 'I must write it down.' Heather was always writing things down in a notebook for the novel she was determined to write one day. 'It doesn't mean anything, Frankie. She's gas, your mother.'

'Yeah, gas.' Frankie's mouth smiled but her eyes didn't.

Noreen Brennan was in the kitchen putting the finishing touches to her toilette when Frankie arrived. Not for Noreen the time-warp make-up that made some people hold on to bright red when it no longer suited. No, she'd had her colours done in the poshest local beauty salon and never went outside the door without the full works from Estée Lauder and lashings of Youth Dew.

She also considered herself an expert in beauty and was keen to initiate her daughter into the secret.

'Get rid of that old silver eyeshadow,' Noreen had counselled Frankie the previous week. 'It's so ageing. Look what it does to your crows' feet. I'm using Typically Taupe, isn't it great? And this coral, it's much better on your lips when you've mature skin.'

Frankie and her mother were physically quite similar: both were small women, with neat figures, big dark eyes and sallow skin. The difference was that Frankie's hair was still a glossy dark brown, making her look younger than she was, while her mother's was now silver grey. Frankie sincerely hoped that the other differences were visible too, because she'd tried very hard all her life to be not like Noreen.

'Hi, Mam,' said Frankie cheerily, greeting her mother with a small kiss in the vicinity of one cheek so she wouldn't interfere with the application of the first few layers of cosmetics.

'Luke phoned, God love him,' her mother said as she rubbed what she insisted on calling rouge on to her cheeks with professional skill.

Frankie often thought that an outsider would assume her younger brother's name wasn't just Luke Brennan but *Luke-God-love-him-Brennan*. This was her mother's way of telling all and sundry that things were not well in Luke's life. The main problem, according to Noreen, was his wife, or *Celia-wouldn't-I-love-to-give-her-a-piece-of-my-mind*.

Luke, as the oldest, had been rewarded with the whole Irish Mammy syndrome where Noreen adored him and considered no woman on earth, with the exception of that nice Princess Caroline of Monaco, possibly, as suitable for him; she was the image of her dead mother, Princess Grace, God rest her, and she had that royal style, class, *breeding*. Noreen had idolised Princess Grace.

121

'He and Celia are going to Portugal for two weeks. Just like that. Her idea. God love him, I know he hates the sun. *She* loves it. Isn't happy until she's baked like an old lizard. I said I don't know why you're not taking a nice house in Kerry again where we could all drop in and have fun like in the old days,' her mother went on.

Frankie, who knew that the ructions from last year's trip to Kerry, where her mother had arrived for a three-day visit and stayed for ten, were the real reason Luke and Celia were hotfooting it off to Portugal, kept silent and began to wash the dishes. She liked the soothing familiarity of the job and she could look out the window into the garden and think about other things while her mother talked to her. Or at her.

'Have I news for you,' Noreen was going strong and told with relish a story about a girl from the road who was going out with two men and there had been a bitter fight *in public* the night before over her.

'Not that I'm surprised, mind. Well, she was reared on the road. Sow as ye shall reap or whatever it is. Go easy on that dish, Frankie. You'll scrub the pattern off if you're not careful.'

Frankie reflected that she'd have loved to have been one of those women who got on with their mothers. The sort who said things like 'she's my best friend', or the ones who nominated their mothers for bouquets of flowers in magazines because they saved their daughter's life every day. Frankie and Noreen did not have that sort of relationship and they never would. Their thinking was totally different on everything.

Frankie did yoga, toyed with the idea of her and Sam walking the Inca Way, and felt ridiculously pleased that

122

Michael gave her an awkward hug and said she was a 'cool mum'.

Noreen wore shoes with a little heel, even when her ankles swelled, said a novena every night, and had fond hopes that people would think she'd always behaved like a lady, no matter what she'd had to put up with in her life. Noreen had no interest in talking about feelings: actions were what mattered. And she thought yoga, with all its touchy-feely-ness, was plain daft.

'Her parents, mind you, they're to blame,' Noreen was still on the topic of the girl from the street with the complicated love life. 'Wouldn't recognise a day's work if it bit them. The poor child will end up pregnant and they'll wonder why. Why, I ask you? With parents like that, it's a wonder she's not in a PVC miniskirt down on the docks looking for work.'

Without pausing to wonder exactly what her mother knew about where the city's hardest working professional women plied their trade, Frankie kept washing up.

'How's Michael?'

Her mother switched topics with frightening speed.

The CIA occasionally used the same technique for interrogating prisoners, Frankie had read: move on to a totally different subject, so you forget the first one and think you were going mad.

'Great. Packing mostly.' In just four days, Michael was heading off for a gap year travelling. He and a pal were starting in France, and after that, it was anybody's guess. Frankie's maternal radar was on overdrive, thinking up calamities as she wondered what would happen if something went wrong when Michael was in India, say. How could she get there quickly enough to sort it all out?

'Ah, isn't he a wonder.' If her son Luke was the first person who made Noreen go misty-eyed, her grandson was the second. 'You're not to go sloping off into misery when he goes, you know,' Noreen continued. 'He's an adult. You can't keep them tied to your apron strings forever.'

'I know,' said Frankie from between gritted teeth.

'I'm only saying,' her mother pointed out, admiring the effect of her labours in her small mirror.

First port of call was a trip to the hair salon to get some of Noreen's 'special shampoo'. This was wash-out hair colourant and Noreen liked to imagine that nobody knew she put a rinse in her hair.

For once, Frankie felt like saying that she'd known for years that it wasn't shampoo because normal shampoo wasn't a silvery purple colour that stained the hands.

She was still hurting after the barb about Michael. He'd been away on holidays before, but only for a few weeks. A year was such a long time.

Roots and wings.

Weren't those the gifts parents were supposed to give kids? Not guilt trips. Frankie thought with a grin of the sticker somebody had put up on the wall at work: *My mother's a travel agent for guilt trips.* Frankie refused to be that sort of person.

Except that Michael's trip had somewhat pulled the rug from under her feet and made her feel that the guilt-trip mom was a trap she could fall into all too easily. Her baby was going away. It was the first step into his future and Frankie was reeling.

Honestly, why couldn't her mother understand that?

She followed her mother out of the House of Elegance Hair Salon, determined to say so.

'Marietta knows what suits me and the shampoo really keeps my curls in place,' Noreen said, patting her hair self-consciously.

The bitch in Frankie died a death. How could she dream of saying something so cruel to her mother?

They were just different people. Frankie had to accept her mother for what she was. After all, it wasn't surprising her mother was tough. She'd had a hard life. Frankie's father had been handsome, charming and feckless. Everyone adored him, but he'd never been the bill-paying kind of dad. Frankie decided that if she had her mother's vigour and liveliness at her age, then she'd have achieved something.

'Ah, Frankie, cheer up. Michael will never want to come home from wherever he's going if he's coming home to your sad face. If the wind changes, you'll be stuck like that! Wouldn't that be gas!'

Frankie snatched the carrier bag from her mother with slightly more force than was required. 'I'll hold the special shampoo, Mam,' she snapped and set off down the road.

Next stop was the cake shop for a few éclairs, where Noreen got the dreadful news that Mr Heron from Stoneyville had died and was laid out in the house for his funeral that evening.

'Oh my Lord,' said Noreen when she heard. 'I thought he'd turned the corner, didn't you, Antoinette?'

'I did,' replied Antoinette, laboriously putting the éclairs,

125

one by one, into a waxed paper bag. 'He was never the same after the operation, was he?'

'True.'

'Who are you talking about?' asked Frankie.

'Eamonn Heron,' said her mother. 'Lived a mile from us, had one of those old pushbikes with a basket on the front. Lived with his sister, Josie. They had a cocker spaniel.'

Exasperation shone in her eyes, as Frankie still looked blank.

'Worked for the council,' Noreen went on. 'Ah, your mind must be going, Frankie, you must know who he is.'

'Very tall and no hair,' said Antoinette helpfully. 'Never married.'

'No, never married. Just as well,' Noreen added, with meaning.

'Just as well,' agreed Antoinette. 'What else would you like, Noreen?'

It took ten minutes to package up what they wanted, due to Antoinette's lack of speed and stream of chatter.

Antoinette had to be at least as old as her mother, Frankie thought with irritation as they waited, so what was she doing working in the bakery? She asked her mother this when they'd left and were heading briskly to Mr Heron's house with the special purchase of a slab of Tipsy cake for the wake.

'*Why does Antoinette work?*' Noreen repeated in surprise. 'It keeps her young. Isn't that what life's all about?'

Frankie was the youngest person in the Heron family home. The people who'd come to pay their respects were uniformly

126

well past seventy, but there was no sense of misery that yet another person of their generation had died. Eamonn was dead, his sister Josie was bereft, and the crowd was there to comfort her and tell her that he'd be missed but her life would go on.

'You've to come to bingo with us,' Noreen told the bereaved woman, who was a strong woman of eighty with a shock of beautiful white hair held up with mother-of-pearl combs.

'No staying at home on your own,' added another old lady, waggling a finger painted with strawberry red nail polish. 'Eamonn wouldn't have wanted it.'

'Poor fellow never knew what he wanted when he was alive,' Noreen whispered to Frankie out of the side of her mouth. 'He was an awful eejit. But that's no help to her. Better to let her think she'd be doing him a favour by having a life.'

Frankie smothered a grin. Her mother could be very funny. Her friend Heather was right. It was just that it could be painful when she turned that sharp humour in your direction.

'Frankie, lovely to see you,' said Mrs Stanley, one of her mother's cronies and a woman she'd never have dreamed of calling by her first name. 'Why don't you ever come to bingo with us?' Mrs Stanley enquired.

'Well, I'm busy, you know,' Frankie started off. God, bingo. She'd rather chew her own leg off without an anaesthetic.

'Ah now, you're not busy,' insisted Mrs Stanley. 'Your mother told us that your lad is all grown up and he's off travelling the world. Lovely Planet or Lonely Planet or some yoke like that. He's reared. You can do your own thing now. The freedom! You won't know yourself.'

'I, I, have to – ' Frankie broke off in confusion. For Mrs Stanley had gone right to the heart of the problem. She didn't have anything to do any more, apart from her three mornings a week in the shop. Her job as a hands-on mother had ended abruptly.

Being the mother of a vibrant son had made her feel young and now that Michael was heading off to another phase in his life, Frankie realised she was left with what the psychiatrists cheerily called empty-nest syndrome.

She wasn't the sort to play bingo and get a blue rinse, but these people thought she was. She'd gone from being an energetic mother to a woman on the verge of a bus pass and all it had taken was a round-the-world ticket for someone else.

Sitting amid a group of much older people, all of whom were clearly enjoying life to the full, Frankie felt like Methuselah's granny.

'Penny for them?' It was her mother, tea in hand, fresh from working the room to glean the latest neighbourhood gossip.

'Nothing,' said Frankie.

The gimlet stare that had seen through all mischief when she was a child was turned on Frankie now.

'Frances?'

'Mum, don't nag me, will you?' Frankie begged. She never spoke to her mother like that. But today, now, she felt sad and defenceless. She didn't feel like putting on the cheery façade that acted like a shield against her mother's hard edges.

Noreen perched on the arm of Frankie's chair.

'Don't mind Anna Stanley, love,' she said. 'She knows you hate bingo. I've told her often enough. She was trying to help.'

'It's not what Mrs Stanley said,' began Frankie and the tears came at that moment, great noisy sobs that made people look up.

To her utter surprise, her mother didn't tell her that this wasn't the place for crying as she once might have done. Instead, Noreen put an arm around Frankie and blithely told the assembled crowd: 'She's a lovely soft girl, always was. Hates to be around bereaved people.'

'Sorry,' muttered Frankie.

'Not a worry,' Noreen said, handing over a bit of tissue. 'If there's one thing you learn at my age, it's that nobody really takes any notice of what other people do. You could strip down to your knickers here, and nobody would notice. They're all tied up in their own dramas. Now listen, love, I know what's wrong with you. It's Michael, and he will come back, love. You're a great mother. Softer and kinder than I was. Although,' Noreen added reflectively, 'it was for your own good. Your Sam is a decent man, but if you'd ended up with a husband like your father, God rest him, you'd need to have been strong. I was trying to prepare you.' She sighed. 'I suppose I got it wrong, but you can only do your best, can't you?' And she smiled at Frankie, her big dark eyes shining, looking for reassurance.

Frankie was silent, digesting it all as she wiped her face. It was a day for firsts. Her mother never spoke to her like that, either. Or looked for reassurance.

Noreen did not belong to the school of mothering where

you explained your motives and actions to your child. Until now.

And then it hit Frankie. Despite it all, despite the difference in their opinions on every subject, she and her mother were very alike.

Both loved their children and wanted the best for them. They just did things differently.

Frankie's generation allowed themselves to say they'd miss their eighteen-year-old son. They were in touch with their feelings; they'd read magazine articles on emotional intelligence. They understood the inner child.

Noreen Brennan had had no time for her inner child when she was having so much trouble surviving – feeding, schooling and caring for her family. Everyone else's inner child had to look out for themselves.

Yet when her grown-up child burst into tears, Noreen had known what was wrong with her.

'You're great, Mam,' Frankie said suddenly, with a pang of love for this tough woman who'd had so much to put up with. 'You did a good job, you know. Rearing us on your own.'

'Ah, go away out of that,' Noreen said, flapping her hand in her familiar way. But she looked pleased. The Estée Lauder coral lips were curved up into a smile.

'What do you say we go into the beauty salon next week and get a makeover done? And you'll have something to tell Michael when he rings, so he won't think you're sitting at home in his room moping?'

Frankie laughed. Her mother knew her so well. Funny she'd never realised that before.

Cassandra

Cassandra always had a very complicated private life. Like, incredibly complicated. We're talking about the sort of relationship twists that would make an episode of *Grey's Anatomy* look straightforward. All of which was a million miles away from my personal life, I might add.

I was Ms Sensible to Cassandra's Femme Fatale.

We met as gangly five-year-olds in junior infants. To be accurate, *I* was a gangly five-year-old and Cassandra was a serious contender for the Miss Pears Soap contest. Blonde ringlets, blue eyes the colour of holiday brochure swimming pools, and endearing dimples. Naturally, by the time we hit our twenties, she lost the ringlets and went for the sort of sleek crop with razored edges that you see in the trendier hairdressing magazines.

She got it cut in Trevor Sorbie and needless to say, she never had to wait three months for an appointment, either. Cassandra kept telling me I should do something different with my hair, which was exactly the same as it was when we first met twenty-three years ago, but I'd got used to having it long and loose. I'm not cut out to be chic and besides, long hair hides a multitude of sins.

'Molly, curls are so last century,' Cassandra liked to say, trying to be helpful. 'The bed-head look would be so you.'

Personally, I could never see me in the bed-head – you know, the short, messy, just-out-from-under-the-duvet look. You need cheekbones and teeny elf ears to carry that off. I'd just look as if I'd spent the night sleeping in a cardboard box in a shop doorway.

Cassandra can wear it, though. She's stunning. Doesn't need to wear make-up, although she loves it and looked totally amazing when she did that heavy kohl thing that makes her resemble a *Vogue* cover girl when the *Millennium/ Barbarella* vibe was hot. As I said, we're very different.

So where was I? Oh yeah, the reason I'm telling you this story. You see, it was Cassandra's personal life that got me into this in the first place. Cassandra and a man, to be exact. She was always the one with more boyfriends than you could shake a stick at.

During our college years, she had a string of besotted men hanging around her.

I know, it's weird that we went to the same college, but at school I had my heart set on journalism, and when Cassandra thought about it, she decided not to bother applying for her drama course after all and went for journalism too. I was a bit surprised, because she'd never been too keen on writing, but Cassandra is so good with people that she was a natural at journalism. She's got that charm thing.

People wanted to talk to her. Being glamorous and wearing sexy clothes helped, or so my mother said a bit snidely. (Mum and Cassandra have never seen eye to eye. They haven't talked since Cassandra ended up going to our graduation dance with Ted. He'd been my date originally, but there'd been a bit of a mix-up and I was quite happy going with Cassandra's younger brother Mitch, who was quite good fun when he wasn't bitching about his sister.)

She and I shared a flat in college and spent lots of time working on assignments together. Cassandra is very clever but she loved talking to me about my opinions. I thought she'd got an incredible mind, really.

There was that time she had to write an in-depth piece about the UN and she'd been too hungover to do much research in the library.

Well, all I had to do was sketch out the briefest idea of the whole thing for her and she went on to get an A+ for it. The tutor loved my point about how giving humanitarian aid made the wealthy West feel better about itself. I didn't put that bit in my essay though, because it would have sounded as if we'd copied each other.

During our student days, Cassandra's biggest problem was getting rid of boyfriends. She liked to be a free spirit: 'Can't stand long-term relationships,' she always said, usually after she had to dump some guy who'd been getting annoying. 'Men get so clingy after a week or so.'

She simply wanted to have fun and not be tied to one person. She loved partying and I couldn't always keep up, especially close to exam time.

'I really should be staying home,' she groaned one

December night when she was racing out to an Arts student bash and I was planning to stay in studying. 'Can I borrow your notes tomorrow?' Her heavily mascaraed eyes were on the mirror as she adjusted the straps on her Wonderbra.

There was once a bit of trouble when three of her exes joined forces and sent this horrible note around campus about her, saying she was a one-woman demolition squad who ate men for breakfast, or something nasty like that. It was terrible. I'd thought they were lovely guys, particularly Joshua, whom I'd had hopes of myself until he clapped eyes on Cassandra. That seemed the one negative thing about being best friends with Cassandra: once a guy saw her, I hadn't a chance. Not that I minded, or anything. Cassandra was special, as her dad used to tell her all the time. We couldn't all be like that.

'Beauty's a curse, Molly,' she insisted. 'Everybody wants a piece of you. They don't treat you like a person but like a beautiful object. You're lucky not to have this problem, you don't know how I envy you.'

I thought she was right, poor love. Everybody did want a piece of her. I tried to help out when I could.

One time, I had to keep her current boyfriend in the kitchen so she could sneak an old flame out of the bedroom.

Which is, incidentally, a bit like what recently happened.

I'm deputy features editor on *Your Kind of Woman* (*YKOW*) which is a totally gorgeous women's magazine in London. We both started working there on a college work placement scheme a few years ago. I'd actually applied for a job in *YKOW* and Cassandra had applied for a job at the *Independent*. When she didn't get in there, it was sheer coincidence that they had a second student vacancy at *YKOW*. We both stayed a year and nobody was more amazed than me when I was offered a full-time job. I mean, *me*, not Cassandra.

Startled and thrilled, I did once pluck up the courage to ask Madeleine, the editor, why they'd hired me. I never really understood her answer: 'Because we want someone with originality and talent, who doesn't need to rip off other people's ideas,' she said.

It was puzzling because that's Cassandra to a tee. Plus, she's gorgeous, which is always useful in our business. Not that I need a brown paper bag over my head at all times, but I'm not a patch on Cassandra with her feline beauty.

'Mol, you're one of a kind; quirky, fun . . . er, and you've got a great personality,' she says to me when I'm feeling insecure about my looks.

That's the nice thing about Cassandra, I always thought. She's truly beautiful but she never made me feel insecure. Instead, she bolstered my confidence and used to help me buy clothes. I was totally hopeless at fashion then and she was like someone from *The Hills*: clothes were her hobby and *Elle* was her bible. She had a positive fetish about making me wear fleecy tops. She insisted I was a fleecy top and denims sort of girl.

'Casual chic, that's you, Moll,' she'd say thoughtfully.

We made an odd combination: her in head-to-toe second-skin garments with Gucci shoes (her father did spoil her with an allowance), me in casual, sporty stuff that wouldn't look out of place in the gym. In our flat – didn't I mention that? We are still sharing, this time in a two-bedroomed shoebox in Clapham – Cassandra had to have the bigger bedroom so she'd have somewhere for her two clothes rails. Every penny of her wages went on clothes and there were weeks when I don't know how we paid the rent because she'd blown her cheque on *an adorable pair of boots, Moll. I simply had to have them!*

She used to march into my office – I always felt bad that I had a tiny office with a window and she was stuck out in the freelance desert where everyone shared desks in that horrible hot-desking system – and beg me to borrow the fashion editor's Karen Millen discount card for her. (She and the fashion editor had this hate:hate thing going on, so she couldn't possibly ask herself.) Even though I felt guilty about going behind the fashion ed's back, I could never say no. Cassandra looked perfect in Karen Millen. Nobody could wear those body-con clothes like she did. She was wearing one at the magazine's birthday party when she met the publisher, Rudy Milano, which was where the trouble started. Rudy was in his forties and wasn't bad-looking in an Italian wide-boy sort of way. Not Cassandra's type, but she fell for him big time.

I didn't see the attraction myself. Rudy might have had three homes, four sports cars and several offshore accounts, but he also had three chins and no sense of style. Oh yeah, and a wife. That was the real problem. Cassandra didn't see it as much of one, although I did.

I can't tell you how often I said: 'Cass, he's married. Don't go there.' But, there has never been any point in talking to her when she's got her mind set on something or someone.

I didn't think she was in love, to be honest, but once Rudy

had taken her to St Lucia for a week and given her the Rolex, well, she never stopped talking about him. 'He says I'm not to wear the Rolex to the office,' she said in a dreamy voice. We were in our messy sitting room, her trying on lots of different outfits to see which ones had the shortest sleeves and would therefore reveal the best expanse of slender, tanned, Rolex-encrusted wrist. 'But nobody will notice, will they, Moll?'

I cautiously said that I thought they might, but Cassandra was determined to have her own way, and besides, I was busy trying to organise an interview with Neil Morten, this gorgeous young rock musician who'd just been on the cover of *Rolling Stone*, so I left her alone. Big mistake.

Two weeks after Cassandra had got the Rolex, the editor called me into her office at lunchtime and launched into this speech about how I was a talented journalist but as naïve as hell and needed to cop myself on pronto or I'd end up in serious trouble thanks to that 'scheming bitch of a friend of yours. Who isn't much of a friend, if you really want to know,' Madeleine finished up.

I goggled at her. 'You mean Cassandra?' I said, startled.

'Molly, will you wake up,' screamed Madeleine. 'Of course I mean Cassandra. She rides around on your coat-tails, steals all your ideas, does her best to get your job when your back is turned, and is now ruining your career thanks to her affair with the publisher.'

I goggled a bit more. I wanted to get her to explain, but I couldn't, could I? It was my job to stand up for Cassandra, like I'd been doing for years. I couldn't stop now.

'I think that's most unfair, Madeleine,' I said pointedly.

'She's my best friend and I can't listen to you say terrible things about her.'

'Have it your way,' Madeleine interrupted wearily and went back to her cottage cheese and crispbread.

Everyone in the magazine was always on a diet except me. I was 'sickeningly thin', as Cassandra put it and could consume vast quantities of just about anything I liked and not put on weight.

I went home early because I felt unsettled and also because the next day I would be taking Neil Morten to The Ivy for lunch to interview him and I wanted to be prepared. I mean, I know it was a bit daft to bother putting on fake tan and applying all-night conditioner just for an interview with a guy who is so devastatingly handsome he could probably date all the current Miss World hopefuls. But a girl can dream. I'd invested in this soft-as-kitten-fur vermillion cashmere cardigan that made my hair look dark and lustrous, and even gave me a bit of cleavage because it was so clingy.

But when I went looking for it the next morning, the cardigan had disappeared from my drawer along with my new burgundy filigree necklace and the gel-filled bra which was the only item of lingerie I'd ever owned that made me look bigger than a 32A.

Sorry, Moll, knew you wouldn't mind me whipping these, went the note scrawled in Cassandra's trademark gold handwriting.

I did mind, but there was no point crying over spilt milk. It'd have to be my boring old black suit. Again.

I tried not to think about Cassandra as I sat in the taxi

on the way to The Ivy. It was uncanny how people had loved her to bits in college and how everyone at work disliked her. Well, not everybody liked her in college, but most people did, surely? So why did Madeleine and the fashion editor and actually, most of the rest of the *YKOW* staff loathe her and slam their office doors when she strode along the corridors in the mood to chat? And what exactly had Madeleine been trying to warn me about? I felt so terribly unsettled by it all, and had been ever since Cassandra had taken up with Rudy Milano. I didn't like him or approve and Cassandra just didn't care what I thought. Which wasn't the way friends were supposed to behave.

Neil Morten was just as gorgeous in the flesh as he looked on the cover of *Rolling Stone* and on his new album. Tall, lanky, with straw-coloured hair, blond stubble, greeny-grey eyes like Pernod with water added, and this sweet, almost anxious smile that lit up his face. He was nicer than I'd expected and we just, well, this is going to sound stupid, but we got on like a house on fire.

Most of the time you interview famous people and they talk to you as if you're a tape recorder without a real person attached. They emote, get all their charming little anecdotes out, tell you how much they loved working on the album/movie/soap show and then they're gone. But Neil talked to me as if we were on a date and as if he'd seriously consider going out with me. He was funny, charming and very normal. By dessert, we were finishing each other's sentences and talking so fast, we were running out of breath. The interview hadn't even happened. It was simply two people talking nineteen to the dozen, laughing and smiling, falling in love, practically. I was, anyway. Falling in love.

He had this spiky fair hair that stood up, but one bit drooped over his left eye. I had to stop myself from leaning over the table and pushing it back tenderly. Did you ever feel like that about someone: that you can't help wanting to touch them? He must have felt the same, I thought ecstatically, because he stroked my hand across the pristine tablecloth with his long, guitar-player's fingers.

We'd gone through a bottle of wine and were thinking about wandering off to a little pub somewhere to actually do some interviewing when it happened.

This blonde woman marched into the restaurant and after a consultation with the maître d', marched over to our table. She looked vaguely familiar and because she was one of those elegant types who shop in Dior and have diamond rings the size of gobstoppers, I assumed she was somebody semi-famous whom I had written about in our gossip pages.

'Are you Molly O'Rourke?' she said between clenched, beautifully polished teeth.

I nodded, feeling a prickle of anxiety as I stared up at her. Despite having the best part of three glasses of wine inside me, I instinctively knew something was wrong. So did Neil. He leaned towards me protectively, but wasn't fast enough for Ms Dior.

'You bitch!' she howled. 'You've been having an affair with my husband and you don't even have the shame to pretend to be someone else when you ring up. I'll see you out of your job, you cow! The magazine belongs to me, not Rudy Milano. And he's out on his ear, too!'

With that, Mrs Milano leaned over and belted me. Thank God she got me with the ringless hand or I'd be in serious trouble, I can tell you. Not that a black eye isn't serious trouble, but it's marginally better than having your eyebrow painfully removed by a massive diamond with no anaesthetic.

Luckily, the maître d' calmly escorted her out before she could black the other eye and before Neil could throw a glass of water over her. He was quite white with rage.

'It's Cassandra,' I managed to say in shock. 'My flatmate Cassandra is having an affair and it must be with that woman's husband. Mrs Milano.' I shook my head in bewilderment. 'I can't imagine why she thought it was me.'

With Neil hugging me and petting my battered face, we made it home to my apartment where he put ice on my eye and fed me hot chocolate all afternoon. I explained a bit about Cassandra, and Neil became quite grim the more I explained. It did make sense of what Madeleine had been trying to tell me.

When I rang Madeleine, she explained in greater detail.

'Rudy Milano,' she said his name as if she was spitting simultaneously, 'talked to me about firing you to give Cassandra your job. She's using him to crawl up the career ladder and she doesn't care who she walks all over to get to the top, including you, Molly. I'm sorry. I know you think she's your friend, but she isn't. She's also wrong about Rudy. His wife's family own the magazines and without her, he's got nothing. I don't know how Mrs Milano got the idea Rudy was having an affair with you, but I guess it's some fiction of Cassandra's to keep herself out of trouble.'

Neil was in the kitchen draining pasta when Cassandra

walked in, wearing my new cashmere cardigan and with a self-satisfied expression on her beautiful face. She was terribly shocked when she saw me with my rapidly blackening eye.

'You poor thing,' she said. 'Whatever happened, Moll?'

'A woman hit me, a woman who thought I was having an affair with her husband – Rudy,' I said.

My eye was very painful and I felt like crying all the time: not just because I'd been hit but because I'd realised that my so-called best friend wasn't really my friend at all.

She did a double take when Neil came out of the kitchen with the pasta in one hand. He really was amazing looking. Cassandra's expression changed in deference to both his fame and his gorgeousness. Off went her normal face and on went the Athena the Huntress expression she adopts when she sees a man she likes: her mouth curves up into this wicked smile and her eyes glint with an arch look that says *You'd never believe how sexy I am, much sexier than any other woman you've ever met in your life*. It always works. Or it did, until this occasion.

Neil didn't look impressed. In fact, he looked angry and contemptuous.

'Molly has a black eye because your lover's wife hit her in The Ivy.'

'I rather thought she'd been hit in the eye,' quipped Cassandra, obviously misjudging the way this conversation was going. Under normal circumstances, the object of her attentions would be gazily mistily at her by now, not staring at her harshly and being nasty.

'Why do you think this man's wife thought Molly was having an affair with him?' Neil asked coldly.

Cassandra tittered, a sound which had never seemed irritating to me before.

'It's silly,' she said, turning to me. 'Sorry, old thing, but when I rang his house looking for Rudy and he wasn't there, I said I was you.' She must have noticed my eyes widen, because she rushed on: 'Their housekeeper is Puerto Rican or something and she can barely speak English, so I didn't think it would matter. You do understand, Moll, don't you?' she wheedled.

I wondered suddenly how many other times she'd fooled me? And I felt so foolish and so sad.

Neil, however, wasn't sad at all: he was furious.

'Could it be that this mistaken identity prank was part of a plot to help you get Molly sacked so that you could get her job?' Neil asked. He'd grasped the whole idea so quickly. No wonder he was a multi-millionaire songwriter. Brains as well as beauty.

'Don't be silly. That was nothing to do with it,' Cassandra said crossly. 'Rudy would give me a job anytime I wanted. I said I was Molly because, if his wife ever met her, there's no way she'd think Rudy was seriously contemplating an affair with her. Molly's, well . . . she's not his type. He prefers blondes.'

'I happen to think Molly's very beautiful,' Neil said softly, looking at me. 'I like the natural look as opposed to the done-up-like-a-dog's-dinner look.'

He cast those Pernod-with-water eyes over Cassandra in a manner which left her in no doubt that she was the dog's dinner in question.

She quivered indignantly. 'It hardly matters any more.'

143

'Just one thing, Cassandra,' I said, speaking for the first time. 'I'm afraid you miscalculated with Rudy. He can't give you a job. In fact, I daresay he'll be looking for the Rolex back when his wife throws him out. You see,' I paused, amazed to find that I could even speak, 'he's not the real boss of the magazine. His wife is. The publishing empire belongs to her family and Rudy is utterly replaceable. I've told Madeleine the whole story and she's told his wife. Mrs soon-to-be-ex-Milano was most apologetic about the black eye. But I rather think you've lost your job. You and Rudy can visit the job centre together.'

Cassandra's mouth hung open, giving both of us a good view of her expensive dental work.

'You're joking,' she gasped. 'He promised . . .'

'You were my friend, Cassandra,' I heard myself saying. 'I trusted you. Have trusted you for years. How could you do this to me?'

But Cassandra wasn't even listening. She was jabbing at her mobile phone, dialling Rudy and leaving a message on his voicemail.

'Rudy, baby, call me.'

She babbled away to the phone, totally ignoring me, and I wondered how I could have possibly spent twenty-three years of my life standing up for a woman who rode rough-shod over me in her stilettos. She stole my men, my ideas, my self-confidence and had tried to steal my job. The real Cassandra was revealed to me after years of blinding myself to her true character. It was like scales falling from my eyes, which is how Neil puts it.

The true Cassandra was a selfish person and it must

144

have been some flaw in my own character that kept me in thrall to her for so long. Neil says I'm a good person and I simply assume everyone else is nice too, so I was easily taken in by Cassandra, who needed me to clean up after her messes, take notes for her in college, and help smooth her path through life.

I haven't seen her for months. She keeps phoning me at work but I don't return her calls very often. Not surprisingly, she got fired from *YKOW* and she's now freelancing for the *Tree Surgeon's Gazette*, desperately trying to get a foot in the door of women's magazine journalism again.

Mind you, Rudy Milano's ex-wife has put the word out on Cassandra, so it's doubtful if she'll ever get another job in our tight-knit little industry. Neil and I are living in a lovely old house in Islington and, despite having the builders in all the time, putting in a recording studio downstairs and renovating the nursery upstairs – yes, you've guessed it: the baby's due in March and Neil is over the moon.

Sometimes when I'm alone, I think back to all the years with Cassandra and I feel terribly sad. We shared so much together and it's hard to look back at it through the prism of what I know now.

We're invited to all sorts of trendy parties but we don't go. Cassandra would have a fit if she knew about the invitations we turn down. She'd never understand how wonderful it is to be with a kind, lovely man and want to sit at home and watch telly with him, feeling the baby wriggle inside my belly. So you see, I feel sorry for her. She taught me so much, after all.

Letter from Chicago

Elsie loved her letters from Chicago. She adored the fat envelopes with their colourful American stamps. Even the postmarks looked exotic and exciting. On the first Monday in March, she was as usual the first person up in the McDonnell house. She was making a cup of tea in the kitchen when she heard the rattle of the postbox.

She put down the milk carton and went slowly into the hall to collect the mail. Elsie went everywhere slowly. She was sixty-five and suffered from arthritis. Sometimes, every part of her body ached. This morning, only her hands were sore, which was a mixed blessing. Good in that her knees weren't hurting, but bad in that it had taken her ages to turn on the tap to fill the kettle. Tom, her son-in-law, said he'd get her a special gadget to help her turn the tap on, but Elsie had said no. She wasn't an invalid. She didn't want to be treated like one. Once you yielded to the arthritis, it was winning. And she didn't want it to win, not yet.

There was only one letter on the mat. It was for her and it was from Chicago.

Smiling, she went back into the kitchen and sat at the table to read it over her tea.

From upstairs, came the sounds of activity.

Kim was begging the twins to get out of bed.

'I won't let you watch television late on Sunday if you can't get up for school,' she warned.

She said the same thing every Monday morning. She was too soft on those girls, Elsie thought.

But then, Kim was soft on everyone. Elsie had no idea how Kim managed to keep a class of eight-year-olds under control at St Mary's Primary School.

Elsie heard Tom stomping into the bathroom. He was a big man and made as much noise as an elephant.

Next, the twins turned their CD player on. Loud music could be heard all over the house. It was all incomprehensible to Elsie. When she was alone here, she liked a bit of gentle music, something classical from Lyric FM, perhaps.

'Turn that rubbish down!' roared Tom at his daughters.

He had a headache, he added.

Emer roared back that it wasn't loud at all. Just because he didn't like Lady Gaga, didn't mean the rest of them shouldn't listen to her.

Satisfied that everything was normal in the McDonnell house, Elsie began to read her sister's letter. Maisie had emigrated to America forty-five years before. And every month since, she'd written home. In the early years, the letters had been short, but these days she had time to sit and write at length, telling her sister all about the wonderful life she now had.

Elsie loved hearing about Maisie's two children and her four grandchildren. Maisie liked to detail every proud moment in their lives, from school and college, to work successes and first homes.

In turn, Elsie wrote happily about her own three children. She had six grandchildren, two more than Maisie. Elsie was pleased about that.

Dear Elsie, today's letter said,
I have the most amazing news for you. Charlene is going to visit you in Ireland in the last week of August. Isn't that exciting? She wants to meet all the family. I can't tell you how happy I am that my grand-daughter is going to visit Dublin.

I told Charlene she'd be welcome to stay with you. Her friend is going with her as they are only eighteen. I hope I did the right thing.

Elsie stopped reading and took a shaky sip of tea. She was stunned. No, it was worse than that. She was shocked, really shocked. Whatever was she going to do?

Kim McDonnell was the last person to get into the bathroom. That was the routine in their house. Tom used the bathroom first.

It was go first, he said, or never get in the door, what with two fifteen-year-old girls in the house.

He somehow managed to leave a mess behind him, no matter what Kim said. He didn't mean to, she knew that. It was his upbringing. Tom had been born into a house with four older sisters and an adoring mother. When he'd married Kim, he had never washed up after a meal in his life. He had to be told how to use the washing machine, and he still thought you could wash black clothes with white clothes. Kim wasn't the sort of woman to think her marriage was over because Tom was hopeless at putting towels in the basket. He was such a good man in every other way: she could cope with tidying up towels.

The twins used the bathroom after Tom. They left more towels on the floor and forgot to close the shampoo bottle properly. Toothpaste would be smeared all over the sink and smudges of sparkly eyeshadow – forbidden in school but somehow worn every day anyhow – would dust the basin.

'Ah, Mum, don't nag,' they would say when she complained.

They were studying for their exams. As a teacher, Kim knew that it was important not to upset kids before big exams.

'Young people doing exams need to have a calm home life,' said all the experts.

Kim liked a calm home life herself, but it wasn't easy to feel calm with two fifteen-year-olds in the house. The exams were in three months and Kim couldn't wait for them to be over. On the first Saturday in August, the whole family were going to the beautiful beach in Brittas to stay in a mobile home for three weeks. Kim thought about relaxing in the sun and not having to go to work. She thought about nice meals on the deck outside the mobile home, time to lie on a sun lounger and read. Roll on August.

Kim had a quick shower and washed her long, dark hair, which she didn't have time to dry. Instead, she brushed it neatly and tied it back with a band, which was pretty much all the styling it ever got. She put on a bit of lipstick and mascara, and thought of how the girls used far more make-up than she did. Tom said she didn't need it.

'You're gorgeous as you are,' he'd say, kissing her.

Tom was an awful liar, Kim thought with a smile. She wasn't bad looking. She had big dark eyes, creamy pale skin and nice hair. But she wasn't Julia Roberts.

People who looked like Julia Roberts didn't have to work long hours to pay the mortgage. They didn't worry about money or about the children doing well at school. They went to parties in big cars and bought expensive clothes. Kim buttoned up the pink blouse she had bought for twenty euros. Still, she was happy.

The twins listened to their new Lady Gaga CD and put on their make-up. The principal might not like students to wear make-up, but Emer and Laura didn't care.

Emer closed one eye as she put on black eyeliner.

'Mum will kill you if she sees you wearing that much,' Laura said.

Laura was generally considered to be the more sensible twin, but it was a limited distinction.

'She'll get over it,' said Emer confidently. She did the other eye. 'Do I look like Gaga?' she asked.

'You'd need more than that!' said her sister, laughing.

Emer grinned.

'I wish we didn't have a test in Irish today,' Laura said. 'I know I'll fail.'

'It'll be easy,' said Emer. She was good at Irish. She didn't understand how Laura wasn't good at it. Twins were

150

supposed to be the same at everything. But then, Laura had no interest in clothes. She didn't get excited by the thought of a sale in Top Shop. And she didn't seem that keen on guys either. Not really, anyway. She agreed that Hugh O'Regan in the year above was handsome. But she'd never dream of chatting him up. Emer smiled at him for all she was worth every morning at assembly.

'Girls, come down for breakfast!' shouted their mother.

Emer sighed. She put on another bit of eyeliner for luck and blended it in till it was blackly smudgy. When she was sixteen, she was going to dye her hair blonde. She was fed up with brown hair. She fancied bright blonde, the sort of hair that exquisite women from Sweden had. Boys loved blondes. Emer thought of Hugh and smiled to herself. Perhaps she wouldn't wait until she was sixteen.

Tom McDonnell didn't sit at the kitchen table for breakfast. He ate a piece of toast standing up. He had a rewiring job in Rathfarnham at half nine. The traffic would be mad at this time of the morning. His mother-in-law usually gave out to him when he didn't eat a proper breakfast. Today, she said nothing but stared into the distance. He ate his toast and wondered if she was sick.

At ten to eight, he was ready to leave the house.

'Bye, love,' he said to Kim and kissed her. 'Bye, Elsie, bye, girls.'

'Bye, Dad,' answered the girls.

Elsie didn't speak. She had to be sick, Tom thought. Elsie never stopped talking usually. Elsie had lived with them for two years, since she'd been widowed. She talked about the neighbours, about bingo and about her sister in America. Tom had learned not to listen. He loved Elsie, but she talked enough for four people.

He shut the front door and thought it could do with a lick of paint. The whole house could do with a lick of paint. There just weren't enough hours in the day, Tom decided as he got into the van. McDonnell's Electrical Services said the writing on the side. It had been a big step to set up his own business. That was five years ago. Now, he was always busy. But money was still tight. Every time he looked, the twins needed new clothes or new shoes. Kim's car needed replacing. It would fall apart one of these days. He might buy a lottery ticket with his lunch.

'What's wrong, Mother?' asked Kim when Tom was gone.

She knew that *something* was wrong with her mother. Elsie's face was white under its dusting of pinky face powder. She had said no to a second cup of tea, an unheard of happening. She had stared into space for ages. Even worse, she hadn't given out to the twins about their loud music. Rows about music made up most of the arguments in the house.

'Nothing's wrong,' said Elsie. She drained the rest of her cold tea.

'Mother,' warned Kim, 'I'm not blind. Please tell me what's wrong.'

Elsie knew it was time to be honest. 'This came this morning.' She handed the letter to her daughter.

Kim read it carefully. Her face got grimmer with each word. 'Aunt Maisie has a nerve!' she said when she had finished. She was furious. There was no room in their house

152

for two American visitors. There was no room for any visitor. They only had three bedrooms. Where did Aunt Maisie think the Americans would sleep? In the garden? On the roof with next-door's ginger cat?

'What's wrong?' asked Laura, her mouth full of muesli.

Kim's voice was furious. 'Your aunt Maisie in Chicago has told us that Charlene is coming to stay. In late August, and with a friend.'

'Cool!' said Emer. She had never met her American cousin. She wondered if Charlene would look like a movie star. American teenagers on television all looked like movie stars. They never seemed to have spots or puppy fat, and they all had long legs and tanned skin. Emer dreamed about having long, long legs and tanned skin instead of pale Irish skin.

'Where will they sleep?' asked Laura. She was the practical one.

'I don't know *where* they'll sleep!' Kim was still angry. 'This is a small house. Why does Aunt Maisie think we have room for two guests?'

Elsie bit her lip.

'I think that's my fault,' Elsie said in a small voice.

The eight o'clock news began on the radio.

'Blast. We're going to be late,' said Kim crossly. She always left before the news. 'Come on, girls, you'll be late too if you don't get a move on.' Kim quickly shoved the breakfast dishes in the sink. 'I'll do them tonight,' she told her mother. 'And then you can tell me what this is all about.'

The school where she worked was very near the twins' school, so she dropped them off every morning. Emer and Laura always fought about who sat in the front of the car.

The Mini was nearly twenty years old and the back seat was uncomfortable. This morning, they didn't discuss where they'd sit. They knew that their normally easygoing mother was in a rare temper. Laura hopped quietly in the back.

'I bet your grandmother has been inviting Maisie's family to stay with us for years, without telling me!' Kim raged. 'I don't want them turning up here. I've never met them in my life! We can do without rich relatives landing here.'

The twins said nothing.

Laura wondered what it must be like for Gran to have a sister she hadn't seen for over forty years. Gran had told her about growing up on the farm in Leitrim. She and Maisie had been the youngest in a big family. There was a year between them, so they were almost like twins.

'I remember spending hours getting ready to go to dances,' Gran had recalled fondly. 'Maisie would try and sneak out of the house without Da seeing that she was wearing red lipstick.' Maisie had a great romance with a local lad round about the time Gran had met Granddad. But the lad Maisie liked was the oldest son and he was getting the farm.

'Maisie wasn't one for being a farmer's wife. She couldn't wait to get out of the West,' Gran said sadly. 'She had her heart set on America for years. When this lad came home from Boston to his mother's funeral, Maisie dumped the farmer's son and upped and married him.'

'Why did she never come back to visit, Gran?' Laura asked.

Gran shrugged. 'It wasn't like now, Laura,' she said. 'We had an American wake for her – in those days when people left, they were never coming back. Maisie lived in Oregon

154

for years. That's a very long way from here. She always meant to come home when they had more money and flying was cheaper, but it never happened. And then, her children were growing up.' Elsie didn't tell Laura that she'd often wondered herself why Maisie hadn't wanted to come back to Ireland. They'd shared so much as children. It hurt that her sister could stay away so long.

Elsie and her husband, Ned, God rest him, had never been rich. They couldn't afford to fly to America. But sure, wasn't Maisie as rich as sin? She could have afforded to fly home. And her two children had great jobs as a doctor and a dentist. They could have given her money, too. Elsie would never understand why Maisie hadn't ever come home.

Sitting in the back of the car, Laura looked at her twin sister. Emer was tapping her fingers along to the song on the radio. Sometimes Emer drove her mad. But Laura would hate to spend forty-something years without seeing her.

Third class were quiet as mice all day. This was not normal. But sweet Mrs McDonnell looked so angry today that they were all scared of making a noise. Even Barry Smith was good and he was the boldest boy in the whole school. Barry had a water pistol in his pocket. He'd planned to fire it at everyone when the teacher wasn't looking. Until he saw the fierce look on Mrs McDonnell's face. He hoped she wasn't angry with him. She was never angry, but right now she looked as if she might kill him stone dead. Barry was used to seeing that look on people's faces and it was never a good sign. Just in case, he put the water pistol back in his school bag. There was always tomorrow.

At the front of the class, Kim McDonnell tried to concentrate. It wasn't really that she didn't want to see poor Charlene. They'd love to see her. But where would she sleep? And why did Aunt Maisie think they had loads of room? Number 23 St Jude's Villas was not a big house. Not like her brother Rob's place. He lived in a detached house in Raven with a spare bedroom for guests.

Kim's house didn't have a spare *seat* for guests. The kitchen was so small that there wasn't room for a dishwasher. The things Kim would do for a dishwasher. She sighed. Whatever her mother had said, it was all a big mess.

Emer and Laura sat beside each other in school. Between classes, they talked with their friends.

'I bet she's got blonde hair,' Emer said dreamily.

'Who?' asked Laura.

'Charlene. Will she bring presents, do you think? I'd love real American jeans, not ones like you get here.'

'The ones you get here *are* American, stupid,' said Laura.

'They're cheaper over there,' retorted Emer. 'People are always flying to New York to buy cheap jeans!'

The Irish teacher marched into the classroom. Laura felt sick. She hated Irish and she hated exams.

'Will you help me if I get stuck on any questions?' she whispered to her twin.

But Emer wasn't listening. She was in dreamland, thinking of the American visitors.

Elsie was off her food. She had a cup of tea with Veronica across the street but didn't fancy one of Veronica's scones.

Veronica was talking too much to notice. Her eldest grandson was in trouble at school for vandalism. He might be thrown out, Veronica said. She suffered with those children, Elsie thought. Veronica's troubles made her feel guilty. After all, there were no real problems in Kim's house. The twins were good girls, for all their loud music. They wouldn't dream of vandalising anything at school. Their father would kill them. Tom might be a man of few words, but he wouldn't stand any nonsense from the girls.

After tea with Veronica, Elsie walked to the chemist for her tablets. The chemist always chatted to her. Today, Elsie didn't chat back.

'Are you not feeling yourself, Elsie?' asked the chemist.

Elsie said she was fine and tried to smile. There was no way out of it. She had to tell Kim the truth.

When Kim got home that afternoon, there was a great smell of cooking in the house. Things must be really bad, she thought. Elsie hardly cooked any more. She baked cakes and her lemon sponge was admired at local church sales. But she didn't cook dinners.

'I made a chicken casserole,' said Elsie brightly when Kim went into the kitchen.

She looked up from peeling potatoes and saw Kim's pale, angry face. Kim was a good daughter. She had a lot on her plate, what with teaching those youngsters in school and worrying about money. Elsie felt her heart heavy with guilt. She left the potatoes in the sink.

'Sit down,' said Elsie. 'I'll tell you. It's all my fault. I lied to Maisie.'

157

She looked so miserable that Kim felt sorry she'd been angry. She patted her mother's hand. 'Go on,' she said.

Elsie sighed. 'You remember that Maisie's eldest is a doctor and that Sandra, Charlene's mother, is a dentist.'

Kim nodded. She knew all this. When she'd been growing up, she got fed up hearing about her clever cousins, the Madison family from Chicago. Aunt Maisie's letters had been full of praise for her children. Cousin Sandra was the prettiest girl in her school and was so clever. The teachers had never seen anyone so bright.

And popular, Aunt Maisie always added. Malcolm was the best in the school at science. He was marvellous at sports, too, a real all-rounder.

Kim had hated the sound of her goody-two-shoes cousins. They sounded awful with their perfect grades. She hoped she never had to meet them. And she never did. She'd never met her aunt Maisie, for that matter. The Madisons hadn't even come for Kim's dad's funeral two years ago. Elsie had been very upset at that, Kim knew. But she'd never said anything.

'You're going to be so mad at me,' said Elsie miserably, thinking of the letter.

'I won't, Mother,' replied Kim. 'Tell me the story, will you?'

'Maisie was a great one for boasting when we were children,' Elsie said. 'She always had to have the nicest dress or the best toy. She loved to show people that she had the best of everything. When she told me how well they were all doing in Chicago, I got fed up. I told her all about you and your sister, but – ' Elsie looked really miserable now. 'I lied. I told her that you were the principal of the school.'

Kim gasped.

Elsie ploughed on. 'I told her Tom was the boss of a big company, that you had a huge house in the country and that the girls had ponies and you had a housekeeper.'

'Mother!' said Kim finally. 'How could you make all that stuff up?'

'I never thought she'd find out,' protested Elsie. 'She was always going on about her pair and how successful they were. Sandra has a housekeeper, so I said you did too.'

'And now Sandra's daughter is coming here. And she thinks we have a big house and a housekeeper,' Kim said. She looked around the kitchen. The wood-effect lino on the floor was ten years old. The kitchen units were orange. Orange had been big in the seventies when the house had been built. Kim hated orange, but kitchen units cost a fortune. There had been no money to spend on the house for ages. Setting up Tom's business had been tough. The twins had wanted to go on that school trip to France and Kim hadn't wanted to say no. Clothes for teenagers cost a fortune. The kitchen had been last on the list.

'What are we going to do?' wailed Elsie.

'You'll have to tell Maisie the truth,' Kim said finally. 'We don't mind Charlene and her friend staying here. But they'll have to sleep in sleeping bags. We can turn the dining room into a room for them. I'll push the table back, but that's it.'

Elsie looked as if she could cry.

'What else can I do, Mother?' asked Kim. She felt like crying herself.

Miles away, Clodagh Dunne sat at her big desk in a city-centre office. She stared through the glass doors in front of her. Clodagh was Kim's younger sister and Elsie's youngest child. In her letters to Chicago, Elsie always said Clodagh worked in Ireland's top advertising company. Elsie made it sound as if Clodagh ran the company. In a way, she did. She was the receptionist and took all the phone calls. The boss joked that the company would fall apart if Clodagh didn't keep them all on their toes. She was very good at her job, but she was also fed up. She was twenty-nine and she didn't want to be a receptionist any more. Even in a trendy advertising office. She wanted to be creative. She wanted to do more than say: 'Hot Flash Advertising, can I help you?' a hundred times a day and organise couriers left, right and centre.

Her boyfriend, Dan, was torn. He wanted her to be happy, but he knew she had no training for a creative job. And if she gave up her good job in Hot Flash, how could they afford the lovely luxury flat they were renting in Ringsend? That was why he never said anything when Clodagh got into one of her creative moods. During the last one, she'd repainted the bathroom bright blue and made fish patterns in navy blue all along the bath. She had made a blind for the window all by herself. It looked beautiful, Dan admitted. But God knows what the landlord would say.

'Hot Flash Advertising, how can I help you?' said Clodagh wearily. It was nearly half past five. She wanted to go home.

'Clodagh, it's me,' said Kim.

'Hello!' said Clodagh happily. She loved talking to her sister.

'Are you at home tonight?' asked Kim. 'I need to talk to you.'

'Yeah,' said Kim. 'It's *Coronation Street* on the television tonight. Where else would I be?'

'I'll ring you after that,' said Kim. She said goodbye.

What was the big mystery? Clodagh wondered. She looked at the big silver clock on the wall. It was exactly half five. She put her headset down and got up from her desk. If anyone wanted to phone now, tough bananas. They were too late.

That night, Kim and Clodagh spent half an hour on the phone.

'Poor Mam,' said Clodagh when she'd heard all the details.

'What do you mean "poor Mam"?' shouted Kim. 'It's me you should feel sorry for. These American girls are going to come and look down their noses at my house. They think I've got a housekeeper.'

Kim was getting more upset.

'Charlene's in college. She's very clever, Mother says. She probably has her own car at home. All American kids have their own cars. We can barely afford the van and my rust bucket. The house hasn't been touched in years. Tom painted the hall two years ago, that's it. He did the girls' bedroom the year before. The living room is a mess and I hate that green colour in the bathroom. I can't have two strange girls moving in and seeing the state of the place.'

'Calm down,' said Clodagh.

'I can't,' said Kim. She burst into tears. Her mother was ashamed of Kim and her family. That was it. Why else would she lie about Kim and her job? Why else would she lie about the big house and Tom's job? Because she was ashamed of Kim. That had to be the answer.

161

'She's not ashamed,' said Clodagh, when Kim explained how she felt. 'Remember when I was ten or eleven and Miriam from across the road told me she was getting a bike for Christmas. I told her I was getting a bike *and* a dolls' house. I wasn't. I just didn't want her to think she was better than me. That's all.'

'Yes, but you were ten. Mother is an adult. She should know better,' said Kim sadly.

'Don't be silly, Kim. Of course Mam is proud of you. She drives me nuts every time she sees me. "Why can't you be more like your sister?" she says. It's like listening to a broken record. "Why can't you get married and settle down?" She thinks that Dan and I are living a wild life, going to night-clubs all week. She wants us to be like you and Tom.'

'Do you think so?' asked Kim. She wiped her eyes with a tissue.

'Yes.' Clodagh was cheerful. 'Don't panic. I have a plan. Let's all meet up in your house on Friday night. Tell Rob to come.' Rob was their older brother. He worked in the bank. He had four sons and was married to Stephanie. Stephanie was tall, blonde and thought she was the last word in style.

Elsie hated Stephanie. That was why she lived with Kim and not with Rob. Rob and Stephanie's house was bigger than Kim's. But if Elsie and Stephanie had to live together, even the UN wouldn't be able to keep the peace.

Clodagh wasn't fond of her sister-in-law either. Stephanie had once told Clodagh that she felt sorry for her for having red hair. Clodagh's hair was long, curly and the colour of flames. Clodagh had never forgiven Stephanie. Poor Rob was stuck in the middle. Family get-togethers could be deadly.

At Christmas, Stephanie, Clodagh and Elsie had to be kept well apart from each other. After the argument last year about whether to watch *Titanic* or a ballet special, Kim had decided against having Christmas dinner in her house.

'I bet Mother didn't have to tell Aunt Maisie lies about Rob,' said Kim bitterly.

'Don't be silly,' Clodagh said. 'She probably said Stephanie was a nice person. That's a lie, for a start.'

There were eight of them round the small dining-room table. Clodagh had brought her boyfriend, Dan. Rob had brought a pot plant for his mother and a box of chocolates for Kim. He hadn't brought Stephanie.

'Thank God for that,' thought Elsie. Stephanie would look down her long nose at Elsie when she heard what had happened.

'What's the plan, Clodagh?' asked Tom McDonnell. He felt sorry for his mother-in-law. She'd been boasting a little bit. So what? Lots of people did it.

'Interior decoration,' said Clodagh proudly.

'What?' said Tom.

'We're going to do up the house,' Clodagh said simply. 'We've loads of time. They're not coming till August.'

'We can't afford an interior decorator,' Kim said, shocked. Those people charged a fortune to tell you what colour wallpaper to use. She'd seen them on the telly. They never used the cheapest wallpaper. Oh no. They went mad and did things with paint and bits of scarves draped over lamps.

'We're not hiring anyone,' Clodagh said. 'I'll do the designing and the rest of you will help out with the donkey

163

work. All you need is clever ideas. You can do it really cheaply.'

'Like you did our bathroom,' said Dan. Clodagh had primed him beforehand on what to say.

'Exactly,' said Clodagh, beaming at Dan. 'I've got some wonderful ideas. You've been saying for ages that it needs to be repainted, Kim. We'll all help and it will be beautiful. Then you won't mind Charlene and her friend staying. If they ask, you can say you got tired of the country and the horses. They won't ask,' she added confidently. 'Say you like the city air and the fact that you are in the centre of everything. You have shops and cafés round the corner. You can hear the bells of Christ Church. You're minutes away from Stephen's Green. Tell them you wanted to be more cosmopolitan.'

'I thought that was a girls' magazine,' joked Dan.

Clodagh shot him a fierce look. 'It means that you wanted to live in the centre of a big, exciting city.'

'We'll say we're far too old for ponies,' Laura said. She loved this idea.

'We can say we wanted to be nearer the shops,' said Emer. That was true. Emer lived for the shops. Her side of the bedroom was like a sale of work with clothes everywhere.

'I've got great ideas for painting up the bathroom and the kitchen,' Clodagh said.

The rest of the family began to get excited too.

'I could put up those shelves in the sitting room,' said Tom. 'They're still in the box under the stairs. And I could make a special shelf for the television and video.'

'We could have window boxes,' said Elsie. She loved

164

gardening. She had magic fingers with plants. But she hadn't bothered since her husband had died. This was Kim's garden and it would be rude to take over. Kim was bad with plants. She had only to look at a rosebush and it dropped dead. 'We could re-do all your garden pots, Kim,' she said.

'Exactly,' said Clodagh. 'Dan can help with the garden.'

'I sell insurance,' said Dan nervously. 'I don't know how to garden.'

Clodagh tickled him under the chin. 'You know how to dig, don't you?' she said.

Rob said he had a load of paint in his loft. It was left over from the last time he'd had the house done. He knew where they could get nice patio slabs cheap and he had a friend who ran a garden centre. They could get lots of plants at cost price.

Kim was the only one who was quiet. 'We can't afford it,' she said. 'What's the point in painting the kitchen when the units are orange?'

'We can paint them too!' said Clodagh cheerily. 'I've seen them do it on the TV. You buy this special primer to cover the orange and then you can paint it any colour you like. You can even paint wall tiles, did you know that?'

'We'll all chip in, Mum,' said Emer.

'I'll buy the extra paint,' offered Rob.

'I'll buy patio slabs,' said Tom.

'I'll buy plants,' said Elsie.

'And we can do all the work ourselves,' Clodagh added.

'What about the housekeeper, and me being the school principal?' demanded Kim. 'I'm not lying to those two girls. I won't do it. It's wrong.'

Kim believed in telling the truth. She spent her entire life telling the children in school that the truth was important.

Tom decided it was time for his opinion. He'd been worried about how upset his wife was about the whole stupid thing. 'There'll be no lying in this house,' he said firmly. 'You *aren't* the principal, we *don't* have a housekeeper and there are *no* ponies.'

'They'd never fit in the garden,' joked Emer, looking out at the tiny square of grass.

Tom continued. 'Nobody is going to lie to Charlene and her friend. They can stay here and be welcome. That's all we're doing, making them welcome. The house could do with a lick of paint. And if the house looks nice, you'll feel better about the visitors, Kim. But if they ask, we'll tell them the truth. There's no housekeeper and there never was. Nobody will mention anything to do with ponies and you being the principal.'

'Ah come on, Mum,' said Emer. 'It'll be a bit of fun. You're always saying I spend too much time doing nothing in the summer holidays. It'll be cool to have Charlene here.'

Kim looked at the eager faces. 'As long as I still get my holiday on the beach,' she said.

Clodagh's project filled her mind all day. When she wasn't answering the phone in Hot Flash, she looked through magazines for ideas. She got gardening books from one of the women at work. She watched television programmes about gardens. Her favourite was one where Alan Titchmarsh transformed a garden totally in two days. The revamp was always a big secret. The owner was nearly always speechless when they saw how different it all looked.

Clodagh had dreams at night about what she would do to Kim's garden. She woke Dan up one night with her muttering.

'Pink, pink, I want pink pots,' she said in her sleep.

The next day, Dan teased her about it.

'Aren't you lucky,' she laughed. 'I could be shouting out another fella's name in my sleep.'

'If you shout another fella's name, it'll be Alan Titchmarsh's,' Dan said.

In the evenings, she sat at the coffee table and drew plans. She had different pages with colour schemes for each room. Dan said it all looked great.

'I don't know,' Clodagh said slowly. She stared at her plans. 'How hard is it to lay patio slabs?'

Dan hadn't a clue. 'Tom will know,' he said hopefully.

'Tom's an electrician,' Clodagh pointed out.

The plans for the inside of the house were simpler. Everyone knew how to paint. The twins had promised to help her with the special details.

She was going to paint sea creatures in the bathroom. Emer and Laura were going to paint the fish. Clodagh was going to do the seahorses herself because they were hard to do.

The living room was very dull, so Clodagh planned to make it look lively. Bright sunshine colours would be great. And she had a plan to get plenty of big, bright pictures for free. Ones in shops cost a fortune, but Clodagh knew a man who had art on the brain. He worked in a boring job and painted at the weekend. He'd be pleased to have his paintings hanging somewhere other than his mother's house.

Kim would have to make curtains, Clodagh decided. She had a sewing machine. Elsie could help her. Clodagh had already bought some of the material in a fabric sale. Yards of cheap muslin in cream. In one of her decorating books, it explained how to paint a pretty gold pattern on to muslin. She was longing to try it. Then, you draped the muslin on the window. That couldn't be too hard, could it?

But what she really couldn't wait to start was the dining room. Charlene and her friend were going to sleep there. Clodagh had it all worked out. She had her eye on a sofa bed that would look perfect with her colour scheme. Kim would probably be a bit shocked by the colour of the walls. Kim liked everything cream or white.

Clodagh was planning on a bold russet. She decided to paint that room while Kim and the twins were in Brittas. That way, her sister wouldn't get upset at the sight of the paint in the tins.

Dear Maisie,

We'd love to have Charlene and her friend stay with us. We will be delighted to meet them at the airport. Kim's two daughters are lovely girls and very clever. They will show Charlene around if she would like. They have lots of trips lined up. Did I tell you that Emer got first place in her class in Irish recently?

Elsie paused. She was going to mention that Clodagh was going to give up her job to do a course in interior design.

168

But she thought better of it. Clodagh had talked about giving up her job, but she hadn't. And Elsie had got into enough trouble stretching the truth. She didn't want to push her luck.

Clodagh would love to give up her job to do a course in interior design. But it would be hard with such a good job. And the course is very expensive.

That sounded better.

The third Thursday in June was the end of term. Kim decided they'd celebrate. She bought wine in the supermarket and picked up a big cream cake. She had steak, chicken and potatoes wrapped in tin foil all ready to go on the barbecue. Elsie helped her set up chairs and the picnic table in the garden. But where were the twins?

Emer and Laura went into the big chemist in Stephen's Green to buy hair dye. There was an entire section-ful. They stared at the shelves.

'How do you pick one?' asked Laura. She had never really looked at all the different hair colours before. She was amazed there were so many.

Emer was a bit surprised herself. On the television ads, they only showed a few colours. One blonde, a red and a dark brown, maybe. But here, there were hundreds of boxes of colour.

There were white blondes, golden blondes and ash blondes. There were ones that you had to paint on, like highlights from the hairdresser. Laura picked up one with a picture of a woman with huge blue eyes and a golden mane of hair.

The sisters stared at the picture. The woman looked as though she'd just stepped off a movie set. She looked stunning. She looked like Emer wanted to.

'That's the one,' said Emer.

Every time there was a noise on the street, Kim jumped. She was waiting to hear the twins come home.

'You're like a cat on a hot tin roof,' said Elsie when Kim jumped for the third time.

'It's a big day,' said Kim, 'the last exam. I hope they did all right.'

'No matter, don't mention the exam,' Elsie advised.

Tom arrived home at six.

'Where are the girls?' he asked.

Kim sighed. 'There's no sign of them,' she said. 'I don't know what can have happened. They said they'd be home by now.'

The doorbell rang but it was only Clodagh and Dan.

'Where are the girls?' demanded Clodagh. She'd brought a big box of chocolates for them.

'They're probably still with their friends, laughing their heads off because they're on their holidays,' Tom said.

Kim was still worried.

'I'm starving,' Dan said hopefully. He looked at the wine on the picnic table. 'I could kill for a drink.'

By half six, the barbecue was cooking away. Dan had had two glasses of wine. Clodagh had opened the chocolates and eaten four. She'd go on a diet tomorrow. She couldn't diet when there was barbecue food around. Elsie sat in the most comfortable deckchair and rested her feet.

Suddenly, they all heard the front door slam.

'Thank God,' said Kim.

Laura appeared, still in her school uniform. 'Sorry we're late,' she said. 'We went to Fiona's house.'

Her mother hugged her. 'I was worried about you. How did you get on?'

Laura looked a bit nervous. 'Oh, all right,' she said.

'Have you left any food for me?' said a voice. It was Emer. Emer with bright blonde hair.

Everyone stared at her in shock.

'So that's why you were late,' said Clodagh.

'Emer!' said Kim.

'Look at your hair!' said Elsie.

Tom McDonnell stared at his daughter. She had left the house that morning with long dark hair. She'd be sixteen soon. She was growing up. 'I suppose you want the first baked potato because you've finished your exams?' he said.

Emer grinned. 'Yeah, Dad, that'd be cool.'

Laura sighed with relief. If Dad didn't mind the hair, everything was going to be all right.

'Why did you do that to yourself?' asked Elsie.

Emer patted her long blonde curls. 'I wanted to look nice for Charlene,' she said. 'Plus, there's an end-of-exam party tonight in Fiona's house and I thought it was time to show-case the new me.'

On the first Saturday of the great decorating job, everyone wanted to use the wallpaper stripper.

Emer demanded the first go: 'I've seen them do this on the telly,' she said. 'It's easy.'

After ten minutes, she wanted to give it back. It was the hottest job ever. Steam rose from the stripper all the time. The person using the stripper was permanently covered in a cloud of steam.

'You asked for it,' said her father from the top of the ladder. He was slowly stripping wallpaper with a scraper.

'Think of it as a type of skin treatment,' Clodagh said. 'People pay good money to have their faces steamed.'

Emer was stuck with the steamer.

By six that night, they were all sick of it. But the walls in the sitting room were bare.

'Tomorrow, we'll do the hall,' said Clodagh. She was in charge of the plans.

'Can't we have tomorrow off?' begged Emer. Watching television shows about doing houses up and actually doing them up were very different.

'No,' said Clodagh. 'Dan and I are going to get us a takeaway from the chipper for a treat. Who wants what?'

It was a fantastic summer. As good as being in Spain, thought Kim as she lay on the deck outside the mobile home on their last day away. She'd got a tan from the sun and so had the twins. Even Elsie had freckles on her arms. The only person who was still pale was Clodagh, back home.

'I'm as white as a milk bottle. I haven't had a chance to sit in the sun,' she told Kim the last time they spoke on the phone. Clodagh was spending every spare moment doing up the McDonnell house. In the two weeks that Kim and the girls had been away, she'd been finishing it.

'What have you done, exactly?' asked Kim. She was a bit

172

nervous about the whole thing. When they'd gone away, there hadn't been much painting done. Tom, Rob and Dan had laid a patio. Elsie had bustled about with plants. Kim hadn't seen her mother so happy in ages.

'You need a couple of geraniums there,' Elsie would say, looking at a patch of earth. 'And I love roses. A small bush would be nice. Bright pink is my favourite colour.'

Bright pink was Clodagh's favourite colour too. She couldn't wear pink, not with her red hair. What Kim was really afraid of was that Clodagh would have gone mad and done the walls pink. Kim didn't think she could live with pink walls. What was wrong with cream wallpaper, anyway?

The following day, Kim parked the Mini outside the house in Dublin. Emer, Laura and Elsie got out. Clodagh's car, which was even more rusty than Kim's, was parked outside.

'I can't wait to see what Clodagh's done,' said Emer eagerly.

'Neither can I,' said her mother.

Kim opened the front door nervously and stepped into the hall. For a moment, she thought she was in the wrong place.

'Oh,' she said. Her hall table was still there and it was the same old lamp she'd got as a wedding present. The coat stand was the same too. But the walls . . . Kim stared around in wonder. The cream wallpaper with a pale pink stripe was gone. Now the walls were a pale green colour, with deep green ivy carefully hand-painted as though it grew there. The painted ivy trailed along over a mirror. Kim looked more closely at the mirror. It was her old one. But it had been treated with gold paint and made to look really old and expensive.

A huge real ivy sat on the hall table. There were photo frames beside it, gold, hand-painted, full of pictures of the family.

Kim peeped into the living room. It had been a mushroom colour once. Now, it was bright cheery yellow with bits of blue here and there. It looked like a different room. Kim realised that her old cream curtains had been dyed a sunshine yellow. The armchairs and couch were covered with soft yellow throws. Fat bright blue cushions lay on the armchairs. Clodagh was lying on the couch.

'I'm exhausted,' Clodagh said. She had a cup of tea in one hand and she wore jeans with paint marks all over them. Clodagh's fingers were covered with paint too. Her red hair had wild yellow and green streaks in it.

'But I enjoyed it, you know,' she said.

Kim looked around in awe. The room was like one from a magazine. Everything looked incredible because of Clodagh's bright new colours. She had turned a tired room into something special.

'It's like a different house,' Kim said.

'I know,' said Clodagh proudly. 'I think I'm good at this interior decoration stuff.'

'Good isn't the word,' said Kim. 'You're brilliant.'

Emer and Laura grinned. 'Wait till you see the bathroom, Mum,' said Laura.

They all trooped up to the bathroom. It was like diving into the sea. Clodagh had painted it in deep blues like the ocean. At the bottom, there were fishes and sea creatures like starfishes. The tiles had fishy designs on them too. Higher up, the walls were a paler blue, like the sea near the surface.

174

There were aquamarine towels and an aquamarine blind. It must have taken days to paint.

'I dyed the towels,' Clodagh said quickly. 'They're not new.'

Kim hugged her sister tightly. 'You've worked so hard,' she said.

'Do you like it?' asked Clodagh.

Kim could barely speak. She wanted to cry instead. 'It's beautiful,' she said finally. 'Really beautiful.'

Charlene and Pamela looked eagerly out of the plane window. Thousands of feet below them was Ireland. From the air, it looked like a pretty green patchwork quilt. It really was emerald, Charlene thought in surprise. Grandma was always talking about how green Ireland was. And how friendly the people were.

On St Patrick's Day, she would have a sip of sherry and get tears in her eyes. She would cry a bit. 'I'm sorry I never went home to Ireland,' she'd say sadly.

'Chicago is your home now,' Charlene's mom would say firmly.

Charlene's mom, Sandra, had never wanted to visit Ireland. She preferred Florida. She liked the sun.

'I don't get much vacation time,' she said. 'And I don't want to spend it in the rain.'

'It rains in Chicago,' Grandma would argue. 'It snows too. It doesn't snow that much in Ireland.'

Charlene wished Mom and Grandma wouldn't argue so much.

As the plane landed at Dublin airport, Charlene began to feel really excited.

175

'We're in Europe!' she whispered to Pamela.

The two girls grinned happily at each other.

'I hope the McDonnells are nice people,' Charlene said then. That was the only scary thing. She'd never met her Irish family. Now she'd be stuck with them for two weeks.

'They sounded nice in the letter your granny's sister sent,' said Pamela.

'Yes,' said Charlene nervously. Grandma had told her lots about her cousins. They sounded very different from the Chicago side of the family. Grandma said they were very clever girls and had been to France and everything.

Emer was wearing new jeans and high boots. She had put half a can of hairspray in her blonde hair to make it sit the right way. Her make-up had taken an hour. It was very hot in the airport and her high heels were killing her. But she didn't care. She looked good. That was the most important thing.

Laura was wearing her old jeans and flip-flops. If Emer was going to dress up to the nines, she would dress down. Whoever said that twins did everything the same was mad.

Elsie and Kim looked as if they were going out to a party. Elsie was in her Sunday best outfit and was carrying her good white handbag.

'Mother, sit down,' said Kim.

'It would be rude to sit down,' said Elsie. Despite the house being done up, she was still nervous.

'Mother, they're two eighteen-year-old girls,' said Kim crossly. She was nervous too. 'They could be ages getting their luggage. I wonder where Clodagh is?'

They needed two cars to bring everyone and the luggage

from the airport. Clodagh said she'd come to give moral support.

She arrived just in time.

Two very ordinary-looking girls in jeans came out of the Arrivals door. They were pushing a trolley. They looked around and saw the sign that Emer had made.

Welcome Charlene and Pamela, it said in big writing.

'That must mean us,' said Pamela, seeing the sign.

The Dublin branch of the family smiled at the visitors.

'Hi,' said Charlene nervously. 'Are you the McDonnells?'

'Yes,' said Kim. 'Welcome, I'm your aunt Kim.'

She was pleased to see that both girls looked friendly and unsure. They weren't wearing lots of expensive clothes. They looked like ordinary teenagers.

Elsie was pleased to see that Charlene looked a little like Maisie.

Emer was pleased that the American girls looked very normal, not like movie stars at all.

Laura was pleased that they were wearing jeans. She didn't want to spend two weeks with people who wanted to dress up all the time. It was bad enough sharing with Emer. Emer put on make-up to answer the front door.

Why were they all standing around like dummies? Clodagh wondered. Somebody had to take action. 'Lovely to meet you!' she said, and hugged Charlene. Then she hugged Pamela. 'I'm Clodagh. Which is which?'

There was nobody like Clodagh to break the ice, Laura thought.

Soon, they were all smiling and hugging. It was as if they'd known each other for years.

There was a big discussion on which car everyone was to go in. Clodagh took charge again. 'Right,' she said, 'Emer and Charlene can go with me. We'll take half the bags. Pamela and Laura can go with Kim and Mum. Right?'

Charlene had never seen a car as old as Clodagh's before.

'Hey, this is cool,' said Charlene. 'A classic car.'

'Yeah, right,' said Clodagh as she crunched the gears. 'A classic car.' She opened the window to let some air in. 'It's got classic air conditioning too.'

'What's that?' asked Charlene politely.

'No air conditioning!' laughed Clodagh.

Emer giggled and so did Charlene. Everyone relaxed. Everything was going to be fine.

At the house, Kim put the kettle on and the twins showed the visitors where they were going to sleep.

'This is normally the dining room but we fixed it up for you,' said Emer.

The visitors looked around at the warm red walls. They looked at the huge watercolour pictures that Clodagh had got for next to nothing from her friend.

'No mad modern stuff,' she'd warned him. 'I want flowers, right?'

They admired the floaty cream curtains and the sofa bed covered in the same cream material. Clodagh had even dyed sheets and pillowcases to go with the walls.

'I love this house,' said Charlene. It was so different from her home in Crystal Lake. Her mom and Grandma liked pale colours. But this Irish house was really unusual. Artistic, that was the word for it. The dining room was like a painting and the bathroom was something else. Charlene hoped she'd get a chance to lie in the bath and light all the tiny vanilla candles that surrounded it. She could lie back and look up at the rich blue walls. It was supposed to look like the sea and it really did.

The kitchen made her think of the pretty pale buildings in Miami, Florida. Charlene decided she'd take a photo to show her mom and Grandma. They'd love the McDonnells' house.

'Do you like Italian food?' asked Emer.

'Sure,' said Charlene.

'Great. We're going to an Italian restaurant tonight to celebrate your visit.'

Charlene smiled with pleasure. Her Irish family were so nice. The way Grandma had described them, she didn't think they'd be friendly. But they were so warm and kind.

The Italian restaurant was lively and good value. The family sat at one long table and everyone talked loudly. Clodagh told them all that she was going to do part-time interior decoration.

'She's so clever,' said Dan proudly.

Emer said she'd help out as long as she didn't have to use the wallpaper stripper.

'I'd love to do something like that,' said Charlene. 'I don't know what I want to do in college.'

'I thought you were going to be a dentist like your mother,' said Elsie sharply.

'Mom's not a dentist,' said Charlene in surprise. 'She works with a dental surgeon. She's a nurse. She would have liked me to be a dentist or a nurse, but I flunked chemistry and biology.'

Elsie's eyes were like saucers.

'I was sure she was a dentist. Tell me, your uncle is a doctor, right?'

'No,' Charlene said. 'He works in a lab, though. He'd like to be a doctor but it takes years.'

Elsie's eyes got even bigger. What had Maisie been telling her all these years? That Sandra was a dentist and Malcolm was a doctor. It hadn't been true at all. She was about to say something about all of this when Kim looked at her.

'Mother,' she said firmly, 'would you like garlic bread?'

Elsie looked back at Kim. She could tell what Kim was really saying: *Let's forget all about doctors, dentists, school principals and houses in the country.*

Elsie could take a hint.

'I'm so hungry,' she said. 'I'd love garlic bread.'

That night, Kim sat at her dressing table and rubbed cream on her face.

'I thought Elsie's eyes were going to pop out of her head,' said Tom with a smile. 'She looked amazed when Charlene said her mother wasn't a dentist. It sounds like your aunt Maisie was telling the odd fib too.'

Kim smiled as if she'd known all along. 'No harm was done,' she said.

Tom thought of all the hassle of redecorating the house. He thought of how upset both Kim and Elsie had been. He thought of Kim worrying herself sick about the visitors before they came. He smiled back at his wife. 'No harm was done,' he agreed. 'And aren't Charlene and Pamela lovely girls?'

'Lovely,' Kim said. 'It's a pleasure to have them here.'

*   *   *

180

It was a warm afternoon a week later. The four girls had gone off into town shopping. Elsie finished weeding the flower bed under the window. The bed on the other side needed weeding too. That was the thing about weeds. Once you finished one side of the garden, the other side was full of weeds again. Her knees didn't hurt a bit any more because she had a weeding stool. She sat on the stool and used the weeder with the long handle. A bee buzzed by lazily. On the wall, a robin sat and looked at Elsie. She made a tweeting noise to the bird. He put his tiny head to one side and looked at her with his shiny black eyes. At that moment, she felt very happy. She loved gardening. Tom had given her a bit of the garden shed to use for seedlings. She planned to grow bulbs in there in the winter.

Maisie sat in the den in the house in Crystal Lake, Chicago. She had her old photo album on her lap. Maisie had felt sad ever since Charlene's phone call from Dublin.

'I'm having a great time, Grandma,' Charlene had said happily. 'I love it here. Everyone's so nice to us. And Auntie Elsie is just like you, Grandma. She's really kind.'

Maisie opened the first page of the album. The pictures weren't anywhere near as good as the modern pictures that Malcolm took with his digital camera. With that, you could have big photos or small ones or any size you wanted printed from your own computer. But Maisie still loved the old ones best. She stared at a hazy black-and-white shot of herself and Elsie. She had been around eighteen, so Elsie must have been seventeen. They were posed in their best dresses outside the farmhouse. Behind them, their mother's rambling rose climbed up the wall. Their father's old sheep dog sat at Elsie's feet, enjoying the sun. Maisie's dress had a big full skirt and she had a flower brooch on her collar. She could remember that dress as if it was yesterday. It had been a rich French blue with a white collar. Elsie's had been pale pink with a cream collar.

They looked so young and so happy. Funny, she couldn't remember where they were going, all dressed up. Or who had taken the picture. Elsie would remember, she was sure. Elsie had the best memory.

They used to talk about the old times in their letters. Elsie would write *Do you remember the day we went to McNiffe's for the hay-making? You said you were in love with young Billy McNiffe and he got all shy?*

And sure enough, Maisie would remember it. She could almost smell the hay and the fun they had when it was dinnertime. The woman of the house would come down the field with the dinner. Everyone would be mad with hunger. There would be hot, sweet tea, thick home-made bread and plenty of cold meat.

Everyone would sit and eat. They'd laugh and joke. Life was so simple then. Elsie didn't write about the old days any more. Her letters had been sadder since Ned had died.

Maisie felt a pang of guilt. She should have gone back to Ireland for her brother-in-law's funeral. She should have been there for Elsie.

The tears started to fall down her face. She and Elsie had been so close and now look at them. They wrote letters out of habit. They talked about houses and jobs and clever grandchildren. Not about the real things in life. They hadn't talked on the phone since last Christmas. That had to change, Maisie decided suddenly.

She got to her feet and went to the phone in the hall. She sat down at the small table and thought for the hundredth time that the hall furniture was getting tatty. It wasn't that she couldn't afford to replace it. Her late husband's insurance policy had left her well off. But she was nervous of spending the money. She'd never been used to spending. Now, she was worried about the kids. Sandra had always had trouble getting alimony out of her ex-husband. Malcolm never had a cent. He was hopeless with money, even though he was well paid at the university. Maisie liked to think that, when she died, her children and grandchildren would be looked after.

But why not spend the money now? Why not visit her beloved sister in Ireland? Didn't they always say at home *There's no pockets in a shroud*. The kids would manage without every dollar of the insurance money. They never asked for it anyway. Maisie had a right to use her own money.

It took Maisie a while to find the number and a bit longer to dial it.

'Hello,' said a tired little voice at the other end.

Maisie felt the tears come to her eyes again. When had her sister started sounding so old?

'Elsie, love,' she said hoarsely. 'It's me, Maisie. I don't suppose I could come for a visit?'

'Oh, Maisie,' said Elsie. 'I thought you'd never ask.'

Bride and Doom

Lily hated weddings. With a vengeance. Not just because the very thought of walking down the aisle turned previously intelligent women into simpering idiots obsessed with oyster satin bodices and antique lace veils. No.

Lily hated weddings because at some point in the day she'd inevitably overhear a murmured snatch of conversation. It always ran along the same lines: 'That's poor Lily Fitzgerald. Got stood up at her own wedding. She was devastated. I don't think she ever got over it. And she's well over thirty now.'

At this point, Lily had taught herself to smile radiantly and grab some unsuspecting man and drag him on to the dance floor where she did her best impersonation of someone who didn't know the meaning of the word 'devastated'. The latter course of action had caused a bit of trouble on several occasions because she then abandoned the man in question at the side of the dance floor when she'd finished with him. Men didn't take kindly to being used.

Tough, thought Lily grimly. Get used to it, boys.

Consequently, there was a raft of reasons for Lily's wedding-o-phobia but the only person she'd ever been able to confide in about this had been her best friend, Shauna.

A scientist with a doctorate in medical microbiology, Shauna was not one of the hand-clasping, lip-biting sisterhood (that included Lily's mother, all her aunties and her older sister, Jen) who watched Lily anxiously at family weddings, hoping that she wouldn't break down in sobs and throw herself on to the wedding cake in the manner of a distraught spinster.

'I wish they'd stop watching me!' Lily hissed at Shauna as they stood and raised their glasses at the wedding toast for Lily's cousin. None of Lily's family was watching the bride and groom – they were all worriedly staring at Lily. 'It was five years ago, I'm over it. I was over it as soon as I heard that Mr Bloody Perfect Richard had been two-timing me for so long.'

Lily's small, firm jaw was clamped fiercely and her normally shining toffee-coloured eyes glowered.

'Your mum just worries about you, Lily,' said Shauna, helping herself to another glass of champagne from the tray of a passing waiter. 'Ignore it. One day they'll realise you had a lucky escape from that moron. Have a drink.'

Plain-talking Shauna was a breath of fresh air. *She* never urged Lily to get out more or to take up evening classes so she could meet nice young men. *She* never suggested that Lily go out for a drink with Mrs Redmond's son, Monty, who had always liked her, really, and had his own house and everything, and no longer wore those strange nylon trousers or talked to himself.

'He's a lot better these days, Lily,' Mrs Fitzgerald insisted. 'Much chattier, doesn't mutter to himself as he walks down the road, you know.'

Nobody could accuse Mrs Fitzgerald of not doing her level best to find Lily a man. It wasn't as if Lily wasn't pretty. Well, Mrs Fitzgerald thought, she might be if she made a bit of an effort. It was as if Lily was determined to look frostily untouchable, what with all her staid clothes and her hair tied back tightly. What was the point in being pretty with all that nice shiny hair if you didn't make the best of it?

No, Mrs Fitzgerald thought darkly, Lily didn't make the best of herself because she was still broken-hearted.

Mrs Fitzgerald didn't believe in voodoo and such carry on, but there were occasions when she seriously thought of making a wax dummy of Richard, the two-timer who'd broken her daughter's heart. She knew just where she'd stick the first pin.

'Why doesn't Mum understand that I don't want a man?' wailed Lily. 'I don't want any man, ever.'

'That's the older generation for you,' Shauna sighed. 'They think a man is the be all and end all of life. In a few years, we won't need men at all. We'll be able to reproduce human life without them, they'll be obsolete.'

She grinned with satisfaction. Shauna had her own war stories from the front line of dating.

'"Reproducing human life" doesn't have quite the same ring to it as "mad passionate lovemaking", though, does it?' said Lily thoughtfully.

'No, but test tubes don't get out of the bed and go home straight after sex,' Shauna added.

Lily laughed. 'It's so long since I had sex, I have no idea what you're talking about.'

'You're better off without it,' said Shauna. 'Sex – who needs it?'

Not me, thought Lily. She was perfectly content with her life as it was. A geography and English teacher in a girls' school, Lily was happy living in her tiny mews house in a picturesque harbour village, and she had enough friends and interests to keep her occupied. Men were not on the list.

Shauna, her partner in crime, felt the same way.

Which was why it all came as such a shock to Lily when she heard the news.

She was sitting on her tiny patio, enjoying both the early evening sun and a glass of crisp, cool Pinot Grigio as she marked English homework. Her long dark hair hung loosely around her face and she wore a pair of ancient jeans and an elderly grey sweatshirt that had been washed to a comfortable level of softness.

The girls she taught at St Imelda's certainly wouldn't have recognised her or the delighted squeal with which she greeted her best friend, Dr Shauna Zaidan, who let herself in the back gate, waving delightedly and saying she had 'the best news ever'.

'Welcome back,' said Lily, hugging her friend before nipping barefoot into the kitchen to get the wine bottle and another glass. 'I can't believe you've come back from a disease conference with the best news ever, unless you've finally cracked Ebola.'

Shauna didn't notice the gentle teasing. She was staring dreamily into space.

'You won't believe it,' she said, sighing. 'I almost don't believe it myself.'

'Tell me!' urged Lily. 'It's bound to be more fun than my news, which is that half of 3a *still* don't know the difference between verbs and adverbs.'

'I'm getting married.'

Shauna hadn't touched her wine. Lily took a huge gulp of hers.

'What?' she croaked.

'I know it's sudden,' Shauna said, still speaking dreamily. 'It's Patrick Taylor, remember? We met at the airport on the way to the conference in Paris. It was like nothing had changed, we were still crazy about each other, it was incredible.'

'I knew it was a mistake to have a medical conference in bloody Paris,' said Lily, joking to hide how jolted she was at the news. She remembered Patrick, all right. How could she forget? Drop-dead gorgeous, clever and kind, he'd been the love of Shauna's life for four years and nobody had been more surprised than Lily when they'd split up. The normally voluble Shauna had never wanted to talk about what had gone wrong. It had been easier not to talk about it recently, anyway, because Patrick was a reminder of Lily's earlier life, when she had been one half of Lily 'n' Richard.

Patrick and Richard had been consigned to history. That was then, this was now: she and Shauna in single, all-men-are-pigs bliss.

'I know you'll think we're mad, but I've never really got

over him,' Shauna said slowly. 'He was my one, *the* one. And when we met again. I can't explain it, Lily. I had to tell you first. Are you shocked?'

'Me, shocked? Don't be silly. Not at all,' said Lily, sure that her face was bleached white. 'We all have to settle down some time, we can't be wild young things forever,' she added in a hollow voice. 'You are sure, aren't you? It is a bit sudden, Shauna.'

'But it's right,' Shauna said fiercely. 'I love Patrick. I know everyone will think we're mad, but it feels so right and life's too short to waste time. What if we let each other escape again – what then? Will I wake up one day to find I'm seventy and alone, thinking of what could have been with Patrick? And I've missed him, Lily, God I've missed him.'

It was the faint cracking in her voice that made Lily realise she was serious.

'You've always been the smartest person I know,' Lily said, moving closer to clasp Shauna's hands tightly in her own. 'If this is your decision, I'll support you. As long as you've thought it out. I'll kill him if he hurts you.'

Shauna didn't say anything. She just put her arms round Lily and hugged her tightly. 'You're my best friend, Lily, do you know that?'

'Yeah, sure. I'm just wondering what the alien body-snatchers have done with my friend, Shauna Zaidan, the one who famously asked why, if NASA had put one man in space, they couldn't put them *all* there?'

They both laughed. 'Toast,' announced Lily, raising her glass. 'To the marriage of my best friend, the fabulously clever Dr Zaidan, and Dr Patrick Taylor, who is living on borrowed time if he doesn't treat you like a princess and instantly learn how to empty the dishwasher.'

'Just one thing,' Shauna added. 'I've always wanted an autumn wedding, so we're going to get married next month. I know you hate weddings, but this is different and you're over Richard, I know that. You've told me often enough.' She smiled at this. 'You will be my bridesmaid, Lily, won't you?'

Lily remembered her joke about alien body-snatchers many times over the next month. Because they'd definitely done a job on Shauna. Within one week, Shauna had changed from a sensible person into someone who admitted to having nightmares over the wedding arrangements.

'Why worry about the damn seating plan?' raged Lily to herself after yet another phone conversation where Shauna had actually cried at the thought of integrating all her difficult relatives with all Patrick's difficult relatives.

'Why bother inviting them?' Lily had said on the phone, which was actually quite a restrained response from a woman who really wanted to ask why didn't Patrick and Shauna either elope or, better still, just live together like millions of other perfectly happy people? Who needed a piece of paper to prove their love? Who needed the opportunity for their beloved to humiliate them in front of all their friends and family in an eighteenth-century stone church in a pretty village with a horse and carriage outside and a champagne reception for a hundred and fifty all lined up in a charming hotel, followed by a glorious meal of wild Irish salmon and strawberries?

Not that it was personal, Lily convinced herself.

'Shauna, why don't you let me organise the seating plan?' she suggested, gritting her teeth. 'Then we can tell all the out-of-sorts relatives that I did it and they can scream at me if they want to.'

'Lily,' said Shauna, 'you're so good to me.'

Lily could tell Shauna was on the verge of crying. Weddings were worse on female stress levels than a year's worth of pre-menstrual tension, Lily decided glumly.

'I know this must be hard for you,' sniffled Shauna, 'what with memories of me and Patrick, and you and Richard, but – '

'Nonsense.' Lily did her best to sound jolly. 'Richard did me a favour. He was seeing someone else for the last year we were together – what sort of a marriage could we have had under those circumstances? No, I'm glad he's gone. Now, what else do we have to organise?'

Shauna ran through her list. 'The dresses are fine. You do like your dress, don't you?'

'Lovely,' Lily said automatically.

She had recently realised that burgundy was not her colour, but Shauna was her best friend and it was her big day, after all.

The wedding was only a week away and the chief bridesmaid was utterly miserable. Patrick and Shauna's happiness was incandescent: it lit up everybody who came near them. Lily, who loved Shauna like a sister, was thrilled for her. But Shauna's happiness suddenly magnified all that was wrong in Lily's life.

Before, they'd been single together. Lily felt that her life could be classified as perfectly normal because Shauna's life was the same. And now it was all different. Shauna was joining the world of coupledom, while Lily was still buying dinners for one in the supermarket and making arrangements to spend Christmas at her mother's.

Stoically, she'd helped Patrick and Shauna organise practically everything at short notice. The main problem had been finding a suitable venue for the reception. As the wedding season was still winding down, there wasn't an unbooked hotel for miles. So Patrick had come up with the solution: the local hotel in his rural hometown of Macready.

Shauna had cooed with delight at the thought of the pretty village she remembered from their early days together, and even Lily had to admit that the brochure of the Coaching Inn looked straight out of central casting as Ye Olde Cute Pub.

'Four-poster beds, inglenook fireplaces and black beams,' sighed Shauna, looking at the brochure.

Lily ordered and helped write out the invitations, she organised the flower girls' dresses (fairy princess visions in cream taffeta with burgundy silk ribbons), found a string quartet, and spent many hours on the phone with the local florist discussing the table and church decorations.

Patrick's best man, Rene, whom Lily hadn't even met and who had done precisely nothing to aid the preparations, had been charged with supplying the wedding carriage: his classic old sports car, which Patrick adored.

Once married, the happy couple were going to drive to the ferry in the borrowed car and tour Brittany for a glorious, wine-soaked two weeks. There was just one problem: the best man had damaged his ligaments playing rugby and couldn't transport the car before the wedding. In the face of such unreliability, only one person could help.

'You'd be doing us a huge favour, Lily,' Patrick said gratefully. 'I wouldn't trust anyone else to drive her down. She's Rene's pride and joy.'

After a moment's irritation wondering why men called all cars 'she', Lily agreed.

Instead of going down on the morning of the wedding with Shauna and her mother, Lily decided to drive the car to Macready the night before. That way she could take her time, and also she wouldn't have to endure Shauna's highly strung mother for the journey. Shauna's mother was still in shock over the speed of the wedding and alternated between delight ('You'll be a beautiful bride!') and doom ('Marry in haste, repent at leisure!').

'Lucky you, travelling on your own,' said Shauna. 'Mother is driving me nuts. If I don't turn up on the wedding day, it'll be because I've killed her somewhere on the road between Dublin and Macready.'

'Just think that you're driving to your wedding,' Lily said. 'Think of Patrick, a four-poster bed, and of it all being over. That'll keep you going.'

Patrick delivered the car to Lily's house late in the afternoon. 'Don't crash it,' he joked, as he climbed into a taxi.

'As if,' said Lily.

She collected her luggage, locked the front door and then stared at the classic 1960s Jaguar. What was it about men and cars? Sure, the car was sleekly cool, but all Lily was interested in was how many miles it would go on one tank of petrol.

'Gas guzzler,' she said, opening the door and flinging her belongings in. She sank into the driver's seat and gunned the engine. It did start up with a gratifying roar; like a tiger waking from a deep sleep.

Maybe it wouldn't be so bad, she decided.

At the first petrol station, she reconsidered.

'What a car,' said the forecourt attendant.

'Yeah, lovely,' Lily said, watching the gallons mount up. 'Expensive date.'

Back on the road again, Lily began to relax and enjoy herself. Patrick Taylor's home county was certainly very pretty and in the first flush of autumn, the countryside seemed dusted with a hint of gold. Graceful beech trees trailed bronze and green leaves on to the roadside, while the hedges still had clusters of fat blackberries. Even when the mildest sprinkling of rain began to fall, Lily didn't mind. She drove happily through the mist, enjoying the evening and being on her own. It was the calm before the storm of the wedding and she was looking forward to a quiet dinner by herself.

The manager of the Coaching Inn seemed startled when Lily rolled up and said there was a reservation in her name for the night.

'Are you sure?' he asked anxiously.

'Yes,' said Lily confidently. 'Shauna Zaidan booked it. I'm with the Zaidan/Taylor wedding party.'

The hotel was certainly attractive, she thought idly as the manager flicked through the big reservations book. It had a huge welcoming fire in the hallway surrounded by lots of faded red squashy chairs. The sounds of a jazz band coming from one of the function rooms and the presence of lots of laughing people in evening dress made it look as if another wedding was on. Maybe there was no chance of her enjoying a quiet evening in the hotel, but she could have a room-service dinner and watch a movie, perhaps.

The manager cleared his throat nervously. 'I'm really sorry, Ms Fitzgerald, but there's no reservation here for you. There are three rooms to be ready by half ten in the morning for the wedding party, but nothing for tonight. And we're packed to the rafters with another wedding. There must have been a mix-up.'

Lily grimly hauled her luggage back out to the Jag, cursing loudly as she hurried through the now heavy rain. What had she done to deserve this? She flung her luggage back into the car, flung herself in after it and then looked at the small map of the village which the manager had given her with directions to the only other hostelry in the whole place. The Lake View Hotel sounded all right. All she had to do was take two right turns, one left, then follow a windy road for about a mile. Simple.

The rain pounded down on the windscreen and Lily wished she was driving her nice modern Toyota and not an unfamiliar sports car. The thought was barely out of the dim recesses of her brain when she lost control of the vehicle. It swerved suddenly, veered wildly to the left and ploughed into the grass verge before coming to a shuddering stop at a small stone wall. Shocked, Lily sat shaking in her seat. She wanted to cry. She *would* cry. Tears streamed down her face as she thanked God she'd been wearing her seatbelt. What if she hadn't? What if the car had gone on fire. *Fire!*

With trembling fingers, she unfastened the seatbelt, grabbed her handbag and threw herself on to the muddy verge. Half crawling, she managed to drag herself out on to the road where she could view the scene from the distance. It didn't take a brain surgeon to see that the car had skidded on a huge slick of oil before plunging into the wall. Rene's pride and joy now sported a crumpled bonnet and front fender, both of which would probably cost the Gross National Product of some small country to fix.

Shock made Lily cry more, and the tears mingled with the rain that lashed down on her. It was cold too; cold and wet. She was standing in a country lane in the middle of nowhere with not a house or a car in sight. It was getting dark and she should be curled up in a nice hotel room.

The sound of an approaching car startled her. She began to wave frantically at the thought of rescue. Then, she realised that the car was a battered taxi containing two men and she began to think how scary movies always started with a lone female helplessly waving down the serial killer.

The taxi stopped and the passenger got out. He didn't look like a serial killer, Lily thought doubtfully, unless serial killers wore nice blue shirts and had short chestnut hair and deep brown eyes set in a concerned face. He was hot, as the girls in St Imelda's would probably say in appreciation.

'Are you hurt?' he asked, rushing towards her as fast as someone could with a mild limp.

'Fine,' sobbed Lily, still in tears.

'You're not fine,' said the man firmly. He peered into her eyes in the gloom. 'You're probably in shock. You need to see a doctor,' he added, putting an arm round her.

'I don't need a doctor,' said Lily. 'I just need to get out of the rain. And what about the car?' She had stopped crying but the sight of the crumpled classic car almost made her cry again. Shauna and Patrick's honeymoon was ruined.

The man's eyes lingered for a while on the car. Lily could have sworn he grimaced as he looked at it, but then he turned back to face her.

'I'm pretty sure it won't catch cold, whereas you will,' he said with a certain stoicism.

He had a nice grin, she thought irrationally.

'Have you anything else in the car?'

'My suitcase,' sniffed Lily.

Before she could make up some story about how she'd already phoned for help on her mobile (a useful ploy to deter would-be abductors), Lily found herself sitting in the back of the taxi with the man in the nice blue shirt holding her hand and telling her it would be all right.

'I think we should call a doctor,' he fretted.

'I'll be fine,' Lily insisted. 'I just want to get to my hotel and call a garage to pick up the car.'

'Where are you staying?'

'The Lake View,' she said.

'Me too,' said the man.

'What would it cost to fix the car, do you think?' Lily asked him.

He considered this. 'Thousands, I daresay,' he said slowly. Then he gave himself a little shake. 'But who cares. It's a car, right? You're fine, that's all that matters.'

The Lake View was not a patch on the Coaching Inn.

'It's not the nicest hotel in the town,' Lily murmured to

197

her rescuer as they went into the big, sparse lobby, him limping and her dripping.

'I'll get them to phone for a doctor,' he said.

'No you won't,' Lily retorted. 'There's nothing wrong with me. I just got a bit of a shock. Thank you for your help.'

'I can't leave you like this,' he said tetchily.

'I'm not a puppy you've rescued,' she pointed out.

'More drowned rat, actually.'

The crinkling round his eyes showed her that this was meant as a joke.

Lily, knowing that her hair hung in a tangled mess around her face and somehow not minding, smiled back at him. 'I don't even know your name,' she said.

Something flared in the dark eyes. 'RJ,' he said.

'Thanks, RJ,' she said. 'I'm Lily.'

'I know,' he said.

Lily glared at him suspiciously, her visions of a serial-killer conspiracy worsening.

'It says so on your suitcase,' he said quickly.

Lily looked down to her case where an old holiday address tag still hung on the handle.

'Oh, well, bye.'

Lily's hotel room was decorated in a style she decided was Seventies Hotel: mahogany veneer furniture, mushroom walls with damp in two corners, an elderly television bolted to the wall, and a carpet of the same colour and texture as wire wool. After a blissful enough hot bath, she wrapped herself in her dressing gown and turned the TV on to find it was showing snowstorm on all but one channel. The news channel, naturally.

She poured herself an orange juice from the mini bar and was lying on the bed feeling sorry for herself when the phone rang.

'I hope you got the Presidential Suite. I'm in the Prisoner Cell Block H room,' said RJ.

Lily giggled. 'I don't think there is a Presidential Suite in this establishment.'

'Fancy dinner, then? Perhaps good food and wine will make us forget how ugly the rooms are.'

'Good food and wine *here*?' joked Lily.

'Burger and chips then?' he asked.

'Done.'

The food was surprisingly good. Over some fantastic sea bass, they talked so much that the restaurant was nearly closed by the time they'd finished. Lily didn't know if it was the shock from crashing the car or the sense of unreality about the whole evening, but she found herself telling RJ how much she hated weddings. He was a good listener. There was something about his kind face and those deep, warm eyes that made her feel he'd gone through his own pain. And he asked such intelligent questions.

'You must have some dark history in your life,' she said when she'd given him chapter and verse on Richard and being stood up at the altar.

They'd left the table and were sitting in a small corner of the hotel bar with a fire in front of them and no one else in the whole place apart from a young barman.

RJ smiled. 'Do you have all night?'

'Yes,' said Lily, surprising herself. For the first time in years, spending hours with a man felt like a wonderful prospect. RJ told her about his teenage sweetheart and how they'd split up three years ago, and he told her about working in Cincinnati for a multinational company, only returning home occasionally. But he didn't mention how he'd injured his leg. That was the only negative. Lily didn't like mysterious men. Look where it had got her with Richard. His air of mystery meant he could date another woman at the same time as being engaged to Lily.

It was after one in the morning when they left the bar. Lily felt tired and something else, something she had difficulty identifying. Excited? Was that it? She smiled to think how happy her mother would be if she could see Lily now: chatting and flirting with this delectable man. The man who'd rescued her from the rain. Lily allowed herself to fantasise about her and RJ telling people how they'd met. They could celebrate their first-date anniversary with a romantic roadside picnic before making love . . . Lily dragged herself back to earth.

'I'll walk you to your room,' RJ said.

At her hotel-room door, he brushed his lips gently across hers. Lily felt as if she was attached to a whole wall of electrodes, all of which were turned on and driving her wild. It was a heady feeling, redolent with erotic memories of her last kiss, a very long time ago.

'I'll see you in the morning,' she murmured, pulling away regretfully.

'You may not like me in the morning,' RJ said, pulling her close again and nuzzling her ear.

'I promise, I will,' Lily said. 'Goodnight.'

*   *   *

Lily had breakfast downstairs the next day but there was no sign of RJ. He'd left a note for her in reception with his phone number on it.

Don't hate me, it read.

Why would I hate him? thought Lily suspiciously. Then it clicked: he had a wife and seventeen children, that was it. That had to be it.

Well, it wasn't going to ruin her day. No man was ever ruining her day again. Right?

Shauna was remarkably relaxed when Lily returned to the Coaching Inn to help. Her make-up was done, her dress was hanging up and ready to go, and her mother was lying down in her own bedroom. Peace reigned.

'Patrick's sorting out a hire car for the trip to the ferry,' Shauna said idly as she plucked a stray eyebrow hair out.

Lily looked up from her wedding arrangements list.

'What?'

'Nobody blames you for crashing the car, Lily. Rene told me it was an oil slick and nobody could have avoided it. He told me how well you'd got on. Isn't he cute?'

'That wouldn't be my word for him,' Lily said slowly as all the pieces of the jigsaw fell into place.

Don't hate me. Now it all made sense. Rene was RJ. No wonder he'd looked a bit shocked at the state of his car when he'd seen it crashed into a wall.

Shauna turned from the mirror to see Lily's furious face.

'I thought he'd told you everything this morning!' she said in shock. 'I've put my foot in it, haven't I?'

'You didn't, he did. He told me his name was RJ and I told him everything about myself,' Lily said grimly. *'Everything!'*

'Did you sleep with him?' asked Shauna.

'Thankfully no,' said Lily. 'If I had, I'd murder him right now and then throw myself off the roof.'

'He said you were lovely and he knew, because Patrick had told him, that you'd been badly burned by Richard. He wanted you to be friends first.'

'He should have told me it was his blinking car I'd just crashed!' said Lily crossly. 'I'll be back in a moment, Shauna.' She marched out of the hotel room.

RJ, or Rene, was sitting in the bar with Patrick, looking very pleased with himself.

'A word, please, outside,' commanded Lily, glaring at Rene.

Both men's eyebrows shot up. Rene obediently followed Lily outside to the hotel garden.

'Now don't get all angry with me,' he started. 'Patrick told me you'd had a tough time with men and I thought if you liked me first as a friend, then we could become more than friends.'

'You lied to me!' yelled Lily.

'I didn't mean to and it was harmless. And I didn't even mind that you crashed my car, now, did I? I love that car. How many men would say nothing about that? How many, tell me?'

'Excuses, excuses,' Lily said. 'Who cares about the car? It's insured. How dare you lie to me and let me tell you everything about myself when you knew it all anyway.'

'I was going to confess today,' Rene protested.

'Forget it,' Lily said. 'I suppose I should be grateful to you. You've taught me one thing,' she added, suddenly gentle.

Rene's eyes went all meltingly gorgeous, the way they had

the night before when he'd stared into Lily's as though he could see into her soul. When she'd told him all her inner secrets. 'Yes?' he breathed.

'Never to trust a man ever again.'

'What!' Rene tried to grab hold of Lily's arm but she was gone, a whirlwind in burgundy silk.

'I thought you liked him,' Shauna said, as they stood in the hotel foyer waiting for the cars to bring the wedding party to the church.

'I do,' Lily said grudgingly. 'But he lied to me. Still, he's done one fabulous thing for me.'

'You *did* sleep with him!' said Shauna triumphantly.

'No, I didn't.' It was Lily's turn to look triumphant. 'He's given me my confidence back. I enjoyed flirting with him and talking to him – it must have been the shock of the crash. But it was fun. Mum's right: I do need to get out more.' She winked at Shauna. 'I'm going to make him suffer just a teeny, weeny bit. Just to get him back for lying to me last night.'

Shauna relaxed.

'But you're going to forgive him?'

'Yes.' Lily beamed at her friend. 'I think both of us are really going to enjoy your wedding, Shauna.'

You've Got Mail

Dear Jess,

This is my first ever e-mail! Well, my first *proper* one. The nice man who brought the computer and set it up made me send one as a test, but that doesn't count. He was so lovely and I was so delighted to get the computer, that I kept telling him how kind and clever he was. You know how I talk when I'm nervous. I think it annoyed Archie. He is very sensitive, actually.

It might be his age. We are none of us getting any younger. I did tell him that sixty was the new forty, but he growled something about 'how would I know that?' since I'm only fifty-six. I think it must be the male menopause. He wasn't like this before he moved in – which is only since January, come to think of it. Men are even more confusing now than they were when we were teenagers, don't you think?

How is everyone in Cork? I haven't visited for ages. We must come to see you soon. Archie just wasn't in a good mood that first time. It's hard to visit a girl's family, with them all watching his every move and seeing if he's the right one or if he's just after her money.

I can't lie to you, Jess. He *was* upset but he's fine about it all now.

Grandpa's money does carry a big burden with it, doesn't it? But Archie didn't know I had money until I told him. How would he have known? It's not as if I advertise it. I live so quietly and am not a dressing up kind of girl. I do wear Grandma's pearls, but only under my cardigans, which all have holes in them.

It's very quiet here in Claddagh, although Millie's Wool Shop is doing very well. I said to Doris that we should add a little café section so people could have a cup of tea or coffee on the come-and-knit evenings and it has all worked out really well.

love,

your big sis,

Millie

Dear Jess,

Please order me one of those silk pillows that keep your face unwrinkled during the night. I can't remember where on the Internet you said you'd seen them but I know you said they were proven to give you baby-smooth skin. I could do with some help in that department and you know I can't order things on the computer. I am afraid I will do it wrong and those people in Nigeria who want to give me a million dollars to invest in my country will get my credit card and I will be banjaxed. Oh yes, remember those eye bags Mother used to have? I have them now too. They just arrived one night. I wake up with wrinkles and puffed-up eyes like a fish, and I have to get to the bathroom before Archie does because he would notice something like that. And I used to think morning breath was a problem!

Archie is very keen on the computer now. He says it's just the thing to check out the competition in the shoe business. He is such a sweetie.

He says perhaps we should go on a holiday soon. I suggested Scotland but he has his mind set on a cruise of the Med, taking in Ephesus, Rhodes and Capri. He's never been. I am not telling him about how we stayed with Grandpa for four months in Capri that time. He gets upset by things like that.

Your loving sister,

Millie

Dear Jess,

Forget the silk pillow. Can you get me some of those pyjamas and pillow cases that don't get wet when you sweat? I am waking up looking like a wet poodle every morning, now. The fleecy pyjamas are fine but the wet sticks to them and it's like being wrapped with cold bubbles of water stuck to you. Plus, I cannot have that twelve-week blow-dry EVER because you can't get your hair wet for three days and I cannot keep my hair dry for more than twenty-four hours.

At best, I look as if I have been plugged in every morning. I think Archie is going off me. He never signed up for this when we met at the Dance and Dine in McGurk's Lounge and Bar.

I am so tired, you see, that he wakes up before me now and I don't have a chance to do damage limitation in the bathroom first. He's stopped wearing his glasses in bed, if you must know.

Plus, the computer is playing up. I get a lot of messages

from girls who 'just want to talk to me' and I am constantly being offered cheap watches and penile implants. A word of advice from your older sister: never say anything about penile implants to a man, even as a joke. They don't think it's funny.

Hugs,
Millie

Dearest Jess,
Bio-identical hormones are where it's at! You rub them on and you no longer feel like you are going to kill the girl at the café when she takes a long time getting your cappuccino because she's gossiping to her friend about last night's party.

Archie is hoping the hormones work. I think he believes that sorting this out will turn me into a tiger in the bedroom. I think it will take more than a cream to do that. Sometimes, I long for the days when I could lie in bed with the pugs beside me and watch *Criminal Minds* non-stop.

Thank you for the pyjamas. They are kind of unsexy-looking but if they work, it will be worth it.

I'm going to have to get the nice computer man, Patient Fred, to come to the house to help me stop all those e-mails. I think they're called scam.

On the phone, Patient Fred says he thinks I have spyware in my computer – I didn't like the sound of that.

'Can they *see* me?' I asked. I have got into the habit of wearing my trackpants and my very oldest cardigans when I'm at home, although Archie doesn't really like sportswear unless you're doing sports.

Luckily, Patient Fred explained that it's not that type of spyware. He really *is* very patient. I do hope he's married or has a girlfriend. He's only just moved into Claddagh and probably doesn't know anyone in town.

Doris says Archie should have sorted it all out for me – between us, I don't think she likes Archie very much. But Archie says he doesn't have time to sort out my computer. He runs a business. I wanted to say that I run a business too but, as we both know, dear Doris *does do* all the computer stuff and ordering with the wool shop, so he has a point when he says being a partner in the business isn't the same as doing it all yourself. Doris says one shoe shop in the city is hardly an empire, but I reminded her that Archie is sensitive and men prefer to earn more than their partners. You see, he's *not* after my money!

Love,
Millie

Dear Jess,
Bunny and Sherry, my dearest pals from school, are coming to stay! I am so excited. Although it nearly never happened because when Bunny phoned for a chat, I happened to mention that I was lying on the bed with my head hanging backwards and she hung up.

When I phoned back, I explained that this is the only way to put nose drops in. Poor Bunny had got entirely the wrong idea and had hung up in shock. She is still quite innocent, despite all those years travelling with darling Lloyd in the diplomatic service.

I told her I wanted her to meet *my* special someone and she said she couldn't wait. Sherry can't drive after some mishap involving driving with an untethered Great Dane in the car, so

Bunny's driving them both. I can't wait. To think it's been thirty-eight years since we left Miss Minchin's Academy!

Archie isn't all that keen to meet them, but I think he just likes having me to himself. Which is a sign of great romance, I think, isn't it?

Hugs,

Millie

Dearest Jess,

I am terribly sorry to have to say that Bunny and Sherry's visit was not the success I had hoped for. Bunny cannot drive at all. It took them five hours from Boyle and we are not that far off the beaten track. She kept saying she was used to having drivers in their foreign postings or even walking when her hip wasn't bad.

Archie got in a terrible mood because dinner was so delayed and then he had to haul their suitcases up to their rooms. Sherry's weighed a ton, apparently. She explained that she'd brought a few bottles of red in case we didn't have enough. She brought half a crate. She had a whole bottle in the car on the way down from Dublin, as it happened, and she was only in the door when she got stuck into another bottle. Between us, I think there may have been more to her not being allowed to drive than the Great Dane, but you know us Miss Minchin's girls, we stick by our friends! And I do love dear Sherry.

Bunny and Archie seemed to dislike each other from the start. By the time we were on to the brandy, Archie called her a snob and she called him – well, I can't repeat it. She didn't learn it in Miss Minchin's, I can tell you.

'You learn all sorts of handy phrases abroad,' she told me

briskly as they left the next day. 'I love *you*, Millie,' she said. 'But I don't like that oik. Fortune hunter if ever I saw one.'

I had to stand waving until she got Sherry settled in the passenger seat with her bottle and the corkscrew before they could drive away.

Archie still isn't speaking to me. He gets so upset by people not understanding that he loves me for me.

It's a cruel world.

Love,

Millie

Dear Jess,

Archie thinks we should cruise the Mediterranean on our own yacht. This is not a mistake in my typing: he wants to buy a yacht. Frankly, I am unsure as to what to do. In the old days, I'd have asked Mr O'Gorman for advice. He was so wonderfully reassuring when it came to keeping an eye on the old pennies. I don't want to start slicing into my capital, I told Archie, who then snorted 'nonsense'.

'You're rolling in cash, Millie,' he said.

I retired to the bedroom with the dogs, which made him even more annoyed as he hates dog hairs on the sheets. Froufrou never moults and Pansy is the same colour as the sheets, so it's not as if you'd notice. But Archie says it's the principle of the thing. Dogs should be kept out of the bedroom.

I turned on my CD player and played Mario Lanza as loud as I liked. The dogs prefer Barry Manilow but I needed to think and I can't think when Barry sings.

Your confused sister,

Millie

Dear Jess,

Archie and I are still barely speaking. I think his plan to buy a yacht is rather more advanced than he originally told me. A man in a flashy car turned up yesterday to see him and he had a stack of brochures with him. They were all to do with ocean-going vessels.

In Archie's defence, I do wonder if I made a mistake early on in our relationship by letting slip that Grandpa had his own plane years ago. Archie thinks our family is used to things like yachts and planes. He doesn't realise that Grandpa only got it so he could frighten people in it when he did loops. I do miss old Grandpa, don't you?

Archie doesn't understand that I'm not pushed about shiny cars or yachts.

I mean, I'm entirely happy with my old car. She's been with me seventeen years and I like that. Mother never spent money on cars. She liked the odd fur, of course, and I still have her mink coat somewhere, along with all the jewels (in the bank, I promise!). But she drove the same dreadful old rust bucket for years and she'd have died at the thought of having a yacht.

Couples argue, though, don't they? I suspect that's all it is.

Hugs,

Millie

Dear Jess,

Disaster! I reversed the car into Archie's today. Last night, he apparently mentioned to me that he had to park his car behind mine on the driveway instead of *beside* mine, because I had parked so badly.

The thing is, I had been in urgent need of the bathroom when I came home yesterday, so I did abandon it somewhat. My bladder has a mind of its own.

Anyways, I forgot he was behind me and *smash*. There were bits of cream vintage Mercedes all over the driveway. He loves that car. Really. I had never seen him cry before. Not even when he told me about his marriage breakdown, although he was tearful when he talked about the divorce settlement, but that gets a lot of chaps, doesn't it?

He says you can't get a car like his fixed around here. I said, why not? This was a mistake. It seems he's been harbouring a silent hatred for Claddagh for some time. He is fed up with the commute into the city to the shoe shop. Sorry, Shoe Empire. This is the last straw.

He says he will go in the morning. I got an e-mail offering me low-cost drugs, shipped from India, what do you think? Archie is in the study with the last of the Scotch. He has locked the door.

xxx Millie

Dear Jess,

I *promise* I won't click on the buy button but that's a good deal for Xanax. They do a price comparison thing and you can see how good value it is. You see, I could do with a little soft-focus right now.

Archie has gone and he took the CD player with him, which is unfair because we bought it together. I had got into the habit of listening to Barry Manilow records at night, it was very peaceful. I miss my Barry time.

I miss Archie too, although I don't miss having to rush

212

to the bathroom in the morning. I can be sweaty and wrinkly and nobody minds. Plus, the dogs are back sleeping on the bed. Archie had banished them to the utility room, poor puplets.

Miserable in Claddagh,

Millie x

Dear Jess,

The hormones are really working! So is the agnus castus and the black cohosh. I no longer look like a poodle in the morning. Result! My breasts even seem bigger. The doctor is as astonished by this as I am.

I was never able to tell you this before because it was humiliating, but Archie had made a few remarks on my lack of endowment in that department. He wouldn't say that if he could see me now!

Doris says good riddance to him, but she just didn't know him properly. I'm still very sad but I guess sometimes you have to accept that what will be, will be. That's what Mother said when Sir Rollo turned out to be a bigamist insurance salesman from Ballyporeen. I will never forget how brave she was when she turned up at bridge the day before she was supposed to be getting married. She even brought the wedding cake along for the bridge tea.

'Terrible to waste it,' she insisted.

Mother really was a lioness, wasn't she?

At times like this, you have to rely on inner strength.

Your big sis,

Millie

Jess!
I am in shock. I think Archie must have been using my computer to look at . . . I'm embarrassed to say it: porn. I keep losing things on the computer and I opened a file to find lots of pictures of girls in their twenties with no wrinkles and big boobs. I don't think the boobs are real, by the way. You have no idea how big they can get. Well, maybe *you* do. But I can tell you that *I* was surprised. Those things look sore and I hate to think what would happen if they travelled by plane. The thought of a pressurised air cabin . . . well.

I'm going to write Archie a strongly worded e-mail. But first, I have to get these things off my computer. I'm going to phone Patient Fred. Apparently, he isn't going out with anyone – or at least that's what they say in the chemist.

Love,
Millie

Darling Jess,
The most wonderful news – Patient Fred asked me out on a date. I went and we had the most fabulous time! I would never have thought a picnic by the lake was a good plan, but it is, when the man brings a lovely basket of nice things, has rugs for us all to lie on – he insisted the dogs came too – and he had a radio tuned to the classical music station.

He is a truly lovely man. I'm not calling him Patient Fred any more. He is Gorgeous Fred and Kind Fred.

He does not own a vintage car to get upset about if it got bumped into. He says I'm amazing the way I've built up Millie's Wool Shop over the past ten years and he says I should be proud of myself for being such a great businesswoman. Even better, he says I'm beautiful and when he says it, I believe him. Do you know, I don't think I really believed Archie when he said nice things to me. But I do with Fred.

Plus, Doris likes him and she is a good judge of character. She says I should have listened to her about Archie.

I am so happy!

Kisses,

Millie

Jess,

My first e-mail from overseas! How thrilling. We landed in Istanbul two days ago and Fred, Sherry, Bunny and I have been having the most marvellous time.

Turkey is still lovely. Sherry is off the drink, which is handy as I have no idea how we'd have managed otherwise. She can be quite wild if she gets enough Montrachet into her, Bunny says.

Incredibly, it turns out that Fred was here years ago on a degree course about the Byzantine Empire. He wasn't always in computers, he says. He knows so much about all the sights in Turkey, and Bunny and Sherry are terribly impressed.

Bunny knows a lot of diplomats in Istanbul and we have been having the most fabulous time going on excursions and to little parties.

Fred steers Sherry away from danger zones like fruity cocktails, which look innocent but are actually seventy per cent proof. She looks like her old self again, which is wonderful.

Fred got me a golden amulet as a present. It has my name in hieroglyphics inscribed on it and love from Fred at the bottom. It's quite the nicest thing I've ever been given.

Bunny said I should send Archie a card from Ephesus but I don't think I could.

A St Minchin's girl could never be so cruel.

Love,

Millie

Christmas Post

To Joseph the postman, the houses on Sycamore Lane looked the same most of the year round. A row of terraced redbricks, the most obvious differences between them were the colour of their doors and whether they had dogs or not. Number 21 had a tiny white fluffy dog who hissed with ferocious intent from behind a wrought-iron side gate, while the Callaghans at number 40 had a giant horse of a dog who lay on the front doorstep and would do nothing more dangerous than lick you to death.

It was at Christmas that the houses came into their own and looked truly distinctive. Joseph liked it when everyone's Christmas decorations went up. You could tell a lot about people from their decorations.

Miss O'Shaughnessy, who lived alone and got lots of letters from far-off missions, had the Holy Family in her window as soon as Advent began. The Carters, a young professional couple who'd tarmaced over the grass because they never got round to cutting it, were keen on wrapping plastic tube lights around the sole tree in their garden. Neon pink last year.

The Callaghan family, who'd lived on Sycamore Lane for longer than Joseph had been working the route, twenty years at least, were madly into skeins of those tiny twinkling lights you had to staple to the eaves.

There were so many Callaghan kids that he never could work out which was which. They all looked the same, too: mops of coal-dark hair, startlingly blue eyes and freckles. One of them was just about to climb up a ladder, staple gun at the ready, as Joseph went up the path that morning in mid-December.

It was one of the girls, twenty-something, Joseph reckoned, and clearly ready for Christmas-light application in her cosy fleece, a hand-knitted hat and jeans. The horse-sized dog sat happily at her feet.

'Hello, Joseph,' she said cheerfully, and Joseph said hello back and wished yet again that he knew which one was which. They grew so fast. One moment, there had been a house of toddlers flinging themselves on tricycles around the garden, now they were all grown.

'Letter for your mam,' he said, handing over a lilac-coloured envelope. 'No bills, thank God.'

The dog tried to lick him.

'Down, Fang,' said the girl, and Fang sank gloomily to the ground.

Alice Callaghan was sitting at the kitchen table when Fiona swung in with the envelope. They both knew who it was from. Only Charlotte, Alice's sister-in-law, sent her heat-seeking missives on lilac stationery.

'Do you want a cup of tea to face it?' asked Fiona, patting her mother on the shoulder as she went to put on the kettle. 'Or a Valium for us both?'

Despite herself, Alice laughed. 'Terrible child,' she said. 'Even if we had it, Valium wouldn't work. Any sensible drug would leave your system in terror at the sight of a letter from your aunt. Besides, you'd fall off the roof putting the lights up. I wish you'd wait – '

Alice had been about to say – *until Isaac comes home and we can celebrate properly*, but she stopped herself just in time.

Just because she didn't want to even think about Christmas until her youngest was home, didn't mean it was fair on her other five children. They deserved a proper festive season without her waiting for Isaac like he was the prodigal and nothing could start without him.

Fiona Callaghan wanted to say, *He'll be back, Mam, I know he will. He wouldn't stay away over Christmas*.

But she didn't. Saying it was promising something she couldn't deliver. Who knew if Isaac would be home for the holidays. His five siblings had e-mailed him and left increasingly annoyed messages on his phone. But there had been no contact since late October, when he'd been in Bangkok.

Having fun. With a great crowd. Talk soon, love, Isaac.

When Fiona got her hands on him, she'd kill him, the little brat. Her mother was trying to hide her devastation at the lack of contact. But everyone, even Cara and Joanna, who were more or less self-obsessed, could see how upset their mother was.

No, Fiona decided: killing wasn't good enough for Isaac. There had to be something worse. She'd rip his passport to shreds. That would put a stop to his gallop.

Alice scanned the letter. Her sister-in-law Charlotte was coming to stay for Christmas.

True to form, Charlotte wasn't asking, she was announcing in the manner of a royal personage circa the fifteenth century.

Charlotte wrote that she'd like the purple bedroom, she'd need an extra oil radiator in her room and goose for lunch gave her wind.

It was like a booking form for a fancy hotel, Alice thought grimly, although their crowded house was anything but.

Fiona was back in the purple bedroom since she'd lost her job and given up the flat. To make room for Her Majesty, Fiona would have to squash in with the twins in the attic. And in the fifteen years since Gordon had died, there hadn't been anything as rich as goose in the Callaghans' for Christmas. As a young widow with six children to bring up, Alice had considered herself lucky to be able to put turkey on the table.

But Charlotte lived in another world: a world where life was fabulous, everyone had money and Alice ought to be grateful for the small crumbs of wisdom that Charlotte dropped when she arrived.

'I hate to say it,' Charlotte had murmured last Christmas, 'but those lights outside the house are very tacky. Gordon would have hated them.'

Alice hadn't been sure what had annoyed her most, but it was possibly that Charlotte was sure she alone knew what

220

her dead brother would have wanted. Alice's husband and his sister had never been close and Charlotte certainly hadn't been a support to his widow when his fatal heart attack left her alone with six kids, ranging in age from fifteen to seven. Now Charlotte was insisting that she knew what Gordon would have wanted with regards to Christmas decorations. It had made Alice's blood boil and the memory made her furious all over again.

'Forget about making tea, Fiona,' Alice said now, getting to her feet. 'I'll help you put up the lights. I love them. Christmas will be here before we know it.'

Joseph loved the way the Kents decorated their house for Christmas. It was like Santa's grotto with signs telling the reindeer where to graze, and a plastic snowman on the lawn. It was so joyous, the sign that a happy family lived there.

They were nice people, too: both probably in their early forties with a sweet, blonde kid named Loulou who had adorable dimples and an impish smile.

Siobhan Kent was leaving the house with her little girl when Joseph got there.

'I think I have a letter from Santa for a young lady by the name of Loulou,' he said to the child.

'Oh, Loulou! Santa's replied to the letter you sent him!' said Siobhan with delight.

She and Joseph exchanged smiles, but Loulou didn't notice. She was ripping open the letter.

If only, if only . . .

I know you've been a very good girl, the letter said.

Loulou realised that Santa had replied to the letter she'd

written with her parents watching fondly. In that letter, she'd asked for new DS games, Hello Kitty stuff and a surprise.

Loulou Kent, aged ten and a half, wanted to cry.

She had another letter to Santa, her *real* one, but it was a secret. She hadn't been able to let Mum or Dad get even a glimpse of it because, then, the wish wouldn't come true. When you wanted really big, important things from Santa, you had to write in secret. The secret letter was still upstairs.

Dear Santa, I don't want any presents if you can make my mum and dad love each other again and not fight.

Nobody would answer it because nobody had seen it. Loulou had hoped that Santa was magic enough to know when there was a secret letter and to answer it, but she was wrong. There was no magic.

Two days before Christmas, Alice took Fang for a walk. He liked to meander, snuffling his velvety nose into every gateway. A ten-minute walk could stretch into half an hour with Fang investigating every smell within a five-mile radius. Alice didn't really mind. She'd known as soon as she'd got Fang's predecessor, Prince, all those years ago that she was going to have to walk him and clean up his poop, despite all the outraged 'No, we will, Mum!' comments from the kids.

Fang – named by Andy after a family vote – was the family's second band-aid dog. There to fix what might never be fixed otherwise. When the children's father had died, if someone had told Alice that a tank of boa constrictors would cheer everyone up, she'd have got a tank from somewhere. Prince and then Fang were easier to manage than snakes. All these years later, most of the walking of slobbery Fang fell to Alice, but she didn't mind. Walking with him was wonderfully meditative.

They were at the Kents' house when Alice noticed Loulou in the garden. The child was holding an envelope made with copybook paper and staring at the postbox on the other side of the road with an anxious expression on her face.

'Hi, Loulou,' said Alice warmly. 'Is that your Santa letter?'

Fang pushed his soft face into Loulou's hand. She sank down to hug him and burst into tears, holding Fang as if he were a lifesaver.

'You poor darling,' said Alice. 'What's wrong, Loulou?'

On Christmas Eve, Joseph spread the word that Miss O'Shaughnessy had twisted her ankle and couldn't walk, which meant she wouldn't be able to go for the Christmas overnight dinner with her friends in Bettystown. They had stairs and she'd never be able to cope.

'She'll come here,' said Alice decisively. 'I couldn't bear to think of the poor thing on her own on Christmas Day. Andy and David will carry her down.'

The Kents were coming after lunch too.

'I can't thank you enough,' Siobhan Kent had said to Alice over and over again. Her voice was breaking as she spoke. 'I had no idea Loulou could hear myself and Neil arguing. The fertility treatment isn't working and we can't afford any more and – well, it's hard on us all. We love each other, truly we do. We just thought that, if I'd got pregnant once, I could again and we'd have another child. Not that we're not happy with Loulou – we adore her. I promise.'

Alice had patted the younger woman's hand affectionately. 'Trust me, I never judge anyone,' she said. 'Life can be hard and we all struggle along doing the best we can. I'm just glad we found out what was upsetting Loulou. Christmas is a great time for putting the worries on hold, spending time with the people you love and starting again in January – at least, that's what I try to do.'

Charlotte Callaghan prided herself on both her fine mind and her lovely manners. She arrived at her sister-in-law's house on Christmas Day with an anaemic prayer lily as a gift because she thought poinsettias were too bright. She had a white silk scarf for Alice. White was far more appropriate than those jewel colours Alice always wore. Alice was nearly sixty, after all. High time she stopped with lipstick and crimson cardigans.

Using a small windfall Alice had won on the Prize Bonds, the house had been enlarged with an extension into the backyard which made for an airy, open-plan kitchen-cum-dining area. There were decorations everywhere and festive music played in the background. The table was set with a jaunty red tablecloth, sparkly table confetti and lots of crackers.

Cara and Joanna, twins of twenty-four, had made eggnog.

'Well, *sort* of eggnog,' they explained to Miss O'Shaughnessy, and gave her a tiny glass. 'We don't want it to interfere with your medications,' they said.

They poured Aunt Charlotte one too.

'It's made with advocaat from Fortnum and Mason's,' Joanna said, which was a blatant fib. Apart from the dregs of a banana liqueur from the Canaries, the ingredients had all come from the off licence down the road.

'I used to love tea in Fortnum's,' Charlotte said mistily, taking a huge gulp. She rarely imbibed, but this was a special day and one wouldn't hurt. Or two, for that matter. 'I think I might have another little one,' she said.

Great merriment was had with the crackers.

Fiona, who'd bought them all in the two-euro shop, said that even if the gifts were hopeless, the jokes were good. And cheap crackers meant there were so many of them.

Loulou wore a pink paper hat and insisted everyone else wore one too, even Fang.

Miss O'Shaughnessy loved being part of it all.

'You're so kind to have me,' she kept saying.

'Nonsense,' said Alice. 'You're so good to come to us. Christmas is always better with guests – otherwise this lot would slope off to watch *It's a Wonderful Life* and leave me to do the washing up!'

It was such fun that nobody was in any mood to leave the table, and they lingered for a long time, nibbling cheese and talking fondly about Christmases past.

Alice told Miss O'Shaughnessy about when Gordon was alive, and for once, it wasn't a tale tinged with sadness. Fiona could remember her sixth birthday and how Dad had blown up a roomful of balloons for her. Alice talked of how she and Gordon had first met at a party, and how they'd been inseparable afterwards.

Siobhan Kent told them all of the day Loulou had been born, of how it was the happiest day of her life.

'Really?' asked Loulou.

'Really and truly,' said her mother.

Cara and Joanna told how they'd streaked their hair red when they were sixteen.

'Not a nice red,' Alice said cheerfully to Loulou. 'A scary, fire-engine red.'

The only person who was silent was Charlotte, and Alice watched her anxiously. There was something wrong, but what?

After dinner, the five Callaghan children and Loulou cleared up, stepping over a sleeping and happily full Fang. Charlotte slumped in an armchair and tears began to fall down her cheeks.

Alice sat on the arm of the chair and held her sister-in-law's hand.

'What's wrong, Charlotte?' she asked quietly.

'I miss Gordon so much,' Charlotte sobbed. 'I'm so lonely.' She looked up into Alice's eyes. 'I know I've been a bit of an old trout, Alice, and no help to you at all, but it's been so hard. You've had the children. I had nothing and now –' she wiped the tears that were coursing down her face '– you're the only family I've got left. I want us to make a fresh start, if you can bear it. It's not the eggnog talking, it's the truth.'

Perched on the arm of the chair, Alice felt something she'd never felt before for her sister-in-law: sympathy. All these years, she'd thought Charlotte was looking down her nose at her when in fact, she'd been grieving silently. It was sad that it had taken fifteen years and some dodgy Christmas concoction to make Charlotte open up, but what was important was that she *had* opened up. Alice was determined to take this chance and run with it.

'We all miss him,' she said softly. 'I miss him every day, but we have to keep going, Charlotte. You're a strong woman.' She leaned in and hugged Charlotte in a way she never had before. 'And we are your family, if only you'll let us in.'

Charlotte nodded tearily. 'Thank you,' she said. 'Thank you.'

By seven, Loulou Kent sat playing Monopoly with her parents and the twins. Fang was at her side, delirious at being petted so lovingly.

Miss O'Shaughnessy was telling Loulou's parents about her years teaching in Kenya. Andy and his girlfriend, Susie, were fiddling with the iPod to find more Christmassy songs.

Nobody even heard the door open quietly as Isaac Callaghan, suntanned and with a bag of presents, let himself into the house. He felt the warmth of number 40 Sycamore Lane envelop him. It was good to be home for Christmas.

The Trouble with Mother

On the first Wednesday in August, Marjorie called a family meeting to discuss *the trouble with Mother.*

'I'm telling the whole family to come to Castle Wood House at three on Sunday,' Marjorie bossily informed her younger sister, Sadie, over the phone.

Sadie resisted the impulse to stick her tongue out childishly at the receiver. Marjorie had that effect on her.

And why, Sadie wondered, didn't Marjorie ever refer to her home as just 'my house' or 'my place'? No, it was always *Castle Wood House*, just in case someone overheard and didn't get the full impact of the imposing address and thought it was an ordinary two-up, two-down on some anonymous housing estate.

Marjorie's home was a stately pile on ten acres in the countryside with electric gates, a gravel drive, a stable block and a granny flat, or *guest cottage*, as Marjorie grandly referred to it. Was Marjorie really so shallow that she imagined her new, big house concealed the O'Brien family's origins in a tiny council house in the city centre? Sadie knew the answer to that question.

'You're not going to make some excuse and fail to turn up, I hope?' Marjorie said imperiously to Sadie. 'This problem won't go away. Mother is becoming impossible. It's her age, of course. You have to expect problems from a seventy-year-old, but she is utterly unbelievable. I live closest to her so I have to deal with her, you don't.'

Marjorie's voice was tinged with the inevitable trace of martyrdom.

Sadie had been sitting at her desk finishing a lunchtime latte and doing the crossword when the phone had rung. Now she clutched her blue biro so tightly that the plastic casing broke in two. No matter what age her mother was, she would never cause Sadie the grief that Marjorie did.

Marjorie had never understood their mother. Mary O'Brien was one of life's free spirits, while Marjorie was the sort of woman who thought free spirits were what you got when the supermarket was having an alcohol promotion and staff were handing round drinks in minuscule plastic cups.

'You will be there, won't you?' repeated Marjorie shrilly.

'I'll be there,' Sadie said grimly. She wanted to yell at her sister and call her an unfeeling cow, but people were streaming back to their desks for the afternoon and everyone in the open-plan office of Merrion Mortgages would be astonished to hear easygoing Sadie, who could deal with the most irritable customer the bank possessed, screaming into her phone. 'Will there be food?' Might as well get fed if she was going to have to hike all the way out to Marjorie's on two buses.

'Agnes can rustle up something,' Marjorie replied, pride resonating in every syllable.

Agnes had come with Castle Wood House, a housekeeper straight out of *Upstairs Downstairs* who addressed Marjorie as Mrs Wilson and managed to starch Phillip's shirts to such a degree of stiffness that they could probably stand up on their own.

Sadie privately thought that Phillip was such a stuffed shirt that he didn't need any more starch in him. But despite that, she felt sorry for her brother-in-law. She felt sorry for anyone who had to live with Marjorie.

'Fine,' Sadie said tersely, and hung up.

Nothing annoyed Marjorie more than being hung up on. As their mother often said, Sadie had two degree-level skills: business studies and irritating the hell out of her eldest sister.

Sadie abandoned the crossword, even though she had five minutes of lunch left. She was too furious to concentrate. How *dare* Marjorie even mention trouble and their mother in the same breath. It was about time Marjorie heard some home truths and on Sunday, Sadie was going to tell them to her. She might be the youngest member of the O'Brien clan, but she was more than able to stand up to Marjorie.

Rhona wasn't at home when Marjorie phoned. And, to Marjorie's intense irritation, the answering machine was so full of the day's messages that its electronic voice informed her that she couldn't leave a message either. Grimly, Marjorie dialled her sister's mobile phone, remembering how it had been exactly the same when they'd been children. Marjorie, as the oldest of the O'Brien sisters, *should* have been the popular one. Instead, Rhona, two years younger and a dark-eyed beauty, had been the one everyone adored. The doorbell in the O'Brien house had rung ceaselessly for Rhona, and Marjorie had done her best to pretend that she didn't care.

Since marrying Phillip fifteen years before, Marjorie hoped she'd redressed the balance. Phillip was a hugely successful businessman and his job meant loads of entertaining and entire weekends when Marjorie's diary was gratifyingly full.

But Rhona had fought back by marrying a hotshot lawyer, which meant elegant legal parties that featured heavily in the gossip columns. Even worse, Rhona had joined a tennis club, the one club that was well-nigh impossible to get into. Not to be outdone, Marjorie was working feverishly on a golf club membership. She'd also become involved in two children's charities. Children's charities were very fashionable at the moment and Marjorie occasionally indulged in daydreams of herself at some glorious black-tie gala, modestly accepting an award for her services to mankind and saying how she'd meant her charity work to be anonymous, honestly.

She wouldn't invite her family to witness her triumph, of course. Marjorie tried very hard to forget her humble roots. Rhona was the only member of the family who'd managed to elevate herself to a social level that Marjorie found acceptable, but there was too much rivalry there for the sisters to ever be comfortable with each other.

They were united on just one issue: their desire to keep the past firmly in the past. If anybody ever found out that Marjorie and Rhona had grown up in a council house with a humble bricklayer for a father, and an outside loo, they'd have both died with shame.

Marjorie left a message on Rhona's mobile. 'Mother has become unmanageable, we must do something. It's at crisis point now. You have no idea what she's just done.'

Last on Marjorie's list was Denise, who wasn't actually one of the three O'Brien sisters but was married to Ger, the only O'Brien brother. Denise was, inevitably, at home. Marjorie didn't know why her sister-in-law never had her hair styled properly or had her nails nicely manicured. It wasn't as if she didn't have the time to visit the hairdressers or the beauty salon. She was always at home, gardening or doing laundry or some other domestic drudgery involving the triplets. Marjorie would have died if she'd had triplets. It was so low class. Marjorie had made it her mission in life to avoid the taint of being working class.

She'd told Phillip from the start that one child was quite enough. And she had her hands full with nine-year-old Serena as it was. Imagine getting *three* kids off to ballet and violin and chess club. Not, of course, that Denise's three would ever aspire to violin and chess club. They were madly into football and never went anywhere without a ball.

'It's about Mother,' she said now to Denise. 'The time has come when we have to do something. Her behaviour is dreadful.'

'Well, she was fine last time I saw her,' Denise replied, the phone jammed against one ear as she tried to wrench open a jar of pasta sauce.

The kids, a trio of energetic six-year-old boys, were waiting to be fed. So was the dog. The kitchen looked like a disaster zone with the boys' castle – made from cushions off the couch and several cardboard boxes – in the centre, and toys scattered all around. Denise didn't mind. Kids made mess. She'd sort it all out later.

'Denise,' said Marjorie with a resigned air, 'Mother is anything but fine, believe me. I've had enough. I've called a family meeting for three on Sunday, at Castle Wood House. I trust that you and Ger will be there. And the boys, of course,' she added as an afterthought.

She'd tell Agnes to keep an eye on them in the garden. They couldn't get up to much mischief there.

A rare surge of anger gave Denise the strength to wrench the pasta jar lid off.

'We'll be there,' she said grimly, realising that Ger's plan to put up the final roll of wallpaper in the dining room was now out of the question. She and Ger would have to go to Marjorie's, if only to put her right on the whole question of Mary O'Brien. Denise knew exactly what Marjorie was getting at when she spoke about her mother's behaviour: she wanted her mother as far away from her as possible, where she didn't have to see her or deal with her.

'Over my dead body,' thought Denise.

Rhona was still at lunch with her four best girlfriends when she decided to check her phone messages. It was a rule that they left their phones switched off during their weekly lunches. Otherwise, nobody would ever be able to talk, what with the constant buzzing of phones. Today was the turn of Maison Chevalier, the newest restaurant in town, where the portions were doll-sized and the waiters suitably attentive.

Rhona waved away the dessert menu as she listened impassively to her elder sister's message. Her expression never softened but her jaw tightened.

'Rhona, sweetie, are you all right?' asked the beautifully preserved blonde on her left.

Rhona bit her glossy bottom lip, dabbed a tissue to one exquisitely made-up eye and sighed 'yes' dramatically. 'It's my mother,' she said, putting her mobile phone back in her YSL handbag (waiting list of five weeks for normal people but Rhona had got hers from Paris, naturally, and hadn't had to wait at all). 'She's at that difficult age. There's always some drama. My sister has just left me a message about her . . .' Rhona's voice trailed off.

Everyone around the table in the restaurant made sympathetic sounds. A waiter was summoned to bring more wine.

'Poor you,' sighed the blonde. 'Is she too frail to live on her own?'

Rhona nodded. 'That's it,' she agreed. 'She really can't be left alone. Poor Mummy.'

'More wine, mademoiselle?' asked the waiter.

Rhona dimpled up at him. He really was cute.

'Just one more,' she murmured.

On Saturday mornings, Sadie met her best friend, Dominique, for brunch. Together they would trail through the big second-hand market on the quays, admiring glittery forties necklaces, faded evening dresses and bias-cut nightgowns in the clothes stalls.

In their favourite vintage stall, Sadie found the sort of handbag her mother had always loved: heavily embroidered, beaded and with a fat silvery chain, looking as if it had just slipped off the arm of some fluffy pre-WW2 debutante. Her mother adored eccentric clothes, heavy jewellery and cosmetics.

When Sadie had first experimented with make-up, her mother had toyed with too much eyeliner too.

'Your father never approved of make-up,' she'd say, squinting to see if she should attempt to put eyeliner on the other eye too. 'Poor darling thought only loose women used more than a little lipstick.'

Sadie, fifteen years younger than Marjorie and the afterthought in the O'Brien family, didn't really remember her father. He'd died when she was small. Ger, ten years older, had been her father-figure and older brother rolled into one.

Rhona and Marjorie had been so much older and so busy with their lives that they'd seemed more like distant relatives than sisters. They'd adored Dad. To Sadie, he sounded like a male version of Marjorie: hard-faced and constantly worried about what other people thought.

Her mother, who never worried about what other people thought, was her idol.

Mary O'Brien had always welcomed her youngest daughter's friends into their home with a warmth that made Sadie's friends envy her. When teenage boyfriends left them in tears, Mrs O'Brien consoled them. She never dismissed their heartbreaks as teenage crushes. She took them seriously, while supplying hot chocolate and advice.

With her tumbling honey-blonde hair, her shrewd kind eyes, and her lively outlook on life, she had the attitude of a much younger woman, even though she was one of the oldest mums.

'Age is just a number,' was one of her favourite sayings.

That and: 'A woman is like a teabag – you don't know how strong she is until you put her in hot water.'

It was only years later that Sadie realised what had made her mother different from so many of the other mothers. Freed by widowhood from the domineering husband she'd loved but who'd clearly stifled her, she had recovered from her grief and decided that life was too short to waste.

It was a message she'd transmitted to her youngest child.

When Sadie had wondered whether she should take a gap year and go travelling instead of going straight to college, her mother had been the one who'd encouraged her to see the world.

'Get out there and live!' she'd said. 'The college will still be here when you get home.'

Marjorie had nearly passed out with shock when Sadie had dutifully phoned from Greece with news that she was working as a bar tart. Sadie explained that bar tart wasn't anywhere near as bad as it sounded and just meant chatting to passers-by and trying to make them have a drink in the bar where she worked. All the bar tarts vied for customers, each trying to make their own bar sound like the most fun. Sadie was a natural at the job. Her smiling face and huge blue eyes, just like her mother's, charmed tourists and they gladly chose her bar above the others.

'It's a laugh,' she'd written. 'I tell them about the special offer ouzo shots and the sundowners. You get to meet so many people.'

Sadie later heard that Marjorie told friends that her youngest sister was nannying for a year 'for a professional couple. So suitable.'

Mary O'Brien told friends that she was so proud of her youngest for having the courage to travel alone.

Mary had been so encouraged by Sadie's travels that she decided to do some travelling of her own. By then, she owned the small council house where she'd brought up the children and, thanks to her husband's insurance, she had a nest egg stashed away for a rainy day. With her customary brio, Mary decided that it was a better idea to use the money for a sunny day instead.

She'd always loved Spain, so she rented out her house, took a plane to Madrid, and immersed herself in Spanish life.

Sadie smiled at the thought of her mother's time in Madrid and the exciting holidays Sadie had spent with her. Her mother's gift for finding friends meant the holidays passed in a blur of fascinating people and marvellous parties, with Mary at the centre, being adored. No matter what happened in the future, that was how Sadie would always remember her mother: laughing, talking nineteen to the dozen, wearing her favourite colour, red, surrounded by people.

Sadie picked up the cream brocade handbag and dangled it by its silvery chain.

'I think I'll buy this for Mum,' Sadie said. 'I'm going to drop in on her on the way back from Marjorie's later tomorrow.'

'What's going on at Marjorie's?' asked Dominique, who'd met Sadie's social-climbing sister too often. 'Don't tell me.

She's having a garden party and she wants you in a black dress, pretending to be a waitress.'

'Worse,' said Sadie. 'She's having a family meeting to discuss my mother, who is becoming "a problem", according to Marjorie. Ger, Denise and I are all going.'

Dominique grinned. 'I wish I could be a fly on the wall for *that* meeting.'

Saturday night was their special night for Ger and Denise. They rarely went out to dinner. With Ger's landscape gardening business in its infancy and with Denise only working part time in the boutique, they didn't have the spare cash for either fancy dinners or babysitters. So they had romantic dinners at home, every Saturday night. Even Adam, Chris and Guy knew that Mum, who was a complete softie most of the time, put her foot down about bedtime on Saturdays.

At nine on the Saturday before Marjorie's big family meeting, Ger decided that his cod kebabs were ready. He enjoyed cooking and fish was his speciality. By the time he'd carefully carried the plates over to the table, Denise had opened the white wine.

'You're a great cook, love, do you know that?' said Denise as she savoured the subtle flavour of the lemongrass that Ger used in his marinade.

'Perhaps I should give up landscape gardening and become a chef,' joked Ger.

'You're brilliant at whatever you do,' Denise replied, her eyes full of love.

By the time they'd finished the bottle of wine, they were

both mellow and relaxed. They tidied up and then sat in their cosy lounge with a CD playing in the background.

There was just one little niggle at the back of Denise's brain. The thought of Marjorie and her plans for Mary O'Brien.

Denise's own mother was dead and she could honestly say that her mother-in-law had been like a second mother to her. Mary was a million miles away from the stereotypical interfering mother-in-law. She was practical and kind. If it hadn't been for Mary's generous cheque four years before, Ger would never have been able to set up his business. And Mary had never mentioned the money since.

'I'd prefer you to enjoy the money when I'm alive and not when I'm dead,' was all she'd said at the time. 'Now let's forget about it. There's nothing worse than people who go on about money all the time.'

Emotional thanks to half a bottle of wine, Denise felt her eyes prickle with tears at the thought of dear Mary. She didn't deserve a daughter like Marjorie. Or one like Rhona, for that matter. They'd never appreciated their mother. Whatever stupid plan Marjorie had, Denise was determined that she, Ger and Sadie would put a stop to it.

Marjorie had ironed out her arguments by Sunday morning. She practised them in front of the long mirror in her dressing room.

'My only concern is Mother's well-being.' That sounded good.

'She is clearly losing her mind and should be looked after.' Not so good. Mentioning that Mother was losing her mind

239

was such a negative statement. Sadie, Ger and Denise were always so protective of Mary O'Brien that they'd rear up in anger if Marjorie put it like that.

She tried again.

'Ever since Mother became difficult, I have been researching – er – where she could live. I've discovered this fabulous sheltered accommodation complex in Cork. She could live in one of the one-bedroomed apartments and have her meals in the main house.'

The complex was quite expensive, but they could all chip in to pay for it. Some things were more important than money. Ger and Denise were always whingeing about having to be careful financially, but hadn't Mother given them that huge cheque a few years ago? That money was part of the whole family's inheritance. Marjorie hadn't forgotten about it. She only hoped the money had been taken into consideration in her mother's will.

She faced herself in the mirror and moved on to her next point.

In case there was any chance of the family pointing out that Marjorie had a perfectly good granny flat that her mother could move into, it was important that Marjorie had an answer ready.

'Just because Phillip and I have space is no reason for Mother coming to live with us. We need the guest flat for, er, guests.'

No, that didn't work.

'Phillip often has people coming for the weekend and the guest flat is for them. That's why we bought Castle Wood House: for ease of entertaining. The complex in Cork is definitely the best option.'

She fiddled with her glossy dark hair. The stupid girl in the hairdresser's had put too much hairspray on it the previous morning and it was as hard as a board. Marjorie hadn't left a tip. If the hairdresser couldn't get Marjorie's hair right, then she didn't deserve one.

At least Agnes had agreed to work today. She normally had Sundays off. If Marjorie didn't know better, she'd have thought Agnes looked irritated when she'd been asked to work on her normal day off. Surely not.

Rhona shifted the BMW into fifth gear and cursed her mother. Trust her to cause trouble. Why couldn't she be one of those sweet, sedate, little-old-lady-mother types all Rhona's friends had? Marjorie was right: a home somewhere was the answer. Preferably somewhere far away from Rhona.

There were two camps in the drawing room. On one side sat Sadie, Ger and Denise, who were glaring fiercely at Marjorie and Rhona. Marjorie was doing her best to look regal. She'd told them about the sheltered accommodation in Cork.

'Of all the hare-brained schemes, this has to be the worst,' Ger said angrily. 'How dare you even suggest it. You're pathetic, Marjorie.'

Agnes stepped away from the door as the voices got more heated and her ladyship's brother began to really shout at her. Agnes would have liked to have eavesdropped some more but someone might catch her at it and she had to get tea organised.

She hurried into the hand-painted cream kitchen and began to lay out the tea tray when she heard a car on the driveway. Peering out, she saw a clapped-out purple Mini race wildly up the drive, sending gravel flying. Agnes put on her glasses to have a proper look. She knew most of Marjorie's friends by now and they all drove enormous Range Rovers or Mercedes station wagons with dog wire partitions in the back. Her bitch of a sister drove a sporty BMW.

Agnes would never forget the first time Marjorie had asked her to clean out her car. Agnes had been stunned. The woman had no class, that was for sure. The previous owner of Castle Wood House, Mrs Smyth, now she was a true lady. She'd treated Agnes with respect and wouldn't have dreamed of asking Agnes to clean her car.

Mrs Smyth did the garden herself and cleaned out her own car.

Marjorie Wilson thought she was so posh with her marble bathrooms and her designer clothes, but everyone in the village knew she was the worst sort of nouveau riche snob. Agnes wasn't the only one who'd noticed that, when Marjorie was angry, her carefully cultivated accent slipped. Agnes would have bet a month's wages that Marjorie was nowhere near as grand as she made out.

The Mini stopped and the door opened. Agnes's mouth fell into a surprised oval at the vision that emerged from it. A blonde woman who wasn't in the first bloom of youth got out. Very blonde, Agnes noticed, eyeing up the bouffant cloud of honey-coloured hair. The woman wore a fitted red dress with a short skirt that showed off good legs.

She was accompanied by a tall, exotic-looking man who

wore a velvet smoking jacket and had a white handlebar moustache that he was now twirling.

Agnes grinned. It was the couple who'd just moved into the village. Eccentric was not the word for them. Rumour had it that they were naturists and traipsed around their rented cottage in the nude. Or so the milkman said, and he was usually very reliable. The husband was Spanish and they'd just moved back from Spain. His wife . . . Agnes peered closer for a better look. His wife was a dead ringer for Marjorie, aside from the fact that she had a smiling face instead of the sour lemon one Marjorie usually adopted.

Agnes threw the tea things on to the tray and raced out of the kitchen. She was not going to miss this.

'She's gone too far this time.' Marjorie's voice resonated throughout the house. 'We must do something!'

Agnes opened the drawing-room door and gleefully waved the visitors in.

'Really, Marjorie, you are such a prude,' said Mary O'Brien, arriving in a cloud of Opium perfume.

In her exquisitely cut dress, with her blonde curls framing the heart-shaped face and her soft mouth curved into its familiar smile, Mary O'Brien looked ten years younger than her threescore years and ten. She kissed Ger, Sadie and Denise.

'Your sister's furious because I'm going to ruin her reputation by living in her precious village. Darling –' she turned to face her eldest daughter '– I promise I won't embarrass you any more by going into the village shop in my dressing gown, but Antonio hasn't finished my portrait and I can't keep shoving my clothes on and off every five minutes just because we've run out of sugar. The man in the shop doesn't mind. He was quite complimentary, actually,' she said dreamily. 'It was my pink silk dressing gown, very flattering.'

'You're seventy, you're too old for nude portraits!' shrieked Marjorie. 'What will people think?'

'You're going to make us all look ridiculous. Why couldn't you have stayed in Spain?' demanded Rhona.

Mary O'Brien regarded her two oldest children shrewdly.

'I wanted to be closer to my family and Antonio wanted to see my home,' she said equably.

Antonio, who looked unperturbed by this family row, twirled his moustache and smiled at everyone.

'By the way, we've an announcement,' added Mary, shooting a look of affection at Antonio. 'We're getting married.'

'Wonderful, Mum!' said Sadie, kissing her mother.

'Congratulations!' Ger shook Antonio's hand.

'But everyone thinks you're married already,' snarled Rhona, thinking of the shame. She'd be the laughing stock of the tennis club. And she'd led her friends to believe that her mother was a frail little widow, instead of this blooming woman who was clearly still enjoying a riotous sex life. At her age! Her mother had always embarrassed her and she was still at it. Rhona glared at her stepfather-to-be, resplendent in his velvet jacket with the wooden toggles.

Marjorie thought of the gossip columnists having a field day on septuagenarian wedding stories and felt weak. If Mary and Antonio lived in the village and continued their outrageous carry-on, what would people think? How could Marjorie continue the fiction about her genteel background

244

with her mother around, behaving wildly, talking about the past, making Marjorie look like a liar? Imagine the parties, the card games, the inevitable drinks' bill in the off-licence.

'A wedding's always fun,' Mary said serenely, blowing a kiss at her fiancé. 'When your father and I got married, it was so traditional. I think we might do something crazy this time. I'm thinking flamenco, something wildly Spanish. Antonio's such a wonderful dancer.'

Sadie stared at her sisters. She didn't know who looked more horrified: Marjorie or Rhona.

'Mum,' she said fondly, 'I'm so glad you're back.'

The Paradise Road
Book Club

Marsha Reid's birthday loomed. Not any old birthday, mind, but a significant one. In the leafy suburbs of Paradise Road, a winding cul-de-sac lined with houses of every variety, it was the sort of birthday that beloved husbands normally celebrated with a trip abroad (two nights on the Orient Express, then a week in a palazzo in Venice: Ella and Marcus, who lived in Paradise Villa) or a long weekend away in London (Ruth and Arthur, Sorrento Cottage).

For such a birthday, grown-up children would club together to buy jewellery; friends would discuss whether a big surprise party was in order; and girlfriends from the book club would plan a night out in a wine bar where cocktails would be ordered with glee and everyone would discuss how fifty was the new forty.

Except that none of Marsha's neighbours in Paradise Road knew quite what to do for her significant birthday. Because she and her husband of twenty-five years had just split up.

When he'd left their pretty detached house on the south-facing side of Paradise Road, Dan Reid had taken his fishing rods, his half of the furniture and everyone's expectations of precisely how Marsha's fiftieth should be celebrated.

Even worse, Marsha was keeping her great pain and suffering to herself. Still clear-eyed and serene, not a wisp of dark hair in her sleekly elegant knot out of place, she smiled at people as she headed off to work in her little silver Golf, and hadn't been seen sobbing in desperation outside the supermarket.

'Honestly, it's better this way,' she told Elizabeth serenely when Elizabeth spotted Marsha putting out the bins and had run downstairs and across the road in her nightie to say hello, that she'd heard the news and *if there was anything she could do?*

'Thank you, Elizabeth,' Marsha had added, smiling. This had taken Elizabeth aback – *smiling* when your husband had just left you? 'You're so kind and I appreciate it, but honestly,' Marsha had patted Elizabeth's bare arm at this point, 'it really is better this way.'

'*Better this way!*' demanded Elizabeth of the assembled room. She'd known Marsha over years of chatting idly at the school gates. 'Better for whom? I daresay he's run off with some bimbo half her age. It's the male menopause, isn't it? Dump the first wife for a trophy blonde with a French manicure and a degree in male manipulation.'

Elizabeth, who'd reached the dreaded fifty a whole seven years ago, shook her head in temper, although her artfully streaked blonde hair was glued into place with hairspray and vast quantities of product and not a strand stirred. 'I hope Marsha takes him for every penny he's got!'

Naturally, Elizabeth didn't say this to Marsha. She said it at the book club, where discussions on Anita Shreve's themes had been wilfully abandoned for detailed analysis of Marsha, Dan, what to do about poor Marsha's impending birthday, and *what must the children think?*

Thankfully, the Reid children had both left home and, therefore, were not around to witness the horrific break-up, the shattering of plates and whatever terrible things must have gone on behind the solid doors of the Reid household.

Hanna, the elder of the two, was studying science in Cork, while Oliver, who had left home only last year, was studying surfing on Bondi and had a girlfriend named Roxie, of all things. To the more conservative denizens of Paradise Road, Oliver's life choices were upsetting, but these flaws now seemed immaterial in the grand scheme of things. Their parents had split up and the Reid children must be devastated.

The mothers among the book club thought of their own children and how age was no barrier to worrying about a six-foot rugby player when you could remember him as a six-pound baby with a piercing cry and eyes that pleaded for Mummy.

'Typical, isn't it? Clearly Dan only stayed with Marsha for the children,' said Ruth with a shiver.

Ruth lived in the rounded cul-de-sac part of Paradise Road in an ugly 1960s bungalow that had resisted all attempts to make it look outwardly modern. She'd often envied Marsha Reid's lovely house with the climbing rose that draped itself fragrantly over the porch. She didn't envy poor Marsha now.

Ruth was in her late forties and Danny, her youngest, would be eighteen soon. He was currently planning his gap-year trip instead of burying himself in books for the forthcoming state exams. It didn't seem to matter how often she chided him about surfing websites for the best beaches in Thailand, he still hadn't touched a textbook.

Now, Ruth suddenly imagined how quiet and tidy the house would be with him gone. She'd have plenty of time to read the book club choices, but wondered how she would really feel when the weight of silence hung around the house every day, with no Danny ambling in at odd hours wondering if his jeans were washed and could he borrow ten euros?

It wasn't as if Arthur was around much either. *Work* was his perennial excuse. Could work be the be-all and end-all of her husband's existence? And what about her? Didn't she count for something in Arthur's life too?

'I think it's awful for a man to march off into the sunset as soon as the kids are old enough to fend for themselves. It's an insult, isn't it?' she said now. 'Like saying you don't mean anything to him as a person and he's only stayed until the children were old enough not to care. And just two months before her fiftieth birthday too. It's callous, that's what it is. Poor Marsha.'

The book club went silent. This was the stuff of tragedy, just as heart-rending and real as anything they'd ever read about. And so sudden. It was the very suddenness that shocked them all. One minute, you had your life planned out. The next, your husband had run off with some gold-digger who could overlook age, male-pattern baldness and a paunch for the heady lure of a lucrative milk-carton-packaging business and the latest S-class Mercedes.

'I wonder, did Marsha notice Dan change when he started seeing this other woman?' Elizabeth said thoughtfully. 'You know, like they say in magazines, if he was coming home late, losing weight, making lots of whispery phone calls and saying he was working all the hours.'

The other ten members of the book club turned to look at her.

'I was just wondering,' Elizabeth said hastily. 'Right: the book. Who wants to go first?'

The Paradise Road book club had been Elizabeth's idea initially and had been running for two years. In that time, the eleven women had had enjoyable dalliances with the classics, lots of fun with contemporary literature and a few argumentative nights over whether *The Da Vinci Code* was fabulously compulsive or not.

Not, insisted Amelia, a former English teacher, who kept her Booker, Orange and Costa prize winners in a well-dusted line in the hall where everyone would see them.

Compulsive, illuminating and *true*, argued Ruth, who'd gone to a convent where the head nun had been heavily involved in Opus Dei and so keen on finding new recruits that it was considered dangerous to be alone in a room with her in case you were indoctrinated and had your mind wiped or whatever it was they did.

Elizabeth herself was a Jane Austen fan, favouring *Mansfield Park* as the finest example of Austen's work, while the Colin Firth version of *Pride and Prejudice* was her idea of perfect television viewing. She loved the combination of clear-sighted social comment with a suggestion of closely reined-in passion restricted by the social mores of the time. Not to mention Mr Darcy dripping as he emerged from the lake.

Marsha Reid had been in the book club for the first year and then had gently bowed out, saying she had somewhere else to be on Monday evenings and, although she loved the book club, she couldn't manage it any more.

Nobody had thought much about her leaving at the time. Marsha was a publishing illustrator who often worked to difficult deadlines. But now they all began seeing more sinister reasons behind her departure. She just couldn't cope with a social, chatty group of friends at a time when her personal life was in flux, that had to be it. Think how hard it would be to pretend everything was all right between her and Dan when she knew it wasn't.

When that night's book club was over, everyone tidied up and checked the rota to see in whose house the next meeting would be held. Inevitably, the conversation slipped back to the Reid family.

'We've got to do something for Marsha's birthday,' said Elizabeth with determination. 'She's our friend, one of us. We should make her birthday go with a bang, even if her lying, cheating husband won't. It's only six weeks away – any suggestions?'

'Perhaps we ought to talk to her first,' Mildred said doubtfully. Mildred was the newest member of the book club, having only recently moved on to Paradise Road with her sister, Winifred, and their pugs, Tristan and Isolde.

Mildred loved books and had eclectic tastes, but her

absolute favourite bedtime reading had to be the historical romances where a strong, fierce warrior tamed a gentle maiden's heart, killed all her foes and carried her off to bed as if she was as light as a feather. Of course, Mildred didn't let this preference slip at the book club, not even when it was her turn to pick the book of the month. Everyone needed their little secret.

'No, let's not say anything to Marsha,' Ruth insisted. 'Imagine how awful it must be for her, everyone knowing he's gone and people guessing about the other woman. She probably thinks we all knew anyway. The wife's always the last one to know, isn't she? Marsha must be hurt and raw, imagining her husband with this other woman, with her callously left behind while he heads off to another life. She deserves a wonderful night out somewhere and I think she'd appreciate it much more if it was a surprise.'

A night away in a small hotel where there were spa facilities was the plan. The book club would each pay their own way and pay for Marsha too. They'd tell her a few days before. After all, it wasn't as if Marsha appeared to have many pressing engagements these days.

'She goes out on Monday nights,' said Gloria, the club busybody and a woman who felt that people didn't take the whole neighbourhood watch scheme seriously enough. Everyone listened, shocked, as Gloria recounted how she'd discovered that if she stood halfway up her stairs, she could see Marsha's gate. From her vantage point, and with her opera glasses on, Gloria had seen Marsha coming home one night with red eyes, a pale face and a tissue in her hand.

'Bet she's been round Dan's lovenest, sobbing her heart out,' Gloria sniffed.

'I might cry if my husband left me,' said Elizabeth sharply.

'I was only saying – ' Gloria began.

'We're supposed to be her friends, and friends rally round in time of need,' Elizabeth shot back.

It would have been nice to have been in Marsha's confidence and hear all about her problems at first hand instead of relying on conjecture to work out the truth, but really, Gloria took the biscuit. Support was what Marsha needed, not surveillance.

As Marsha's birthday drew near, Ruth and Elizabeth checked on hotels where the club could enjoy the whole spa experience. They couldn't spend too much money, but they wanted somewhere where Marsha would feel pampered.

Ruth enjoyed the research. She liked taking charge: it felt invigorating and made her see that it was a mistake to wallow in self-pity and wait for whatever life would bring, instead of going out and getting it yourself. She didn't want to end up abandoned like Marsha Reid.

She booked a table at the local Italian restaurant and took her surprised husband out to dinner.

'What's this about?' said Arthur as they sat with menus in front of them and an open bottle of wine.

'It's about us,' said Ruth. 'We've been talking in the book club.'

'All you do is gossip at that club.' Arthur smiled.

'We've been talking about how, when the children leave home, lots of people discover that they don't want to be married any more,' Ruth went on as if he hadn't interrupted.

'I wondered what you thought about that – should you have an affair, or will I? Or should we make a stab at actually being a couple again? Any thoughts?'

Arthur needed the waitress to bring him some water because a bit of wine had gone down the wrong way.

He wasn't interested in an affair, it turned out.

'I love you,' he blurted out, for once not caring that people might overhear in the busy restaurant.

'Great,' said Ruth, smiling back. 'Hopefully, you'll stop treating our home like a hotel, then, and talk to me as if we love each other, not as if I'm the head of hotel housekeeping.'

'I don't.'

'You do,' she shot back.

By dessert, Arthur was apologising and saying he hadn't realised she felt that way.

They sat in the back of the taxi on the way home, holding hands, and Ruth felt a surge of pity as they passed Dan and Marsha's house. If only Dan and Marsha had been able to have such a discussion, perhaps they'd still be together.

Elizabeth had been thinking too. Dan and Marsha had seemed like the perfect couple and look what had happened to them. What hope was there for people whose marriages were nowhere near as perfect?

She phoned her grown-up daughter, Mia.

'Do you think your father is happy?' Elizabeth asked, when they'd gone through half an hour talking about Mia's job, how she'd left her latest boyfriend and what she was going to do about the holiday to Greece she'd booked for two.

'Happy? I don't know, Mum,' said Mia, startled.

'Happy with me, I meant,' Elizabeth went on.

'I think he can be grumpy, unappreciative and hopeless showing his feelings,' Mia said, thinking that seeing as how her mother was asking, she might as well tell the truth.

'You know the way people look at their parents and can see that they should never have got married,' Elizabeth went on. 'Do you think that about us?'

'What's brought this on?'

'Marsha Reid's husband has left her. We're pretty sure it's for another woman and, you know what, I find myself wondering if Marsha's better off without him after all,' her mother replied candidly.

'Wow, Mum, that's serious.'

'Yes, it is,' agreed Elizabeth. 'It's just that Marsha has set me thinking.'

'Dad doesn't appreciate you, if that's what you're asking,' Mia said quickly. 'Hey, I've had an idea. Why don't you come to Greece with me? Let Dad see how lonely it is to be grumpy and unappreciative on his own without you.'

Elizabeth began to cry. 'You're a great daughter,' she said. 'I'm not going to end up like poor Marsha Reid, am I?'

The day before her birthday, Marsha Reid was surprised to be asked at the last minute to a coffee morning in Elizabeth's house across the road.

'Yes, I can come,' she told Elizabeth, 'but I'm wearing my ancient jeans and a shabby old sweatshirt because I'm putting stuff in the attic. I'm hardly dressed for socialising.'

'Don't worry about that,' Elizabeth said warmly. 'It's you we want to see, not your clothes.'

Before she left for Elizabeth's, Marsha looked around the house she loved, with boxes waiting to be stored in the attic, and thought how lucky she was to be starting a new life. She was leaving in a week, so today would give her the chance to say au revoir to the women in the book club. She hoped they'd understand when she told them and not think she was being horrendously selfish.

It wasn't easy, being selfish. Not after a lifetime of looking after other people. Women looked after people: it was that simple. They put their own needs after other people's. And she'd done that. She'd cooked, cleaned, worked part time, stood in the freezing cold at football matches.

Two months previously, she'd finally taken that big, final step.

'I know it's the right decision, but I don't know how to tell Dan,' she'd said to the counsellor she'd been seeing every second Monday night for the past year.

The counsellor refolded her arms and said nothing, which seemed to be a bit of a counselling habit.

'OK, I *do* know how I can tell him,' Marsha agreed. 'I have to tell him that I want some time out of our marriage, that I don't want to hurt him but that I'll hurt both of us if I'm not honest now. If he doesn't want to wait for me, that's his choice, but my choice is to travel the world on my own for a year and find out who I really am under all the roles I take on: wife, mum, chief bottle washer.'

'Well done,' said the counsellor. 'I couldn't have put it better myself.'

The kids leaving home had forced her to take stock of her life. For years, they'd needed her and she'd needed Dan. But need was surprisingly reversible. Hanna and Oliver suddenly didn't need her in the same way, and Marsha found, to her surprise, that she didn't need Dan so much either. He'd moved in with his bachelor brother to give both of them space, and Marsha relished the freedom.

Once she'd realised that life was very different now – no children to consider and a grown-up to share her life with – she'd realised she could change the rules. After all, she was only answerable to herself.

'Just take care,' Hanna had told her mother.

'I'll join you in India,' said Oliver in delight. 'Roxie and me were thinking of going to India anyway, and it'll be cool to hook up with you.'

'I wish it wasn't like this,' Dan said helplessly. 'I don't understand.'

'I know, and I'm sorry, but I can't make you understand,' Marsha said. 'I still love you but I've got to do this.'

Across the road in Elizabeth's house, the book club surveyed their efforts. The prospectus of the spa hotel was laid out on the coffee table, and everyone had brought something along as a mini-gift for Marsha: flowers, chocolates, self-help books, although there were two copies of *Feel the Fear and Do It Anyway*.

Marsha took one look at it all and burst into tears.

'You're so kind,' she said, hugging everyone in turn. 'This will be a lovely way to send me off on my trip, and I'll tell you all about that in a minute, but first, I've got a favour to ask.'

The Paradise Road book club leaned forward in one

enthusiastic group. They would do anything, *anything*. This was what sisterhood was about. They had the names of lawyers with ice running through their veins; they had willing shoulders ready to be cried on.

'I'm going away for a year,' Marsha announced, her eyes alight as she thought of her fabulous trip, 'and while I'm away, I'm going to be renting out the house. A lovely couple are taking it for the whole year and I told the wife all about the book club and how gorgeous you all are, and guess what – she'd love to join. What do you think? Will you take her on?'

The Angel Gabrielle

As Claire shut the front door behind her, the warmth of 7 Redmond Villas embraced her in a giant hug. It was an icy December night and three hours earlier she certainly hadn't felt like heading off to her evening class when the rest of the family were sitting down in front of a cosy fire.

But tonight had been the last computer class and with a determination Claire had thought she'd lost a long time ago, she was not about to miss a single lesson.

By the time she was finished, the teacher had said confidently, Claire would be able to organise folders, blithely send e-mails off into the ether and use Power Point. Quite what she was going to need Power Point for was another matter. There wasn't much call for it at home as Lorraine, Claire's nineteen-year-old daughter, had merrily pointed out.

'Will you be printing off the shopping list on Excel Notes, Mum?' she teased.

Charlie, who was two years older, joined in: 'No, Mum's

259

going to start flirting with strangers over the Internet, now she knows how to use it!'

Even Steven, her husband, seemed to find it all very funny. 'You shouldn't tease your mother,' he told the kids, although he was smiling. 'When she's running some big computer company, you'll be sorry. Next stop, chairmanship of Microsoft, eh, Claire?' he joked.

Though she managed to smile back at them, Claire felt strangely wounded.

After twenty years raising a family, she'd decided to change her life. And they all thought it was funny.

Nobody at home seemed to realise what it had cost her to enrol on the course in the first place. It had been twenty-one years since she'd been a student of any kind. She was two months into a management training scheme with the hotel company when she'd become pregnant with Charlie. Instantly it had been bye bye books, hello nappies. Charlie was twenty-one now. In some ways, the time had flown. When it came to going back to work, twenty-one years was a very long time.

'We don't need the money, you know,' Steven had said in September, when Claire had broached the subject of doing an evening course and explained how having a new skill could help her rejoin the workforce. 'But if you want a job now the kids are seen to?'

Steven's mother said she didn't see the point of all that computer nonsense.

'It's for young people,' Mavis had sniffed. 'You're nearly fifty, dear. You can't turn the clock back.'

Claire, who was forty-nine and a half, thank you very

much, held her tongue. Mavis lived in the street behind them and spent a lot of time in Claire's house.

I don't like interfering, was her mantra.

Claire often wondered if mantra was the correct description for a phrase someone used a lot but didn't adhere to in any practical way.

Now, she hung up her coat, tidied away the canvas bag that contained all her coursework, and went into the living room. Her family, mother-in-law included, were watching the television with mugs of tea and a packet of chocolate biscuits on the small table in front of the couch.

'Bet you're glad that blinking course is over,' Steven murmured. 'I'm sick of seeing your head in a book. Now you can relax and enjoy Christmas. I'm really looking forward to tucking into your special Christmas pudding, love.'

'Oh yes, Mum,' Lorraine said. 'Did you make two puddings this year? You said you would because I hate currants and if we could have one with currants and one without, it would be brilliant.'

Four eager faces turned towards Claire and she had a sudden flash of reality: she was no longer a person to any of them. She had morphed into Robot Mother, who cooked, cleaned, took orders for festive meals and had no needs of her own. This Christmas would not be any different from all the others.

Claire shut her eyes and wished it was January.

Shelley found that the trouble with lying was keeping track of all the lies.

The first lie was telling Mum and Dad that she wasn't

going home to the farm for Christmas because she was spending the holiday with her friend, Adele, in Greece.

She'd decided to phone them with the news because she was actually a hopeless liar face-to-face. Over the phone, lying was much easier.

'It's a week-long yoga thing and it just came up. It's impossible to get places on it but someone pulled out and Adele and I thought it would be just what we need,' she'd bluffed. She couldn't help thinking that God, if *He* was listening, would burn her to a cinder for such fibs. And fibs about Christmas weren't the half of it.

As if a week doing yoga could possibly hold any attractions for her. She could be going to Greece, in fact. Adele had asked her along. But even twenty-four hours away would be torture unless she was away with Ken. And that wasn't going to happen anytime soon. The lie was necessary because she couldn't possibly tell her parents she was going to stay on her own in her flat in Dublin just in case Ken managed to sneak over to see her during the holidays.

The next lie was to Adele.

Adele and Shelley worked together in marketing and Adele made no pretence of her dislike for Ken, who was one of the directors of the large estate agency where they'd both worked for three years. Adele was much shrewder than Shelley's parents and lying to her was undoubtedly trickier. So Shelley gritted her teeth, tried to look blasé, and told Adele she was going home to her parents as usual.

'You're sure you're not staying in Dublin because that lying scumbag wants you on tap in case he gets away from his wife for five minutes?' Adele had asked suspiciously.

''Course not. I'm not stupid, you know.' Shelley smiled as she lied.

Adele was *amazing*. How had she figured it out?

'Good,' said Adele. 'I'm glad you're finally listening to me. He's using you.'

Adele had spent hours the previous week telling Shelley what she called the Facts of Life.

'He won't leave his wife, Shell: get used to it. Dump him. You're just a soft touch and he's taking advantage of that fact.'

Adele just didn't understand, Shelley thought. Love didn't always work out in traditional ways. Ken loved her. He wanted to be with her whenever he could manage it and he'd already worked out how they could sneak some precious hours together over Christmas.

Shelley thought about the last conversation she'd had with Ken as they lay in her bed, cosy after making love.

'Maura and her sister are sales mad. They'll be in town waiting for the shops to open on Boxing Day. I'll have plenty of opportunity to slip away,' Ken had assured her.

Maura was Ken's wife; a source of huge guilt and sadness in Shelley's life. If only Maura wasn't so emotionally fragile that she'd fall apart if Ken left. If only there weren't two innocent children involved, then it would all be so much easier.

But still Shelley felt the wrongness of the affair like a weight on her soul.

There were so many lies, Shelley thought sadly. A person shouldn't have to lie about Christmas, should they?

*   *   *

Mavis had an early Christmas present for her daughter-in-law: an hour-by-hour guide to cooking Christmas dinner which she'd clipped from a magazine.

'It says keep a lipstick handy in the kitchen so you don't end up looking a wreck just because you're standing over a hot oven all day,' she explained kindly as she gave the clipping to Claire. 'And a bit of powder too. Nice to get the shine off your face.'

Claire stopped herself from asking why *she'd* been chosen to receive the guide. There were three other adults in the house. Why was cooking Christmas dinner solely her prerogative?

Since the night she'd come home from her last computer lesson, Claire had been having lots of similarly strange thoughts. She felt the buzz of pride from the hard work she'd put into learning about software and e-mail. The rest of them seemed to think it was nothing more than a blip that kept her from more important duties: looking after all of them.

At lunchtime on their second-last day at work before the holidays, Shelley went with Adele to buy both last-minute presents and yoga gear for Adele's Greek idyll. Adele was flying off to Athens early on Christmas Eve. Shelley was supposed to be spending the same morning driving a hundred miles to her parents' small dairy farm. In fact, she and Ken were going to spend as much time as possible in her flat, enjoying their Christmas dinner a day early.

Shelley had already bought a tiny turkey crown from M&S, a miniature cake, and splurged on champagne for the occasion. She'd spent all week imagining their wonderful day together: making love; talking about future holidays when they'd be together.

'Why are all sports bras ugly?' Adele demanded, holding up a solid-looking white thing with disgust and prodding at the straps, so big they looked as if they might possibly be used to bind up some big rugby player's legs. 'My boobs are too big to do yoga in a vest.'

'Probably to keep the lust out of yoga,' Shelley said absently, eyeing up a very sexy peach lingerie set. She was getting her hair done that evening just round the corner, so she'd be able to pop back later and buy it.

'S'pose,' Adele agreed. 'Yoga isn't supposed to be sexy, is it? Neither will I be in this thing. Hope there's no gorgeous sinewy yoga fellas on this trip, because they'll ignore me once I've got this mammoth bra on. Probably think I'm an Olympic shot-putter.'

'Stop it. Nobody's going to think you're a shot-putter, you mad thing,' Shelley said, looking at her watch. The office drinks party started at four.

At six that evening, Claire sat in a chair in Gabrielle's Hair Salon and stared at herself in the mirror. She'd been shopping for groceries and presents all day. She was exhausted and she'd just received a text from Steven: **Forgot Mum's gift. Cud u get something? What wud u like from me & kids?**

She liked Gabrielle's, but normally only got her hair cut there. Today's wash and blow-dry was a special treat. However, as she sat there, the face in the mirror looked older than forty-nine and a half, and her plan to look different for Christmas suddenly seemed futile. After twenty-five years of marriage, her husband still had to ask what perfume she liked and she still had to buy every single present for everyone. Tiredness washed over her along with a tidal wave of feeling unappreciated.

'What are you thinking of having done today?' the stylist smiled.

Claire burst into tears.

Shelley almost didn't notice the woman crying in the chair beside her. She was still in shock, trying to make sense of what she'd overheard at the office drinks party. It had started at four: drinks and nibbles in the boardroom and, traditionally, it all went crazy at six when the partners went home and the real fun began.

That's what Adele said, anyway, but for Shelley, the real fun was a social occasion where she could be near her darling Ken. Not together, of course. Nobody could know about them, he'd said. He didn't want people talking. It wouldn't be fair to her.

But that afternoon, Shelley had felt the magnetic pull of Ken's presence. She couldn't stop herself from trying to stand near him, although not exactly in his company, and she'd been near enough to overhear him talking to one of the other directors about what they were giving their respective spouses.

'You always give Maura great gifts, you clever git,' the other man was saying to Ken. 'What's it this year? The Hope Diamond?'

'A week's skiing in Courcheval.'

Shelley could hear the smile in Ken's voice.

'We love skiing and Maura's a real daredevil at it. She did

a black run last time. I'll tell you, she frightened the life out of me.'

A daredevil? Surely that couldn't be the same Maura who'd fall apart if Ken left her? And wasn't a week spent skiing a very intimate, coupley present – the sort of holiday you'd share with a lover and not with a woman for whom you had 'brotherly' feelings?

Shelley had kept it together enough to put down her glass and not drop it on to the grey office carpet, then she'd rushed out of the boardroom.

In the hairdresser's, with her hair stuck wetly to her scalp and a glass of office wine rattling round inside her, Shelley felt emptier than she'd ever thought possible. And then, the sound of crying filtered in through her own misery and, like seeing someone else yawn when you're tired, the tears started to pour down her own face.

Across the salon, Gabrielle – or Peggy to her friends – saw the two women sobbing. *Christmas*, she thought, shaking her head. It got to the best of them.

Installed in Peggy's office above the salon with two cups of hot, sweet tea and a pile of mince pies in front of them, Claire and Shelley began to feel better. It was impossible not to cheer up in Peggy's comforting presence. In the salon, as Gabrielle, she was a stately sixty-something blonde with a fat gold-and-diamond Cartier watch and a slightly imperious manner. In her office and as Peggy – '"Peggy O'Riordain's" doesn't have the same ring to it as "Gabrielle's",' she'd said wisely when she'd started the salon many years ago – she was kind and warm.

'You don't have to tell me, girls,' she said gently. 'It's just the Christmas blues. If all's not rosy in your world, you can be sure Christmas will make you want to cry.'

The two women nodded.

'I'm fine,' said Claire, finishing her tea. She felt terribly embarrassed about letting herself down in the salon. What had come over her?

'Thank you,' Shelley added, taking Claire's lead. How awful to break down like that. What was wrong with her?

Peggy watched both women put on their emotional armour again and pretend everything was all right. She knew the drill: she'd done it often enough herself until she'd stopped hiding her feelings. What a liberation *that* had turned out to be.

'I have a party every Christmas in my house,' Peggy said, handing them each a pale pink card with her address on it. 'It's for all my friends who feel like spending a bit of time without family or loved ones. They drop in, have something to eat and chat, and somehow, it's all very relaxing. Everyone comes on their own, so nobody feels like the odd one out. You're both welcome.'

'I've a family Christmas lined up,' smiled Claire, back in control.

'Me too,' said Shelley. 'But thank you so much for the invitation.'

'If you change your mind,' Peggy said, 'the offer stands.'

After their blow-dries, both Shelley and Claire ended up at the cash desk at the same time.

'Your hair is lovely,' said Shelley to Claire.

'I was about to say the same to you,' Claire said, smiling back.

They walked out of the salon together and it seemed natural to start chatting.

'I love the sound of Peggy's party,' Shelley said, not quite believing she'd said that. Christmas Day was going to be spent waiting for Ken to phone and daydreaming about the following Christmas, when they'd be together.

'It does sound nice,' said Claire. 'I'll be at home standing guard over the oven. There's no way I could escape for an hour.'

Outside the shopping centre, they stopped, awkward again.

'Well, if you do decide to go –' began Shelley. She fumbled in her bag and found a pen to write down her number. 'Phone me and I might come with you.'

On Christmas Day, Claire's cooking was timed with military precision. Everyone had loved their presents and after Mass the Christmas spirit went into overdrive as they sat back to enjoy the day while Claire headed back into the steamy kitchen with her bottle of Chanel No. 5 (from Steve and the kids – although she'd originally said she'd love a bottle of Allure) and a furry hot-water bottle cover with a bunny face (from Mavis). The scent of No. 5 hung about her. She hated No. 5, always had. Hated it. How come nobody knew that?

This time, Claire didn't cry. Instead, she thought.

The problem wasn't about presents: it was about respect and about people taking heed of her and her opinions. Perfume she disliked and no help in the kitchen to cook a meal they'd all eat was part and parcel of this.

* * *

Shelley couldn't help herself. She phoned Ken on his mobile to wish him Merry Christmas.

'For heaven's sake,' he hissed down the phone at her. 'You know I'm at home, Shelley. Do you want us to get found out?'

Shelley hung up. Surely if they were going to be together – as discussed the day before from the luxury of her bed – then getting found out was a given? Or perhaps not.

When Claire phoned, Shelley was sitting numbly in front of *Gone with the Wind*, too stunned to turn it off.

'Do you know,' she said, 'I think getting out of the house is just what I need right now.'

Claire and Shelley arrived at Peggy's front door at exactly the same time.

'I feel better already,' said Claire, who was wondering how she'd found the courage to walk out on her family, leaving the Christmas puddings simmering away and the oven fit to burst with turkey and all the trimmings. They probably wouldn't miss her for hours.

'So do I,' grinned Shelley, who felt remarkably happier now that she wasn't going to be on her ownsome at home waiting for the phone to ring.

'I'm so glad you both came!' Peggy flung the door open. Behind her, the lovely house was full of laughing, chattering people, clearly having a ball. There were no rows or moods floating around: just music and enjoyment.

'My husband gave me the idea,' Peggy said, filling crystal flutes with champagne for her two new guests. 'He left me just before Christmas twenty years ago. Said I was a boring old bag, he couldn't bear to stay married to me a moment longer and he was off. He didn't leave me much, either. He was a bit of a gambler, you see. The day after he went, I found out that the house was going to be repossessed. It was a terrible Christmas, that first one. I was alone in a house with no TV and very little furniture – the bailiffs had been and taken nearly everything. And then I thought that it couldn't just be me, there must be other people on their own at Christmas, staring at the wall and feeling sad, and we couldn't all be total rejects, so I came up with this idea: the Old Bags' Christmas Party. Welcome, girls. Just be sure to leave your baggage at the door.'

Lorraine smelled it first. 'Is that burning?'

The water under the two Christmas puddings needed to be topped up constantly and, without Claire to do it, both saucepans had dried out.

Steven, Charlie and Mavis glanced up from the television.

'No, surely not,' said Steven with a satisfied smile. 'Your mother will have it all under control.' And they all swivelled their eyes back to the TV.

Ken dialled Shelley's mobile. He was puzzled to hear party noises in the background. Shelley had said she wasn't going anywhere and he'd quite liked the idea of that: her waiting patiently for him.

'Sorry, Ken,' Shelley said, sounding merry. 'Can't talk. See you in the New Year, I imagine.'

She hung up.

She couldn't mean what he thought she meant, Ken

pondered. Surely not. His wife was off to the sales the next day, as he'd known she would be. He was tired of the house and the kids yelling at each other. A bit of pampering from Shelley would be lovely in the sanctuary of her little flat where she'd fuss over him and tell him he was wonderful. He'd phone in the morning.

As Peggy moved through the room, refilling glasses, she smiled contentedly at her guests. It had taken her a long time to get to this place, but she felt she could truly say that there was no better way to spend the holiday than by adding a little sparkle to other people's lives. After all, wasn't Christmas supposed to be about giving?

Lizzie's Fling

Lizzie stared at Oscar grimly. He looked back sheepishly, dark spaniel eyes doing their best to appear sweetly soulful in the hope that she'd forgive him. Even at the age of six months, he was smart enough to know when he was in trouble.

'Bad dog, Oscar,' she snapped before trudging back into the kitchen to get some kitchen towels, the carpet cleaner and a bucket of water. By the time she got back, Oscar was gone. The small pile of doggy poo on the new caramel-coloured hearth rug was still there, however, and no amount of air-freshener was going to take the smell away.

'Jason, Naomi, I thought I told you to let Oscar out first thing!' Lizzie roared as she wrinkled her nose and starting cleaning up.

There was silence from her offspring. Well, not exactly silence. Justin Bieber music blared from Naomi's bedroom. But silence on the who-was-supposed-to-let-Oscar-out front.

Lizzie scrubbed and raged. What a great start to Monday

morning. She'd known exactly who was going to end up looking after that damned dog when her husband Scott had arrived home with the little bundle of black fluff the previous Christmas.

'I don't have time to take care of a dog!' she'd told him.

'We'll take care of Oscar,' Naomi had said in outraged pride.

'OK, I believe you.' Lizzie had smiled, ruffling her eight-year-old daughter's dark hair.

'They've wanted a dog for so long,' Scott said, delighted at the effect his Christmas present was having.

Naomi was bright-eyed with happiness and Jason, a quiet, bespectacled twelve-year-old who was normally glued to his PlayStation, was rolling around on the floor with the puppy and demanding to know when they'd be able to take him out for a walk.

'You should have discussed it with me first,' hissed Lizzie, *sotto voce*.

'I thought you liked dogs,' protested Scott, doing his best expression of injured innocence.

'I do, that's why I feel sorry for a dog that's going to be on its own all day and who won't be walked if it's raining or cold. I'm out at work until four, you're out at work until God knows when and the kids are at school all day. Who's going to take care of it and who's going to tidy up after it?'

'Don't be so negative,' Scott had said huffily. 'We'll all muck in.'

'Yeah, right. *We'll all muck in*,' muttered Lizzie as she finished cleaning up Oscar's little present. He was normally quite good about doing his business in the yard, but he had to be let out in the first place.

'Kids! Come down and get your breakfast,' she yelled, 'or

you'll be late for school.' It was already a quarter to eight and they all had to be out the door by ten past. Whizzing around the kitchen with the ease of someone practised at doing four things at once, she made toast, coffee, assembled sandwiches for the kids' lunch breaks and heated milk for Naomi's cereal. Hot milk with cereal was the latest fad. Next week it would undoubtedly be yogurt.

Naomi, pretty in her blue school uniform with her long hair held back in a girlish headband decorated with tiny flowers, ate her breakfast daintily, one hand patting Oscar's soft head. Jason arrived in the kitchen five minutes before they were due to leave and wolfed down cereal and a piece of toast, cramming his food into his mouth without looking, engrossed in a computer magazine.

Leaving them to it, Lizzie went up to her and Scott's bedroom to collect her things. She did no more than glance at herself in the mirror. Looking at your reflection when you hadn't had time to wash your hair that morning was too depressing, she felt. When it was freshly washed and blow-dried, her shoulder-length chestnut hair swung glossily. But she'd been too tired to dry it this morning and it would look terrible and limp all day. Lizzie wanted her hair to be to blame for the way she felt. She didn't dare think that the two pounds she'd put on that weekend (two to add to the stone by which she was already overweight) were responsible for making her feel about as alluring as a sumo wrestler. It was her hair's fault. She coiled it into a knot and promised herself she'd stick on a bit of make-up in the car. Grabbing her coat in case of April showers and her huge, bulging shoulder bag, she yelled at the kids:

275

'Let's go.'

She was holding the door open when she spotted the note Scott had hurriedly scribbled when he'd left the house at six that morning. 'Back late, don't wait up.'

Lizzie scrunched it up. Perfect. That would make it the sixth week-night in two weeks where Scott had been home after eleven o'clock. Marrying a plumber meant you never set eyes on your husband. She might write in to a women's magazine helpful hints section with that information: *How to avoid ever seeing your annoying spouse: make sure you marry a plumber. He'll spend all day thrilling other women with his handsome, flirty face and dazzling them with his ability with a monkey wrench, and no time at all with you. Perfect for the woman who doesn't want any affection in her life.*

'Kids!' roared Lizzie more loudly. 'Get a move on.'

The traffic had been bad but not bad enough to give Lizzie the chance to apply a bit of eyeshadow or lipstick in the traffic jam. So when she ran from the car park towards the imposing office block that housed Oak Leaf Life Assurance Inc, she was still barefaced, panting and only just on time, so there'd be no chance to slope off to the canteen to get a quick latte.

She nearly tripped over a bit of scaffolding from the building site next door. A gang of builders on their first tea break of the day watched her impassively. Nobody whistled or called out to her.

Nobody whistles at frumpy forty-year-olds, she thought miserably as she climbed the front steps to the office, conveniently forgetting that she used to hate builders catcalling when she was younger, slimmer and more confident. With slinky clothes showing off her curvy figure and plenty of mascara setting off glinting blue eyes, Lizzie had made more than one builder get the cement-to-sand ratio wrong over the years.

'Good weekend?' asked her friend, Margaret, as Lizzie swung herself into her seat on the fourth floor and booted up her computer.

Lizzie typed her password in with more force than was strictly required.

'Don't ask. Scott was gone most of the time. Working, he says. I don't know. If he's not playing soccer, he's round his mate's house watching Sky Sports. I mean, I never see him these days.'

'Oh,' said Margaret. 'I understand. I've been in since seven thirty and have done loads, so I'm going to get a coffee. Will I get you one too?'

Lizzie smiled for what felt like the first time that day. 'You're a lifesaver, Mags. What would I do without you?'

'Die from caffeine-withdrawal symptoms,' Margaret joked.

As Margaret headed off to the lifts, Lizzie berated herself for being ungrateful with her lot. She had a husband and kids, after all. Poor Margaret was childless, recently divorced, and so keen to get out of her house after a lonely weekend that she was always in the office hours early on Monday mornings. She'd have loved to have kids and dogs running around, even dogs who pooped all over brand-new 75 per cent woollen rugs. Feeling guilty, Lizzie attacked the pile of work she had to get through today.

Her e-mails were the usual litany of problems: a woman in the Donegal office was irate because one of her policy-holders had been overcharged for a year and still hadn't received either an apology or back payment. Some new guy working in the Galway office had sent an e-mail saying hello. It was an amusing e-mail, really, much more chatty than the usual ones she received.

Nick, that was the new guy's name, sounded upbeat and good fun in an endearingly youthful way. He ended his e-mail by saying: 'Do the Oak Leaf people ever get together for parties? It'd be nice to meet some colleagues. I feel like the youngest person in this office. The rest of them are about a hundred!'

Laughing, because she'd met all the Galway people and they were anything but staid, Lizzie pressed 'Reply' but with her fingers poised over the keyboard, she hesitated.

She thought of the sort of e-mail she would have written when she was twenty-something, as Nick clearly was. Oh, why not, she thought.

Yeah, sure. You're obviously the life and soul of the party, Nick, like me. Well, us youngsters aren't well catered for in Oak Leaf. I mean, they complain when I get in late on Mondays because I've been out all weekend clubbing. But what can you do? A girl's got to earn a living somehow. Now, if you're taking over from Elaine, we better discuss business or we'll both be fired.
Lizzie

Scott didn't get home until half twelve that night. Lizzie woke up when Oscar started barking frantically, but she was still too sleepy for conversation when Scott slipped into the bed beside her.

'Hello,' she muttered, burying herself further under the duvet. Within minutes Scott was snoring. Typically, Lizzie was now somehow wide awake. She lay seething in wakefulness and watched the alarm clock digits slowly reach two before she fell into an uneasy sleep.

When she dragged herself out of bed at seven, Scott was gone and she felt and looked like a zombie. Her hair would have to go another day without washing.

Nick in Galway was much perkier this morning.

> Nice to meet someone my age. You sound like a bit of a babe, Lizzie. Any chance of you coming to Galway for some 'work'? I bet I'm just your type: twenty-nine, athletic and single.

Lizzie blushed as she read his e-mail. She hadn't meant hers to sound quite so flirty, but she could see that she had. Nick now thought she was his age, a youngster who liked clubbing, instead of a woman who had stopped buying bikini knickers because the big, full briefs held her backside in better.

She was about to e-mail back sternly, telling him she wasn't what he thought. But something changed her mind. What the hell, she thought irrepressibly. It was only a bit of harmless fun, after all.

Bit risky calling me a babe, isn't it? You never know what people are like until you meet them, she typed. I could be some boring, married old dear who lives in thermal vests and woolly tights, for all you know.

Nick answered back quickly. Yeah, but I can tell you're not.

Slow down, Tiger, Lizzie wrote, her eyes sparkling. A guilty thrill whizzed around inside her: she shouldn't be doing this, but it was fun. Nick fancied her. It was nice that *someone* still did. Anyway, nobody need ever know. It was all utterly harmless after all.

'I'm going on a diet, Mags,' Lizzie announced. 'I've got to lose some weight or I'll never be able to fit into any of my summer clothes.'

'We both said that last month,' Mags said gloomily, halfway through an apple Danish.

'This time I mean it,' Lizzie said firmly. She could hardly pretend to be a hot young thing if she didn't make a bit of an effort, after all.

Scott worked late for most of April, but Lizzie didn't nag him about it. Instead, she went for a power walk every evening, striding out for three energetic miles with a delighted Oscar. Tired from the exercise, she fell into bed each night and was fast asleep by half ten, usually an hour before Scott arrived home. She got her hair cut, too; a sharper, chin-length cut that was easier to manage in the mornings and somehow made her look younger. She dyed her eyelashes at home one Saturday and Margaret remarked that it was amazing how much difference it made to Lizzie's beautiful eyes.

'You don't have to bother with mascara,' Lizzie explained, although she did bother these days.

By May, she'd lost seven pounds, had toned up and regained the spring in her step.

'It's not just losing weight that matters,' she told Margaret. 'I feel better, livelier, more in control of my life.' She didn't voice the feeling that having a long-distance admirer had something to do with it. Because it wasn't really about Nick.

One morning, he wrote that he was going to Morocco with some pals for two weeks and Lizzie gaily replied that she and the girls were thinking of spending two weeks in an apartment in Ibiza in June.

I don't know if the local lads will cope with us, she wrote. Five prime specimens of Irish girlhood launching ourselves on them.

Nick replied wistfully: Sounds great. Any room for a bloke on this trip?

At lunchtime, Lizzie raced into the city centre to go shopping. It was Naomi's birthday the following week and she'd said what she really wanted was a voucher for Planet TweenGirl, a trendy new shop full of adorable little T-shirts and cotton dresses with flowers embroidered all over the place. When Lizzie sprinted back to the office with the voucher, hair flying and her flirty pink linen skirt riding up firm thighs as she ran, the builders next door went on red alert.

'Come in here, darlin',' one shrieked. 'You'd make an old man very happy.'

'Forget him,' shouted another. 'I'm your man.'

Lizzie laughed and blew them a kiss. Men, huh.

In June, Nick sadly told her he was going to work for another company. Guess we'll never meet up now, Babe, he wrote. Pity, we could have had such fun together.

Lizzie was sad he was going. He'd meant a lot to her, more than he would ever know.

It's been great, she wrote. But life goes on, Nick. Meeting would have ruined it all. Take care of yourself.

She felt a smidgen of remorse as she pressed the 'Send' button, but it was only a smidgen. Nick had been fun; better than Prozac, that was for sure. His long-distance admiration had given her back her zest for life. It was weird, she knew, but having someone to flirt with in that cybernet way had been what she'd needed. A pick-me-up. Something to remind her that she was more than a mum and a wife. She was a person, maybe even a babe. She had a husband she loved and kids she adored, but she was still a person someone could fancy.

That weekend, Scott's mother came to babysit while he took her out to dinner. He had special news for her, he said.

Lizzie, looking healthy and glamorous in a slinky grey dress she hadn't worn for years, thought how exhausted the poor man was looking. His handsome face was pale because he never had a moment to enjoy the sun and he looked older than his forty-two years. Poor darling, she thought, stroking his hand across the dinner table. He needed a break.

'I know I've been working really hard and that it's been tough on all of us, particularly you, love.' He looked searchingly at Lizzie. 'I wanted to keep this a surprise until I knew for definite that I could afford it, but I've been trying to earn some extra cash because the guys at work want to buy a holiday cottage in France and I needed my share of the money. But,' he hesitated, 'only if you think it's a good idea,

Lizzie. I'm sorry for keeping it a secret, but I didn't want to get your hopes up until I knew I could manage it . . .' His voice trailed off, unsure.

Lizzie took both his hands in hers and smiled a heartfelt smile. 'I love you,' she said, 'and I think it's a wonderful idea.'

Margaret had a copy of the company newsletter and was looking through the gossip section at the back where photos of company parties were usually printed. 'There's a picture of that nice bloke you know in Galway,' she told Lizzie. 'It was his leaving do. They hired a kissagram, according to this.'

Lizzie peered over Margaret's shoulder at the photo. Looking mildly drunk and very happy, the Galway office crew were scrunched up beside a bar, all waving glasses or balloons. Lizzie looked carefully for Nick. She recognised everybody apart from one person: a portly, shiny-faced guy in his late thirties who'd clearly lost the battle to keep his hair and had long since given up the fight to keep his waist-line. Beaming at the camera, he had one hand around a full pint of Guinness and the other round a girl dressed as a policewoman with most un-police-like fishnet stockings.

Lizzie scanned the caption. There it was in black and white. The handsome, young, lively Nick was really a sweet-faced, thirty-something bloke.

'Funny,' she said smiling, 'that's just how I pictured him.'

Thelma, Louise
and the Lurve Gods

The taxi driver thought Becky was a bit of all right.

'Got any room for me in your rucksack, love?' he said, turning to wink at us and showing an expanse of nicotine-stained teeth. As if a twenty-nine-year-old blonde babe would be even vaguely interested in some fat slob who'd never see fifty again and who had the remains of his breakfast on his beard.

Becky gave him her 'drop dead, moron' look, a fierce glare which usually made even the cockiest bloke gulp and start examining his cuticles. Not this bloke. Mr Missing Link just grinned even more.

'Bet your friend isn't so choosy,' he said eagerly, giving me the eye.

It was the story of my life. Guys who'd been given the cold shoulder by Becky Hill (twice voted 'girl most likely to succeed' in St Mark's Community School) always assumed that her not-so-stunning red-headed friend would be sufficiently desperate for male company that she'd give them a mercy snog. Whoever said there were advantages to being best friend with a supermodel lookalike was wrong.

'I like a girl with meat on her,' slobbered the driver, admiring the size-12 denim shirt I was bursting out of in the hopes that I looked a bit like either Thelma or Louise.

Becky's blue eyes narrowed to deadly slits. I recognised that look. Missing Link didn't.

'OmiGod!' she roared. 'I think I'm going to be sick. Please stop the cab!'

The thought of having his sticky, filthy upholstery made even more sticky and filthy prompted Missing Link to slam the brakes on faster than Michael Schumacher on the chicane at Monaco.

Becky winked at me. 'Ready, Suze?' she whispered.

I nodded. Once the car was stopped, we dived out, clutching our rucksacks and running away.

'Oi, come back here!' yelled the outraged taxi driver. 'You owe me money!'

'He catches on fast,' giggled Becky as we risked life and limb by running across the road, on to the central reservation, and then over to the other side.

'It'll take him at least five minutes to get up to the next junction and come back,' she crowed as the taxi driver waved his fist at us menacingly from the other side of the road.

'I'll get you little bitches!' he roared.

'Oh yeah? We'll report you to the police as a pervert first!' Becky roared back.

At that precise moment, a clean and respectable taxi, as opposed to Missing Link's ramshackle Cortina, cruised along.

Becky flicked back her long, streaky blonde hair, angled one tiny black-leather-clad hip forward and gave the piercing wolf whistle she'd mastered at the age of twelve. The taxi backed up.

Of course, if it had been me, no taxi would have appeared and I'd have been stuck on the Shannon airport road for another half an hour until the Missing Link man turned up with the police and had me arrested for non-payment of my fare. Then again, if it had been just me, I wouldn't have got out of the original taxi in the first place and would have endured drooling sexual harassment all the way to the airport. But that was the difference between me and Becky.

Becky grabbed Life by the throat and shook it: I was the sort of woman who'd politely ask Life if it minded me breathing.

The airport was jammed with harassed families manoeuvring over-packed luggage trolleys around and trying to hold on to Granny, a couple of toddlers, and the bag with all the nappies in it. Your average pre-holiday hell.

Becky and I grinned at each other in delight. Our holiday was going to be a million miles away from that. We weren't going to be ordinary tourists – we were going to be travellers for twenty-one glorious days. Forget a week in Benidorm, or a fortnight in Greece with nothing more thrilling to look forward to than which sun lounger to lie on. We were trendy travellers who wouldn't be seen dead in a touristy joint and shunned the idea of comfortable, normal travel. We were Stateside Twenty-Oners.

In case you haven't heard of this, I'll explain. Unlike your average holiday, a Stateside Twenty-One holiday is a trip into the unexpected: twenty-one days in the US where the travellers are given a car, a map, hotel vouchers and a designated final airport from which, twenty-one days later, they're flown home. Some people fly into Los Angeles and their meeting point is Denver. Others go for New York with Atlanta as the final destination, which was what we were doing.

It had been my idea to sign up for the trip. When I'd read the piece on the Internet about the cool new way to experience the buzz of travel without spending months away, my pulse raced. This was just what I was looking for. A one-woman odyssey into the heart of America where I would be my own boss, travelling at my own pace through the recesses of the country where the tour buses never reached. All this with the added safety factor that there were five hotels on the tour that we had to use on each scheduled trip. So people would be keeping an eye out for me and if I was kidnapped by a serial killer, Mum and Dad would soon hear about it and I'd be rescued, preferably by some hunky FBI person with big muscles and a gun. Or would it be CIA? I can never remember.

Anyway, this trip was the answer to my dreams: my dreams being how to get out of my BORING life.

Boring is the only way to describe being the telesales manager in a double-glazing firm in Limerick. Mind you, since Paul and I got disengaged (my mother hates when I say that, but how else are you supposed to say it? 'We've broken it off' sounds like something painful that involves a sudden snapping noise and male howls of agony) I am slightly less boring.

Because being the sedate, double-glazing telesales manager

fiancée of a bank official has got to be up there at the top of the Boring-ometer. I think there's got to be some kudos about a broken engagement; a sort of mysterious, tragic thing in a Marlene Dietrich way. Me, heavy-lidded in a cocktail bar somewhere with a handsome man gazing deep into my eyes as I twirl the olive in my martini and languidly purr: *There was a man, long ago, a man I thought I could marry.* Sorry, daydreaming again. My mother said it'll be the end of me.

'You're always in a fantasy world, Suzanne,' she says in a worried voice. 'You want to spend more time in the real world, love, for your own sake.'

If you ask me, the real world is not all it's cracked up to be. Give me Fantasy World with Jake Gyllenhaal any day.

In the real world, Paul and I had the house (a two-bedroomed townhouse), the beige three-seater with two armchairs (complete with fabric protector in case of stains), the savings plan, and the wedding booked for next summer. We were *that* organised. Even our sock drawers had those divider things in them so that Paul's fawn argyle socks wouldn't dare get squashed up beside his best black ones. Our holiday plans never varied from two weeks somewhere hot that wasn't more than four hours' flight away (Paul hates flying), and our idea of total, untrammelled excitement was not having a Chinese takeaway on Friday nights but – shock, horror – having a pizza instead.

Do you see where this is going? Yes, Boring City. So when Paul and I parted mutually (this is what we've told everyone because he's so sorry for what happened and promised never to reveal anything about his one-night stand with that slut in New Accounts. If he does, he can kiss goodbye to his share of the money from selling the furniture), I moved home to my family and decided a holiday was in order. Not a two-weeks-anywhere holiday, but something exotic to wrench me out of being dull as a dodo. An adventure.

'An adventure!' yelled Becky over the phone when I told her about my plans. Becky has nearly burst my eardrums on several occasions. She says it's her job and that she's always yelling because she has to talk to clients on mobile phones in bad signal areas. She's a booker in a model agency, the same agency which couldn't hire her as a model because they told her that sadly she didn't have what it took to be a photographic or a catwalk model. I and most of the men on the planet think that Becky has just what it takes, but she's remarkably OK about it all and says that she just didn't photograph right.

She photographs better than me. I'm five foot four, built along curvy lines (which is shorthand for saying that I'll never need one of Marks & Spencer's padded bras but am an ideal candidate for their tummy-flattening knickers) and have the sort of Celtic complexion that looks great on glamorous, misty-eyed women in adverts for Ireland but not so good on anyone with less visible bone structure. My hair is my best bit, I suppose: long, wavy and the colour of molten bronze, as my father says fondly.

Well, Becky said she was boring too. How can she think that when she was going to wild model parties every night of the week during those years when I was stuck at home with Paul, circling interesting documentaries in the TV guide? Anyway, she was determined to go with me.

'We could be like Thelma and Louise in a soft-top sports car,' she said excitedly.

'I think it'll be more on the lines of a jeep thing,' I pointed out, in case she started getting too carried away with visions of the two of us belting down the Interstate in a blue Thunderbird with the wind in our hair.

Becky grinned. 'Suze, you've got to have a spirit of adventure,' she said.

She was right. Thelma and Louise it was. Which is how we ended up in the airport with rucksacks filled with denim garments, with me wearing lots of silver jewellery like Susan Sarandon, ready to board the flight to New York.

I spotted them first: two gorgeous guys alone amid the throngs of couples and families. They were stocking up on magazines in the bookshop, talking and laughing and generally having the sort of great time you have when you're among the world's top ten per cent of hunks. One of them had cheekbones you'd cut yourself on. Dark-haired, melting dark eyes, with a bod to die for. You know the sort of thing: big shoulders and proper biceps that stick out all the time and not just when he flexes them in desperation (like Paul's). His friend was taller, leaner and a paler version: the same cheekbones and the same bone structure but with chestnut collar-length hair and a lop-sided, sexy grin. He looked like the clever one; it was the intelligent glint in those expressive eyes. Brothers or cousins, definitely.

Being me, I turned away and looked at my watch again. I was off men, for understandable reasons.

Then Becky spotted them. She's very good at spotting blokes. She claims it's because she's on the lookout for possible male models for the agency, but I know it's because she has an insatiable hunger for men. I used to have an insatiable hunger for men too, but when I met Paul, I stopped looking, naturally. When Paul had his fling with that slapper, the only insatiable hunger I was left with was for Mars Bar ice creams, which are not good for your backside on a long-term basis.

'Suze,' she hissed, 'get a look at those two guys.'

'Cute,' I said dismissively.

'They're not cute, they're lurve gods,' she drooled. She was just starting to sashay over to them when our flight was called.

'We better board,' I fussed, stopping her mid-sashay. Becky never bothered being on time for things but I did.

'You're worse than my mother, Suze,' she grumbled, but she followed me all the same. 'There'll be loads of time for men in America,' I said consolingly.

On the plane, Becky picked at her meal (the secret of staying thin, obviously), drank two Bacardis and fell asleep, while I ate every last forkful of my meal, had my dessert, her dessert, drank two little bottles of wine, watched two films, half-finished a detective novel, and wondered if I'd ever want anything to do with a man again.

'Suzanne, there's plenty more fish in the sea,' my mother said stoically when I arrived home after the break-up, complete with four suitcases and a face swollen from crying. 'I admire you so much for deciding that you'd made a mistake. In my day, we'd have been too scared to end an engagement. Modern women know their minds and that's great.'

I burst into tears again, wishing I could tell her what had really happened, but not wanting to humiliate myself by doing so. The party line was that we'd decided to take a break. I couldn't, just couldn't, tell anyone except Becky that Paul had cheated on me.

Mum hugged me and then made me tea and toast with honey, my favourite comfort food when I was a teenager. We went through a lot of honey when I was a teenager. 'You'll be back in the dating game in no time,' Mum assured me.

'I don't want to be,' I sobbed. 'I hate men. They're all bastards.'

'I know. But, sure, they have their uses,' Mum said kindly. 'Look at your father. He did a great job putting up those shelves in the kitchen, didn't he?'

That was a month ago. The house Paul and I had bought was up for sale, I was still in my old bedroom at home (there wasn't much room for me there, actually, seeing as it was full of things from the house; Paul was not getting his hands on the CD player and speakers I'd spent a year paying off) and Paul had phoned me four times in the last week begging me to reconsider.

'Hang up on him!' said Becky in outrage when I told her he'd had the temerity to call me at work. 'Tell him you'll nail his kneecaps to the floor if he bothers you again. No, better still, tell him *I'll* nail his kneecaps to the floor!'

Becky was very loyal and I suspected that nothing would give her greater pleasure than to nail any part of Paul's uptight anatomy to the floor. His knees would not be top of the list, either.

I felt a bit groggy and uncoordinated when we got to JFK. Becky was bright as a button thanks to five hours' sleep.

'Look!' she squealed in my ear as we emerged into the Arrivals hall and spotted the two lurve gods ahead of us.

'Those gorgeous guys. Maybe we should ditch our plans and just follow them.'

'Yeah right,' I grumbled. 'And forfeit all the money we've already paid for the holiday.'

'I thought you wanted an adventure,' Becky said.

'Not tonight,' I said. 'I want to climb into a nice hotel bed and fall asleep.'

Becky smirked. 'If we hitch up with those two blokes, there's no reason why hotel beds can't be involved.'

After a certain amount of grumbling as we dragged our rucksacks along, we finally made it to the Stateside Twenty-One office, which was close to all the rental car agencies. There were lots of those sports utility jeep things around. Becky was a little miserable to see no sign of any Thelma and Louise-type sports cars.

'I'd hoped we could do a deal and maybe upgrade to something sexy and sporty,' she said as we hauled our luggage up the steps. 'I really wanted to feel the wind in my hair as we drive through Utah.'

'You can hang your head out the window like a dog,' I suggested. I *was* tired.

Inside the office, a bored-looking young woman was sitting behind a high counter, chewing gum and talking at the same time. Guess who she was talking to? Yes, our lurve gods. Beside me, I could feel Becky adopting her model pose of stomach in, boobs out. My stomach was already painfully in thanks to my too-tight jeans and my boobs always stick out, so no action was required on my part.

'Hi,' Becky said throatily to the guys.

Both lurve gods smiled, displaying lovely teeth. I'd been

wrong with my previous assessment: they weren't in the top ten per cent of hunks, they were definitely in the top five.

'Are you Suzanne O'Reilly?' the girl behind the counter asked Becky, not bothering with the whole 'hello' business.

'No, *I* am,' I said.

'Now you're all here, we can process your tickets,' the girl said.

'Now we're all here?' I repeated. 'What do you mean?'

'There's four people to every sports utility vehicle,' she said, as if she was talking to a moron.

'Four people?' I repeated, probably intentionally making it look as if I *was* a moron.

'Yeah, four people to every vehicle,' said the taller, and to my taste, sexier lurve god. The one with the glinting, intelligent eyes. He did not sound pleased. 'It's in the small print apparently. We thought we got our own car, but it seems that we're sharing with you two.'

Becky's face grew radiant.

'Great. Hey, it'll be fun,' she beamed at the other lurve god with an unmistakable I've-just-won-the-lottery smile. 'I'm Becky Hill.'

'I'm Tony Stewart,' he said, also with an I've-just-won-the-lottery smile. 'And this is Liam, my cousin.'

Liam didn't look too pleased, probably because it was obvious that Becky fancied Tony, which left him with me. The expression of irritation on his face was the sort of look that's not good for a girl's morale.

'There must be some other way of sorting this out,' I said to the girl behind the counter in my firm but confident voice, a skill which I have honed over two years as the telesales manager. A managerial tone of voice is very important, as they told us on the management training course. 'I'm afraid this isn't satisfactory. We were led to understand that we got our own vehicle and, if this isn't the case, then your company is guilty of misrepresentation, which is illegal. If you don't have the authority to sort this out, we'll need to speak to the manager or whoever is in charge.'

The girl looked as if she couldn't give two damns either way. She kept chewing. A dentist with a loaded drill couldn't have got the gum out of her mouth. 'It's like, seven o'clock on Saturday, like, there's nobody to talk to. If you wanna complain, you'll have to wait for Monday.'

I dragged Becky away from batting her eyelashes at Tony and we went outside for a confab.

'This is terrible,' I said. 'I vote we stay in New York until Monday and come back and get this sorted out then.'

'Suze,' Becky wailed, 'it'll be fun. Think of the adventure we can have with them. It'll be much more fun with four of us.'

'No way, Becky,' I said.

Becky gave me a poke in the ribs that winded me. 'It'll be fun,' she said, between gritted teeth. 'Please, pretty please. We haven't got any choice, Suze, we're stuck with them.'

She was right. I felt like crying. My dreams were going up in smoke. Instead of a male-free holiday where I could wash Paul out of my hair, I was going to have to spend three whole weeks with two strange guys, both of whom had drooled over Becky as if she was Cindy Crawford's better-looking sister. Nobody was looking at me. Mind you, denims always make my backside look enormous. It was going to

295

be like being fourteen all over again. Me, Miss Wallflower at discos despite all my best efforts at looking cool, and Becky with boys clustering around her in the manner of bees and a honey pot.

'Cheer up, Suze,' Becky pleaded.

How could I cheer up when I could see through the glass doors to where Liam was gesticulating wildly at his cousin, obviously making the point that there was no way in hell he was going to end up stuck with me the entire holiday. I could even imagine the conversation: 'Forget it. You get the good-looking one and I get the short, ugly one. No deal.'

Iron entered my soul. Tough bananas. He was going to be stuck with me.

We went back in. 'You better record our complaints,' I said to the girl behind the counter. 'I'm getting a discount when this is over, I promise you.'

She gave me a look that said this was pretty unlikely. 'Sign here.'

It took an hour and a half to get to the New Jersey town where Tony had read about this 'cool hotel Bon Jovi goes to'. I sourly pointed out that any hotel where rich rock stars congregated was going to be a bit out of our price range, but he and Becky chorused, 'Lighten up, Suze!'

'Fine,' I said tightly.

Liam, who was driving, looked just as irritated as I did. I was sitting in the front of the utility vehicle, while the love birds were sitting in the back, bonding. Liam and I were not bonding.

Via Tony, I discovered that they worked together in the

296

family business estate agency and lived in Dublin. Tony was the younger at the age of twenty-eight, while Liam was thirty. Tony's sister, a trainee travel agent, had booked the holiday for them.

'If I'd booked it, I'd have realised we'd have to share a car,' Liam said grimly, 'and we'd have booked another holiday instead.'

Charming. For a good-looking guy with a movie-star profile and lovely long fingers that rested lightly on the steering wheel, Liam could be a total pain in the ass. He had really long legs too, I noticed, legs that looked pretty good in soft canvas jeans, not that I cared.

'But isn't it fun that it's worked out this way?' Becky said happily.

When we got to the Bon Jovi hotel, I asked Tony where he'd read the crucial bit of information that led him to believe it was a nice place.

'In a magazine,' he said, staring at the seedy one-storey building with delight.

'Was it a very old, out-of-date magazine?' I knew I was being a bitch but I couldn't help it. We'd driven ages off the main beaten track to find this place and now that we were there, I realised it looked like the sort of premises that even cockroaches would boycott.

The only good news was that it was cheap. That was the deciding factor. None of us had money to spare and we were all ready to stop somewhere for the night, so we checked in.

'Let's all go for something to eat,' said Becky enthusiastically as soon as we'd dropped our rucksacks on the twin beds in our crummy room.

'The only place I'm going is to bed,' I said, inspecting the sheets for wildlife. It was that sort of place.

'Spoilsport,' she said.

'Trollop,' I answered. 'Wake me in the morning.'

It took Tony and Becky until the second night on the road to reach first base. Beautiful people live their lives faster – or at least that's the conclusion I had come to.

We'd driven to Atlantic City and found a small, pretty motel that we all liked the look of because it was fake fifties. Our room was full of veneer, had frilly curtains, a double bed with ice-pink covers and a squashy purple couch that could have come straight off the *Happy Days* set.

Dinner was in a steakhouse down the road where there was a beer promotion. By the end of the night, none of us could remember how many dollars a giant jug of beer was, but we got through two jugs before we ran out of budget. Booze was certainly easing the tension between us all. Well, the tension between me and Liam, actually. Becky and Tony were about as tense as a couple of carefree teenagers and could be heard screaming with laughter as we all walked home: them arm in arm, myself and Liam walking about a yard apart. When the other pair started running hysterically back to the motel, Liam and I kept walking along in not-very-companionable silence.

I wasn't surprised when I opened our door and found no sign of Becky. She was clearly in Tony and Liam's room. Well, if they wanted a ménage à trois, that was their business. I switched on the TV and was trying to find something to watch from the zillions of cable channels, when there was a knock at my door.

Liam, rangy and vexed-looking, stood on the threshold. 'Can I come in?' he asked.

'Don't tell me,' I said, letting him in. 'Live sex show in your room?'

'Something like that.'

The *Happy Days* couch was quite small really and when we both sat on it, we were quite close together. I kept stealing glances at Liam's profile, wondering if I was so horrible looking that he couldn't be bothered even making a move on me. Not that I wanted him to or anything. But if he tried to chat me up, I'd have the satisfaction of telling him that I had taken a vow of chastity and would never look at a man again. Or something like that.

At half twelve, I said I was shattered and was going to bed.

'Can I stay?' he muttered, eyes glued to the TV.

I nodded.

'I'll sleep on the couch if you'd prefer me not to use the bed.' He looked wary.

Thanks, I thought. Obviously I was so repulsive he preferred to be as far away from me as possible.

'Sleep on the bed,' I snapped. 'I'm not expecting you to hop on me in the middle of the night.' Chance would be a fine thing.

I woke up next morning and rolled over to see Liam lying on his back, half-covered by the pink bedspread. Either he'd been away somewhere hot recently or he used sunbeds, but his body, his perfectly sculpted, ripped body, was a golden caramel colour. Wow. He sure was gorgeous.

I gazed longingly at the hard, muscled shoulders and at

the taut six-pack stomach. I thought briefly of Paul's untoned belly and how he used to drool all over the pillows at night. Liam was not the sort of person to drool. In fact, the only person around here who was drooling was me. I clambered out of bed and threw myself into the shower. It didn't help.

Even when I closed my eyes, I could still see Liam in all his gorgeousness. There was no doubt about it: somewhere inside me, the anti-men icicle had melted. How typical that I'd start getting over Paul with a man who clearly wouldn't touch me with a bargepole.

I dressed in the bathroom, averted my eyes as I walked past the sleeping Liam, and then marched over to the other motel room.

'Let's all get up and get going,' I yelled, sounding like a holiday camp rep with a lust for power.

We soon got into a routine. We booked three rooms every night: one for me, one for Liam and one for Becky and Tony, who couldn't keep their hands off each other. Every morning, we'd have breakfast together and plan the day's driving. We wanted to see Kentucky, Tennessee and go to Memphis, obviously. We were all keen to visit Graceland and see just how madly tacky it all was. Then, it was down to New Orleans, over to Houston (Liam was eager to visit the NASA space centre) and finally, back up to Atlanta. Or at least, that was the plan. We had lots of conversations about how we were going to do all this because there was a lot of driving involved. Well, Liam and I had long conversations about how we were going to do all this, because the other pair were too deeply in lust to think about anything else. Every day when we reached our destination, Liam and I set off sightseeing while Tony and Becky slammed their hotel-room door and did their own personal sightseeing.

'They're missing everything,' I said to Liam one evening. We had walked around downtown Nashville and found ourselves in a little club where you could dance and listen to lively country music all night.

'Yeah,' he said, surprising me by pulling me on to the dance floor to join all the cowboy-boot-wearing dancers. 'It's their own loss. We might as well enjoy ourselves, Suze.'

And we did.

Liam and I started a diary which we wrote up every morning.

We'd sit side by side and laugh as we wrote our own versions of the previous day. Tony and Becky were so late getting out of bed, that we had normally finished our breakfast by the time they joined us.

I had great fun teasing Liam by writing descriptions of our various budget motels in what I called 'estate-agent speak'.

'Let's see,' I said the first morning in Memphis as we sat in a pancake house waiting for our giant breakfasts to arrive. 'Compact and simple accommodation with a comforting police presence.'

Liam laughed uproariously. 'Don't forget to write that the police presence is due to the fact that the area is so bad, the cops have to drive past twenty times a night.'

I giggled. 'The decor is Zen-like.'

Liam laughed again. I loved hearing him laugh. When he did, his face crinkled up in a sexy sort of way and he looked utterly adorable. 'What do you mean, Zen-like?' he asked.

'You should say that there's no furniture in the room apart from the beds, which are probably glued to the floor.'

'I thought estate agents needed to be inventive,' I teased.

'Not that inventive. You sure have a great imagination, Suze.'

Breakfast arrived.

'I'll never get used to these portions,' I sighed, looking at the huge plate in front of me. 'I'll look like a hippo by the time we get home.'

'You look great,' Liam said with his mouth full. He smiled at me before turning his attention back to pancakes the size of dinner plates.

In between bites, he started talking about what we were going to do that day, but I wasn't listening really. I was in a daze thinking about Liam saying I looked great. Granted, I'd got a bit of a tan and it made me look healthy and glowing. And now that I'd made friends with Liam, I was relaxed enough to abandon the big, floaty shirts that hid my bum and had started wearing my little strappy tops, which did suit me, I have to say. With my long hair rippling down my back and with my new American jeans slung low on my waist, I looked as good as I ever had before. But for someone as Grade A gorgeous as Liam to say so, well. That was something else.

There was no sign of Becky and Tony by the time we'd finished, so we walked back to the motel and knocked on their bedroom door.

Becky opened it. She was paler than I was, thanks to the fact that she and Tony spent far too much time in bed to actually get a tan.

'We're going to Graceland now,' I said. 'Are you guys coming?'

'Er no,' she said, and grinned at me.

I shrugged. Tony might not be the brightest bulb on the Christmas tree but he was obviously fantastic in the bedroom department.

Graceland was incredible. Even if you'd never been an Elvis fan, there was something very moving about seeing his house. It was sad too.

We felt a bit subdued after seeing the King's home, so we decided to head for Beale Street and have some fun. It was a bit touristy, we realised when we got there, the sort of place that had lost some of its character and was now just a must-see destination on the tourist map.

'It's like walking down a film set,' I said as we ambled down the street, drinking in the sights and listening to the mellow music coming from B. B. King's club.

'I know, but we'd be furious if we'd missed it,' Liam said.

That was exactly what I'd been thinking.

We found a tiny restaurant that advertised the best steaks in town and plonked ourselves in the corner. Liam ordered a steak that was so big we burst out laughing when it arrived.

'Y'all enjoy yourselves and ask me if you want anythin' else,' said the waitress with that lilting Memphis accent.

We smiled at each other. I loved America. Everyone was so nice and I was having so much fun. The only dark spot in the future was the fact that we only had seven more days to go and then it would be back to normal life, normal life without Liam, life where I dressed in boring office suits, placated irate customers over the phone and limited my chocolate biscuit intake to two a day.

'I might never wear a suit again,' I commented, stretching out my denimed legs and admiring my cowboy boots.

'It's funny, but the first day we met, I could just see you in a suit, all starched up and bossing people around,' Liam said, finally giving up on his huge steak. 'But not any more,' he added quickly. 'Now,' his eyes roamed over my curves, 'I can't imagine you all buttoned up at all. You're perfect as you are.'

I balled up my napkin and threw it at him. 'Stop it,' I said, embarrassed. 'You're such a big tease.' Well, he had to be teasing, didn't he?

New Orleans turned out to be my favourite place on that whole magical trip. Despite the devastation of Hurricane Katrina, the vibrant city was every bit as beautiful as I'd read about. I adored the atmospheric French Quarter with its overhanging lacy balconies, shutters and shady courtyards. Liam and I were like children as we rushed along, desperate to see everything. I insisted we visit a voodoo shop, although I was a bit nervous.

He laughed and squeezed my arm. 'I'll hold your hand, scaredy cat.'

We had sugary doughnuts in a café on Jackson Square, half because we were hungry and half because the combination of humidity and heat was so great that it was impossible to spend too long outdoors without rushing into a shop for a blast of air conditioning.

I'd never experienced such humidity before. My little white T-shirt was stuck to my body and Liam's wasn't much better.

The upshot of this was that we had to keep stopping for liquids. After trailing round Decatur and Chartres streets, we got out of the heat in a little bar off Dumaine and ordered two mint juleps, the traditional Southern drink.

Liam loved his but I hated mine. 'I thought it would be sweet,' I said with a grimace.

Liam smiled and ordered me a Long Island iced tea. 'I thought you were sweet enough already,' he said softly.

Afterwards, we wandered off looking for the voodoo shops. Before we found one, we came upon a little old Creole lady on a street corner with a sandwich board beside her proclaiming her skills as a seer.

'You want me to tell the pretty lady's fortune for ten dollars?' she asked.

'No,' I said, blushing.

'Yes,' said Liam with a grin.

He handed her the money and she took my hand in hers. I looked into her eyes and was disconcerted to see that she was blind, with the milky white pools of cataracts covering the iris.

'You have to make a choice,' she said softly to me. 'You have love. Don't waste time. Life's too short, chile.'

That was it. Liam thanked her and we walked off. I felt a bit dizzy what with the heat and what she'd said.

'You OK?' he asked.

I nodded. 'It's strange, what she said,' I mumbled. 'About a choice.'

'Do you think it's between me and your ex?' Liam asked.

I stared at him.

'Becky told me,' he admitted. 'I wanted to know why you were so hostile all the time.'

'I wasn't,' I protested. 'I didn't think you liked me and – '

He stopped and faced me, tracing the damp line of my collarbone lightly with his finger. My skin, already hot, burned. 'What made you think that?' he said, his voice as soft as a breeze.

'I don't know,' I said. 'I thought you preferred Becky. Everyone does.'

He sighed and gave me an exasperated look. 'Come on,' he said in a normal voice. 'Let's go back to the hotel and rest. We could sunbathe by the pool and come back here tonight for dinner. We've got less than a week left and I want to top up my tan before I go home.'

I felt cheated that the moment had been broken. It was my own fault for mentioning Becky. He liked me and I'd ruined it all by reminding him about her.

Back at the hotel, I put on my bikini, got my book and my sun lotion, and met Liam out by the pool.

He was sitting on a lounger with a can of beer and he looked moody.

'Hi,' I said shortly, doing my best not to look at that lean, brown body, naked but for khaki shorts. I rubbed sun lotion on my front and lay there for half an hour, brooding and feeling sorry for myself. Half an hour was long enough for one side, I decided, unless I wanted to go lobster red. I readjusted my sun lounger and took a surreptitious look at Liam. He looked as if he was asleep. Probably dreaming about Becky, I thought crossly.

I sat up and creamed the backs of my legs before trying to rub lotion on to my back.

Suddenly Liam appeared beside me.

'For God's sake, give me the bottle,' he said in exasperation. 'Lie down.'

Gulping, I lay on my front. 'I only need a tiny bit, you don't need to do my legs,' I bleated.

'You don't want to burn,' Liam said, his voice suddenly unsteady.

His hands felt warm and delicious, spreading the cream gently over my shoulders. It doesn't mean anything to him, I reminded myself miserably. It must be like rubbing sun lotion into his sister's back. Utterly platonic.

'Do you have a sister?' I asked.

'Sister?' he said, puzzled. 'No. I've only got brothers.' I could almost hear him smiling. 'I've never met anyone like you, Suze – your mind works in mysterious ways.'

His hands slid over my back, firm movements. Then I could feel him unfastening my bikini top.

'You don't need to . . .' I began.

'Hush,' he said, pulling the shoulder straps down. I obligingly raised my body and he whipped the bikini away. My heart was beating like a drum with excitement. I could hear Liam breathing more heavily, I could smell his aftershave, hot and lemony.

The slow rhythmic strokes slipped over my rib cage, circling and circling. His touch was exquisite, like finding someone who can play your body like a grand piano after years with someone who hammered away on it like they were playing on a wrecked old upright. Paul's fingers had never electrified me like Liam's did.

Suddenly, I couldn't take it any longer.

I turned over, clutching my towel to my chest, not caring

that he could see every untoned inch of me. His dark, handsome face was close to mine, his pupils large with desire as he stared longingly at me. It was the most erotic moment of my life. No, correction, that was when he moved to sit nearer to me on the lounger, and gently ran one finger along my collarbone, sending ripples down my spine.

'I wanted to do that from the first night I slept in your room,' he said huskily. 'You fell asleep and I watched you for ages.'

I could only stare at him.

'But I was convinced you liked Becky,' I began stupidly.

'I don't fancy Becky. I fancy you,' he said, his voice gentle. 'And you've got to stop thinking you're some sort of second-class citizen just because you hang around with her all the time. She's lovely, but so are you. I'm crazy about the way you bite your lips when you're thinking, I'm crazy about the way your hips sway when you walk, I'm crazy about those sexy little tops you wear. I'm just crazy about you.'

At that moment, I pulled him close and our lips met. I wanted to taste him, to devour him, and it seemed as if he wanted to do the same to me. Our bodies were pressed together and it suddenly occurred to me that we'd better leave the pool area or get arrested for lewd behaviour if my towel slipped.

'Shall we go upstairs?' I said, astonished at my own bravery.

He smiled. 'Absolutely. There are a lot of breathtaking sights I've wanted to explore for a long time.' He playfully twanged the elastic of my bikini bottoms as he spoke.

I grinned back and wrapped the towel around myself.

'Will this be the quick, budget five-minute tour or a long, drawn-out one?' I whispered.

'It's definitely going to take more than five minutes,' he promised.

I was back at work on Monday morning over a week later. Although my own world had shifted on its axis after the holiday, in the office, nothing had changed. My desk was still piled high with the same old queries; Pippa, the new junior, was still spending most of her time flirting with Evan, two desks away; and the air conditioning was still broken, making it a nightmare to work in the sultry August weather.

It was nearly lunchtime when Paul phoned me.

'Suzanne,' he said plaintively, 'I need to see you, please. We've made a terrible mistake.'

I said nothing. It was funny, you see, but I'd spent so long mentally telling Paul what a complete pig he was, that when I actually was talking to him, I'd run out of insults altogether. And besides which, you don't want to scream at your ex-fiancé when you're in the office. Not my office, anyway. Reuters doesn't have as efficient a news service as this place. One word from me about Paul's dalliance and I might as well have taken out an advert in the *Limerick Leader* telling all and sundry that he'd slept with a stick insect named Maura.

'Please talk to me,' Paul begged. 'You mean everything to me and it was all a big mistake. Since you've been away, I've missed you so much.' He paused for breath before starting again. 'Suzanne, we can't throw it all away. We have a house, a life together, a future, and a history. We've been through too much to end it all.'

309

'Yes, we have a history,' I agreed calmly. I'm used to sounding calm in the office.

It was all the encouragement he needed. 'Yes,' he repeated eagerly. 'We've been together so long, Suzanne, we can't ruin it for one meaningless fling. She meant nothing to me, it was a mistake, I never meant to hurt you, honestly. Please let's try again.' He sounded very convincing.

'You want to start again? I don't know, do you think we could? Would we just end up torturing each other over the past?' I asked him.

'I love you, I want to be with you,' he said frantically.

'We have to meet,' I said decisively. 'As soon as possible. We do need to talk.'

Even over the phone, I could hear Paul breathe a sigh of relief. I could just imagine him smiling. He had a lovely smile. It was the thing I liked most about him, the thing that other women admired. Paul wasn't tall or well built, but he was certainly attractive with Nordic blond hair and cool blue eyes.

We arranged to meet on Friday. Paul was eager to see me immediately, but I said no. Friday it would have to be.

I don't know how I got through the week. I thought about Paul a lot, naturally. Well, we'd spent years together and you can't throw all that away lightly, can you?

On Friday, at ten past six, we met up in The Den, a big modern pub near my office. Paul got the drinks and we sat down beside each other. He looked pale and tired, to be honest.

I took his hands in mine. He was smiling, those blue eyes were glinting with delight. I looked at his familiar face and at the blond hair I'd loved running my fingers through. I thought of how sweet he could be on weekend mornings when he'd sometimes bring me a cup of coffee in bed and we'd read the papers and chat. We'd been together since we were twenty, a lifetime. He'd been there for so many of the big things in my life: my graduation, my twenty-first, Granddad's funeral – you name it, we'd been there together. It had been perfect, until he'd ruined it all by sleeping with someone else.

'Will you marry me, Suzanne?' he said softly.

I smiled and kissed him gently on the cheek. He smelled of that musky, expensive aftershave I always bought him at Christmas. It cost a fortune. Last Christmas, he'd bought me bubble bath. Really cheap bubble bath and not the dear stuff I'd actually asked for.

'No, I won't marry you,' I said.

His face was a picture. Shock, astonishment and disbelief fought for control of his features. Disbelief won by a narrow margin.

'B-b-but you love me, Suzanne. You're heartbroken about me, I know you are,' he stammered.

'I *was*,' I corrected him. 'I got over you.'

Paul stared at me, shocked.

'I don't believe you,' he said. 'You're just trying to hurt me, to make up for my fling.'

'I'm not,' I said. 'I'm in love with someone else.'

'You're just saying that!' Paul raged. He was getting red-faced and angry now. Pale-skinned people can go amazingly red in the face. His eyes were no longer warm and kind: they were a strange combination of enraged and astonished.

Paul couldn't believe that I was turning him down. He'd thought that all he needed to do was snap his fingers and I'd come running. Well, it *had* worked in the past. But not this time. Things had changed. *I* had changed.

I got to my feet. 'I'm not just saying it,' I said kindly. 'It's true.'

I looked over to the bar where Liam was standing, looking ruggedly handsome in a very nice grey suit, his face anxious as if he was dying to rush in and punch Paul for daring to hurt a hair on my head. I smiled at Liam and he walked over. If Liam looked good in jeans, let me tell you, you've got to see him in a suit. Those big shoulders were made for Italian tailoring.

You see, I *had* thought about Paul a lot since he'd rung me. We'd been in love once and it had seemed like a good idea to get married. But not any more. I'd spent a whole week thinking of how he'd bossed me around, how we'd never gone anywhere thrilling for holidays, how he'd always picked what we watched on the telly. And then I thought about Liam, lovely Liam, who couldn't bear to be away from me and who was running up an enormous bill on his mobile, phoning me night and day. Sexy, funny Liam, who liked me for who I was rather than for the sort of person he could mould me into.

I suppose I forgot to mention how well Liam and I got on after New Orleans. Well, we had a lot of stuff to write in the diary, but we'd never have been able to show it to anyone else, so we left it out.

Paul's eyes nearly popped out of his head as he stared at Liam, my own personal Lurve God. He stood up, which was a mistake. Beside Liam, Paul looked scrawny and badly dressed. Liam also looked as if he could flatten Paul in a second, so Paul sat down again and took a deep slug of his beer.

'You can't be serious, Suzanne,' he said weakly, but I could tell his heart wasn't in it. He knew serious competition when he saw it.

I patted him on the arm. 'We'll talk about the house,' I said confidently. I took Liam's hand and we walked out of The Den. We were picking up Becky and Tony and the four of us were driving to Kinsale for the weekend. We wanted to get a move on to beat the traffic. You see, Liam and I were keen to do some sightseeing.

The Office Christmas Party

Five people wanted it to be fancy dress with everyone dressed up as elves or Santas or even Rudolf.

'I've got the ears and the nose and everything,' said Freddie, from the post department. 'The nose glows: it's got those tiny batteries in it, like the ones in watches.'

'Mrs Claus isn't sexy, though,' protested Mary, accounts. 'Why can't we do superheroes? I could be Catwoman.'

There was a moment's silence in the canteen of Kennedy Engineering as everyone pictured Mary in shiny PVC with a cat tail swinging behind her. Mary is one of those people who dresses with total disregard for their actual body shape or fashion. She wears what she wants and to hell with everyone. I envy her, to be honest. Mary always has a fleet of men after her. I do not.

Mrs Dineen, who runs the office catering and is dedicated to St Padre Pio, attempted to take charge. Mrs Dineen doesn't like talk about sex or anything close to it. A Christmas party with people in PVC catsuits would be Mrs Dineen's idea of the work of the Devil.

'Wheesh,' she said, fanning herself with her hand. 'We must remember what Christmas is all about.'

'Yeah: presents,' chirped in Fifi, who is on work experience in reception and has brightened up the place no end with her pink hair, graffitied nails and interesting belly-button jewellery.

'There'll be a lot less presents this year,' murmured Bianca to me.

Bianca and I both work in sales and although Kennedy Engineering are riding out the recession better than many companies, we've all been hit with cutbacks.

Last year's office party had been a shadow of previous events and had taken place in a big hall of a local pub with free drink for an hour, baskets of chips and sausages, and a karaoke machine for anyone who was in the mood. Bianca and I had sung 'Dancing Queen', as usual, and then we'd sat and talked for the rest of the evening. The end of year always makes me maudlin because it's inevitably a time for looking back, and looking back is depressing. I had achieved none of the great plans I'd made the previous New Year. I had not learned how to speak Italian, I hadn't checked out the Zumba class and even though I'd bought the sunshine yellow paint, I still hadn't painted the en suite bathroom in my one-bedroom apartment by the river.

After the party, I'd been home in bed by twelve and had read a thriller till two because I'd been to the library that lunchtime. Yes, I *am* a wild and crazy woman.

'Remember two years ago we went to Wexford for the

night?' said Seth, also sales, shortly to retire. 'Wasn't that a great night?'

Seth has become misty about the past now his time in Kennedy Engineering is coming to a close. He remembers us all sitting up in the Wexford hotel bar till three singing folk songs while Sive and Noel played the flute and bodhrán.

I remember little Ciara, newly hired, getting sick in the MD's wife's handbag, and subsequently sobbing in the ladies' about how she was going to be sacked, no matter how much I told her she wouldn't be. It's all about what you remember, isn't it?

That was a wonderful night, agreed everyone, including Bianca, who'd said it was boring at the time.

But Bianca is now in love and sees the world – especially the past – through an entirely different prism. This time last year, she was the same as me: permanently single, thirty-seven (our birthdays are a month apart) and bemoaning going to our parents' for Christmas *again*.

This year, she is living with a physiotherapist named Robert, they are engaged, trying for a baby and she is off wine, chocolate and carbohydrates.

I am still single, still like a glass of wine on a Friday night, and if it wasn't for carbohydrates and the lovely new HD television I got for my bedroom, I'd probably have gone completely mad. I wasn't even going to my parents' for Christmas this year. Although they'd never gone further than Portugal for a holiday before, this time they were going skiing.

'We've saved for a decent holiday for three years and we want to do something different this Christmas,' Mum had

316

told me months before. 'It's been your father's dream but we never had the money for it. People keep telling us that we're too old to learn. But you're never too old. And if I wreck my whatchamacallit ligament, well, there you go.'

'Cruciate ligament,' I said. Bianca's Robert liked to talk about his work.

'Whatever,' Mum said. 'Your father and I are a pair of old crocks anyway, so we might as well go out with a bang. And Larissa, I feel awful that you never get to do anything thrilling at Christmas because you're coming to see us. This year, you can do what you want!'

The irony was that I hadn't anything thrilling to do at all.

My brother, Roan, lives in New Zealand, so it wasn't an option to see him and his family over Christmas. Bianca and I might have once gone off somewhere, but now that she was in baby-making bliss with Robert, that wasn't an option either.

So far, the office Christmas party was about the most exciting thing I was going to be doing over the festive season, and if Mrs Dineen had her way, it would be a night of hymns in the canteen with a fruit scone and a cup of tea.

Suggestions were being flung around:

'Karaoke night.'

'Pub quiz in the Fiddler's Arms.'

I began to wonder if it would be all right to skip the Christmas party altogether and have another evening at home with my library books and whatever I'd recorded on the Sky box. But then, that was how I spent every other night. I didn't have loads of party invitations over Christmas. I rarely did. So many of my friends were now married with children, and people with small kids didn't want to go out at all. When they did go out, they fell asleep over the main course or else got pie-eyed on one gin and tonic due to sleep deprivation and had to be manhandled into a taxi at half past nine. No, whatever our Christmas party was, I'd have to make myself go.

Desmond Kennedy marched into the canteen. Desmond is the boss and he's a good boss because he's fair, doesn't get too grumpy, has been doing his best to keep us all in jobs despite the economic crunch and has a decent sense of humour.

He'd actually laughed when poor Ciara told him about getting sick into Moira's handbag.

'No, I wasn't laughing *at* you,' he said, patting her shoulder when Ciara burst into tears. 'I was laughing *with* you. Moira has shedloads of handbags. She loves them big banana-shaped ones and then she can't find a thing in them. 'Course you're not fired, you daft thing. Go on, back to work.'

Desmond had his announcement face on. I tensed because it could be bad news.

'We got the McCarthy contract!' Desmond yelled, and the whole place erupted.

It was a huge contract and would ensure Kennedy Engineering's security for several years to come. We'd hoped, but nobody had been totally sure.

Congratulations flowed, people hugged other people. Desmond stood there with a look of pure pride on his face.

'Can we have a decent Christmas party, then?' asked Seth.

'A night away!' squeaked Freddie. 'Fancy dress optional!'

*　　*　　*

318

Are there any words more quietly threatening than 'plus one' on an invitation? The answer is no, if you're a single woman. Single men can rock up with nobody and people don't look at them wondering if they have an extra toe or halitosis. But single women – it's a different story.

'Drive down with me and Robert,' insisted Bianca, when the venue was announced.

It was the Castle Hotel in Kilkenny, a large hotel built for conferences, and the party was to be held on a Friday, two weeks before Christmas. Desmond had organised two buses to transport us all, but lots of people were driving there themselves in order to turn the night into a weekend.

Bianca and Robert were clearly going to do the same. The day after the party, they were going to tour the city and stay another night.

'If they *let* us stay, after whatever devilment the rest of them get up to,' she added.

'It's a giant of a hotel,' I said, 'and if they're booking in seventy people plus partners for a Christmas party, they know what they're letting themselves in for. It's like a hen party with added madness. If anyone ends up in the fountain in their underpants with reindeer ears on, the hotel can only blame themselves.'

Plus one was the problem. I was plus nobody.

Two Fridays before Christmas, not a tap of work was being done in Kennedy Engineering. Discussions on dresses, lunchtime hair appointments and beating the rush-hour traffic to Kilkenny were the main topics among the female staff members in sales.

319

Corinna, who had three small children, the youngest being just a year old, worried if her mother-in-law would be able to mind them all.

'We haven't been away since Rory was born,' she said anxiously, chewing a fingernail.

'It'll be good for you,' said Eileen, who had teenage sons and was worried they'd throw their own party as soon as she and her husband were a mile outside Dublin. 'You need time together as a couple.'

'I'm not sure I want time together as a couple,' Corinna said. 'I just want to lie on the hotel bed and sleep.'

'You will not sleep!' insisted Eileen. 'Myself and Larissa will march into your room and drag you down to the party. Won't we, Larissa?'

'Yes,' I said automatically. 'You have to party!'

I had been thinking that, if I got too miserable, I might go and hide in my own room. But if Eileen was determined that our department was going to have fun, she'd hunt me down and make me join in.

I went by bus. I didn't want to spoil Bianca's fun with Robert. Just because I had nobody to drive on a romantic trip with, didn't mean she should miss out.

I didn't get my hair done, but I was wearing a new dress – a dark purple v-neck wrap in a silky jersey that made the most of my figure. The big advantage of being a single woman at thirty-seven is that you have lots of time to go to the gym. Well, you need to do something to offset all the hours consuming family-sized bars of chocolate in front of the telly. I could crack walnuts with my thighs thanks to sessions on the cross trainer. Unfortunately, there isn't much call for cracking walnuts with your thighs, so this skill was largely unrecognised; but it was nice to know I *could*, should the need ever arise.

'Lovely dress, Larissa,' said Mary, who was wearing a gold sequined mini-dress and looked like she should have been on Christina Aguilera's tour bus instead of a Kennedy Engineering Christmas party one.

'Thanks, Mary,' I replied. 'Love yours, too.'

'It's great, isn't it?' she said. 'It's got matching knickers, but nobody's going to see them. Still, it's nice to know they're there.'

Fifi was wearing black, thigh-high suede boots, stripey tights with holes in them, and a lichen green cobwebby dress that was either an expensive designer thing made to look like it had loads of holes in it, or had been viciously attacked by moths. She had black nails in honour of the party and all her piercings in. Normally, Desmond only allowed her to wear earrings and one belly-piece on reception, but now, she was a metal detector's dream.

The bus filled up and it became clear from the air of merriment that many of the people on it had already started partying. Cans of beer and a cocktail shaker appeared as we set off, and an argument started about the bus soundtrack.

'Shakin' Stevens!'

'Tina Turner!'

'Kings of Leon!'

Mrs Dineen won and we listened to Shakin' Stevens for forty minutes, by which time the excited chatter was drowning out the music.

321

It was a full hour before my single status was brought up.

'What's a lovely girl like you doing on your own?' said Seth, who was holding hands with his wife in the seat opposite me. 'Look at me and Regina. Married forty-three years. Never a cross word.'

'Ah now, Seth,' said Regina, 'we've had the odd row.'

'Well, the odd row, I'll give you that,' he conceded. 'But we've never let the sun set on our anger.'

They talked about marriage, kids and grandkids all the rest of the way to Kilkenny. I managed to pick the nail varnish off most of my nails. I'd have done my feet too if I hadn't been wearing tights.

Quite a few of our bus conga-ed into the Castle Hotel reception. I lurked near the hotel entrance until they were all safely checked in because I wanted a room on my own and checking in was a danger zone. People were ending up sharing rooms and, since I couldn't share with Bianca, I wanted to be on my own. Fifi and Mary agreed to share a room. As they waited for their key they did an excited little dance, part Riverdance, part *Saturday Night Fever*. The receptionist didn't bat an eyelid. When they'd danced off towards the lift, I decided that it was safe to approach the desk.

'Now, *they* are definitely going to an office Christmas party,' said a voice.

I looked around and found a tall, dark, undeniably nice-looking man at the reception desk beside me. *He* didn't look as if he'd just come off a tour bus that reeked of cheese-and-onion crisps, Southern Comfort cocktails and beer. He looked as if he'd been giftwrapped in an elegant men's store and set down beside me. He had dark curly hair, a five o'clock shadow – did I tell you that I love dark men who need to shave twice a day? – and his eyes were glittering. He even smelled nice: lemony with spices. Yum yum. I drew myself up to my full five foot four and did a bit of eye glittering back. Just because I hadn't been on a date since Adam was in short pants, didn't mean I didn't know the drill. I tried to look like I was an interesting, mysterious woman, which is apparently the key to getting men to chat you up. Since she got engaged, Bianca has become an expert on what men want – Robert keeps telling her – and where I've been going wrong is by looking too approachable. Men like the movie-star-Megan-Fox/exotic-mystery vibe instead of the *I sit at home alone a lot with wine and watch reruns of* Sex and the City vibe. According to Robert, women like me frighten men because they're afraid we will jump on them, drag them to our lair and never let them go.

The Megans are too cool to want to drag anyone to their lair. They look like they might possibly want wild sex and then stalk off never to be seen again, which is a plus to the male mind. Therefore, the mysterious Megan thing is actually less threatening than us telly-watching girls. Who knew?

'Are you here for the weekend?' he asked.

'Just one night,' I said. Very mysterious, that. Score one to me.

'Me too,' he said.

I looked for evidence of a wedding ring, or a wife or a trail of adorable children with him, but he seemed to be on his ownsome.

'And you're here for a Christmas party?' he asked.

I needed to think quickly. A true-blue Megan wouldn't set

foot at a Christmas party unless it was at Chateau Marmont and featured rockstars.

'I just needed some time on my own to think,' I said, a scenario which even surprised me. I had been reading too many thrillers. In thrillers, people are always checking into hotels on their own to think. The killers always find them, though. 'What about you?' I purred, still doing my mysterious thing.

'I'm here for a Christmas party,' he said.

'Really?'

Was it too late to say, *I just lied to you in order to sound more interesting, I'm at a Christmas party too*? Yes. Far too late. Just below the 'too much telly and wine' women on the AVOID list were women who tell lies, giggle and think it's hilarious. This is apparently a sign of mental instability, and that really scares the heck out of men. The mentally unstable types go for one date then turn into stalkers, phoning at all hours of the day and night, screeching that they'd been promised marriage and eternal love.

'Right,' he said, nodding in a way that said *you're interesting*.

Or I *hoped* that's what he was thinking.

'I might see you later. When you're thinking,' he said.

'Yes,' I nodded gravely. 'Lot of thinking to do. Lots.'

'Bye,' he said, and walked off.

Myself and the receptionist watched him walk to the lifts. He even walked nicely, and it was clear that the big shoulders on the coat were filled with actual big shoulders and weren't just a big coat on a skinny guy. All in all, he was pretty delectable.

'Don't see many of them round here,' the receptionist said with a little sigh.

'Men?' I asked, thrown.

'No, you moron,' she snapped. 'Total hunks.'

'What's his name?' I asked, ignoring her rudeness.

'I can't tell you that,' she said, going all prim.

'You want him for yourself, don't you?' I leaned over and peered at her computer screen. 'Jack Mitchell. See,' I said triumphantly, 'I'm not that much of a moron.'

In my room, I did my make-up (bit of lipstick) and fixed my hair, which basically involved a blast of the hairdrier and a brush to settle it down. I put on dangly earrings and pinned my hair up, then took out the earrings and let it down again as it didn't look right.

I am not back-of-the-bus material. I am girl-next-door, according to Robert, which is OK, I suppose, but men do not die of lust over girls next door. My last boyfriend, Peter, did not even have palpitations of lust over me, although he did say I was very funny.

'Larissa, you're a scream!' he said, a lot. I *am* funny, but there are times when a girl wants to be told she's lovely/sexy/any-of-the-above instead of hilarious. By the end of my relationship with Peter, it was like going out with my brother, which is the death knell for any relationship. Besides, I already have a brother.

For some reason, I kept thinking about the guy at the check-in desk, but I had already messed that up by telling him I wasn't here for a Christmas party. If I saw him again in the company of all my office colleagues, he'd know I'd

lied, thereby placing me into the Mental Instability category
of women. The only other option was to somehow pretend
not to be with everyone else.

Or maybe I could look so different that he didn't recognise
me, then, sneak into his Christmas party, flirt with him,
and make it back to my room again before he found out
the truth. Yes, that sounded truly impossible. However, he
looked gorgeous and I'd been boyfriend-less for a long
time. I'd try it.

When I asked, Bianca didn't want to lend me her other pair
of reading glasses, the black-framed, scary professor ones.

'I'm blind as a bat, Larissa,' she said. 'You won't be able
to see wearing them.'

''Course I will,' I said confidently.

I needed glasses as part of my disguise. I also needed to
have my hair curly to make me look totally different. Bianca
didn't have her heated rollers with her – she has a man now,
therefore no man-trapping carry-on is required. But Mary
would. Mary would have a whole beauty salon of gizmos
to make herself beautiful.

I knocked on her door and found her and Fifi in hotel
dressing gowns, hotel slippers, wearing face masks and
drinking hot chocolate as they watched the telly.

'I thought you were already dressed?' I said, looking at
the golden dress which was now hanging up.

'What's the point of being in a lovely hotel if you can't
enjoy it?' Mary said with a contented smile. 'Besides, I
mightn't wear that dress at all. I have another one, it's got
silver sequins and I have shoes to match.'

I perked up. In Mary's gold dress, with curly hair and glasses, there was no way my new love would recognise me. I could dance at our party, change briefly back into my purple dress to see if I could find him for a bit of flirting, then bob's your uncle. I could tell him the truth later.

'Mary,' I began, 'there's this guy I met downstairs.'

An hour later, I daresay that my own mother wouldn't have recognised me. Fifi – I should have *known* – was a dab hand at make-up, Mary deserved an Oscar for hair, and in the gold sequined dress (wearing my own underwear), I looked entirely different.

I put on Bianca's scary professor glasses and looked at myself in the mirror.

I was part-cabaret, part-pole-dancer-o-gram, with rich lustrous curls, snaky black eyes and huge sheeny lips. I was also mysterious. Well, mysterious in that I looked like an entirely different person.

Mary and Fifi were dressed to kill too, Fifi still in cobwebby-moth thing and Mary in full-on silver sequins. The three of us looked like we were in a strange band.

The Kennedy Engineering party was in The Old Lounge, a ginormous room with a bar, French windows opening out into the terrace, a dais for any karaoke later and a dance floor where a man was setting up a music system.

'Drinks!' announced Mary, heading for the bar.

'Let's go slowly now,' I said, the voice of reason.

I wanted to be stone-cold sober for later on when I got out of my golden dress and back into my normal self for flirting with Jack.

'It's the Christmas party, Larissa,' said Mary. 'Don't be such a bore. It's time to let your hair down!'

My hair didn't come down but only because Mary had sprayed an ozone-depleting amount of spray into it.

Surprisingly, it was fun to morph into Mary in her dress. I felt like I was a different person. I was mysterious and beautiful, all the things I'd always wanted to be but was too shy to try out. And wearing Bianca's glasses meant I was so blind, I couldn't see if anyone was looking at me in horror. Result.

Mary, Fifi and I stayed on the dance floor all night, pretending we were Beyoncé in *Dreamgirls*.

Seth and Regina waltzed the whole time, irrespective of the beat of the music. Desmond and his wife were doing something that looked like a jive, but I'm no expert. Bianca and Robert gazed into each other's eyes as if there was nobody else in the room. The music was so loud, sign language was surely the only way to communicate. Waiters and waitresses drifted in and out, tidying away glasses, bringing more drink. Any moment soon, someone would be sick in someone else's handbag. It would have been any normal Christmas party except that I was different. I was having fun and it had nothing to do with drinking three cocktails with Mary and Fifi. I was really letting my hair down.

I did think about lovely Jack from reception and how my plan to find him had gone awry, but I cast him mentally aside. Who needed men? I was having a wonderful time and it was all to do with Mary's sequined dress and my plan to be different.

This was where I'd been going wrong all along. It had nothing to do with trying to be what men wanted me to be:

it was about being who *I* wanted to be. There might never be a man out there for me, but I'd enjoy myself anyway.

When it got too hot on the dance floor, the three of us shimmied out on to the terrace where people from other Christmas parties were sitting to smoke, and we did an impromptu performance out there too. I had never realised I could sing without the karaoke machine and Mary's dress was so much fun to dance in, what with the sequins rattling adorably as I wiggled.

'Do another song!' roared the people from the party next door, which was apparently an Internet start-up company – or so Fifi said – and was full of gorgeous young men.

A couple of tables were shoved together to make a stage for us, so we did requests.

There was quite a crowd round us and we were halfway through our version of 'Diamonds are a Girl's Best Friend' when I spotted a man who looked a bit familiar. I shoved Bianca's glasses down my nose to get a good look.

It was him: tall, dark hair, glinting eyes, probably hadn't had a chance to shave when he'd got to his room earlier. Someone had given him a Santa tie with lights on it and he was smiling up at me as I shimmied. Lovely Jack from reception.

'Can I make a request?' he asked, when we'd finished.

'Anything you want, babyeeee,' said Mary, who'd had more cocktails than me.

'Can I dance with the one in gold?'

If he hadn't been ready to catch me, I'd have fallen flat off the table because Mary and Fifi pushed me forward delightedly.

'We can go solo,' yelled Mary.

'No – doublo,' said Fifi.

'Whatever.'

'Have you managed to get any thinking time in?' Jack asked me when we'd put a few yards between ourselves and the girls' rendition of 'Son of a Preacher Man'.

'Very little,' I said, grinning idiotically. 'I'm sorry, I lied. I *was* going to my office Christmas party.'

'I saw you get off the bus,' he admitted.

'Right. Sorry again,' I said. 'It's just that I wanted a go at being a Megan.'

'OK,' he said thoughtfully. 'What does that mean, exactly?'

'It means that men like mysterious women who do mysterious things, not ordinary, sensible ones who watch too much television and wear normal clothes, and I wanted to be mysterious instead. Sensible girls never meet men at their Christmas party,' I pointed out, 'so I thought I'd do something different—'

'What is this "sensible" word you keep applying to yourself?' said Jack. 'Because you do not fit into the sensible box in my version of the word.'

'I don't?'

He gave me another of those glittering smiles. I took Bianca's glasses off so I could see it better.

'You don't.'

'I do sometimes,' I said.

'I find that very hard to believe. I may need to hear more before I make a decision either way,' he added. 'I might need to spend more time with you.'

In the background, Mary was doing a solo version of

'I Will Always Love You'. She has a lovely voice, actually. Normally, I hate that song, but at that exact moment, it was perfect.

'How much time?' I asked.

'Lots of time.'

It's funny, but I had the weirdest feeling that Christmas was never going to be the same again.

A Family Christmas

Stevie woke every morning and felt around in her head to find what it was like in there.

Still bright? Or, God forbid, dark and gloomy?

It was early December now, three months since she'd started taking the new tablets; wonder drugs, she called them. Until the doctor had come up with them, Stevie's head had been darker than she'd thought it was possible to be and still be called human.

The darkness made her feel *in*human: a sort of half-being who didn't care about existing and who even walked as if she were part of a zombie tribe on earth, one foot in front of the other because she knew that was how it was done. She couldn't hear properly, either. Not standard deafness; instead, a disconnection from the world which meant speech sounded muffled and she had to tilt her head all the time to tune in.

Not that there was much to tune in to. She stayed in bed

a lot, not reading or watching television, just lying there, eyes open. Hurting.

She'd known that Carl was heartbroken seeing her like this and, even though she adored him, she couldn't break out of the darkness to reach the old Stevie.

The only faint pleasure was in knowing that Max, her darling boy, wasn't here to see this. In fact, Max's going off to college in Edinburgh the year before was partly what had brought her to this place.

'Severe reactive depression in a person with a predisposition for depression in the first place,' said Dr Zelda, who looked as if she'd never had a depressive moment in her life, and yet was kind and understanding when Stevie arrived in the surgery. Not crying, no. She wasn't even able to cry. The hopelessness didn't allow for that relief.

This December morning, Stevie lay in the big double bed beside Carl with her eyes closed and gently probed around inside her head.

Every time she did it, she held her breath and ran through her mental checklist: Max was fine, Carl was cosy under the duvet beside her, they could pay the mortgage and she had things to look forward to today. Best of all, there was no dark hole inside her. Instead, wonderfully, joyously, there was still the golden warmth she'd begun to feel a few weeks after taking the new drugs.

Over the previous eight months Dr Zelda had prescribed therapy and three types of anti-depressant and suddenly, randomly, the white oval ones had worked.

Perhaps she should put an advert in a local paper to say thanks to the pharmaceutical company, she thought with a wry grin, the way people of her mother's generation used to do when novenas worked.

Even the fact that she could have a humorous thought made her smile. No darkness. No high anxiety over her family or crazed fears over the catastrophes that could occur to them.

She breathed an almost silent prayer of gratitude to whoever was helping her, and to her new tablets.

Carl stirred beside her. It was still dark, nearly seven, and in a moment his alarm would go off. Their home, Woodbrook Farm, was in the lush Golden Vale, land of the dairy cow. It was a busy dairy farm with two hundred and fifty Holstein cows. There were no lie-ins for the dairy farmer. The cows were milked twice a day in the bank-owned, state-of-the-art milking parlour. Early in the morning and at six each evening, the herd was brought in and funnelled into the milking parlour, ten cows each side of a pit in the middle. Carl and his young Polish farm manager, Olev, would stand in the pit to hook each cow to the milking machine and, finally, the milk would flow into the giant, sterilised glass containers, and from there into huge vats.

When those twenty cows were finished and unhooked, gates clanged open, they walked dutifully out, and the next twenty were led in.

Once the cows were milked, there began the cleaning and sterilising of the parlour, then the feeding, then the cleaning of the giant cowshed. It was hard work and still money was tight.

To help out, four years ago, Stevie had the idea of turning the old labourers' dwellings into summer cottages for visitors who fancied staying on a working farm. A petting farm of goats, sheep and rabbits was brought in to add fun for small children. Stevie had taken a strange yearning to have a yak with dark dreadlocks, but Carl had put his foot down and said he knew nothing about yaks, and could they not get a pig instead?

Which had turned out to be just as well. The cottages and the petting farm had been Stevie's baby but she'd barely been able to function the past summer, so Carl had taken responsibility, delegating some of his other work to Olev. Olev lived in one of the cottages with his pregnant wife, Veruschka, who was tall, slender and now boasted a baby bump like a pumpkin hidden under her sweater.

For much of the past eight months, Stevie had barely ventured beyond the farmhouse. It was a big rambling place with plenty of bedrooms and not enough decent carpeting. Despite that, it was homely and well loved. Flossie, her grey silken whippet, liked to lie on the old floral couch in the kitchen, close to the giant range that heated the whole place. The well-scrubbed table where Max had done his homework for years was big enough for ten, although it was a long time since they'd had guests for dinner.

Just then, Carl's alarm sounded. He reached to turn it off then rolled over to snuggle up to his wife.

Stevie relaxed against him, grateful for every moment of this happiness because she could still recall the absence of it.

Carl normally had nothing but a banana and a swift cup of tea for breakfast, and after milking, he'd have porridge in the kitchen with Stevie. Just after ten, he was back in the kitchen where Stevie was folding laundry.

'Everything all right?' she asked automatically. She was frowning at a worn shirtcuff.

For once, Carl didn't reply.

Stevie looked up anxiously.

Her husband had his mobile phone in his hand, and there was a certain whiteness around his mouth.

'Ma just phoned me,' he said.

Stevie's hands began to shake.

Her mind was speedily running through the disasters: his mother had cancer, someone in the family was bankrupt . . .

Her therapist had tried to work on her anxiety, but it didn't take much for Stevie to career back into terror.

'You know Ma asked everyone to Maryfield for Christmas?' Carl said hoarsely. Maryfield was his family home, a big but shabby country house which Carl's mother, Louise, shared with his sister, Joan.

'Mmm,' Stevie said. She was still wondering if she could face going or if she'd prefer to stay at home with just her, Carl and Max.

'Well, she's fractured her ankle. Apparently she slipped in the garden. She was in Casualty all night, but she's finally sorted, poor darling. She was crying on the phone. She asked if we could have Christmas here and I said yes because I felt so sorry for her.'

'Oh, Carl.'

Husband and wife stared at each other.

Stevie's fight with depression had been kept private, just between them. Louise hadn't known and, if she had, she'd

336

never have asked such a thing, for them to host a family Christmas which meant at least a dozen people. Including Lillian.

Lillian was the real reason Stevie hadn't wanted anyone to know how she'd been.

There was a long silence, eventually broken by Stevie.

'We can't tell them now,' she said. 'We'll have to do it.'

There would be many guests. Louise, who was one of life's shining stars, and Joan, who was besotted with her giant Persian cat, Pushkin, and couldn't see the point of people at all. There would be Louise's brother-in-law, Denis, a shy, single and long-since retired civil servant who was invited to all family events because he had nobody else to go to. There would be –

'– Great-Aunt Jack,' said Carl miserably.

Great-Aunt Jack could start a row in an empty room, and frequently had.

Stevie thought there was no point worrying about Jack. Give her a bottle and a seventies thriller with lots of sex in it and she'd be fine.

'Uncle Denis will be no trouble,' Carl said. 'There's plenty of racing on the television at Christmas.'

'Edward, Belinda, Katie and Meribel.' Stevie ticked them all off on her fingers, Carl's eldest brother, his wife and two teenage daughters. 'The girls get on so well with Max. It'll be nice for him to have people vaguely his own age.'

'What about your parents?' said Carl. 'We can't have the house full of my lot and not invite yours.'

'No, not this year. They'll want to bring some stray person they'll have picked up on the motorway.'

Stevie's parents were free spirits in their seventies who travelled a lot in a camper van and adored inviting total strangers who'd run out of money/phone credit/clean laundry to travel with them.

'OK. But there's Kevin, Lillian and the children,' said Carl.

Kevin was the youngest of the family, a man so gentle that Stevie had never been able to work out quite why he'd married someone like Lillian, who appreciated only herself.

Her sister-in-law was the star in her own world and dressed at all times as if she might be attacked by photographers for a society shot. Lillian ran a publicity firm and believed that she, herself, was the firm's best advertisement. She'd had a BlackBerry back when most people still thought it was a lovely autumnal fruit, and had moved seamlessly on to all the i-electronic devices with delight, keen to explain to everyone that she never had to wait for the latest version of the phone. No, it was biked over to her as soon as the first one arrived in the country.

Two Christmases ago, Lillian, Kevin, with their two small children, had descended upon the farm and had stayed in the best bedroom, naturally, leaving Carl's mother to have the one next to it, a much smaller one at that. Lillian's much-talked-about Filipina helper hadn't been able to come and for an entire week Stevie had become the de facto child minder, rescuing Sebastian from the silage and stopping Tallulah from being gored by a goat. Lillian hadn't lifted a finger to help, either with the cooking or with the caring for her own offspring. Instead, she'd lounged around, perfectly dressed, permanently attached to her phone and a gin and tonic.

'Work is so busy, they won't let me have a minute's peace,'

she'd say as Stevie lurched past with another tray of lunch, red in the face from all the cooking and cleaning.

Carl pulled Stevie away from the laundry and into his arms. 'I'll phone Ma and say we can't do it. She'll have to un-invite them all.'

'No,' said Stevie. 'We can't do that. Let's think about it, OK?'

Stevie was having lunch in town that day with her friend, Dot. Dot and her husband had a herd of Friesians and a hand-made cheese business, which was exhausting work. The two women tried to meet once a month just to have one single day when they got out into the world.

For once, Dot was on time, there being no last-minute emergency with the vet or trauma over one of her two part-timers not being able to come in to work.

Stevie had found a window table in The Elder Tree and was already ravenous after passing the counter jammed with quiches, wraps and vegetable bakes.

'Sorry I'm late,' Dot said, slumping into her seat with a giant breath of relief.

'This isn't late,' said Stevie, smiling. 'You're here, that's all that matters.'

Dot had been the only person beside Stevie, Carl and Max to know about Stevie's depression, and Stevie would never forget Dot's endless support. Dot had sat in the house with her on days when Stevie had only been able to cry. There weren't many friends who would do that.

They had lunch and talked about family, life and farming. Inevitably, the conversation moved to Christmas.

Dot had one son at school locally and a daughter in college in Dublin. Her Christmas was already planned out: a joyous and rare four days' family holiday at a hotel. It was Dot and her husband's twenty-fifth wedding anniversary and, as a gift, his younger brother was coming to run the farm over the holiday.

'I can't wait,' said Dot. 'I am going to lie in bed till twelve all day. No, make that one o'clock. I'm going to watch rubbish on the box, eat sweets and do nothing more physical than order my dinner in the restaurant. Gracie says I should go and use the pool and such like. I said, "Gracie, love, I'm fed up with getting physical. I want to slob around my hotel room."'

'I'll be thinking of you,' said Stevie. 'Our quiet Christmas is a non-starter. Carl's mother's fractured her ankle and she'd invited the whole clan to hers. So now they're coming to us instead. Including Lillian.'

'Oh, merciful hour,' said Dot, who'd met Lillian and hadn't been impressed. 'That's not Christmas, that's Armageddon. Can't you get out of it?'

'I feel I owe it to Carl, really,' Stevie admitted. 'He's been so good to me, you know that. He said yes to his mother and I know he'd like it. Louise isn't strong. Who knows how many more Christmases she has before her. And Max would love it. I read once that only children value family parties, and it's true. He'd love to have the whole crew around. It wouldn't kill me to do this.'

'It might,' said Dot grimly. 'If you have to do it, you need help and a plan.'

'We can't afford any help,' Stevie said. 'It's just going to be me.'

'Well, you need a brilliant plan, then. You had it all wrong last time,' advised Dot. 'With women like Lillian, you give an inch and they'll take a yard. You need to set up the parameters better. Get her out of the house, for starters. Stick her in one of the cottages.'

'They're pretty, but they're a bit basic for the likes of Lillian,' said Stevie. '*I* like bare floors and IKEA throws on the couches, but she'd hate that. She's used to luxury hotels.'

'Ha!' said Dot. 'That's where you're going wrong, Stevie pet. You're worrying about her. *She* won't worry about you, you can bet your bottom dollar. Allocate all the rooms in the farmhouse to other people before she gets there and give everyone their little chores. You can't spend the whole of Christmas peeling spuds. Then when herself and Kevin roll up, stick them in a cottage. The furthest one from the house, too. Plus, you are not to let her dump those children on you. She can pay Belinda's girls for babysitting. Insist on it. New rules!'

Stevie drove home feeling buoyed up after her lunch. She could do this. It was ridiculous to let one woman ruin her entire Christmas. If it weren't for Lillian, Stevie would probably have enjoyed the prospect of having the whole clan to stay. Lillian was the problem.

Suddenly, the therapist's oft-repeated words rushed into her head: 'It's not what other people do that's the problem, Stevie: it's your reaction to what they do.'

Lillian didn't have to even turn up to stress Stevie, but that was because Stevie let Lillian's behaviour have that effect on her.

Lillian didn't have to do a thing – Stevie did it all by herself.

If only she could train herself to imagine that Lillian wasn't there, then it might work out. Of course, this was an ambitious plan at the best of times, and for a woman who was only months free of the darkest depression of her life, it was monumental.

Stevie reached the farm and drove through the gate where the hand-painted sign, *Prize Holstein Dairy Cattle*, hung. This would be her way of breaking with the pain of the past year: everyone would come to Woodbrook for Christmas, she would enjoy it and bloody Lillian would not get on her nerves.

Max came home three days before Christmas and Stevie went to collect him at the train station.

Her son had grown in the months he'd been away. He wasn't taller and, if anything, he looked thinner, probably from the craziness of student life. And yet he seemed older, a little grown apart.

Stevie hugged him and reminded herself that accepting the distance was part of being a mother. She might always love him the same way and with the same intensity, but his love would change, ebb and flow.

'I could have got a taxi, Ma,' Max said, walking beside her to the car.

'Not after a flight and a train ride,' she said fondly.

Beside her on the ride home, Max broached the subject of her depression.

'How are you feeling, Ma? I was worried about you.'

So like his father, she thought with affection. Both more comfortable talking on car journeys.

'I'm great, Max. Really great.' Eyes on the road, she put one hand on his arm and patted it gently. 'I don't want you to worry.'

'Ma, I do worry, so it's easier if you talk to me.'

'I know,' she said. 'I hate talking about it with you. I hate admitting how fragile I was, like I couldn't cope with being your mother. Mothers hate their kids seeing their vulnerability,' she added, trying to sound light. 'We want to be all-powerful so you trust us to save you from anything.'

'Yes, Ma,' he said, his tone gentle, 'but I'm not a kid any more. I want to be involved.'

Stevie drove along the familiar roads blindly. She would not tell him how his leaving had affected her.

'I'm seeing a lovely therapist and these new anti-depressants I'm taking are brilliant,' she said. 'I'm me again, Max. And we're going to have a wonderful Christmas.'

Two days before Christmas Day, the clan began arriving. Great-Aunt Jack, Uncle Denis, Louise in plaster, Joan and a deeply annoyed Pushkin in his cat carrier all came in the same car.

'Nobody told me it was in the middle of nowhere!' yelled Aunt Jack, as soon as she got out. 'I hate farms! Hope there's telly in my room.' She stomped off indoors, Max following her and trying to hide his mirth.

Uncle Denis didn't want to be any trouble and insisted on trying to carry cases indoors, even though Carl and Olev stood ready to do all the heavy lifting.

Stevie's whippet, Flossie, danced around Pushkin's carrier and Joan whisked him inside, talking to soothe him and ignoring Stevie and Carl.

'I'm so sorry to have landed all this on top of you,' Louise said guiltily to them both, as Carl helped her from the car.

'Nonsense,' said Stevie and Carl at exactly the same moment.

'It'll be lovely,' Stevie said warmly.

An hour after everyone had eaten lunch on Christmas Eve, Flossie started barking and Stevie looked up to see a glossy silver four-by-four driving into the farmyard.

'Kevin, Lillian and the children are finally here,' she said, and went out of the kitchen door to greet them.

Kevin climbed down from the jeep first and hugged her.

'Merry Christmas, Kevin,' said Stevie, 'we're delighted you're here.'

'Hello, Tallulah, hello, Sebastian,' she added as the two children jumped out, looking rather warily round the muddy yard with its smell of cows. They were wearing little designer clothes. Tallulah's skinny white jeans and sparkly shoes were particularly unsuitable for a visit to a farm. Lillian should have thought of that.

'Right, since we're all full up in the house, I've put you in the cottages,' Stevie went on breezily, not waiting for her sister-in-law to emerge.

Kevin and the children followed her round to the front of the house and up a path to the left where the biggest cottage lay cleaned to within an inch of its life.

Stevie opened the door and stepped inside. 'I think it's nice to have your own space,' she said.

Sebastian and Tallulah immediately ran upstairs to the bedrooms, yelling at each other about wanting the biggest one.

'Thanks, Stevie – ' began Kevin and was interrupted by Lillian arriving late to the party.

She was a tall woman, and dark hair blow-dried into a full style made her look taller. Beside her, Stevie always felt a little unkempt and today was no different. Lillian was in tailored trousers and a smart jacket and wore bright red lipstick. Stevie was in her old jeans and a grey sweatshirt. But for once, the clothes didn't matter to Stevie. This was about inner strength.

'Lillian, lovely to see you. Here's the cottage. I've put some basics in the fridge and a Christmas tree in the living room. It's only tiny, but I know Sebastian and Tallulah will like it. I've got a spare electric blanket if you need it, but you shouldn't.'

Lillian wasn't listening.

'We can't stay here,' she said. 'It's basic. Why aren't we in the house?'

Stevie had spent twenty minutes meditating that morning to ready herself for this moment.

'We've a full house for Christmas, Lillian, and you and Kevin are the last to arrive. There's nowhere else on the farm for you to stay. If you don't want to stay, of course, that's entirely up to you,' she said. 'You can check out some of the local hotels. I'm sure you can get a list on your iPhone. We'll expect you tonight for dinner at seven and tomorrow's lunch is at three. You might come earlier, though, to get your presents.'

Stevie walked to the front door. 'You're welcome to have a cup of tea with everyone else up at the house before you go.'

Lillian glared at her. 'We haven't had lunch,' she said. 'The children are starving.'

Inside, Stevie was quaking.

'Gosh. Well, we've all had lunch,' she said cheerfully. 'There's probably no point dropping in for a cup of tea if you're that hungry. The Elder Tree in town is very popular and they have a kids' menu. I think they're staying open till five this evening.'

She didn't wait to hear Lillian's response, just walked out of the door.

'See you later,' Stevie called, and kept walking.

'Aren't Kevin, Lillian and the children coming in?' said Louise anxiously when Stevie arrived back in the house. Louise liked to sit on the old couch near the range where she could watch snatches of television on the tiny old portable television on the counter, and chat while Stevie cooked.

'No,' said Stevie. 'Lillian doesn't like the cottage. So I suggested they try some of the hotels nearby—'

'She can have my room,' said Louise instantly, and looked so upset that Stevie felt some of her own anxiety over the whole affair melt away. Bloody Lillian bullied everyone so much that everyone leapt to do her bidding. Not any more, Stevie decided grimly.

'Actually, Louise, I think Lillian would be far happier in

346

a hotel. Woodbrook doesn't really do the sort of luxury she likes.'

Stevie found that she didn't mind saying this. It was no slight on her home. It made life easier if Lillian stayed elsewhere.

Hours later, dinner was nearly ready and Stevie's sense of calmness was growing. She didn't care if Lillian turned up or stayed in a rage in whatever hotel she'd managed to book into. Everyone at Woodbrook Farm was happy.

She was listening to Carly Simon in the kitchen, Louise was lying down upstairs, Max and Carl had just come in from milking, and Aunt Jack, Uncle Denis, Belinda, Katie and Meribel were all playing Monopoly, while Joan sat with Pushkin on her lap, petting him as he purred in great growls of pleasure. Flossie the whippet had to be kept in the kitchen. 'Hello, love,' said Carl, kissing her on the neck as she stood at the stove stirring gravy for the roast.

'Hello, you,' she said back, smiling.

Flossie began to bark and Stevie tested herself for the anxiety to rise.

It didn't. She still felt calm. Amazing.

Lillian, Kevin, Tallulah and Sebastian burst into the kitchen bringing a flurry of cold from outside with them.

'Did you get sorted at a hotel?' Carl asked, hugging his brother and planting a kiss on the top of Tallulah's head.

'No,' said Kevin. 'All booked out within a fifty-mile radius. We've moved into the cottage.'

'It's great fun,' said Sebastian, eyes shining. 'Me and Tally have to share a bedroom. I got the top bunk!'

347

'We're going to swap!' shrieked Tallulah, but she looked happy enough.

'Your cousins are playing Monopoly,' said Stevie. 'They're dying to see you.'

The only person who remained standing near the door, still as a statue and just as cold, was Lillian.

As if on cue, Carl, his brother and the children rushed off, leaving Stevie alone with her sister-in-law.

'I hope you got lunch, but dinner's going to be ready in about fifteen minutes,' said Stevie, going into cheerful mode. Then, thinking that at least some wine might soften Lillian up, she added: 'I've opened some red wine, if you'd like a glass.'

Lillian still looked frozen but her face softened at this.

'Thank you,' she said, and put her handbag on the edge of the kitchen table.

Flossie put her paws up to have a look and suddenly the whole glossy, patent thing fell to the kitchen floor and out flew the contents.

Blast, thought Stevie, bending to help pick it all up. Lillian would probably insist that Flossie be banished outside for such naughtiness.

And then she saw it: a discreet white box with the two blue lines on the side.

They were the second brand of anti-depressants she'd tried. She'd recognise the little diamond pattern on the box anywhere.

Lillian was whisking all her stuff away anxiously and when she spotted the box, she grabbed it.

Stevie blithely picked up the innocent things further out, a sun-glasses case and a lipstick.

'No wonder we have achey shoulders with all the things we carry in our handbags,' she said chattily.

'Yes,' said Lillian.

Her sister-in-law would never guess that she recognised exactly what was in the little box. But seeing it had made all the difference to Stevie.

Perhaps she and Lillian weren't as far apart as she'd thought. They might never be friends, but they could get along. It was, as the therapist said, all about how *she* reacted to other people. And the knowledge that Lillian took anti-depressants too had changed how she saw her sister-in-law. She wasn't the scary monster; she was a flesh-and-blood woman with problems of her own.

'Now sit down there and I'll get us some wine,' Stevie said.

Lillian did as she was told.

Stevie turned off the oven and grabbed two glasses and the bottle of wine. She turned up the music, shut the door firmly and sat on the couch, whereupon Flossie instantly leapt on to her lap.

Dinner could wait a while. There was no pressure. It would all happen when Stevie decided it would.

Just before it was time to serve Christmas lunch, Stevie surveyed her dining-room table, a masterpiece of festive pretti-ness as Katie and Meribel had spent the morning arranging tea lights, Christmas roses, dried rosemary and the old delicate china. From the depths of a cupboard, they'd found old-fashioned rose-coloured napkins that Stevie had forgotten she'd had.

'Aunt Stevie, I love these!' Katie had said, and even ran the iron over them to smooth out old creases.

Max had insisted on doing the milking with his uncle Edward, and Carl had had his first lie-in in years. When he'd come in from milking, Max had got into the spirit of it all by searching for his mother's favourite Christmas CD, so that music rang through the whole house.

Carl had enjoyed a leisurely breakfast in bed and he'd hugged Stevie proudly and told her how lovely it was to see her well.

'I know how worried you were, love,' she replied. 'I'm me again. I said that to Max and it's true.'

'I love you, no matter what,' Carl said fervently.

'Thank you.'

And somehow, they'd nearly spilled the coffee and it was another half an hour before Stevie was up again to check on the goose.

Joan, somewhat tempered by the gospel at Midnight Mass, which had specifically mentioned kindness to all men, had left Pushkin in her room and was sweetly dispensing drinks and Christmas crackers.

Uncle Denis was busily studying a racing paper to check the form for the next day's horse racing at Leopardstown.

Flossie was in seventh heaven in the kitchen from smelling the scent of cooking goose and from chewing on her Christmas chewy shoe, a giant thing she could barely hold on to. Everyone was happy, Stevie thought, including her.

'It's time for lunch,' Stevie said, popping her head round the door to the sitting room.

'We can't leave *Chitty Chitty Bang Bang* now!' shrieked Aunt Jack in outrage. 'It's coming up to the bit where the Baron gets his comeuppance!'

Max shot his mother a compliant glance and went off to explain the mysteries of modern televisions and how a programme could be taped from the exact moment you stopped watching it.

Katie, Meribel and their mother, Belinda, followed Stevie into the kitchen to help dish everything up.

'Just tell us what to do,' Belinda said.

'I wish I could help,' said Louise, at the door on her crutches. 'Nobody's seen Kevin, Lillian and the children yet, have they?'

Stevie intercepted a look between Belinda and her daughters, a look that seemed to say that Lillian wasn't their most beloved person either.

With her newly acquired knowledge about Lillian, Stevie felt a pang of pity for her sister-in-law. Lillian was simply one of those people who rubbed everyone up the wrong way. She was vulnerable too, except that nobody could see her vulnerability.

'We're here!' said a voice, and Lillian appeared at the kitchen door, followed by Kevin and the two children, who each had an armload of toys.

'Great,' said Stevie in genuine welcome. 'Come on in, you're right on time.'

'I couldn't get them to leave anything back at the cottage,' Lillian said tiredly as Sebastian and Tallullah dropped things in their progress across the kitchen.

Stevie smiled at Lillian with true warmth. 'It's fine,' she

said. 'Kids will be kids. Seb, Tally – your cousins are inside and they're dying to see you.'

The children responded to Stevie's voice of calm authority and obediently went on through to the living room.

'Thank you,' said Lillian wearily and sat down on the couch beside Flossie the whippet, seemingly not caring that her clothes would get covered in dog hair.

Stevie poured her a cup of coffee from the percolator and Lillian took it gratefully.

She looked exhausted underneath her carefully applied layer of make-up, Stevie saw, knowing that, in the past, all she'd have seen was the make-up and not the exhaustion.

'That's it, we're ready,' Stevie said when the last dish had been carried into the dining room.

She smiled as she looked around, stroked Flossie and then hung her apron on a cupboard knob. The past year had been a difficult, painful journey and yet she'd learned so much because of it, things she might never have learned without the darkness. Among those valuable lessons was the fact that other people couldn't make you happy. Or sad, for that matter. You had to do both by yourself.

Last but not least, she'd learned that the parts of themselves that people hid were often the most revealing parts of all.

She pushed open the kitchen door and listened for a moment to the happy sounds of her family opening Christmas crackers and reading out silly jokes. It was going to be a lovely family Christmas.

Afterword

For the writer, going back to your past work is a little spooky. You've changed, your life has changed and the world has changed, but the words on the page from ten years ago are exactly the same. I encountered this culture shock when I began compiling stories for *Christmas Magic*.

For many years, I was short-story phobic. I loved reading them but I didn't like writing them. Sometimes because the criteria for magazine short-story writing can be exacting: two thousand words by Monday, split into two exact one-thousand word pieces with a cliffhanger in the middle. Or else, because a short story was required for a fabulous charity collection and I'd be overwhelmed by the charity's inspiring work, feel how inadequate my story was and think: *I should be doing more for this wonderful charity!*

And then I wrote *The Perfect Holiday*, a literacy novella for World Book Day, and I fell in love with writing short stories. Suddenly, a sliver of an idea – not enough to sustain an entire novel – could be used and oh, the fun of using it. I was flooded with ideas for short stories and I just had to do something with them. So I began to compile this collection and in doing so, I ventured into my short story history.

Going back over your old short stories is like creeping through the museum of your own mind, seeing themes you loved, phrases you were infatuated with and things you should never have done and, thankfully, no longer do. I edited the past stories and had a marvelous time writing the new ones. In fact, I'm writing this on a computer document filled with ideas for endless more stories.

I really hope you've enjoyed *Christmas Magic*.

Cathy Kelly

Stories previously published

Madame Lucia (originally called The Fortune Teller) *Stories for Jamie*, Blackwater Press, 2002

Off Your Trolley, *Girls Just Want to Have Fun – The Cosmopolitan Book of Short Stories,* Headline, 1998

May You Live in Interesting Times (originally called Interesting Times & The Gravy Boat) *Ladies' Night*, HarperCollins, 2005

Cassandra, *Girls' Night In*, HarperCollins UK & Penguin Australia, 2000

Letter from Chicago – charity literacy novella, New Island, 2002

Bride and Doom – charity anthology written for *Sexy Shorts*, Accent Press, 2004

Christmas Post, RTE guide, December 2010

The Paradise Road Book Club, *The Sunday Night Book Club*, Arrow Books, 2006

The Angel Gabrielle, *A Little Help From My Friends*, Poolbeg, 2007

Thelma, Louise and the Lurve Gods, *Irish Girls About Town*, Simon & Schuster (UK & Ireland) 2002, (USA) 2003
The Gap Year, magazine short story
The Trouble with Mother, magazine short story
Lizzie's Fling, magazine short story

The House on Willow Street

Welcome to Avalon: a quaint, sleepy town on the Irish coast.

Nothing has changed here for generations – least of all the huge mansion on Willow Street; the house in which sisters Tess and Suki Power grew up.

Now, years later, Tess is trying to protect her glamorous sister Suki who has come back home, broken and alone. Similarly, Mara Wilson is seeking refuge from a broken heart at her Aunt Danae's house. But Danae is hiding some shadows of her own.

Now that the big house is up for sale, change is blowing on the cold sea wind. But before they can look to the future, these four women must face up to the past . . .

'Brimming with secrets, passion and tragedy . . . Breathtaking'
Irish Independent

www.cathykelly.com

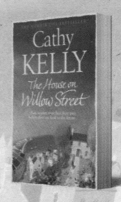

Lessons in Heartbreak

Three Lives. Three Loves.
Three Reasons to Let Go.

Izzie Silver left the small Irish town of Tamarin behind for New York. Life is good - until she breaks her own rules and falls for a married man.

On the other side of the ocean, Izzie's aunt Anneliese discovers the pain of infidelity for herself.

Then Lily, the wise and compassionate family matriarch, is taken ill. At her bedside back in Ireland, Izzie discovers a past her grandmother has never spoken of, while Anneliese feels despair mount. The one person she could have turned to is starting to slip away.

The lessons each of the women learns - both past and present - bring joy and heartbreak. And the hardest lesson of all is learning to let go.

www.cathykelly.com

Once in a Lifetime

Something happens that changes you forever...

Ingrid Fitzgerald is flying high. A successful TV presenter, she's happily married with two wonderful children. But as they fly the nest, she's about to discover a secret that will shatter her world.

Natalie Flynn is falling in love – but the secrecy surrounding her mother's past still troubles her. And Charlie Fallon loves her family and her job at Kenny's Department Store, but could now be the time to fight for her own happiness?

The woman with the power to help them is free spirit Star Bluestone. Experience tells her that the important things in life must be treasured and the chance for real joy comes only once in a lifetime…

'Wise, warm, compassionate, full of characters that I loved and identified with, it's like having a great gossip with your best friends. Her best book yet.'
Marian Keyes

www.cathykelly.com

Homecoming

...because it's where the heart is

Four women. Four lives. One place they call home.

Eleanor Levine left Ireland years ago with just a suitcase and her mother's recipe book. And now, a lifetime later, she returns from New York for Dublin's beautiful Golden Square full of hard-won wisdom. As she watches life unfold from her window, she is drawn into the lives of the women who live in the square...

Beautful actress Megan Bouchier had fame and success in her grasp – then she made the wrong kind of headlines. Now she needs a place to hide.

Big-hearted teacher Connie O'Callaghan is approaching forty and has given up on love. Why does no man match the heroes in her romantic novels?

Rae is a loyal friend and wife, dispensing tea and sympathy from Titania's Tea Room - until a secret threatens everything she holds dear . . .

'An absolutely fabulous read...
warm, touching, funny and
poignant' *Irish Independent*

www.cathykelly.com